I0681149

The White Fleet

Blood on the Stars VII

Jay Allan

system 7 publishing

Also By Jay Allan

www.jayallanbooks.com

The White Fleet

ISBN: 978-1-946451-07-1

Chapter One

The command center was massive, a gleaming open room filled with more than forty workstations, each with a plush black chair positioned behind it. The stations were arranged in circular groupings, each designed to house a specific team—navigation, helm, communications, tactical, fleet control, operations. And in the center, on a small raised platform, was the admiral's chair. It was almost grotesque in its grandiosity, at least to Barron's eyes. To the left sat the flag captain, the officer in actual command of the vessel, and to the right, the fleet commander's senior aide.

The size of the room was nothing compared to the enormous ship that housed it—over five and a half million tons and bristling with weapons. She was the pinnacle of the Confederation's power, the greatest war machine that nation had ever produced, larger and stronger than anything its neighbors could field. Barron was still in awe, still processing the ship's immense capabilities, almost a year and a half after he'd first set eyes on her out at Station Grimaldi. She'd been nearly finished then, but not quite.

She was called *Dauntless*. The name had been official now for nearly six months, ever since the day Barron himself had

1

led the christening ceremony. He'd been surrounded by all the survivors of his old crew, and a crowd of fawning dignitaries the likes of which he had never before seen. He'd spoken the words, bestowed the name on the vast and amazing construct with all the enthusiasm he could muster, but his heart just hadn't been in it.

It had been a difficult day, one he still remembered with some discomfort. Van Striker and Gary Holsten had meant well, and Barron was fully aware that they'd been driven only by a true and deep respect for him and for the last ship to have carried the name. But Barron still felt a bit disloyal calling another ship *Dauntless*. It had bothered him then, and it still did even now, just days before the great ship was set to officially enter service, with him in that monstrous admiral's chair to lead a great fleet deep into the unknown.

Barron fully supported the White Fleet's mission. Twice in the last war, the Confederation had faced the specter of defeat at the hands of an enemy armed with ancient technology. Exploration for and use of such artifacts was strictly regulated by international treaty, but Barron sometimes thought the Confederation was the only nation that burdened itself with compliance to what had to be the most-ignored document in diplomatic history. Certainly, the Union—not to mention the vast network of smugglers and adventurers on the Confederation's Badlands border—plied a healthy trade in bits and pieces of the amazing technology that mankind had lost to the Cataclysm so long ago.

The trade in ancient tech, such as it existed, was confined to black markets and obscured by shrouds of secrecy. It had operated for at least a century, various scraps of ancient devices selling for enormous prices. All tremendously useful technology, but rarely enough to upset the balance of power. Until recently. The discoveries made during the last conflict—the planetkiller and the pulsar, even the stealth generator Barron had used—had threatened to upend the entire international order. Any nation that was able to secure and deploy a weapon of such magnitude would become massively more powerful than its neighbors, with consequences that could only be imagined.

"She's a beauty, isn't she?"

Barron allowed himself a little smile, half forced, half genuine, but he didn't turn around, not yet. He hadn't heard Van Striker coming onto the bridge, but he recognized his voice immediately. "She is that, sir," he said, trying, not entirely successfully, to keep the doubt from his tone.

"But she's not *Dauntless,* is she? Not really."

Barron did turn now, his eyes finding Striker's. "She's an amazing ship, sir. There's nothing else like her." It wasn't an answer to the admiral's question. Barron didn't want to admit just how much he ached for his old vessel. It had been more than a year and a half, and he was becoming a bit embarrassed about how frequently his lost ship remained in his thoughts.

"You can talk to me, Ty. I've been there. We all remember our first commands, but *Dauntless* was something truly special, wasn't she? The two of you saved the Confederation, more than once. At least that's how I see it. Whatever happens, your first *Dauntless* is immortal…she will live forever in the history texts. But your career isn't finished yet, my friend, not by a longshot. The war may be over, but the danger is still there. You know that as well as I do. It's time to go on, Ty. Time to start a new chapter. You didn't die on *Dauntless,* and you can't keep on acting like you did. There's too much ahead of you."

"Of course, Admiral. I'm fine…and I'm ready." Truth be told, Barron didn't want to go at all. He liked the new *Dauntless* well enough, and he'd even managed to think of the battleship as the rightful successor to the sacrificed original. He had almost all of his original crew under his new command, somewhere in the fleet if not on the flagship itself, and he believed completely in the mission. But his heart just wasn't in making such a long journey.

He wasn't sure if it was still fatigue from the war, if he'd simply watched too many of his people die, or if he'd exhausted his ability to face endless crises. But deep down, he wished he could stay. He'd tried to fight it, to embrace the mission. It was an extraordinary chance to explore deep into the unknown, into mankind's mysterious and tragic past. It was something that would have filled his younger self with almost boundless excitement. But the old spirit just wasn't there anymore.

"I wouldn't have asked you to go, Ty, but there's no one else who could take your place. The cream of the navy is serving with the White Fleet, volunteers all, mostly because they wanted to serve under you." Striker hesitated and then continued slowly, "You're the navy's hero now, Ty, as much as your grandfather was in his day. I know that's uncomfortable for you, but it's well-deserved…and you'll have to learn to embrace it, because it's not going anywhere."

Barron just nodded. He would admit he'd done his duty, perhaps even a bit more. He was gratified that he'd served as he had, and he allowed himself to imagine that his famous grandfather would have been proud of him. But the public adoration grated on his nerves. He constantly tried to direct some of the praise streaming his way toward Atara Travis and Anya Fritz. Jake Stockton, Sara Eaton…dozens of others who'd fought and served, and no small number who'd died. All to no avail. The public had made him the symbol of the navy's victory, and he'd had almost no success in deflecting or evading it.

But there was no victory. The Senate threw away the victory. We survived the fight, that's all…and we left the conflict unresolved, condemning another generation to war and death because we lacked the resolve to do what had to be done.

"Perhaps it will be good to get away for a while, sir." It was somewhat of a tangential response, but as he said the words, he realized he truly meant what he had said. He didn't *want* to go, not really, but there was one unmistakable benefit of leaving. He'd be away for months, perhaps a year or more. Away from the interview requests, the parades, the fawning local dignitaries who plagued him everywhere he went. He thought about it all for a few seconds, feeling a touch of excitement build about the impending departure…but then he stopped, a somber look slipping back on his face.

He would be away from Andi, too.

He was hard-pressed to categorize his relationship with the now-retired adventurer. She had the ability to frustrate him like no one else he knew, and she was as pigheadedly stubborn as… well, as he was. She'd also claimed a place like no one else ever had, in his thoughts and in his life, and he hadn't been able to dislodge her from either. He'd even realized somewhere along the line, he didn't want to.

He knew he could never escape the navy. It was an obligation into which he'd been born, and one that his exploits in the war had only made stronger and more demanding…and it complicated any relationships he might have, especially one with her. Andi Lafarge was a lot of things, but no part of her resembled the dutiful spouse of a career flag officer, and Barron knew, as well as he knew anything, that any attempt she might make to pretend that wasn't the case was doomed to failure.

Nevertheless, he loved her. He'd finally admitted that to himself, and he knew she returned the feeling. But, for two people like them, their lives fixed on such diverse trajectories, that just wasn't enough. The most they could hope for was a collection of fleeting moments together. His had been an arranged marriage…to the navy itself, and in the end, he'd remained faithful.

"I think you'll feel better once you set out. You'll leave behind all the cameras and the reporters." Striker's words pulled Barron from his thoughts, at least partially. "They'll probably all come after me when they can't get to you." The admiral grinned.

Barron returned the smile robotically, but his thoughts were still mostly on Andi. He'd remained at the front for almost six months after the destruction of the pulsar, as the temporary ceasefire gradually gave way to a semi-permanent truce and, ultimately, a full-fledged peace treaty. He'd been against the whole thing, absolutely convinced that after four wars, the Confederation should invade the prostrate Union and make damned sure there was never a fifth conflict. But it quickly became clear that the Confederation's population was tired of war. They would never support an offensive of that magnitude, even one history seemed to justify so clearly.

He got an extended leave after the final peace was signed, and he spent almost all of it with Andi. She'd settled on Tellurus, one of the wealthiest worlds in the Confederation, a playground for the rich and pampered. She had bought an immense villa overlooking one of the planet's pristine inland seas, and they'd spent nearly six blissful months there...before duty called again and pulled him back to his real life.

He missed her now, but he was also worried about her. Andi Lafarge had come from grinding poverty so intense, few who hadn't experienced such deprivation could imagine it. She'd been driven since childhood, not just to pull herself up from the bottom, but to gain the vast wealth she'd seen as a child, watching the industrial barons and merchant princes living lives almost beyond the imagination of an orphaned street urchin.

She'd attained that, and more. The stealth generator had been a find of epic proportions, and Gary Holsten had paid her a vast fortune for it. Now, she spent her days walking around a magnificent villa, almost a palace, her ship, *Pegasus*, stored in spacedock, and her crew scattered across the Confederation, spending their own considerable wealth.

She'd been happy during the time they'd been together, he was sure of that. But, he still remembered the look in her eyes when he said goodbye. She'd been sorry to see him go, of course, but he'd seen something more there. She seemed...lost.

Barron had never met anyone as determined and strong-willed as Andi. She'd achieved her lifelong goal, but now, he wondered if she would find contentment in retirement...or if the inaction would wear her down. Those concerns had been there since he'd parted with her, but now, on the verge of beginning a bold new adventure of his own, he wondered if she would find satisfaction in her newfound wealth and luxury, or if she would wither away in her gilded palace.

"I see you're already gone." Striker's tone was genial, amused, but Barron realized the admiral had been talking for some time, and he hadn't heard a word of it.

"I'm sorry, sir. I've just got things on my mind."

"She'll be fine, Ty. It will take more than a couple billion credits to take down Andi Lafarge."

Barron felt a wave of surprise that the admiral knew what he'd been thinking about. Then he realized he shouldn't have.

He and Andi had been about the last two people in the fleet to recognize the obviousness of the connection they shared.

Barron almost denied he'd been thinking about Andi, but then he just gave in. "I know she will, sir. It's just that, well, I'll be gone for so long, and she…" He let his voice trail off. He didn't know what to say. He didn't have any specifics, just a feeling that boredom would drive her crazy, no matter how opulent her surroundings.

Striker didn't say anything else, and neither did Barron. They just stood in the command center for a long time, silent. Then, they turned and headed toward the shuttle bay, for one more trip down to Megara's surface before the fleet departed.

One more damned parade to attend.

Chapter Two

People's New Service Announcement

Workers of Liberte City, rejoice! This morning, seven traitors met final justice in the Place de Revolution on the orders of Citizen Villieneuve. These men and women betrayed their fellow workers and conspired with fugitives from the old government to destroy the ideals of the revolution. Death to all who conspire against the revolution. Long live the People's Union.

Hall of the People
Liberte City
Planet Montmirail, Ghassara IV
Union Year 219 (315 AC)

"I understand your reluctance, Ricard, but I need your help. We have done far better than we could have dared to imagine over the last year and a half, but the situation is still fragile. We cannot take any chances, and I need someone extremely capable—and who I can trust—in charge of the PP. I'm afraid that pretty much narrows it down to you."

"Gaston, it's not that I don't want to help…but administration is not my strength. You know this. You, better than anyone, are aware just where my true skills lie." Ricard Lille sat on the hard, uncomfortable chair, looking across the cheap, mass-pro-duced metal desk at Gaston Villieneuve. The room had nothing of the obscene luxury that had been so prevalent in Villieneuve's old office. It reeked of the workplace of a man of the people, one concerned only with the good of society, utterly uncon-cerned with wealth and the trappings of power. Incorruptible.

It was all a sham, every creaky, rusted millimeter of it.

Lille stifled a smile. The past eighteen months had con-firmed the gullibility of the people, if nothing else. Gaston Vil-lieneuve was a capable man, but his new image as the champion of the masses was a fiction far removed from the motivations that actually drove him…notwithstanding the grubby office and the factory worker's garb he'd taken to wearing in public.

Lille had hoped the assassination of the entire Presidium would allow Villieneuve to escape the retribution of his political rivals, to buy time to figure a way to prevent—or survive—the Union's collapse. But, he hadn't for an instant imagined how far his ally might press his advantage. Gaston Villieneuve had been a member of the now-despised Presidium himself. Worse, he'd been the head of the dreaded Sector Nine, the feared intel-ligence agency. Yet, he'd somehow survived the downfall of the Union…survived and come out on the other side as the reborn nation's sole and uncontested ruler, his power vastly more com-plete and absolute than it had been.

"There may be truth to what you say…but *you* can be trusted, Ricard, and that is true of very few people. You are one of the smartest men I have ever known. I'd love nothing more than to keep you in the shadows, ready to perform your special… skills…when needed. But there is no one else I can rely upon. Not now. Not at this critical stage. I can't trust the PP to some-one who might make a move against me. Not until I've secured a far firmer grip on things."

Lille still wasn't sure how his comrade had managed to achieve all he had…save for the fact that he'd surfed a wave of blood into the top position. Villieneuve had scapegoated every-one he'd considered a danger to his own power, as well as any members of the old government who'd been too well-known, too associated with the repressive past. The executions had gone on for months, retainers and lower-level allies of the murdered Presidium members, government officials, families of the condemned, even enough operatives from the old Sector Nine—his own former agents—to sate the public's hatred.

After the bloodletting, Villieneuve shifted a cadre of surviving agents, those whose identities had been sufficiently discreet, and recreated the discredited spy agency under the amusing title of the People's Protectorate. Now, he wanted Lille to take charge, to step into the very same position Villieneuve himself had held before.

Lille still wanted to refuse, but he knew he couldn't. He and Villieneuve were friends of a sort, but he was well aware that refusing his ally's request could be dangerous. Villieneuve had eliminated almost all his enemies, and he controlled every tentacle of the government. More amazingly, he'd somehow managed to win over the mob. His requests carried the force of irresistible commands, and refusing him would be unwise in the extreme.

Besides, Lille's own fortunes were closely tied to Villieneuve's. If an operative in charge of the reconstituted spy agency, one with his own ambitions, tried to move against Villieneuve, it would be as dire a threat to Lille as to his friend. Lille had no doubts, none at all, that anyone who overthrew Gaston Villeneuve would come for him next.

"Very well, Gaston, but only because you need me."

Villieneuve nodded. "I knew I could count on you. The PP is not yet up to Sector Nine's operational standards, but we must be cautious. We cannot rush recruiting. We must maintain the tightest possible control over security, and particularly the new section heads." Lille knew Villieneuve had kept a tight grip on Sector Nine, but he was just as aware there had always been a fair amount of scheming among the ambitious senior operatives. It seemed his friend was determined to take advantage of the situation to eliminate such problems from the start. Lille doubted that was possible. He had too dark a view of human nature to imagine anything but a swamp of betrayal and corruption surrounding him. But a fresh start would certainly delay the development of conspiracies and plots within the agency. Eliminating such problems, even for a short time, would allow the new regime to cement its position.

"Do I have authority to...handle...anyone I view as a potential problem?" Lille knew his friend was very aware of how he would *handle* something like that.

"Yes." It was a simple answer, more direct and unconditional than Lille had expected. Villieneuve really *did trust* him.

The two men were silent for a few seconds. Then, Lille asked, "What are your top priorities? The...People's Protectorate...does not yet have the resources Sector Nine enjoyed. We will have to be careful where we deploy our limited assets."

"The workers' councils, of course. We need to continue to cement our control over them."

The workers' councils had been Lille's idea, but Villieneuve had taken it further even than his friend had imagined possible. He'd met with them, at least those in the major cities on Montmirail, and he'd passed emergency decrees giving them extraordinary powers to revamp work rules and mete out punishments to former managers, those accused—and nothing more than accusation was necessary—of abuses against the workers under the old regime.

"That is relatively easy on a case by case basis, but we're talking about thousands of individual councils, Gaston. No matter what we do, it's going to take time to get to them all."

Lille was continually amazed at how little it took to entice so many to betray their comrades and their loudly-stated ideals. The efforts to infiltrate the councils had begun with nothing more than extra rations, before progressing to bequests of a more substantive type, such as the homes of former government commissars and promises of political power.

A few men and women had refused such advances, but they were so few, it had been easy enough to do away with them. Some had been killed outright, feigned accidents and the like, but most had simply been denounced to the others as traitors. It was easy enough to create fake trails of payoffs and falsified

communications, and the workers, still charged with revolutionary zeal, spent little time analyzing the accuracy of evidence
before casting their comrades to the rage of the mob.

"I trust you to prioritize the various worlds. Production cen-
ters and resource-rich planets first, of course. As well as strate-
gically-located systems."

"Understood." Lille nodded. "But it will take time."

Villieneuve nodded before continuing. "Barroux is still a
problem of course, though I don't think there's a solution until
we can concentrate enough military power there to crush the
traitors. Still...I don't like the reports I've been getting. My gut
tells me Confederation Intelligence has been assisting the rebels.
We can't allow the situation there to get any worse. I'd like you
to try to get some intelligence assets on the ground there, at least
enough to get a read on the Confeds' involvement. We'll never
retake the planet without a full-scale attack, but I need you at
least to try and interdict Confederation interference."

"I'll do everything I can there..." Lille paused. "...but, I
suggest you also submit a formal complaint to the Confederation Senate. There's no question Gary Holsten doesn't trust us,
but whatever he's doing on Barroux, it's pretty likely he doesn't
have Senate approval. If you can get the Confed politicians on
his back, it will do more to slow his efforts than anything Sect...
PP...agents can achieve, at least in the near term."

"That's a great idea. At the speed they've been demobiliz-
ing their military, the last thing they want is an incident that
might provoke renewed hostilities." Villieneuve frowned. "Not
that we're in any position to start a new fight ourselves. But that
doesn't stop us from expressing our outrage at this blatant viola-
tion of the peace terms."

Lille nodded in agreement. Then, he asked, "Any other top
priorities?"

"Yes...one." Villieneuve sighed. "You're aware that the Confederation is sending a fleet to explore deep into the Badlands?"

"Yes...I'd heard a few reports about that. It's true, then?"

"I'm afraid so." Villieneuve was silent for a moment. "You
know as well as I do how vital old tech is going to be going

forward." His voice tightened, suppressed anger clearly trying to surface. "Tyler Barron and his people cost us victory twice by destroying artifacts we discovered."

Ricard looked quizzically over at Villieneuve. "I agree with the threat the Confederation's expedition presents, but I'm not sure what I can do to lessen that."

"Nothing. At least not regarding the Confederation's exploration fleet. But there are other sources of old tech. Sector Nine always had an extensive intelligence presence along the Confederation's border with the Badlands. It was very productive, and I want it reestablished. Immediately."

"That was a pretty expensive operation, Gaston...bribing frontier prospectors and the like. Are you sure we can spare that much currency?"

"We don't have a choice. We have no hope of mounting the kind of force the Confeds are sending out, so we've got to make do with the closer in worlds. There are still plenty of crews working the border, more than before, now that the war's over and the frontier bars are flooded with discharged spacers looking for new careers. And, don't forget, what they do is still illegal in the Confederation. We need to be in this game, Ricard, any way we can. Rebuilding the Union...the Peoples' Union... is one thing. But we're going to need more tech too, or we'll be left behind."

Lille nodded. "I understand...and I agree completely. As soon as I get the other operations underway, I may even go to the Confederation frontier myself. We've got less to work with now, and that means we've got to get more from what we can deploy."

"Do that...I'll miss having you here, but I'll feel a hell of a lot better knowing you're there. We also need to rebuild our operative network in the Confederation, and the frontier is as good a place to start as any. We need to know if they find anything new."

"Understood." Lille looked down for a few seconds, amused, and mildly depressed as well, at the discolored gray metal of the desk where the effective dictator of the Union—or the roughly eighty percent of it over which he'd managed to retain or regain control, at least—worked every day. It was a far cry from the priceless antiques that had filled Villieneuve's previous office. Lille understood the reasoning, and he couldn't argue with the massive success his friend had achieved through his playacting…but part of him missed the days of more open luxury, at least for those in power. He didn't doubt Villieneuve lived in the same obscene decadence he had before, but now that kind of thing took place strictly behind closed doors.

"Well…" Lille looked up, reestablishing eye contact. "It will take me several weeks to get the operations started that will cement our control over the workers' councils." He paused. "We've picked low-hanging fruit so far, the councils close to home, the ones we could focus on ourselves. You know there's going to be slippage, foul-ups, especially on the planets farther out. I will set forth specific operating criteria, but some agents will screw up, others will run into particularly troublesome councils." He hesitated. "At some point, we're going to have to go back and clean up the problems. Random disappearances and scripted denouncements are useful, but eventually, we're just going to have to send in the Foudre Rouge…or whatever we're calling them now."

"The People's Army, you mean." Villieneuve's eyes were locked on Lille's, and the expression on his face was deadly serious. "And, yes, they will undoubtedly be needed to execute the final stage of the operation. But the more we can handle with clandestine means, the better off we will be. We've done what we had to do, my friend, to survive, and to exploit the situation. It will take time to establish the level of control we need, to rebuild our forces and infiltrate every important group, to establish enhanced surveillance and throw the workers back in their place. But we will get there." There was a silence in the room that seemed to bring the temperature down several degrees.

"When we do, Ricard, these people—these workers—will learn to appreciate whatever we choose to give them. And they will come to understand real fear."

Chapter Three

"Ty, I don't have to tell you how important this mission is…you know that, probably better than anyone." Admiral Van Striker sat at the conference table, his eyes darting back and forth between Barron and Gary Holsten.

The head of Confederation Intelligence had been uncharacteristically quiet, mostly watching as Striker and Barron discussed the mission. He was deep in thought, concerned about sending Tyler Barron and thousands of spacers so deep into the unknown. He'd been a part of the decision-making apparatus that had sent men and women to war often enough, into battles that had killed legions of them. But there was something different about this. Barron and his people would be the first Confederation spacers to journey so far from home…and in a way back in time as well, as they ventured deep into the heart of the dead ancient empire.

"No, sir, you don't." Barron sat upright, looking a little stiff. Not exactly nervous, but a bit agitated, perhaps. "The last war made it pretty clear that the next one won't be won by heroics or economic might. There's too much technology out there, left over from the past, and if the pulsar taught us anything, it's what

15

kind of difference even a single artifact can make."

"You know better than anyone what a close thing that was. If you hadn't managed to destroy the thing, who knows what might have happened. Foudre Rouge could be marching on Megara even now." Striker leaned back and took a deep breath. "We're very restricted by the treaties governing old tech, Tyler… but even if we have to share any finds with the other powers, it's better than risking someone else discovering something like the pulsar…someone a little less…dedicated…to treaty obligations." Striker's tone left little doubt he thought the whole notion of sharing artifacts was ridiculous, and that if it had been up to him, he'd have told Barron to hide anything his expedition found.

"Tyler…" Holsten finally spoke. He'd had something he wanted to say since they'd all sat down together, one last meeting before the fleet set out. But it wasn't based on hard data or intel, only on a feeling that had plagued his gut. "I would tell you to be careful out there, but I know that's not necessary. Still…" He paused, his edginess as clear, he suspected, to his two companions as it was to himself. "It's just that…we like to think of ourselves, this small cluster of habitation so close to the Rim, as all that is left of humanity after the Cataclysm."

"Are you suggesting there are others?" Striker sounded surprised. "We've never had any indications of any other survivors."

Holsten took a deep breath and exhaled. "And, we've never gone as far as we're about to either." He paused. "I'm just saying, we really don't know what's out there…or even how vast the empire was, how many hundreds—thousands—of systems are connected by warp points, how far that web stretches. We've never had any real data on what lies out beyond the limited range that's been explored. Even the hardiest frontier smugglers have stayed fairly close to the border…ten, maybe even twenty transits. What if the transwarp network goes on for scores of systems? Hundreds? Thousands? How could we possibly even guess at what's out there?"

The three men were silent for a moment. Finally, Barron said, "Well, I guess that's one reason we're going. To find out. I'm more concerned right now with locating refinable fuel sources than I am with stumbling on ghosts of the old empire…but I can promise both of you, we'll keep our eyes open for anything that might be out there."

"Do that, Ty. In the war, at least you knew when you were heading into danger. This time, you've got no idea what to expect. Once you get past the close-in Badlands, every jump will be into the unknown. What records we've got of imperial times are so incomplete, they're almost useless. Trust your gut, and remember…you have the authority to end the mission and return at any time. If you run into danger, no matter what it is, come home." Holsten wasn't used to feeling as uneasy as he did. He'd been the leading proponent of the mission, but he'd become increasingly nervous as time passed and the departure date approached. He had no idea what Barron and his fleet would find, none at all. There was no useful intelligence, no real data of any kind. He didn't like shooting blind, and he'd come to realize that, if he could go back a year and a half to when he'd first been one of the plan's enthusiastic proponents, he might pull his support. He didn't have any new knowledge, no more reason to fear what might happen than he had back on Grimaldi. But the ache in his gut had gotten steadily worse.

"I'll be careful, Gary. Don't worry about that. This is just an exploration mission, and as creepy as plunging through dead and haunted systems might be, if I get the slightest idea that something's wrong, I'll be back here in a flash."

Holsten didn't believe that. Barron's career hadn't exactly been a demonstration in shying away from danger. But there was nothing he could do about it, not now. It was far too late to cancel the expedition. And the original impetus, the need to get as much old tech as possible was as valid as ever.

Nothing to do but wish Barron the best of luck and shake his hand. And, he did just that.

* * *

"Welcome, Commander Globus. I am honored by your pres-

ence. I didn't expect an officer of such rank and experience to
command the Alliance contingent." The Palatians had sent a
small flotilla, three battleships and half a dozen escorts. Their
contribution was more about inclusion and helping to sustain
and develop the Confederation-Alliance relationship than it was
about providing needed strength and power to the fleet. Still,
after watching Jovi Grachus and her pilots out at the Bottleneck,
Barron knew he would never take any number of Palatian warriors on his side for granted.

"The honor is mine, Admiral Barron. Your name is as well
known in the Alliance as in the Confederation, and nearly as
revered, I daresay."

Barron suspected there was some diplomatic nicety in Globus's statement. Barron had aided Tarkus Vennius and the Gray
Alliance during the civil war, and the current Imperator, Vian
Tulus, was a man Barron included on the small list of men and
women he called true friends. But he'd first encountered the
Alliance as an enemy, the man who had destroyed *Invictus*, and
killed Katrine Regulus and her crew. It has been less than three
years since he'd led the assault that crushed Palatia's orbital
defenses and laid the planet open to invasion. That had been
done in the service of Vennius and the Gray Alliance forces, but
Barron knew enough about Palatian martial pride to understand
that had to be a cause of resentment among some officers.

It didn't require looking any farther than the vengeful rage
that had driven Jovi Grachus for so long to understand the
mixed feelings many in the Alliance no doubt had toward him.

"Your words do me great honor, Commander. I trust you
are aware how sincerely the Confederation values its friendship
with your people." Barron countered Globus's diplomacy with
a touch of his own. Most of the navy appreciated the Alliance,
and the aid that power had provided in the closing stages of
the war. The Alliance contingent had fought like wildcats, and
though the destruction of the pulsar had been the climactic act
of the struggle, the Palatians played no small part in the overall
battle.

Still, to many in the Confederation, the Alliance seemed…

odd, their warrior culture a little too foreign for the average citizen to fully understand. And, as a power that lay out beyond what most in the Confederation considered the Rim, many thought the Alliance was provincial.

"So, we have both played the parts assigned to us, Admiral." The Palatian smiled. "Perhaps we can go somewhere now and talk a bit more informally. The Imperator gave me some messages for you, words he tasked me to deliver privately." A short pause. "And, he sent several cases of wine as well, the very best from the Tulus vineyards."

Barron returned the smile. He wasn't much of a drinker, but he wasn't about to refuse Globus's hospitality, nor that of Vian Tulus. It would be unacceptable to be ungracious to the Alliance's Imperator—or to a friend with whom he'd shed blood—and Tulus was both. Besides, it was a good chance to get to know Globus a bit better. The two had met briefly during the civil war, but now it was time to build a true relationship.

"Why don't you join me for dinner on…*Dauntless*." He still hesitated slightly when calling his new ship by its name. "My shuttle leaves in a little over an hour." Barron paused, then added, "You can tell me of the fighting with the Krillians." Barron already knew most of what had transpired over the last eighteen months, but he'd become quite adept at handling Palatians, and inviting one to recount the stories of a war in which he'd fought was the height of graciousness in their society.

"I would be happy to tell you of our victories, Admiral."

Barron held back a smile at the predictability of the Alliance officer, and he just nodded somberly. "I will see you in the shuttle bay in an hour then, Commander." He shook hands with the Palatian. It was predominantly a Confederation custom, but it was practiced to an extent in the Alliance as well.

Barron turned and walked down the corridor. His gear had already been shipped up to *Dauntless*, but he had a few things left to do before he left Megara. As he walked down the hall, he found himself thinking about what Globus would tell him at dinner, about all the Palatians had done since the fighting with the Union ended.

According to Gary Holsten's intelligence reports, the Alliance forces had utterly eradicated the remnants of the Krillian fleet, relentlessly chasing down and destroying every last vessel. The dishonorable nature of the initial Krillian attack called for retribution on its own, but the fact that Tarkus Vennius had been killed in the ensuing combat escalated things immensely. Palatian honor had demanded the complete obliteration of the Krillian Holdfast, at any cost…and that was just what it had claimed.

Krillus himself had already been killed, of course, but that hadn't sated the Palatians' rage. As soon as the ships that had been deployed to the Bottleneck returned to the Alliance, they invaded Krillian space, assaulting every world. The Krillians tried to surrender, but their pleas fell on deaf ears as Alliance ships blasted the last of their ships to plasma, and Palatian ground forces landed on their planets, crushing any resistance and brutally seizing control.

Barron suspected the newly conquered subjects would pay dearly for their former masters' perfidy. The leaders likely faced execution—most had probably been killed already. The common people faced an uncertain future, at best as Plebs serving the Palatian war machine, but possibly worse, as virtual slaves, repaying the honor debt incurred by their former masters through their blood and sweat.

Barron saw injustice in that, millions suffering for choices in which they'd had no part, though he also understood the Palatians' rage. It was a reminder just how different the Alliance was from the Confederation, the divergent philosophies that governed their own systems of ethics and morality, and the role the Palatians' past agonies had played in the forging of their hard and merciless culture.

The armed forces of the two powers had begun to develop a kind of mutual respect, one forged in shared combat, but Barron knew the future of friendship and cooperation between Alliance and Confederation would be difficult in many ways. Carelessness and mismanagement could derail it entirely.

* * *

"You're already in deep with the program to aid the revolutionaries on Barroux. The Senate will crucify you if they find out what you're doing there. Now, you want to sponsor exploration crews—pirates by Confederation law—on the frontier?" Admiral Van Striker sat in his palatial office. The vast room took up half the top floor of the skyscraper that housed naval headquarters on Megara. No luxury had been spared in its construction or decoration. And Striker hated it. Every paneled, gilded, antique-filled centimeter. He longed for his office on Grimaldi, for the practicality of that great fortress, so much closer to the recent battle lines than the Confederation's capital planet was.

Gary Holsten didn't answer right away. He just looked thoughtfully across the desk at his friend. Finally, he said, "It's a risk, no doubt, Van. But what else can we do?" Holsten paused, then added, "I mean really…what other options do we have? We got lucky with the pulsar. You know that as well as I do. Tyler Barron's the best damned officer we've got, but there were a hundred ways he could have failed there. A thousand. Is that our strategy? To get lucky again next time? The White Fleet may stumble on something extraordinary out there, or it may find that, once it clears the Badlands closer to the Confederation, there is nothing but blasted and destroyed worlds. There are still artifacts out there, five or ten transits from the border, where we've found them before. Can we continue to ignore that and count only on the White Fleet to find what we need at the old empire's core?"

"I understand what you're saying, Gary, but the doves are strong in the Senate right now, and you've got to know more than a few of them resent you. You've managed to dance your way around a whole string of crises, but if you get caught trafficking illegally in Badlands tech, they'll try to use it to bring you down."

"Everything you just said is absolutely correct. But how does it change anything? If the White Fleet finds anything…well, we'll have to deal with how to handle that when it happens, but in the meantime, if you don't think Sector Nine—or whatever they're calling themselves these days—isn't out there on every border planet, in every spacer's dive bar, looking for any old tech they can get their hands on, you're crazy."

"There's no appetite in the Senate for picking fights with the Union right now. You know that. They won't see this as a counter to a real threat. They'll say you are looking to undermine the peace, that you're violating international law." Striker paused. "And when this latest force reduction bill passes—and you know you won't be able to stop it forever—our navy won't be in much better shape than theirs. Especially not with the White Fleet gone."

"Van, every report I've been able to get from inside the Union says the same thing. Gaston Villieneuve has not only survived, he's managed to seize absolute control. The entire Presidium is gone, most likely assassinated on his order. He's got all sorts of problems—economic collapse, open rebellion...but he's dealing with it. All of it. We can't underestimate him. Two hundred years of Union oligarchy, and on the verge of total ruin he somehow manages to come out on top. You know as well as I do, as soon as he's able to rebuild his military and his economy, he'll be back at us. Long term, they need to grab some of our productive worlds...or at least hammer down our economic advantage." Holsten shook his head. "Do you want to lead your spacers against a Union that's managed to find another artifact like the pulsar? It could happen, and if it does now, we're at peace. There will be no chance to strike while they analyze and replicate it. They'll bring it back to some hidden research facility, and every scientist they've got will be on it. We won't know a thing until they hurl a fleet as us, armed with a weapon we can't counter."

Holsten sighed loudly and shook his head. "Whatever risks there may be, I've got to take them. I'd rather take the chance on my political enemies defeating me, even locking me away in prison, than knowing I'd let Villieneuve gain the edge...and watching one day as Foudre Rouge haul those oh-so-principled Senators out of the Capitol."

Striker sat still, silent for a few seconds. Then, he nodded. "You're right. But I still don't like the risk." He hesitated again. "Be careful, my friend. Don't get too involved, not directly."

Holsten looked back at the admiral. "The funds will be routed through so many intermediaries, it will take one hell of a bloodhound to trace them back to me." He paused, his eyes flashing to the door, almost as if he was concerned someone would walk in and overhear the conversation. "And I've found someone special to lead the effort. Someone who knows the Badlands border better than anyone I'm aware of, and who's far less conspicuous than me. All I have to do now is convince her to do it."

Chapter Four

Coast North of Seahaven
Planet Tellurus, Elicron III
Year 315 AC

The sun streamed into the gallery, through the row of glass doors and the transoms above. The soft, late afternoon light danced over the black and white marble floor, the shadows of branches blowing in the breeze projected across the wall. It was an image most would have viewed as a glimpse of paradise.

Seahaven was an idyllic town, an enclave where many of the Confederation's wealthiest maintained homes. The highlands lying to the north, great rocky heights soaring above the Azure Sea, were extremely sought after, a stretch of magnificent natural beauty, dotted with great estates and mansions.

The villa was as immense as it was magnificent, the craftsmanship that had gone into its construction almost beyond compare. It was only a few years old, unlike most of the well-maintained, but aging, homes that dotted the coast. It had been built for an industrialist who'd grown vastly wealthy on military contracts, and then been indicted on fraud and war profiteering charges. Its former owner was still fighting the legal battle to preserve some fraction of his wealth and stay out of jail, but he'd been compelled to sell off his non-core assets, including the artfully-crafted vacation estate.

Andi Lafarge was wealthy now, richer than she'd ever imagined even as she'd spent her life in pursuit of such prosperity. And, she was liquid. She had no properties, no investments in company stock. She just had cash. Several billion credits in cash, almost all of it courtesy of the immense fortune Gary Holsten had paid her for the stealth generator.

The property's distress sale had promised to be a brilliant investment as well as an almost unparalleled place to live, but she hadn't been the only one interested in the villa. She had, however, been the only one who could move immediately, and that had proven to be an unbeatable edge when dealing with a desperate seller.

For as long as she could remember, she had dreamed of such prosperity, of experiencing the life she'd seen the industrial barons of her home world living. But, even as she closed the purchase and began moving her meager possessions in, she felt strange. Sad? Disappointed? Disillusioned? She couldn't quite pinpoint what was bothering her, save to say that reaching her goal felt nothing like she'd imagined it would.

She had padded around her immense house for the first few months, bought some furnishings—though far from enough to fill all the cavernous rooms—and tried to adapt to the quiet life of leisure she'd wanted so long to attain.

Then, Tyler Barron came. He'd been stuck at the front, serving with the fleet as the ceasefire between the Confederation and the Union gradually solidified into a permanent treaty. She'd sent him messages, told him where she'd settled, and hoped he would come to see her. And he did just that, the instant he'd gotten leave.

He had been there for almost six months, and she'd truly enjoyed their time together. They'd hiked and explored all along the rugged coastline. They'd sailed the pristine waters of the Azure Sea, and they'd sampled the best restaurants Seahaven had to offer. And those nights with Barron lying next to her had seemed shorter, and far less lonely, than those of the first few months in her new home.

But now, after what seemed like a brief and fleeting interlude, he was gone, back to the navy she knew had first claim on him. She told herself she didn't care, that she always enjoyed his company, but she didn't need it. Andi Lafarge didn't need anyone. That was as close to a rigid personal mantra as she possessed.

She tried to keep herself occupied, to embrace her new life of luxury. She decorated more of the house, though she ran out of drive long before she finished. She tried to live the life of those she'd envied for so long, but it just didn't work. She was restless, unsettled, bored. Miserable.

Then Gary Holsten showed up.

Holsten's family had an estate not far from Andi's villa, an immense palace that befitted one of the Confederation's wealthiest dynasties. The house was almost incomparably large, two or three times the size of Andi's palatial property, and the grounds consisted of over a thousand hectares of prime waterfront and woodland property.

Holsten told her he had just come to spend some time at the family estate, to rest a little after the rigors of the war. That made sense, superficially at least, but she hadn't believed it, not for a second. Her suspicions were confirmed when she asked around about the Holsten place. As best she could determine from speaking to longtime residents, Gary Holsten had been there exactly once before…when he was eight years old. Still, she waited, sure he would tell her why he had come. What he wanted from her. Eventually.

She was curious, intrigued, impatient. The whole thing felt like some sort of high stakes test of wills, and she was determined not to ask his real purpose until he chose to tell her. She found herself feeling more alive than she had since Tyler left. She gave Holsten a tour of her villa, and they had dinner twice, discussing nothing more than pleasantries. She'd have made time for the man who made her so wealthy, of course, but she genuinely enjoyed his company. He reminded her of past adventures, experiences she'd considered hard and burdensome at the time, but now remembered more fondly.

Finally, a week after he arrived, he asked to discuss something important with her. She told him to come to the villa, and the two of them sat in the study. It was one of the rooms she'd furnished completely, and surprisingly tastefully for someone who'd risen from the direst poverty and made her fortune as a borderlands adventurer and smuggler.

"We've confirmed that Gaston Villieneuve has secured his hold on power in the Union," he said rather abruptly, as soon as they'd exchanged greetings.

Andi just sat silently, her eyes locked on Holsten's. She felt discomfort, if not outright fear, at the mention of the Sector Nine chief's name, but she did her best not to show it.

"He has his share of problems to deal with before he will be a conventional threat again, there is no question about that. But..."

The word hung in the air as Holsten paused, just for an instant, seemingly trying to decide how to say what he'd come to say.

"But, you think he will try to recover as much old tech as possible...and sooner rather than later." Andi didn't give Holsten the chance to finish. Suddenly, she understood completely why Holsten had come. She knew more about the border areas and the Badlands than almost anyone in the Confederation.

"Yes. That's exactly why I am here, Andi."

"You want to pick my brain about the Badlands? Or you want access to my old contacts?"

Holsten just looked at her for a moment. Then, he said, "No, Andi...I want more than that. I know you've just gotten yourself set up here, and you deserve every moment of your retirement for all you've done. But I need you. The Confederation needs you."

"Forget working me, Gary. Just tell me what you want."

"I want to make you part of Confederation Intelligence. I want you to go to the border, possibly into the Badlands. We have to get our own operation going out there now. We have to find whatever old tech we can, before Villieneuve's people do. And, we've got to root out the Sector Nine influence. We let them throw money around on our own planets and snatch useful artifacts from under our noses. Not anymore."

She looked back at him, and she realized she was shaking her head. She felt a flash of defiance, of anger. Not at Holsten himself, but at the government he'd come to ask her serve. "When I did that on my own, the Confederation called me an outlaw. They hounded us incessantly." She paused. "I assume there hasn't been any recent change in treaty obligations recently. Or Confederation law."

"No," Holsten said softly. "This would be a secret operation, one financed entirely by Holsten family funds. We'll provide anything you need, and we'll split the value of any artifacts you find…with you, and with anyone you recruit."

"Are you crazy?" She wasn't often surprised, but she hadn't expected what she'd just heard. "I had nothing to lose then, Gary. Most of the crews out there don't. And, once we do— if we get lucky enough to get that big score—we retire." She was silent for a moment. "Do you understand the risks in what you're proposing? I could end up in prison, or worse. And you'd be risking your entire family fortune. If we get caught, if the scope of your involvement becomes public, the Senate will crucify you."

"So, don't get caught." It was a flippant-sounding answer to a deadly serious warning, but suddenly Andi realized Holsten *had* thought his proposal through, including the dangers…and he was still there trying to recruit her.

"It's that important?"

"You know how close we came to disaster with the pulsar… and I'm sure you remember the planetkiller too. What do you think would happen if the Union were able to find another artifact like those, especially now, when we're at peace? They'd have all the time they needed to get it back to their space without interference, to study it, replicate it."

She just sat silently, taking a deep breath. She still felt an impulse to resist. She understood the importance of what Holsten was asking, but she'd done her part already. The mission to destroy the pulsar would have been impossible without the stealth generator she'd found. She wasn't a naval officer like Tyler. She didn't owe the Confederation anything. Certainly nothing more than she'd already given.

Could she even go back to her old life, wandering seedy spaceport bars, trading for information that was, as often as not, pure fabrication? She remembered the constant caution, the fear that any meeting could turn into an ambush in an instant.

Most of all, she realized that joining Holsten did not mean going back to the past. Her crew were all wealthy now too, their shares of the proceeds from the stealth generator enough to support them for the rest of their lives in obscene luxury. They were scattered across the Confederation, settled, retired. If she went back, she'd be going back alone. *No*, she thought. *I can't do it. I'm just having trouble getting used to life here. Things will fall into place.*

But then, she realized part of her *wanted* to go. The excitement, the purpose…they called to her. She looked around, at the exquisite room she'd created, and she realized how much she missed her cramped cabin on *Pegasus*. She still had *Pegasus*. She hadn't been able to bear the idea of selling her beloved ship, and since she didn't need the money, she'd kept it. In fact, the old vessel had been upgraded from top to bottom, no expense spared. Her days in that small ship had been full of danger, of hardship. But there was a void in her life now. She was in paradise, living a life few could dream of. And she was unhappy. Her palace had begun to feel too much like a prison.

And she felt an urge to help Holsten. He'd been more than fair with her in the past, and she owed her prosperity to him, at least in large measure. He could have confiscated the stealth generator as illegal contraband. But he hadn't. He'd paid her for it, and a fair price too. But was that debt, and her own restlessness, worth upending everything she'd worked so hard for?

She turned toward Holsten, intending to turn him down. But then she said, "I'll do it." She wasn't sure what made the words come out, and but the instant they did, she felt a burst of excitement that had been gone for too long.

She was going back to what she did best, back to the rough and tumble frontier, the place where she'd first arrived as a destitute teenager seeking her fortune.

She was going home.

Chapter Five

"I want to thank you for the invitation to dinner, Admiral Barron. This mission is a difficult one for a Palatian. I understand the advantages of picking through the rubble of a long-dead civilization, but it is hardly work for warriors such as ourselves."

Barron looked across the table at Commander Globus. The Alliance officer wasn't a bad sort, and Barron had come to genuinely like the man, but he carried his Palatian warrior culture a bit more obviously than Vian Tulus had. Barron knew Globus's tacit inclusion of him and his people in the comment about warriors was a show of respect…no Palatian would say something like that if he didn't mean it. Diplomacy, especially when based on false compliments and feigned respect, was not high on the Alliance's list of competencies, and while Barron knew there had been enough secrecy and backstabbing during the civil war, generally, a Palatian said what he thought. Their honesty could, at times, be a bit brutal to someone used to more…refined… exchanges.

"A warrior faces danger, Commander. While we are unlikely to encounter enemies of the normal sort, I suspect we will encounter more than enough hazards to sate the warriors' need."

Barron glanced around the table. This was the sixth dinner he'd held for his top officers aboard *Dauntless*—though he was still having trouble thinking of his massive new ship by that name— and the fleet hadn't even left Confederation space yet. It seemed to be going well, and he felt a bit of relief. The first few times he'd hosted both his Confederation people and the top Alliance officers, it had been a bit uncomfortable. The two sides had been allies in the closing stages of the Union War, but the two cultures had considerable differences, ones that seemed more pronounced with his own spacers no longer in their wartime frames of mind. He doubted anyone in a Confederation uni- form felt sorrow for the loss of potential combat opportunities.

"Indeed, Admiral. Very true."

Barron knew that Globus understood the strategic need to uncover old technology before the Union or another potential enemy gained an unbeatable edge, but Palatian culture looked down on such peaceful endeavors. The scientists and engineers in the Alliance were ranked substantially below military person- nel in social status, and Barron understood that Globus and his people had to fight against the ingrained notion that the mission was somehow…beneath them.

"Commander Globus, perhaps you could recount for us the conflict against the Krillians. Many of us served closely with Imperator Vennius in the civil war, and I, for one, would be very interested in more details on his last battle. He was a noble war- rior. I will always consider him a comrade I was proud to stand beside in battle."

Barron watched as Atara Travis spoke. He'd served along- side her for almost ten years now, and he thought of her as his best friend, even as the sister he'd never had. But she still sur- prised him from time to time with the tact and diplomacy she could produce when the mood hit her. Her request of Globus might seem a bit obvious to him and to the other Confederation officers present, but she'd clearly learned what he had in fighting alongside the Alliance officers. At least as far as he'd been able to detect, Palatians never tired of telling stories of their battles.

"Of course, Captain Travis. We all mourn the loss of Imperator Vennius, especially at the hands of the deceitful Krillians. But we can take solace that his death in battle was a heroic one, an epic sacrifice that will immortalize his name and his reign. Our fleet was outnumbered, but Vennius ordered us forward anyway…"

Barron sat with an attentive look on his face, but it was a façade. He'd heard the retelling of the battle before, several times, enough that he could probably tell it himself. Still, allowing Globus to continue on had its uses. The purpose of the dinner had been the same as the ones that had preceded it, to forge his Confederation and Alliance spacers into a single, unified force. They'd fought together, of course, but the Palatians had been segregated as their own task force, and they'd only fought a single battle. Before that, his forces had been sent to fight in the Alliance civil war, and the burden of merging the diverse groups of fighters into a unified force had fallen on Tarkus Vennius.

This was different. They were about to head off into deep space, far beyond where any Confederation or Alliance vessel had ever traveled. They would be alone, in a way so profound, it scared Barron when it slipped into his thoughts. They had to be able to count on each other…because there would be no one else there if they ran into trouble.

Barron looked over at Globus and nodded respectfully. The Palatian was just getting started, he knew. The story would go on for quite some time, through multiple rounds of coffee and after dinner drinks.

"So, Imperator Vennius commanded the right wing to advance…"

* * *

"You're in direct charge of *Dauntless*'s systems and maintenance. And damage control, if it comes to that. It's time for you to step up, Commander, to really take control." Anya Fritz was staring at Walt Billings, feeling a little guilty for the hard time she was giving him. Billings was a good officer, one who'd greatly exceeded her initial expectations. He'd had been a bit of a clown at one time, one who'd thought he was funnier than he was. But the realities of combat, and the losses of friends and comrades, had squeezed the excess levity from him, forged him into a strong officer, and a capable one. Billings had learned from her, and he'd become one hell of an engineer in his own right. She was damned proud of him…not that she'd ever let *him* know that.

"I understand, Captain. I've got everything under control. The teams are organized and ready. This ship is brand new… but we've still run diagnostics on a regular schedule. Plus, it's not like…" Billings let his voice trail off, not finishing what he'd begun to say.

She knew what he was thinking, what he'd almost said. The war was over. *Dauntless* was heading off on an exploratory mission. There was a creepy spookiness to plunging into the heart of the dead empire, but the ship's engineers weren't likely to face anything like the desperate attempts to restore systems in the middle of battle. If things went well, she and her people would spend most of their time researching old tech finds.

"Perhaps we should put that to the test, Commander. I think we'll run some simulated damage drills. Then, we'll see just how quickly your people can do their jobs." Fritz was edgy. The *war* was over, but she was nervous about the mission anyway. The fleet was going to be farther from home than any ships had ventured since the Cataclysm, too far to get any kind of help from the Confederation if something…anything…went badly wrong.

Fritz was a hard taskmaster, she knew that. She also knew her teams had come up with a variety of nicknames for her over the years. She'd heard some, but she didn't doubt there were more of them out there. She didn't really care, especially since her people had always given her their best, however much they grumbled when they thought she wasn't listening. She figured letting them blow off steam was helpful. She worked her people hard, and they needed some stress relief. A few of the names were even fairly clever.

"Captain, my people are ready to meet any challenge you put before them."

She held back a smile. She was about to let him off the hook, tell him there would be no surprise exercises, but then the doubts she'd been feeling surfaced again. She considered herself as battle-hardened as it was possible to become, but the unknown was terrifying in ways beyond even the hardship of battle. Barron had given her as much freighter space as he could for spare parts and the like, and she'd wracked her brain, trying to come up with anything she might require. If she needed something fifty transits from home and she hadn't brought it, she was screwed.

She was also unsettled about her job. Barron had made her chief engineer of the fleet, which made all sorts of sense superficially…but she wasn't exactly sure what a fleet engineer did. She was used to working a ship's innards, tracking down damage and problems. Now, she had an office and a big desk near *Dauntless*'s bridge, and a far hazier picture of just what she was supposed to be doing.

"Well, we'll just see how ready you are." She pulled a tablet from a clip at her waist. "Scenario G4," she said, looking down at the small screen. She almost felt bad. She'd designed the simulated damage routines herself, and she'd filled them with tricks, engineering complexities guaranteed to drive Billings and his people crazy. There wasn't a straightforward drill in the group… and G4 was one of the worst.

"We're ready, Captain." Billings sounded confident.

Good…we'll see if that lasts.

* * *

"I don't even know why I'm here. There are no enemies out there. What does this fleet need with eight hundred fighters?" Jake Stockton was lying in bed, staring up at the ceiling as he'd been doing for the past few hours. He'd never slept very well, but now he simply had too many nightmares waiting for him, too many shadowy faces of friends gone, men and women burned alive in their fighters or blown to atoms deep in space. The price of sleep was just too high.

He'd been as quiet and still as he'd been able to manage as he counted the minutes until morning. There was no point in waking up Stara just because of his own insomnia. But, now he could hear her stirring, and he knew she was awake.

"How can anyone know what we're going to need? Nobody's ever done anything like this before. We'll certainly have more than enough scouting duty for the squadrons." Stara Sinclair was awake, but it was clear from her tone she was *barely* awake.

"Scouting missions, yes, but we've got two-thirds of the crack squadrons in the fleet with us. A hundred ships could handle routine sweeps, certainly two hundred. And prowling around empty systems doesn't require a pack of aces with twenty kills apiece."

"Well, I'd wager the fleet's as big as it is as much because some of the higher ups want to protect a portion of the fleet from the downsizing going on. It's hard for even a pacifist Senator to argue that we don't need to take old tech more seriously than before...and the fleet is a place to stash ships that will be outside the cost-cutters' reach. I'm sure that's true for the squadrons, too." She paused, putting her hand over her mouth to cover a yawn. "And, I'm glad you're here...because I'm here. Would you really like to go a year or more without seeing me?" There was a playful tone to her words, but Stockton took them to heart.

Stara had moved into his quarters, more or less completely, if unofficially. It was a scenario that would have terrified the younger Stockton in a way no enemy gunning for him ever had, but now, he realized, he was not only happy to have her there... he was uncomfortable when she wasn't around. Stockton was one of the navy's most renowned officers, and no one would say he couldn't face whatever came at him by himself. But he was well-aware of the scars he carried now. War, especially the way he fought it, left its marks in more ways than one, and Stara's presence helped. She calmed him, softened the screams of the dead.

"No, I wouldn't want to go a year without seeing you. But maybe we both should be back on Megara. Or at Grimaldi."

"Would you really want Admiral Barron to go on this journey without you? I don't believe that, not for a minute. I just think you like to complain." She grabbed one of the pillows and gently hit him with it. Then, she got up and walked over toward the small head. "I'd love to sit here and listen to you complain, my dear, but unlike you, I've got work to do. I'm on duty in thirty minutes." She slipped through the small doorway, and he heard the shower come on.

He knew she wasn't kidding about having work to do. Stara had run *Dauntless*'s—the old *Dauntless*'s—flight operations during the last few years of the war, but Admiral Barron had since promoted her. She was now the fleet small craft operations officer, which made her responsible for not only the massed fighter squadrons, but also the enormous array of shuttles, gigs, and pinnaces locked in the landing bays, waiting to explore any intriguing worlds the expedition found.

It was a massive job, and while his, as fleet fighter commander, was no less vast, it was far less likely to come into play. His squadrons would pull long-range patrols, and likely they would make the first sweeps over any dead imperial worlds. But that was nothing to Stockton's battle-hardened sensibilities, and he wondered if he'd have to program his AI to keep him awake in the cockpit.

Stockton slid out of bed. His own duty period didn't begin for a few hours, but his chances of getting any more sleep were nil, so he figured he might as well get up.

He looked around the cabin. It wasn't exactly large, not by planet-side standards at least, but it was nearly double the size of his cramped quarters on the old *Dauntless*. The new ship was magnificent by any standards, yet he found himself missing the old *Dauntless* and her dingy, gray corridors. He'd walked those hallways for seven years, alongside friends and colleagues he'd never forget.

The truth was, he felt lost. The pressure of combat was gone, and now he had far too much time to think about the losses suffered in the war, the comrades he'd lost. He'd almost resigned his commission, but he had no idea what else he could do, and in the end, he couldn't leave Stara. Perhaps he could have persuaded her to retire with him, but he hadn't been able to bring himself to suggest it, not when he had no idea where they would go or what they would do.

He took a deep breath and stood up, walking over toward the small built-in console. He'd tossed his jacket there the night before. His eyes went right to the insignia, to the four platinum circlets on the collar.

Captain. It was a rank he'd never expected to attain, one that seemed almost out of reach for a wildcat pilot, like himself. He knew he'd earned it, at least on one level. He'd fought hard during the war, and he'd been in the center of the conflict's greatest battles. But it troubled him, too.

He'd had a hard enough time stepping into Kyle Jamison's shoes, assuming the rank his old commander had held. Now, he'd reached a level his friend, and to a great extent, his mentor, had never held. He realized he had to go on, to accept the deaths of Jamison and so many other friends. He had to do it for Stara, and because Kyle and his other lost comrades would have wanted him to.

He knew what he had to do...he just didn't know how to do it.

Chapter Six

Pamphlet Posted Outside Factory 19A6

Workers of Barroux, there have been several instances of disorder and work stoppages at factories around the city. This disloyalty was instigated by dissident groups, criminals seeking to stand in the way of the Revolution. This morning, sixty-three of these traitors were executed in Freedom Square. The Revolution is yours, fellow citizens, and we can tolerate no interference from those seeking to further their own interests at the expense of Barroux's workers. We will show no mercy to those who oppose the Revolution. Those who fight us must be destroyed. Our cause is righteous, and the future is ours. —Remy Caron, First Protector of the People

Barroux City, Capital of the Barroux People's Republic
Barroux, Rhian III
Union Year 219 (315 AC)

"First Protector Caron, I'm pleased to meet you at last. I'm afraid we had some…difficulty…getting past the Union forces blockading Barroux." Mike Hoover stood in front of a massive desk, looking at the man who, at least if the intel had been accurate, had become the effective ruler of the planet.

Hoover glanced around the room, hiding his surprise at

what he saw. Caron wore a well-tailored suit, and his office was plushly decorated. Everyone present was well-dressed. He'd expected to see a group of factory workers, rough-edged men and women who'd launched a bid to free themselves from their oppressors. All the intel reports and propaganda he'd seen had suggested that Barroux's revolutionaries had established an egalitarian socialist republic, but the people in the room with him now looked almost like aristocrats. *It didn't take them long to forget where they came from...*

"It's a pleasure to meet you as well, Mr. Hoover. Words cannot express our gratitude for the help our friends in the Confederation have sent us." Caron's voice had an edge, an arrogance that hadn't been there earlier, in the days when he'd been just a factory worker caught up in the revolution.

"I don't represent the Confederation, First Protector." *What an idiotic title.* "I am here at the behest of private benefactors who wish to remain anonymous. You and your brave revolution have many admirers, as I am sure you can imagine." Hoover sounded sincere, though every word he'd just spoken was a lie. He'd been sent to Barroux by none other than Gary Holsten, and the technical data and supplies he'd brought had come straight from Confederation Intelligence. The purpose of his mission was aiding the revolution, keeping the fragile Union off-balance. It was second in importance only to the number one priority: hiding any Confederation involvement.

"Of course, Mr. Hoover. My apologies." From Caron's tone, it didn't sound like he apologized frequently.

Hoover nodded. There was no one in the room for whom he needed to maintain the charade, but he did it anyway. Openly aiding a combatant engaged in a conflict with a nation was an act of war. It was unlikely the Union could do anything about that right now—they simply weren't in the condition to contemplate a renewal of hostilities with the Confederation. If he fell into Union hands, he was as good as dead. And, from the looks of this blood-soaked revolution, he could imagine the dangers right there on Barroux. No, Hoover was smart enough to know that the true danger was the Senate, and the apoplectic fit they would throw if they knew what Holsten was up to in the Union. What really made him edgy was ending up back on Megara, testifying before a Senate committee looking to lock him up in some deep, dark hole and throw away the key.

"I have brought you technical specifications, First Protector, plans that will allow you to convert some of your manufacturing facilities to weapons production. My ship's cargo hold contains rare elements and other difficult-to-obtain items, but fortunately, Barroux is a planet rich in both resources and factory operations. Given the technology, and the assistance of the experts I brought with me, I believe we can help you fortify your world sufficiently to ward off any attempt the Union might make to invade."

"My thanks again to you, from myself, and on behalf of the citizens of Barroux. We are ready to fight to the end for our freedom…yet we face an enemy of great power, and your assistance is key to our final victory."

"We will begin production of the weapons at once. We have already repelled two Union attempts to invade. I fear the next one will be stronger. The plans and technology you bring will be of great value."

Hoover nodded. "I have several experts with me who can help you with retooling your production facilities. But what we brought in the way of materials, may be the last we're able to get to you for some time. The Union blockade is still somewhat porous, but it appears they're increasing the strength deployed to your system. I have a series of additional ships coming, but it's far from clear whether they will be able to get through." *Or if they will even try.* The delicacy and secrecy of the mission prevented Hoover from using naval vessels. He'd had to recruit a group of rogues and scoundrels from along the frontier, ex-smugglers mostly—and perhaps a few not that "ex"—who'd been enticed by the sums he'd been prepared to pay for what he had to admit was a very dangerous run.

He was confident his compatriots would at least try to complete their trips to Barroux—mostly because he'd assured them all that Confederation Intelligence would track down any who didn't—but he was equally sure none of them would dive head-long into the Union blockading forces. If they didn't have a clear run, they'd bolt.

"Again, Mr. Hoover, your aid is appreciated. We'll hope for the best with your additional ships. Meanwhile, we will proceed with the production efforts." He paused. Then he turned toward a woman sitting next to him. "Citizen Delacorte, would you show our guests to their lodgings?"

"Of course, First Protector." She stood up and turned toward Hoover. She was young, no older than her late twenties. Her hair was short, a spiky cut that matched the angular shape of her face. "If you will follow me." Her voice was pleasant enough, but Hoover felt something...odd...looking at her, and he suppressed a chill.

"Thank you, First Protector, Citizen Delacorte." Hoover turned and glanced back at his comrades. Then he followed Delacorte out of the room, the others right behind him.

* * *

"Mr. Hoover, my name is Henri Bernard." The man was dressed in a rough shirt and pants, both in drab gray, torn in places and stained from long use. "Thank you so much for meeting with me."

Hoover looked around, not because he particularly thought anyone was watching, but because it was in his nature to assume that might be the case at all times. That caution had saved his life more than once, and Barroux was proving to be a surprisingly complicated mission. Hoover had expected danger, but he'd imagined almost all of that would be centered on sneaking to and from the planet. Now, he felt hazards all around.

"We're alone here," Bernard said, before Hoover could answer. "This is one of our safe houses." Hoover realized Bernard had noticed his concern. He was impressed. He'd developed a cool demeanor in his years as a spy, and the fact that this man had caught his concern suggested he was no ordinary factory worker.

Hoover nodded, but he still looked around. In the field, the only eyes he trusted were his own. "My associate seemed to feel I would want to hear what you had to say." Hoover had three other agents with him, and he was still stunned Bernard had been able to intrigue Silvia Breen enough to convince her to set up the meeting. Breen was his number two on the mission, and one of the most stone cold, cynical agents he'd ever known. The fact that Bernard had gotten to her spoke volumes about the man and his story.

"I suggest you get to the point, Mr. Bernard. This may be a 'safe house,' but from what I've seen there are eyes everywhere on Barroux."

"You're right, of course, Mr. Hoover." A nervous pause. "I represent the Resistance on Barroux. The real Resistance."

"I don't understand." But in the pit of his stomach, he did.

"The Revolution has been hijacked, Mr. Hoover. Our people's desperate lunge for freedom has been taken over by corrupt leaders, no better than those of the Union." Another pause. "In some ways, worse."

"So, your group is fighting against the current government, the one that replaced the Union authorities?"

"Yes. You met with Caron. Sorry...*First Protector* Caron. I'm sure he told you how many died heroically fighting the government forces and repelling the Union's attempts to invade. Did he tell you how many his government has murdered?"

Hoover could feel a headache building. He'd gotten a somewhat of a bad impression from the first meeting with Caron... but there was no arguing the man was in firm control right now. Whoever Henri Bernard was, and whatever people he represented, they didn't seem to be remotely close to overthrowing Caron. "No, we didn't discuss such specifics. Are we talking about Union functionaries killed after the revolution?"

"No, Mr. Hoover. There's no doubt that many government officials were slain following the original uprising. But I'm talking about citizens of Barroux, many of whom were in the streets on that first night, risking everything to free this world. It began with Caron's political rivals, the other leaders of the

Revolution, anyone who stood in the way of his seizing absolute power. But then it spread. Any who spoke against his decrees... and anyone associated with those victims—friends, families, co-workers. Then it got worse. Seemingly random mass murders. And forced relocations—whole populations moved, some out into the countryside, to the farms and mines. Remy Caron was an honest man when the revolution began, I still believe that, but he was corrupted...by the power, and by that monster, Delacorte.

"Ami Delacorte?" Hoover had gotten a bad feeling from the revolutionary leader, even in the brief time it had taken her to show them to their rooms. But if what Bernard was telling him was true...

"She has his ear. They're lovers, and their ambitions feed off each other's. I believe she's the true planner behind what has happened."

Hoover listened, skeptical as always. "Are you sure you're not exaggerating? After all, there was lasting resentment toward the old government. Some overreaction to suspected Union leanings, while not admirable, wouldn't be incomprehensible. And, whatever relationship Delacorte has with Caron, it's difficult to believe what you're telling me."

"I'm not exaggerating, Mr. Hoover. That's why I took the risk of contacting your comrade. Do you know what would have happened to me if she'd turned me in to Caron's people? What would have happened to my family? Delacorte would torture my children in front of me, Mr. Hoover. She's evil in a way I cannot even describe." Bernard's composure was beginning to fracture.

"Very well, Mr. Bernard. For the moment, let's assume all you have told me is true." Hoover paused. In spite of his cynical nature, something told him what he was hearing was the truth. "What do you expect me to do?"

"You represent the Confederation. You're the bastion of freedom in the galaxy. The Union authorities lied about you all the time, painting your people as monsters who would nuke our worlds into submission if they were able to defeat our fleets. But some of us refused to believe such lies. We waited, and hoped you would win the war, that your forces would liberate us. Our hearts sank when word of the peace treaty reached us. But then *you* came here. We need your help now, perhaps more than ever. Please, Mr. Hoover. You must do something."

"Wait a minute, Mr. Bernard. I understand everything you've told me, and if even half of it is true, it's an outrage. But I don't represent the Confederation. I don't have any military forces here, nor any way to get them so deep into Union space." He took a deep breath, wondering if he looked as uncomfortable as he felt. "There's nothing I can do. I'm sorry. I'm only here to help fortify Barroux so it can repel the next Union assault. That's the extent of my authorization, and of my resources."

"You must. You *have* to help us. You cannot support a regime like Caron's. That's not what your people stand for. Please…help us."

Hoover just shook his head, trying to ignore the guilt growing inside him. His mission had nothing to do with the government that controlled a free Barroux. He was there to help the rebels defend themselves, whoever was in charge. It was all part of Gary Holsten's campaign to slow Gaston Villieneuve from reestablishing the Union's strength and power. He wasn't there to help the people of Barroux at all, beyond keeping the Foudre Rouge out.

The whole truth was even worse. He suspected Barroux would eventually be reconquered by the Union, despite his efforts. So, he wasn't even there to save the planet and its people…he had come to use them, to ensure that the Union expended the maximum resources in reestablishing control.

"Mr. Bernard…" Hoover didn't know what to say to the man, especially after his impassioned remarks about the Confederation and its ideals. He was there to put a thorn in the Union's side, no more. He had not come to bring freedom to anyone. And yet, a cold feeling spread through his gut, one that told him everything Bernard had said was horribly true. Worse, it didn't change his mission one bit. If he had to support a pack of bloodthirsty monsters in order to defend Barroux from Union attacks, that was just what he had to do.

"I'm sorry." It was miserably inadequate, but it was all he had.

Chapter Seven

Deep in the Zed-4 System
20 Million Kilometers from CFS Dauntless
Year 315 AC

Stockton eased up on the throttle, letting the thrust fall back from a soul-killing 10g to a more tolerable 3g. He wasn't sure why he'd driven his fighter so hard on such a routine flight, or for that matter, the three other pilots in the patrol.

Well, maybe he did. At least to an extent.

He'd taken three rookies out with him. He didn't have many newbs in his fighter force, but he was determined to do all he could to reduce that number to dead zero. He'd seen hundreds of pilots fresh from the Academy arrive at the front, all full of piss and vinegar but short on actual experience, and he'd watched far too many of them get themselves killed on their first missions. He couldn't see how his people were going to see any combat on the White Fleet's expedition, but a puppy pilot could get into trouble on scouting duty as well. Giving them a hard run or two could only prepare them for whatever lay ahead.

He wondered for an instant why fresh meat like the three rookies brought out his sadistic streak, but then he realized he knew the answer. Stockton believed that most useful lessons came from negative reinforcement. Certainly, that had been his experience. Satisfaction and success were pleasurable, but easily forgotten. The experiences that fueled his nightmares had made him into the pilot he was, and probably saved his life more than once. Squeezing his new pilots at 10g, like fresh oranges in the juicer, was a way to get their attention. Plenty of people would pat them on the back and congratulate them on getting through the Academy, but not him. They might hate him by the time he was done, but if he saved one of their lives, it would be worth it.

He was going to do whatever he had to do to prevent them from joining the parade of shadowy faces that plagued his sleep. But that wasn't the main reason he was out on the patrol. It got him out from behind a desk and back into the cockpit, where he belonged.

He was the fleet's strike force commander, and his steady updraft in rank over the past few years had finally reached the point where it removed him from duties like routine patrols. At least in theory. He might be expected to man his ship and launch in a full fleet battle, when every squadron scrambled, but short of that unlikely eventuality, his time in the vast openness of space was sharply limited these days.

Dauntless's vast corridors had begun to feel like a prison already, and by the time the fleet was ten transits from the Confederation border, he'd started to think he was going crazy. Now, over four months and forty transits into the expedition, he might still be hanging on, but he could also feel the thread getting thinner and thinner. He *had* to get out, to climb into the cockpit and try to recapture the spirit he felt slipping away. Training some of the new pilots was just the excuse he needed to justify assigning himself to a patrol.

"How are you all doing?" He spoke into the comm, not even trying to keep the smile from his face. He remembered the first time he'd pulled 10g, and the first time he'd been this far from base. That kind of discomfort and fear tended to plant themselves in one's mind immutably.

"Fine, sir."

"I'm good, Captain."

"Here, sir."

None of them sounded very good, but they were all trying...

and that was the spirit Stockton liked to see in his pilots. They deserved a little break. But just a little one. He had something else in mind, something that would give his wet behind the ears flyers something to think about when they got back to *Dauntless*.

"Relax for a few minutes, stretch out, get loose. Because we're going to run some exercises while we're out here. Set your lasers at one-tenth percent power, just enough to ding a scanner. Then, the three of you are going to try to take me down…" A wicked grin slipped onto his face. "…before I get you."

* * *

"Status, Captain?" Barron walked across *Dauntless*'s massive command center. He thought of it as the bridge, of course, regardless of what the ship's designers had decided to designate it, but he also realized it was so much more. The ship was commanded from its confines, but so was the entire fleet. Its main display was more than double the size of the huge 3D setup on the old *Dauntless*, and there were two more of them on the new ship. They flanked the main display, allowing the officers present to focus on multiple areas of the system at once. It was all very impressive, even a little intimidating, but it seemed a little like overkill, especially for an exploration mission.

"Everything green, sir. All ships report normal operations. No new contacts." The fleet had encountered a few excavation sites while they were still in the explored areas of the Badlands, spots where previous expeditions had looked for, and likely, at least in some cases, found, bits of old tech. But that was to be expected, and from all the reports Barron had seen to date, the current system was devoid of anything save a few gas giants orbiting far from the primary. There had no doubt been other planets along the fleet's path with useful artifacts waiting to be found, but Barron's mission wasn't to nudge the charted areas of the Badlands out another dozen systems…it was to push deep into the unknown, seeking larger caches of ancient technology, closer to the old empire's ancient core…as well as discovering some clues to the cause and nature of the Cataclysm.

"Any word from the patrol?"

"Routine status check…" Travis looked down at the readings on her screen. "…twenty-one minutes ago. The patrol has…exceeded its coverage area. They're at the very edge of our detection range, near the innermost planet."

"Stockton?"

"Yes, sir. Apparently, he reshuffled the patrol roster again and took out three of the rookie pilots."

Something between a snort and a laugh escaped Barron's lips. He was more amused than annoyed at Stockton's restlessness…and the fact that the pilot thought he was fooling anybody. "That's the third time?"

"Fourth, sir."

Barron wasn't surprised. Jake Stockton had never been an easy officer to command, or to control. He'd have ended up booted from the service long ago, or even in the brig, save for one thing. He was *that* good. Stockton was one of the three or four officers who could actually lay a claim to having been individually vital to victory in the last war. The man was moody, irritable at times—and, in many ways, he was his own worst enemy—but Barron had never seen anyone else who could fly a Lightning-class fighter like the legendary Raptor.

No, that's not true. There was one other…

Jovi Grachus.

But Grachus was gone. She had died in the final battle of the war, another of those officers without whom victory would have been impossible. She had sacrificed herself to save *Dauntless*, opening the way for the doomed battleship to ram the pulsar and ending the chances the Union could continue the war.

Barron shook his head as he remembered Grachus. She hadn't been killed in the battle itself…she ran out of fuel and froze to death before the rescue ships could reach her. That didn't make her act any less heroic in his estimation, but he knew in the strange realm of Alliance culture, dying in such a way was considered somewhat shameful. It didn't make any sense, not to him at least, but then for all the time he'd fought at their sides, he had never come to fully understand the Palatians. Still, whatever the tenets of their culture and the somewhat mysterious "way" they all followed, it seemed terribly wrong that her last thoughts had likely been ones of shame.

"Well, Captain Stockton was moved up pretty abruptly in his responsibilities," Barron said finally. "I think we need to give him some room. He'll figure out how to adapt to his new duties. And it can't hurt morale for these new pilots to see the great Raptor flying next to them. At least they're a lot less likely to run into any combat out here." Barron didn't think the fleet would see any fighting at all...unless they ran into a rogue adventurer or some ancient but still operational automated defense system. No random smuggler could pose a serious risk to the fleet, of course, though the thought of some imperial fortress still functioning under computer control gave him pause. Still, even though he didn't expect to see any major combat, that didn't mean the mission wasn't dangerous. Even his war-hardened nerves were a little on edge as each transit took his people farther and farther into the unknown.

*   *   *

"That was good...you guys did well." Stockton knew the psyche of a young fighter pilot well enough to realize that none of them saw things that way. All three of them had come at him at different angles, blasting hard. If they'd been after one of their Academy classmates, the fight would have been over in seconds...but they were chasing the fleet's premier pilot, a veteran of most of the major battles of the war. Jake Stockton had faced off against enemy aces and packs of fighters that outnumbered him five or ten to one. He'd led desperate assault forces, including the one that knocked out the Pulsar's power supply in the Bottleneck. Coming out on top in the impromptu exercise he'd put together for his rookies had been almost comically easy.

He'd changed his thrust vector almost randomly, pulling his ship away from the incoming attack. Then he spun around, targeting the closest of his attackers and scoring a simulated hit the AI deemed sufficient to classify the fighter as destroyed. After that, his killer instinct kicked in. His remaining two opponents were surprised, shocked at the "death" of their comrade…and their reactions slowed. Just for an instant, but against a pilot like Jake Stockton, that was enough.

He'd brought his ship around, firing his engines at full and coming up on his second target. His intended victim reacted, or at least tried to, burning his engines and trying to get out of Stockton's targeting arc. But he had been too late. Stockton's third shot was a hit, and another simulated kill.

That had made the fight one on one, an almost absurdly easy matchup for Stockton. He had even held back his fire to give the pilot a chance to escape. But that only prolonged the exchange for another half a minute. Then, Stockton's finger had tightened, and the trace power of his lasers had hit the target's sensors, causing the AI to declare a third and final kill.

"Seriously," he added, after his despondent opponents remained silent. "I've been out here a lot longer than any of you…and I've seen things I hope none of you ever has to see. I don't give out unearned praise. You all did very well. I'm proud of…"

His voice stopped abruptly as his eyes caught something. His long-range scanner alarm was blinking. He reached out and punched at the controls, directing the scanning beams to converge on the signal.

The last thing he'd expected was some kind of contact all the way out here. He punched at the keys on his panel, directing the AI to start crunching the incoming data.

"Captain?" It was one of the pilots, Grissom, he realized after a brief delay.

"I'm fine," he responded, his voice a little sharper than he'd intended. "You guys just stay put for a minute."

He turned his attention back to the scanning data. Whatever he was reading—and he had no idea what it was, beyond a strange energy source—it was coming from the vicinity of the nearby gas giant. He'd come a long way, at least four million kilometers past the patrol's stated range, and the planet was another few million kilometers out.

His gut told him he had enough fuel—just—for a run out there and a quick pass to gather closer-range data. It would be tight, and nothing he wanted his young pups involved with, but he figured he could manage it.

"I want all of you to fly back to *Dauntless* and land. I'll be there soon."

"Captain, we can't leave you out here, not this far from the mother ship."

It was Grissom again, and Stockton almost snapped at him to obey orders. But he held his tongue. The kid was right, and the regs were on his side. The almighty "book" yet again. And, something more than that. The pilot's urge not to abandon a comrade was commendable, and Stockton didn't want to override that.

"All right, but I want you all to remain where you are. Decelerate to bring yourselves to a dead stop, and stay there. If any of you follow me, I swear to God, you'll be in a space suit scraping residue off *Dauntless*'s hull instead of flying a fighter. Understood?"

He got three nervous versions of "yessir," or words to that effect. Then he glanced back at the small screen on the dashboard…and he kicked in his thrusters.

It was probably nothing, but he was still edgy. They'd passed through nothing but long-dead systems for weeks, without a trace reading of artificial energy output.

Until now.

Chapter Eight

The Promenade
Spacer's District
Port Royal City, Planet Dannith, Ventica III
315 AC

Andi Lafarge moved down the wide stone walkway, her eyes darting back and forth at the seedy bars and cheap restaurants that lined the Promenade. There were copies of the Spacer's District on half a dozen border planets, but none quite matched Port Royal City, for either activity or sleaziness.

The planet, Dannith, was a hotbed of rumor about old tech. Most of the information sold in the taverns and brothels were lies, but Andi knew from experience that some nuggets of truth made their way through the heavy layer of fraud. She had found or bought—usually bought—more than one solid lead in these grungy holes in the wall. Most had been modest scores, broken bits of marginal equipment that were valuable enough to pay for an expedition and turn a tidy profit.

She never thought she'd see the place again, and it troubled her slightly that it felt almost like home to her. She'd never imagined herself as a Badlands captain for the rest of her life—she'd always considered her chosen profession as the means to an end. But she couldn't deny the relief she'd felt as she sat in the captain's chair on *Pegasus*'s bridge. Her beloved ship *had* felt like home, and she was still struggling to explain to herself how she could possibly have been more comfortable in her cramped cabin than she'd been in the palatial villa. It didn't make sense, and part of her wanted to deny it. She didn't *want* to crave this life. But something about it felt...normal.

One other thing that seemed right, something she hadn't realized how much she'd missed, was the pistol slung around her waist. It hung low on the one side, just the way she liked it, and though it had been more than two years since she'd drawn it in anger, somehow, she knew she was as fast as ever.

She wondered if Holsten had really expected to convince her when he'd come to Tellurus. The whole idea seemed absurd. She was a wealthy woman now, one who could buy virtually anything she wanted, indulge in any kind of luxury she could imagine. And yet, he'd convinced her to return to the grunge of the border, to the dark, dangerous, and sleazy world from which she'd extricated herself after years of work and struggle.

It hadn't even been difficult. The instant he'd put the idea in her head, he'd had her. The boredom, the frustration—the feeling of being *lost* that had taken her as she puttered around her giant house—had all conspired to do his job for her. She'd been determined to make a go of it in her new life, even if it drove her mad. At least until Holsten had opened another door for her, given her an excuse to escape.

Her eyes darted back and forth, from one sign to another. Some of the establishments she remembered were still there, others had changed hands or names. She wondered how many of her old contacts were still there. She'd known a few who'd prowled Dannith's Spacer's District for decades, but in most cases, a career as a purveyor of Badlands rumors was a short one. Some made a killing and vanished, to a life much like the one she had just abandoned. Others ended up on the floor of one of the taverns, gunned down by some free trader's crew he'd swindled. Even those who escaped such an end tended to get worn down quickly. The danger, the constant intrigue...they were a heavy burden that few could carry for long.

She slipped inside the Green Star. It wasn't bad as Spacer's

District bars went, at least not to the eyes. The floor was reasonably clean and, if things were still the same as she remembered, they didn't water down the drinks. Not too much, at least.

That didn't make the place safe, and Andi knew it had seen its share of bodies hauled off after one dispute or another. She'd even watched a few of those fights. But the Green Star had also been the headquarters of one of her most reliable contacts, and she decided to seek him out first to see if he was still in business. Drake Trencher would have at least some information on any prominent leads making the rounds...and he'd probably have a good idea of any recent Sector Nine activity along the border as well.

She scanned the room. It was early afternoon, and the place was almost empty. Most of the port's denizens were probably still sleeping off the debauchery of the night before. But Trencher wasn't like the others. He was a cut above, and she figured there was a chance he would be there. He owned the place, after all, though few people knew that.

She walked toward the back, looking at the table where Trencher had held court back during her days on Dannith. The red leather-upholstered booth was empty, so she sat at a nearby table, and she waited.

She wasn't sure what reception she'd get, assuming he showed up at all. They'd worked together more than once, successfully, too. But Drake Trencher had never been above making an exclusive deal and then selling the information to two or three other parties...and that kind of thing had always brought out Andi's ornery side. For all the times she had shared a good payday with him, he'd also seen the business end of her pistol more than once. She wondered which times he would remember when he set eyes on her.

Her old confidence had come back quickly, with one small change. She'd always had her crew with her before. Having backup waiting in the wings was no guarantee of not getting shot or stabbed when a deal went bad, but it was a damned sight better than nothing. Holsten had told her to wait until he arrived before she started poking around looking for information...but then, she'd never been all that good at taking directions.

"What'll it be?" The Green Star was a nice place, at least in comparison to its competition along the Promenade, but that didn't mean they wouldn't bounce her for sitting and not ordering anything.

"I'll have a silver ale." She'd never been a big drinker, though doing business in the Spacer's District usually required at least putting on a show. She'd developed a dozen ways to spill half a drink without being noticed, but it was early enough that she wouldn't draw any attention to herself if she wasn't pounding down double shots.

"Coming right up." The server was a gruff-looking man. The Green Star was famous for its women, both the scantily-clad ones serving drinks, and the even less-dressed ones waiting in the rooms upstairs. But the earliness of the day was in full force, and the normal denizens of the evening were nowhere to be seen.

Andi watched as the waiter walked back to the table and put the mug down in front of her. He paused for a few seconds, but she just glanced up at him and said, "Run me a tab."

He hesitated for a few seconds, clearly concerned that he'd never seen her before and wondering if she intended to stiff him. But she watched his eyes drop to the pistol at her side, and then he just nodded and walked away.

She sipped at the ale slowly, drinking hardly any, looking around the room. She watched a man and a woman at the bar, whispering to each other and looking her way. They were trying to appear unobtrusive, but they were failing badly. She didn't respond or give any hint she had noticed. After all, she was there to be seen. Finding Trencher was a needless effort, at least when she could just sit there and let him find her. She had enough of a reputation on the border—even with the shroud of secrecy that surrounded her greatest find—that word of her return would spread.

The woman slipped through a door behind the bar, and the man stepped forward, trying to look like he was wiping the counter down while his eyes darted her way every few seconds.

She reached out and picked up the mug, taking another small drink. She really just wanted water, but she knew better than to order that in any spacer's bar. Aside from the advantages of fitting in with the drinking culture so prevalent on the border, she could barely imagine the assortment of pathogens in whatever nasty-ass water ran through the Green Star's pipes. A little alcohol was helpful as an antiseptic if nothing else.

"Andi Lafarge…it's been quite some time since you graced my establishment with your presence."

She turned her head and looked up. "How have you been, Drake?" He'd seemed to come out of nowhere, but Andi remembered the Green Star well enough to know the place had more than one unobtrusive door leading out from the back areas.

She gestured toward the bar. "Your people have dropped off some since I was here last. They might as well have stared over here with binoculars."

"Well, you know how hard it is to get good help." He put his hand on the back of the booth. "Mind if I sit?" His eyes flashed down, checking out the gun at her side.

"It's your place." She waved toward the empty seat.

He nodded and slid onto the seat opposite her. "Like I said, it's been a long time. Rumor has it you had a big find…a retirement score."

"I'd wager there are rumors around here that I have two heads, Drake. You can't believe everything you hear."

"I don't believe anything, Andi. You must remember that much, at least."

"I remember everything." She grabbed her mug and took another drink.

"Still, you've been gone for almost two years now. There must be *some* truth to the stories."

She smiled. "We did okay, Drake. A good run, better than most. Enough for one hell of a time, and I've still got a good amount of it tucked away. But, you know as well as I do, it takes a lot to live the lifestyle." She was tense. It had been a long time since she'd interacted with border lowlifes like Trencher, and she was second-guessing every word that came out of her mouth.

But she felt alive, too, in a way she hadn't all those months, prowling around her villa.

"What about your people? I haven't seen any of them around here. I can't remember the last time I ran into you without Vig Merrick lurking nearby."

She hesitated before replying. "Vig and I had…a disagreement, I'm afraid. Last I heard, he was out near the Rim. He bought a place on some two-bit agricultural planet and settled down. As far as I know, the others are all still out there burning through their bankrolls." She looked over at Trencher and smiled. "I have more expensive tastes than most of them… and besides, I want to make damned sure I have enough to last. I don't want to end up back here when I'm sixty, scavenging around for a score to keep me going."

"Well, whatever's behind it, it's good to have you back here, Andi. There's nobody working Dannith now as good as you were, that's for damned sure."

"Is that your way of telling me you want to work together? Because, if you've got any good data, I'm ready to listen." She wondered if that had been too direct. After all, she was sitting there, without a crew, not exactly ready to blast off chasing down a hot lead.

"I might have something in the works, Andi. Why don't you get your act together, and then we'll talk? You'll need a new crew, I guess. By the time you've got that in place and you're ready to go, I should have something worth talking about." He looked across the table, locking eyes with her. "Sound good?"

She had the ale in her hand, and she took another drink. Then, she set it down and nodded. "Sounds good, Drake." She paused. "Say, a week? I don't think I'll need any more time than that. I've got some good prospects to crew up *Pegasus*. Just a matter of picking the ones I want."

"A week it is then." He slid out of the booth and stood up. "One week." He smiled. "It's good to have you back, Andi. Let's make some money, eh?"

"That's why I'm here, Drake."

"Well, you're already in the black. That drink's on me…and

as many more as you want." He flashed a sign to the bartender, who nodded his acknowledgement.

"That's a change. Can't say I remember you giving anything away before. Getting soft in your old age?"

He took a step from the booth, and then he turned and looked down at her. "Let's just say I'm a sentimental sort, and I'm glad to see an old friend. One week from now, right here." He smiled again, and then he walked across the room and slipped through the door behind the bar.

Chapter Nine

Stockton hit the fighter's controls, decelerating as he approached the planet. He was near enough to have visual contact now, somewhat of a rarity with the vast distances involved in space travel and combat.

The planet was a bright, vibrant orange and red, partially obscured by a gauzy lattice of white clouds that wound all around the massive sphere. It was beautiful, almost breathtaking, and he stared at it for a few seconds, appreciating something he rarely noticed. The universe was full of wonders, magnificent sights all around, but to him they had almost always been nothing save small lights on a screen. A planet might be a destination, or even potential cover from an approaching attacker, but he hardly ever took the time to appreciate one's magnificence.

He didn't think the way he was now very often, his thoughts usually on facts and missions...and especially the dangers that had dogged his work for so long. But, being alone so far out, millions of kilometers from the fleet, made him more reflective.

The gas giant was large, even by the standards of such things, and he suspected that in its formative days, it had come close to becoming a star in its own right. But instead, its mass had just failed to create the chain of fusion reactions needed, and it settled into a deep orbit around the Zed-4 primary. The glory of life as a star had eluded it, but it hosted its own vast and complex array of satellites.

The planet had no less than forty-one moons that Stockton's scanners had detected. Some were little more than scraps of barren rock, while others were almost the size of planets, with atmospheres of their own and varied array of makeups. Several were volcanic nightmares, their surfaces pockmarked with deep craters and geysers of molten rock, while others seemed almost habitable, save perhaps for the low temperatures so far from the primary.

Stockton cranked up his scanners to full power. The signal had been vague and intermittent when he'd first picked it up, and now he could see why. Between the planet's massive magnetic field and the volcanic activity of the moons, there was a tremendous amount of natural interference. He'd lost the reading a few times on his way in, but his AI had altered the frequencies, adapting to conditions and always managing to get it back fairly quickly.

Now, however, this close to the planet, the background radiation and the magnetic fields were near to overwhelming his scanners. He wished his ship had a spread of probes to launch, but a Lightning fighter didn't have room for things like that. He thought about pulling out, about heading back to *Dauntless* and suggesting Admiral Barron initiate an intensive scanning effort. That would delay the fleet's journey and cause a lot of fuss. Still, it was the cautious move, and possibly the right call. Probably. But Stockton just wasn't wired that way.

He was going in.

He angled his thrusters, accelerating softly, heading toward the nearest cluster of moons. The planet was frigidly cold, at least by the standards of human habitability, and if it had any kind of solid ground, it was thousands of kilometers into the dense gaseous outer layers. The gravity that far down would be a thousand times Megara-normal, enough to turn him into something resembling strawberry jam, and that made it very unlikely that anything manmade was on the planet itself.

He kept looking back at his screen, watching as more data came in. The energy readings were stronger now, and as he pushed closer toward the planet's orbital track, he began to get better positional readings. He worked through the data, eliminating potential targets one at a time as his fighter moved slowly forward.

He was sure now he was picking up some kind of artificial construction. The rhythm was just too regular to be any kind of natural phenomenon. For an instant, he wondered if some frontier prospector had made it out this far, if he'd found the remains of some kind of salvage operation...or even an active one. That could be dangerous, not so much to the fleet, but to him, alone in a single fighter. The crews that worked the Badlands generally didn't react well to interlopers poking their noses into a new find.

He shook his head. No, that was very unlikely. They had run into signs of prospecting activity far closer in, but they'd passed through dozens of systems since the last traces of exploration activity. The fleet was just too far out, and no expedition less provisioned and substantial could possibly have come this distance from support.

That realization sent a shiver down his spine. Whatever his scanners were picking up, it hadn't been built by anyone from the Confederation. Or the Union or Alliance...or any of the known powers. That energy reading was from some machine constructed by the old empire, centuries before. And it was still functioning.

No one would call Jake Stockton a coward, but the idea of an ancient device still operating centuries after those who built it had died, was chilling in its own way. He'd seen his share of old tech, even items of great power like the pulsar and stealth generator. But none of those artifacts had been found still functioning. Whatever this was, it was still operating now, on its own. That meant whatever fuel powered it had lasted hundreds of years. Its systems had functioned continually, with no repairs and no replacements. As far as he knew, nothing like that had ever been discovered in the Badlands.

This was the kind of thing the fleet had come to find, of course, but Stockton hadn't imagined stumbling on it himself, alone, far out from the fleet. He knew the potential value of functioning old tech, and the importance of the Confederation finding if before the Union or another malevolent force did. Still, he couldn't shake the feeling that the entire expedition was somehow looking for trouble wandering out this far into unknown space.

He tapped the controls again, adjusting his course as the AI tightened the projected location of the contact. He flipped a series of switches, shutting down non-vital systems to free up power for the scanning beams. The dense magnetic activity was playing havoc on his sensors, and the data was crawling in. Even with the power boost, he'd have to get close—very close—to get anything conclusive.

His eyes moved over the screen, watching as he approached a small group of three moons situated within a thousand kilometers of each other. The power source was definitely on, or in orbit around, one of them. His ship was coming in slowly. He'd barely tapped his thrust. He didn't have a choice. He was getting very close to the limit of his fuel supply. If he burned his thrusters too hard, he wouldn't have enough power to get back. Especially since he'd have to match any acceleration away from the fleet with corresponding deceleration to head back.

Coming at *Dauntless* without enough fuel to decelerate and land was unlikely to be the disaster it could be in a battle situation, but it would be damned humiliating for the strike force commander to zip by his mother ship and wait for a rescue boat to catch up and dock with him, all in full sight of the fleet.

There you are…

His eyes focused on a small dot, the closest of the moons. He'd finally managed to pick out the one he was looking for, and as he got closer, the scanner reports became cleaner, more complete. He crept forward, the cockpit silent save for his breath and the occasional beep from one of the instruments. His AI was active, recording everything. He would have sent the data back to his comrades for transmission to *Dauntless* right away, but the magnetic interference had cut off his comm completely. That was annoying, but it didn't seem like a big deal. He could just blast his thrusters and clear the affected area in a minute or two once he'd finished his scanning run. Still, it made him feel even more alone.

All right, just a little closer. Then, it's time to pull out and turn this over to the admir…

His thought was cut off by an energy spike, and then his fighter rocked hard. The alarm began blaring, and he could hear the AI speaking, warning him of system failures. For an instant, he thought was dead, but then he realized that, whatever had happened, his ship had survived. His first thought was that he'd been attacked, and he braced for another shot…but then he realized it had been some kind of scanning beam that had hit him, one vastly more powerful than any he'd been putting out.

His instincts took over. Attack or no, whatever that thing was, it was dangerous. It was time to get out, to report this to the fleet and get some backup. He angled his throttle and pulled it back.

Nothing.

He reached down and flipped a series of switches, rerouting power flow. But the ship still didn't respond.

"Run a diagnostic," he snapped to the AI.

"Incoming scanner beam has burned out a large number of electrical systems. Restoration of thrust control impossible without full repairs in dock."

Damn.

Stockton's hands moved over the panel, checking for himself what the AI had just told him. It wasn't that he didn't trust the computer, not exactly. But he didn't much like the idea of being stranded so far from the fleet, without comm and without engine control.

Most of all, he didn't like the fact that he had no idea what had just disabled his ship with nothing more than a scan. The fleet had come looking for old tech…and they had damned sure just found some. But Stockton was more concerned now about getting back to *Dauntless* than he was about the potential uses of whatever artifact he'd stumbled upon.

He stared at his screens, waiting, his stomach clenched tightly by the sudden and unexpected danger. He was helpless, and if the artifact he'd found was truly hostile, if had weapons of a power commensurate with that scanner beam and programming that directed it to attack, he was as good as dead.

He forced himself to take a breath, and then another, and with each passing second, he felt his tension ratchet down, just a bit. After a minute, perhaps two, he decided whatever was out there, it wasn't going to destroy him. At least not right away.

He looked at the screen. His scanners were still operating, at least partially, and information was trickling in. Whatever he'd found, it was in geosynchronous orbit around the moon in front of him. The moon was very planet-like, someplace he imagined might even be pleasant, if its temperature had been a little warmer than a chilly 198 absolute. It appeared to have seas, though Stockton recalled enough from his Academy classes to realize they were likely filled with methane. Any water, at least on the surface, would be frozen solid.

He took another breath, deeper this time, and he exhaled hard. The fact that he was still alive suggested the artifact's primary purpose was scanning and not combat, though it was just possible he'd only been spared because the sensors were still operative, and the weapons were not. *Or they need longer to charge before they fire…*

The thing wasn't large, no more than a thousand tons, but he couldn't get any more specific data. None of his beams could read anything beneath the device's hull, save for the detection of ongoing energy production that had brought him out here in the first place.

His fighter had limited scanning ability, and even that was damaged now and operating at reduced effectiveness. Nevertheless, there were no signs of hostile activity and, after another few minutes, his unsettled gut finally agreed with his brain. He leaned back and put his hand to his head, rubbing his throbbing temples. He was beginning to truly believe he wasn't about to get blown to atoms.

But it looked like he *wasn't* going to escape the humiliation of needing to be rescued, after all. Now, he just hoped his green comrades waiting four million kilometers away got nervous quickly and called to the fleet for help to arrive.

Before his life support ran out.

Chapter Ten

"I reestablished some old contacts, good ones, at least in terms of getting some credible leads." Andi felt strange talking to the head of Confederation Intelligence in the back room of a seedy Spacer's District tavern…one she'd been in a dozen times, without the slightest clue that it had been owned and operated by a front company for Holsten's agency for more than a decade. "I'd say Drake Trencher is the best, probably by a considerable margin. He's given me good leads in the past. We've made good money together."

"Do you trust him?" Holsten seemed nervous. Andi wasn't sure how much of that had to do with being out of his element on the rough and tumble frontier…and how much was regret and concern over enticing her into an operation that would almost certainly prove to be dangerous.

"Hell no. He's a Badlands border snake who'd sell his own mother if he could get a good price for her. We've worked together, usually successfully, but I've also come close to blowing his brains out a couple times."

"Do you really think he's the right contact? I don't want you taking any unnecessary chances."

"Gary…normal business on Dannith is dangerous enough. You can't get a decent drink around here without taking some chances. If you want to root out Sector Nine, expose their operations on the border…well, that's not going to be safe, no matter what you do." She paused. "Don't worry. I can take care of myself." She looked over at Holsten. He sent men and women into dangerous situations every day…but now, she realized he was having second guesses about luring her into Confederation Intelligence.

"Oh, I know you can, Andi. I'd never have come to you if I didn't believe that. But Sector Nine is…" His words trailed off. They both knew enough about the Union's infamous spy agency to finish the sentence.

"What about my crew? If I'm going to use my return to Badlands prospecting as a cover, I need to look like I'm ready to head out at some point."

"They're ready, Andi. You can meet them all tonight. Let's say…10pm, at *Pegasus*. Inside your ship is about the one place we can be sure no one else is listening."

"Are they good? Reliable?"

"They're the best I've got. Experienced operatives with military combat training. And they're all from my Black Team, which means they basically don't exist—not officially, at least. Even if someone gets a DNA sample, they won't be able to track any of them down."

Andi just nodded. She knew anyone Holsten sent with her would be reliable. But she was still nervous. Coming back, working leads and looking for some old tech…that was one thing. It just wasn't the thing she'd come to do. She was here to root out Sector Nine's influence, and that was more difficult and dangerous by orders of magnitude. She had to push, to poke around places it wasn't safe to poke. If there was a code on the border, it was one of silence. People didn't ask about things that didn't concern them, and when they did, it usually led to trouble.

She'd jumped at the chance to escape from her gilded prison, to flee from the boredom she'd begun to feel was killing her, but now she realized she felt a little out of her depth. She was scared.

She looked up at Holsten, trying to keep the concern from her face. "Okay, 10pm it is. I'll see you there."

* * *

"Are you certain?"

"Of course, I'm certain. Don't you think I know Andi Lafarge?" Trencher was annoyed, but he didn't let it affect his demeanor. It was an hour past closing time, and the bar was mostly dark, just a single light a few meters away throwing dim illumination across the table.

"We'd heard that she is retired, that she's no longer prospecting for old tech." His contact was unemotional, cold. Trencher disliked dealing with the man. He'd almost told the new arrival to get lost when he'd first walked into the bar a few weeks back, but then the stranger recited a list of Trencher's debts, the legitimate ones, and also those he'd owed to…rougher…parties. It didn't take long for him to realize that whoever the new arrival was, he now held most of the ruinous debt into which Trencher had fallen so deeply. It was unnerving, but certainly an attention-grabber, especially when the mysterious man suggested a way Trencher could rid himself of his obligations.

"Yeah, I heard that too, but now she's back. She says her last score was good, but not enough to last. She's back looking to pad her stake."

"Do you believe that?"

"As much as I believe anything. She'd lie to me if it suited her needs, of course, but why else would she be back here? She damned sure didn't miss the food…or the company."

"What did she want from you?"

"What do you think she wanted?" Trencher could see the man was not amused. He'd been dealing with the contact for weeks now, and the stranger had kept all his promises, at least so far. But there was something disturbing about him too, almost foreboding. "She wanted leads on old tech, of course. It certainly looks like she's planning another expedition."

Trencher played his part in the strange eco-system of the border planets. He was a middleman really, and nothing more. Dannith and the other worlds bordering the Badlands were full of people peddling clues about potential old tech finds. Some of them were of the bookish variety, researchers who examined old records and tried to find traces that might lead to something useful. Others were explorers without the resources or guts to follow up on their own discoveries. It was quicker, and safer, to sell off a lead and take a share of anything someone else found…assuming you could trust anyone else involved.

That was where Trencher's value came in. He was a fixture on Dannith's Spacer's District. He owned several of its best-known establishments, and he had at least some degree of cred-ibility with both the sellers and buyers of information.

"Did you make any arrangements with her?"

"No…I just told her to come back in a few days. She was alone. She had to put together a crew, and I wasn't sure what to tell her…until I had the chance to speak to you."

"Very good. Whatever Captain Lafarge is doing here, I doubt it has to do with resuming old business practices. She…" The man almost continued, but then he stopped abruptly.

"She…?"

"Nothing important. The next step is to find out what she really wants."

"And, just how do you propose we do that?" Trencher was hesitant. He didn't have any loyalty to Andi Lafarge, not really. The crazy smuggler had pulled her gun on him…twice. But she'd always dealt with him more or less honestly, and setting her up felt wrong. Besides, he'd seen her when she was angry.

"You will have your talk with her. Pass on the basics of any leads you may have, anything to catch her interest. Then explain that you have a contact with more detailed information. Tell her you set up a meeting…and bring her to us."

"You must be kidding. Andi Lafarge is no fool. She'll never go along with that." He stared at the man. He was wearing a long black coat, and Trencher was suddenly aware that any kind of weapon could be hidden under there. Not that the stranger needed to hold a gun to his head. Trencher was deep under-water, utterly ruined…unless his new associates honored their agreement to forgive his debts in exchange for his cooperation.

"Perhaps she wouldn't if she were operating the way she did before. But, if we're right, she's fishing around for information herself, and I don't mean vague treasure maps leading to questionable chunks of old tech. She'll take chances she wouldn't have before, push harder to get to what she'd looking for."

Trencher was confused. He didn't understand what the man wanted with Andi Lafarge, but he knew he didn't have a choice. He had to cooperate…and hope his new "friends" kept their word and canceled his debts.

And that Andi Lafarge didn't get pissed enough to put a bullet in his head.

* * *

"I may have something for you, Andi. Something big." Trencher's voice was soft, almost a whisper. The bar was about half full, fairly typical for the time of the night, maybe even a bit light, and the tables right around the booth were empty.

Andi stared at him, trying to get a read on his expression. She'd always been good at judging people's motives and intentions, but Trencher was keeping a good poker face. Still, she was suspicious. If he really had something big, would he offer it to her now, like this? Two years ago, perhaps. She had a good reputation on the border, and a number of successes to her credit. But right now, she'd just reappeared after almost two years, with none of her old crew—no crew at all, as far as Trencher knew. She wasn't sure exactly what was going on, but her gut told her it was more than a promising run.

Which is good, right? She'd spent her career being as low profile as possible, trying not to attract problematic attention. But now, she was *looking* for trouble, at least in a way. Still, it felt strange, and it only increased her unease.

"What are the details?"

"I'm just a middleman on this, Andi. The group that found this came to me looking for a reliable crew. I was going to talk to Mercer or Allante…but then you showed up, fresh back from retirement."

Now she was sure something was going on. Tom Mercer and his crew were pretty damned good, but Santiago Allante was another prospector at the top of the heap. His ship, *Sombra*, was almost twice the size of *Pegasus*. She had a decent relationship with Trencher, but she knew he'd never give her first crack at a prime job if he could get Allante and his people instead.

So, it is a trap of some kind.

But the cold feeling in her gut reminded her of the unsettling truth. She was there to walk into a trap. It was the only way she could get the leads she needed to track down Sector Nine.

Besides, if he wanted me dead, he could have had one of his people shoot me down right here.

That made her feel better. A little.

Very little.

"So, how do we proceed?"

Trencher looked back at her. He'd been doing an impressive job of hiding any tension, but now she caught a hint of it. Whatever he led her to, it wasn't going to be just another expedition.

"We go meet them, Andi." He paused. "Now."

She felt her insides tighten. Trencher had taken her by surprise. She'd expected him to lure her somewhere else, but she'd figured she'd have a chance to speak with Holsten first.

"Now? No, that's no good. Let's do this right. You get to your people and set up a proper meeting, either here or…"

"No, Andi. It's got to be right now. The information is time sensitive. The expedition has to leave quickly."

"That's crazy. Set something up for tomorrow." She had to at least seem to put up a fight. If she didn't, Trencher would become suspicious.

He shook his head. "I'm sorry, Andi. It's got to be now. They're very cautious…and the information is *that* valuable."

Andi took a breath and swallowed hard. She almost told Trencher to forget about it. It was one thing to agree to work for Holsten, to come to Dannith and poke around, and quite another to walk blindly into a trap just to see who was behind it. Her eyes darted for an instant toward the door, toward escape. But she'd come here to do a job, and this was the next step.

"Okay, we'll do it your way. But my new crew knows I'm here, and if you pull anything, they'll…"

"Everything is legit, Andi…and this looks promising enough to be that final score, the one that really lets you—and me—retire from all of this." He slid out of the booth and stood, waiting for her to follow.

She hesitated for an instant. It was against every impulse she had to willingly walk into a trap. Finally, she stood up and nodded, and then she followed him toward the door.

"Where, exactly, are we going?"

"Just down the street. There's a transport waiting."

Andi stopped. "A transport. This whole thing stinks like garbage, Drake. What the hell is going on?"

"I told you they're cautious, Andi. They've got a lot of resources committed. This is no ordinary run for a few scraps and parts…it's the real deal. And, it's their way or no way. You want to walk, walk. But if you want to hear about what could be the biggest haul of your career, we do it their way."

She listened, impressed by the sincerity Trencher managed to put into his words, even though she knew it was fake. She could sense the stress below it all. And something else. Fear. Drake Trencher was scared.

"All right, let's go," she said, trying to inject clear discomfort into her response. Which wasn't hard at all since she was well beyond uncomfortable.

The two of them walked out onto the main road and down several blocks. Then, Trencher turned down a side street. It was a particularly dumpy section of the Spacer's District, one frequented mostly by hardcore addicts and drunks, and lined by the absolute bottom of the barrel in terms of bars and other establishments.

There were at least a dozen people passed out on the walkway, sleeping off whatever inebriation afflicted them. About a dozen vehicles were parked along the street. They were mostly ancient, dumpy trucks, more than one of them looking abandoned. One large black transport was parked at the next corner, new and gleaming. And expensive. Very out of place.

"There they are," Trencher said, extending his arm and pointing toward the vehicle.

She glanced over at Trencher, trying to hold back the anger she felt. The bastard was setting her up. All the times they'd worked together, the money they'd both made...and he was selling her out. True, things had almost come to violence between then a couple times, but never due to outright betrayal. *Besides, I wouldn't have really shot him.*

Probably not, at least.

She walked down the street. It was taking all she had not to duck into cover in some ally, or at least to put Trencher down like the miserable backstabber he was. But she held it together and walked up to the transport, standing quietly as Trencher knocked on the shaded window.

The door slid open a second later. It was mostly dark inside, but she could see it was a large space, and as plushly configured as the vehicle's exterior.

"Get in." Trencher was standing behind her, gesturing toward the open hatch. She angled her head back, her eyes catching his for an instant. If the son of a bitch though he was going to muscle her into the transport...

But she remembered why she was there. Whatever was inside the vehicle, it was at least a step closer to what she'd come to find. She took a deep breath and stepped in, sliding into an empty seat just past the hatch.

"Welcome, Captain Lafarge. I am very glad to make your acquaintance at last. We have much to discuss."

The man speaking was sitting directly across from her. It was almost dark in the cabin, and his face was hidden in the shadows. Not that she'd recognize a Sector Nine agent anyway, if that was what she was dealing with. And she'd decided she was almost sure about that, at least.

"And what might that be?" Her voice was hard, but she

held back as much of the caustic tone as she could manage. She needed to get information from these people…and get out of this meeting alive, if at all possible. Needlessly antagonizing them wouldn't help her cause on any of those counts.

"We'll get to that soon enough. But, first, where are my manners? Allow me to introduce myself properly. I'm Ricard Lille, Captain Lafarge. Very pleased to finally meet you."

Chapter Eleven

Hall of the People
Liberte City
Planet Montmirail, Ghassara IV
Union Year 219 (315 AC)

Desiree Marieles sat on the cold metal chair, waiting, tapping her feet nervously. She'd come as soon as she'd gotten the call, but she was still concerned she was late. There had been no time specified for an appointment, just a brief instruction to "come immediately."

She'd waited now for more than a year since she'd gotten back from the Alliance...waited for Gaston Villieneuve or one of his lieutenants to contact her, to bring her back into the fold. Or for his killers to show up on her door.

She'd watched the orgy of bloodletting that had accompanied the former Sector Nine head's transition from entrenched government apparatchik to revolutionary leader. The totalitarian regime he'd served, of which he'd been an integral part, was gone now, almost totally destroyed. Yet, Villieneuve remained, head of a new order that had an iron grip no less powerful than that which had preceded it.

Marieles had always respected Villieneuve, even considered herself one of his protégés, but now she had a new perspective on the depth of his genius. He'd somehow reinvented himself in the eyes of the mob that had murdered most of his former colleagues, and he'd done it with stunning success.

She moved around on the chair, trying to get comfortable. She'd wrestled with how to dress for the meeting. First, she'd put on her black leather outfit, the one that fit her so well...the one she'd used to successfully seduce countless men and women in her previous missions. But then she'd had second thoughts, and in the end, she took a cue from Villieneuve himself, donning an ill-fitting set of gray factory clothes, the kind of proletariat garb he'd worn every time she'd seen him on the vid.

She was uncomfortable in her new clothes, both because the fabric was stiff and course, and because the bulky unisex outfit hid every curve and contour of her body. She didn't like hiding any of her assets, though her looks and seduction skills were far from the only tools in her arsenal. Marieles was a stone-cold killer, a brilliant operative with an enormous skillset ranging from a fair hacking ability to expertise in a half dozen styles of personal combat. But she hated being without even one of her weapons.

She was also nervous, unsure what to expect when Villieneuve walked in. She doubted the absolute ruler of the Union would waste his time calling her into his office just to have her killed. There were far easier ways to see to that, if he'd finally decided to do away with her. But, she still wasn't sure he was going to offer her what she truly wanted...a way back in, a return to her former life as an operative.

Sector Nine was gone now, the buildings—the ones that weren't very well-protected secrets, at least—burned or pulled down brick by brick. Thousands of the agents had been killed, most of them betrayed to the mob and murdered in the streets. The blood of so many of his operatives had greased Villieneuve's route back to power. Marieles knew many people would find that appalling, disgusting...they would hate and despise the man for such callous treachery and disloyalty. But she saw only brilliance in all Villieneuve had done, and she admired her former—and future?—boss immensely.

She indulged a small spark of optimism. She had achieved

considerable success in her mission against the Alliance, almost single-handedly provoking a war between the Palatians and the Krillians. Tarkus Vennius had refused to call back the fleet deployed against the Union forces at the Bottleneck, so in that regard, her mission had failed. But any reasonable analysis would show that she had been as successful as *she* could have been, especially working with as few resources as she'd been given. She'd created a serious threat to the Alliance home world. Vennius's steadiness and courage in facing that danger, and overcoming it, had been a factor beyond her control.

Still, her own opinion didn't necessarily extend to Gaston Villieneuve, and she'd been more than a little concerned when she came back, unsure how much blame for the war's failure he might heap upon her. Her worries had proven to be well-founded. Villieneuve had scapegoated many, shifted the blame from himself to whomever best served his purposes. Marieles had been left alone, though it was unclear whether that was because Villieneuve didn't blame her, or just because the worst of his rage and massacres occurred while she was still making the long journey back.

She'd been uncertain what to expect when she arrived. At first, she'd cowered in a small apartment, one of her safe houses, feeling a wave of fear at every sound from the hallway. But, as time went by, she'd begun to see cause to hope that she'd escaped the wave of terror that had swept across Montmirail.

Survival had been her initial concern, of course, but eventually, she'd begun to worry about a future beyond just another day drawing breath. She had hidden resources, of course, as most agents did, but the widespread crash of the Union's currency had reduced the value of her reserves to almost nothing. She'd eked out a tolerable existence the past year, certainly better than most of Montmirail's inhabitants had managed, but she knew she would have to do something soon. Tolerable had never been Desiree Marieles's target.

Then, she got the message to report to Villieneuve at once. The fact that it hadn't come along with armed guards was cause for some hope, she'd realized almost immediately, but now, sitting there waiting, she was getting edgier as each minute slipped off the clock.

"Desiree…what a pleasure to see you again." The words pulled her from her thoughts, and she stood up, turning toward the door as Gaston Villieneuve stepped into the office. He looked vastly different than she'd remembered, thinner, for one thing, and clad from head to toe in factory worker's clothes, his pants stained, his worn leather boots covered in mud. She remembered him as perfectly groomed and tailored at all times, but now he sported a three-day scruff and his hair was long and tousled.

"Minister Villien…"

"Please, Desiree…I am merely Citizen Villieneuve now." He moved toward her and extended his hand, grasping her arm in the style that had become commonplace on Montmirail since the…revolution.

"Yes, of course, *Citizen* Villieneuve. I'm so glad that you sent for me. I know how busy you must be."

"There is far too little time in the day. Yet, those in the factories work long hours as well, doing their part to bring prosperity to our People's Union. I can do no less."

"I'm impressed, sir…by all you have accomplished."

"Thank you, Desiree. But there are no 'sirs' here. Only two Citizens, both loyal and committed to the new future."

"Indeed…Citizen." Marieles was a little surprised at Villieneuve's intensity. For a moment, she almost believed he had sincerely turned into the people's leader his propaganda had so widely promoted. But then, he sat at his desk, a barely perceptible wince on his face as he landed in the hard and unyielding chair. He pressed a button on his desk, and the door slid shut. A few seconds later, a small yellow light on the desk turned green.

"We can speak more freely now, Desiree." He gestured toward the small device on the desk. "I still have political enemies out there, I'm afraid, and caution is always warranted. The room is secure now."

"I understand…" She wasn't sure what to call him now. "Sir? Citizen?"

"Citizen will do, Desiree. There is no sense in making things more complicated than they need to be, and we certainly don't want to risk carelessness in public now, do we?" He paused for a moment. "I wanted to speak with you about something important."

"I was very happy to receive your communication. It had been so long, I was afraid you…"

"Things have been…hectic. I'm afraid some matters have taken considerably longer than I might have hoped." *And I wanted to wait and see if you had a low enough profile before I decided to let you live.* He didn't say that, but she heard it in her head.

"I understand completely…Citizen." She understood better than she let on. She didn't have the slightest doubt that if her identity as a Sector Nine agent had become public, he'd have sacrificed her to the mob in an instant. The year or more she'd spent in fear and deprivation, waiting to see if she would survive…it had been a test of sorts. And she had passed.

"We're forming a new organization dedicated to protecting the interests of the state. The People's Protectorate. I'm actively recruiting individuals I believe have the ability to undertake certain missions, endeavors vital to the new Union's security."

Ah…The People's Protectorate. She'd heard whispers of the new organization before, mostly hints that its purpose was to root out any remnants of the old regime, and anyone acting against the interests of the Union's workers. At least, that was what people were supposed to think. But she knew better than to believe what she heard. *He's building a new Sector Nine. This is what I've been waiting for…*

"I am ready to help any way I can."

"I was sure you would be." Villieneuve paused, and he smiled across the desk at her. "Desiree, I never had the chance to tell you this, but reviewing what survived of the files and reports, it appears you did an outstanding job with the Krillians. You got the Krillians to attack with no support from us, financial or otherwise." Another pause. "The fact that the Palatians were too… pigheaded…to call back their ships from the front in time is not your fault. You did everything I sent you to do, and far faster than I'd imagined possible."

"Thank you, Min…Citizen."

Villieneuve smiled again. "Don't worry, you'll get used to it." He looked down at himself, at the disheveled clothing he wore. "At least sooner than you will to dressing like a factory laborer. But we do what we must, do we not?"

"Absolutely, Citizen." She smiled, too. The discussion was heading exactly where she'd hoped it would.

"Desiree, I have something in mind, a plan for which I laid some of the framework before the…change of government. It is not unlike what you did with the Krillians, though I'm afraid it is far broader in scope."

"I am with you. One hundred percent. You just have to tell me what you want me to do."

Villieneuve nodded. "I knew you would feel that way, Desiree. I am sorry you were on your own for so long. These are…unsettled…times."

"Yes, they certainly are. So, what can I do?"

"I want you to direct an ongoing operation to undermine a government. It's a longer-term project, one with many moving parts. It is complex, and I'm afraid it will be dangerous as well, but it is also one that offers great rewards. Unfortunately, it is not focused on a single individual, like your mission to the Krillians. It involves manipulating many individual politicians, some with debts or secrets we already control, others who will have to be enticed into the web in one way or another."

"It sounds like a major undertaking, Citizen. I would be honored to be a part of it."

"You're not going to be a part of it, Desiree…"

Her stomach tensed. Had Villieneuve called her here out of some perverse sadism, after all, instead of to recall her to duty? Or had she said something, done something that might have angered him?

"You're going to run the whole thing, from top to bottom."

His words were a total surprise, and it took a few seconds for them to register. Finally, she managed to reply. "I don't know what to say…Citizen. I am very grateful for this opportunity."

"You don't even know where I'm sending you…or which government you will be undermining."

She didn't care. Anything was better than scraping by as she'd been doing, skulking in obscurity with barely enough resources to survive. She'd go anywhere Villieneuve sent her, take on any mission he gave her…as long as it got her back on the inside.

"This mission is of great important, Desiree. I am trusting you with one of the three or four most crucial positions we've got." He paused, and a hint of menace slipped into his tone. "You cannot fail. You will have substantially greater resources than you did on the Krillian operation, both in terms of person-nel and finances. But, you *must* get it done, whatever it takes." He stated across the desk. "Do you understand me, Desiree?"

She understood completely. She could feel the sweat beading on her back, the spark of fear rekindled inside her. Villieneuve was giving her a major opportunity, but the deal was the same as it had always been. Succeed…and reap great rewards. Or fail… and die.

"I understand."

"Good. You have my complete confidence. Go, now, and wrap up any loose ends. You leave in two days."

"Yes, sir." She stood up, turning toward the door, but then she stopped and looked back.

"Where am I going? What government will I be working to bring down?"

Villieneuve had looked down at the desk, but now his eyes darted up and met hers.

"You're going to Megara, of course. You're going to destabi-lize the Confederation government."

Chapter Twelve

"Commodore, we're picking up a signal from *Dauntless*'s patrol."

Sara Eaton turned and looked over at her communications officer. "On the main line, Lieutenant."

"Yes, Commodore."

A few seconds later, the bridge speakers crackled to life. "*Dauntless*, this is Ensign Palich calling from patrol one."

Eaton could tell at once something was wrong. The pilot's voice was tense. And in a rookie mistake, he hadn't stated any details in his report, nothing but his ID. He was acting like he was on some kind of intraship line instead of sending a message from almost two light minutes from his mother ship. *Repulse* was on the far edge of the fleet, which meant a turnaround time of just under one minute for communications, rather than just over three minutes for a message to return from *Dauntless*. If something was wrong, *Repulse* was far better positioned to intervene.

She flipped the switch on her own headset, and said, "*Dauntless* patrol one, this is Commodore Eaton on *Repulse*. Report your situation at once."

She turned toward her tactical officer. "Commander, let's get Gold Falcon squadron ready...just in case we need them." Eaton didn't expect any *real* trouble, at least nothing that rattled her battle-hardened sensibilities, but she was a big believer in being ready for anything.

"Gold Falcon squadron, report to launch bay. Repeat, Gold Falcon squadron, report to launch bay." The officer turned around and looked back toward Eaton. "Gold Falcon commander confirms order, Commodore."

Eaton just nodded. Then she leaned back in her chair and waited for a response from the patrol.

"Commodore, this is Ensign Palich, serial number A456D711, in temporary command of patrol one." Nothing else.

Eaton shook her head. *My God, this kid is a rookie. How did someone so wet behind the ears end up commanding a patrol?* It didn't seem at all like Barron to send out someone so raw, and even less like Atara Travis, who most likely had selected the pilots for the mission.

She shook her head. He still hadn't reported what was happening. "Ensign, report your situation at once, and in detail." She didn't snap, not exactly, but she put a little more oomph behind the command.

She glanced over at the chronometer. *Dauntless* would be receiving the first signal in a few seconds. But it would take more than a minute and a half for any response to reach the fighters...and given the apparent lack of experience of Ensign Palich, she imagined an exchange might go on for quite some time if she didn't intervene.

"Falcons ready, Commodore."

Eaton was a bit surprised by the tactical officer's report. The Gold Falcons were her elite squadron, but they'd outdone even themselves. Their response time was bordering on the impossible.

"Launch Gold Falcon Squadron. They are to move toward patrol one's location, maximum possible thrust." She didn't want to exaggerate whatever was happening out there, but she always believed it was better to overreact a bit than get taken by surprise. And, it was going to take time to get assistance to those pilots if they were in trouble, so the sooner that help started out, the better.

"Gold Falcons launching, Commodore." A few seconds later, Eaton could feel the gentle vibrations from the catapults. It was a softer sensation on *Repulse* than it had been on *Intrepid*. Her new flagship was larger, and outmassed her old vessel by a good million tons.

Perhaps half a minute later: "Gold Falcon squadron launched."

Eaton just nodded. Then, the next signal from the patrol came in. "Commodore Eaton, we detected…some kind of signal coming from the gas giant up ahead. Captain Stockton…he went forward to investigate. We can't raise him, Commodore, and we haven't heard from him at all since he got close to the planet."

Eaton felt her tension increase. It was one thing for some rookie pilots to get into trouble. That could be anything— mechanical failure, an overreaction to natural phenomena. But Jake Stockton was the best pilot in the fleet. If he was having some kind of problem…

It's probably just a system failure. Her discipline slammed down in place. There was no cause to panic, at least not yet. *But, why hasn't he contacted the fleet, or the other ships of the patrol?*

"Gold Falcons, continue to location of patrol one, maximum thrust. Further orders will be available when you get there."

"Yes, Commodore."

"Activate tender one, prepare to launch."

"Tender one crew, to the bay."

Eaton sat quietly as her tactical officer carried out her commands, listening as *Dauntless*'s reply to the patrol's initial communique reached *Repulse*.

Eaton turned toward the tactical station. "Advise *Dauntless* we have responded to the patrol's communique and dispatched assistance."

"Yes, Commodore."

She looked back at the main display. Most likely, Stockton's fighter had just broken down…but there was no room for care-lessness, not hundreds of lightyears from home.

"Bring *Repulse* to yellow alert, Lieutenant." She studied the locations of the ships in the fleet. *Repulse* was well out on the flank. If Stockton had found something…her ship was the clos-est. "And launch tender one as soon as it is ready."

* * *

Stockton watched as the data continued to come in from his partially operational scanners. It was spotty, but his momen-tum was bringing him closer to the…whatever it was…and that increased the clarity of data. He'd done the calculations twice. He was going to come within one hundred kilometers of the thing, and that was practically a collision course in terms of space travel.

He moved his hands over the controls, doing what he could to focus the scanning power he did have. He thought about shutting the scanners down entirely, saving his fuel for life sup-port, but he just kept working the controls. He had enough fuel to get back to the fleet, and he could use that to give him heat and air for a good while. Long enough for help to arrive, at least.

He watched as the distance counted down on his screen. Two thousand kilometers…nineteen hundred…eighteen hun-dred. He was still too far out for visuals on the contact itself, at least with his fighter's limited optics, but he was getting clearer data on the size and power figures. Whatever it was, it wasn't more than a hundred meters in length. *Less*, he realized as he crept closer. But the power figures were way above anything he'd expected. Whatever energy source that thing had, it was far more powerful than anything Confederation science could cram into so small a space.

Antimatter…

That was a guess. Stockton didn't have scanners capable of analyzing the trace radiation completely enough to determine if its source was an atomic reaction…or antimatter annihila-tion. But, somehow, he just knew. The pre-Cataclysm empire had mastered the production of antimatter, that much was well known. He was still stabbing in the dark, but now he was fairly certain he'd stumbled on a bit of old tech…one that appeared to be at least partially operational.

"Captain…read…"

His comm unit came to life, mostly static, with a few words he was able to pick out. "Can you clean that up at all?" he snapped to the AI.

"Already clarifying and enhancing signal as it comes in."

So, that unintelligible blast of noise had been the communication *after* the AI worked on it. *Just great.*

Stockton reached out to the communication controls. The scanner interference near the planet was significant as well, and he figured he'd better give his prospective rescuers an idea where he was. He didn't figure his own message would come through any clearer, but they really didn't need to know what he was saying, as long as they could trace the comm beam back to him.

He put his hand to his headset, but just before he tapped it, his screen flashed, the brightness almost blinding. *Another energy spike?* Whatever it was, it had been strong. For an instant, he even thought the artifact had attacked. But he was still there, and he suspected if the device had wanted him dead, he would be.

He wondered if he'd been scanned again. The last beam had been powerful enough to blow out half the electronics in his fighter. He looked around, checking each system in turn. If another scanner beam had hit his ship, there was no new damage. *So, probably not a scan…*

He sat for a minute, trying to figure out just what he'd seen. Then, he shook his head. It didn't matter right now. There would be time later to analyze whatever his battered systems had managed to record, but the first step was getting back to *Dauntless*.

"This is Captain Stockton. My location is…" He glanced down at the screen. "…102.340.119. I have found a contact I believe to be some kind of artifact, likely old tech. It appears to be operational. I repeat, it appears to be operational." He paused, then added, "It has made no indications of being hostile." He doubted anyone was getting much beyond the general direction of the comm beam, but if his words got through, he didn't want to cause a panic. He was still nervous, of course, and he certainly considered the device a potential threat. But his nerves had calmed considerably as time had passed.

"…Stockton…coming…minutes."

He still couldn't make out more than a few words, but the signal was stronger than before, and that meant the ship transmitting it was getting closer. He had his scanner concentrated on the artifact, but now he switched it back to wide area. The interference was affecting the sensors as much as his comm, but after a few seconds, he picked up a contact incoming. No, multiple contacts.

It looked like a group of fighters. For an instant, he thought his rookies had decided to follow him in, but then he realized there were too many contacts. It looked like a whole squadron, and a larger ship of some kind behind the fighters.

The retrieval boat, he realized. *With a full squadron escort.* Whoever had gotten his patrol's call for help wasn't taking any chances.

"Raptor…is Gold Falcon squadr…here to assist." The signal was beginning to clear up as the contacts moved closer. He could see them shift their vectors slightly, and he realized they had locked onto his comm beam and were following it in.

Gold Falcon…they're on Repulse. *Of course! Commodore Eaton's ship is the closest. She must have responded before the call even reached* Dauntless.

"Gold Falcons, this is Raptor. My thrusters are disabled. Exert extreme caution. I am approximately eight hundred kilometers from a contact I believe to be an old tech artifact."

"Archer here, sir. Sit tight, Raptor. We're on our way, along with a tender to tow your bird back to base. We'll keep our eyes out for your artifact."

"Roger that, Archer."

Stockton let out a relieved sigh. He hadn't been too worried, at least not once he'd realized the artifact didn't seem like it was going to blow him to bits. But knowing help was almost there left him free to feel some excitement at the find, and curiosity about the artifact.

This is what we came to find, after all…

*   *   *

"I've told you everything, sir." *Several times.* Stockton held back the last remark. He'd always been a bit of a maverick, but even his instincts called on him to keep silent with what would undoubtedly come across as a snotty remark to the admiral. "The scanner beam was powerful, strong enough to blow out half my systems. I lost engine control, along with most of my own scanning capacity."

"But you weren't attacked at all."

"No, sir." It hadn't sounded like a question, but Stockton answered anyway.

"Any thoughts?" Barron looked out across the conference table. Atara Travis was there, and Sara Eaton, Cilian Globus—every key officer in the fleet. The first contact with what appeared to be a substantial artifact was the most crucial moment in the fleet's journey to date.

"It has to be an imperial artifact. What else could it be?" Travis looked over at Barron. "I don't have an alternative hypothesis." She angled her head, looking at the others. "Does anyone else?"

"I'm inclined to agree with you, Atara," Barron said, after no one else responded. "So, the key questions are, what is it? What, other than basic chance, explains why it's still working, when all other old tech we've found was in some state of inoperability or decay? Is it dangerous?" He paused. "We picked it up, and that didn't trigger any sort of attack." The artifact had activated its scanning beam several more times since fleet units had put it under close surveillance, but nothing resembling a weapon had been detected yet.

Still, Barron wasn't taking any chances. The thing was likely powered by antimatter, and that alone was a good reason for caution. He'd ordered the shuttles that had towed it back to the fleet to stop ten thousand kilometers from *Dauntless*…and he'd dispatched his engineering teams to inspect the device there. It was far more difficult to analyze the thing in space, but he wasn't about to bet his new vessel's survival on an antimatter containment system he guessed was over four centuries old. It wouldn't take more than a nanosecond's failure in the magnetic field to release enough antimatter to blow *Dauntless* into a cloud of superheated plasma.

He'd hesitated to send the teams at all. Keeping the artifact away from *Dauntless* would protect the flagship in the event of a catastrophic failure, but it would do nothing for his engineers and technicians. Anya Fritz and her best people were clad in spacesuits even at that moment, prowling around the ancient device. It wouldn't take a massive antimatter explosion to kill every one of them. Even a modest defensive weapon, or just an accident in the deadly environment of space, would be enough to wipe out the research party.

He'd led his people into so many dangers, he'd nearly lost count. But it was always hardest to order a small, hand-picked group to put themselves in jeopardy. At least in battle, they all shared a similar danger. He knew Fritz had practically leapt out the airlock, almost overwhelmed by enthusiasm to inspect the new find. He'd have had to have her shackled and thrown in the brig to keep her away, but still, he felt responsible for whatever might happen to her.

"I suggest we wait, at least for the preliminary inspection report." Eaton was tapping her fingers on the tabletop, a sure sign, Barron knew, that she was as edgy as he was. "Then we'll have more to go on."

"What more will we have, Commodore?" Globus had been quiet since the meeting had started, but now he spoke up. "We know that device has to be old tech...and we also know that it was deployed near a transit point. I say it's leading the way for us. We've made mostly random navigational choices to date, but I'd say now the route is clear. We should advance through that point, and see what lies beyond."

Barron wasn't surprised that the commander of the Alliance contingent was in favor of the most aggressive option...but he was a little less prepared for how much he suddenly realized he agreed. The condition of the find suggested that the fleet might run into more functional old tech, and he was nervous that meant possibly hostile artifacts...but part of him wanted to push forward immediately, to see what lay beyond the transit point. The fact that the artifact had been situated so close to one of the system's five points did suggest that perhaps it was indeed a route toward the heart of the old empire.

"Your enthusiasm speaks well of you, Cilian, but I believe we should at least wait and see what the engineering team is able to uncover on their initial inspection." He glanced over at the chronometer. "In fact, we should be hearing something any time now."

Barron leaned back in his chair. "We also have to consider how we'll proceed when we do transit. We will proceed through the one situated near the artifact. Does everyone agree?"

When no one offered a different opinion, he continued. "We must organize the fleet into a more...for lack of a better word, combat ready formation. If we can find one artifact in functional condition, we could find others...including warships and other weapons under robotic control. We have to be ready."

"I humbly request that my forces be placed at the head of the fleet, Admiral, as the advance guard." Globus again, this time acting so much like a Palatian, Barron had to struggle not to grin. He couldn't risk offending Globus by refusing his request, though he knew the Alliance ships were a generation behind their Confederation counterparts in terms of scanning and computer analysis capability.

"I accept your offer, Commander...but I'm afraid your force is a bit smaller than I'd like for the forward unit. So, I will assign a group of Confederation ships to join you."

"Sir, if it is acceptable to you, I would like to take *Repulse* to the front of the fleet."

"Very well, Commodore Eaton." *And thank you, Sara.* Eaton's request would put the fleet's exec with the advance guard. She would outrank Globus, and as such, command the entire advance guard. Barron wasn't concerned about Globus's tactical ability, nor his courage. But he was just a little afraid the Palatian might blast something a bit prematurely. Alliance officers worked on a kind of a partially submerged paranoia, most likely a vestige from the days when their home world was subjugated, and their ancestors slaves. It didn't take more than the slightest signs of hostility to bring out their warlike sides. Sara Eaton was a hell of a fighter, one he'd match against any Palatian in battle…but she was far more likely to try to avoid hostilities than Globus.

"Very well, Commodore. Take *Repulse*, and…" Barron thought for a few seconds. "…*Courageous* and *Defiant*, as well as two squadrons of escorts. You are to advance with full combat protocols, but remember, we're not looking to provoke anything. I want you to exert maximum caution at all times. Is that understood?"

"Yes, sir."

Barron nodded to her. *She understands.*

He was just about to dismiss the meeting when the comm unit buzzed.

"Admiral, I've got Captain Fritz on your line."

"Put her through." He looked up. "If you will all remain for another moment, it looks like we may have some information on the artifact."

"Admiral?"

"Yes, Fritzie. I'm here in conference with the other senior commanders. Do you have anything for us?"

"Yes, sir…we're pretty sure the device's purpose was surveillance, some kind of satellite or drone. My guess is, it was positioned where it was to warn of anything approaching the transit point."

Barron nodded. "That makes sense." He looked up, turning toward the others at the table. "It also supports our theory that this transit point leads toward the center of the old empire." He turned back toward the comm unit. "Anything else, Fritzie?"

"Yes, sir. It's antimatter-powered, as we suspected. As far as we can determine, the containment system appears to be completely sound, but I still recommend we keep it some distance from any of our ships. It's quite advanced, sir, but…" She paused a few seconds.

"But? Speak your mind, Fritzie."

"But, it seems noticeably lower-tech than some of the other devices we've encountered. The stealth generator, and certainly the planetkiller, were more sophisticated in design and construction. I was never able to examine the pulsar, of course, but I feel comfortable in saying that, too, was considerably more advanced. I can't be sure about this, but if I had to guess, I'd say this device was built by a culture several centuries behind the one that constructed the other artifacts."

Barron sat silently for a moment. That didn't make any sense. The old records were spotty and incomplete, but he'd never heard anything about more than one entity existing in the pre-Cataclysmic past. The empire ruled all mankind, for centuries, if not millennia, and it had never encountered any alien civilizations. What could explain two distinctly different technology levels, both far in advance of the Confederation's?

"Do you have any explanation, Fritzie?" He knew the answer even as he asked the question.

"No, sir. None." A pause. "And, I have something else, Admiral. We can't be sure, not until we can bring samples back to the lab aboard *Dauntless*, but...well, sir, we think this artifact is newer than the ones we've found before. Perhaps not much more than a century old, and no more than two."

"Do you know what you're saying, Fritzie?"

"Yes, sir."

Barron shook his head. The empire had been destroyed nearly four centuries earlier. It seemed impossible that anything like the artifact could have been produced after the Cataclysm, even if some vestigial civilization had endured longer than the old records suggested. The Confederation was over a hundred years old, and Megara's history was well-documented back at least another century. Yet, Fritz was saying the artifact they'd just found was from roughly that time period.

Barron almost asked if she was sure, but she'd said flat out that she wasn't, that she needed to verify the results. That meant there was still some doubt. Perhaps the new artifact was simply a cheaper, lower quality item from imperial times. He didn't really believe that—he was inclined to take Fritz's instincts as proven fact—but he wanted as much solid data as he could get. "All right, Fritzie, get your people back here immediately. Run whatever tests you have to, but get me solid information on this."

"Yes, sir."

Barron leaned back, deep in thought for a moment, almost forgetting the others in the room. Then he exhaled forcefully and said, "You all heard Captain Fritz. If she confirms her suspicions, we've got another mystery on our hands, the implications of which I can't even delineate right now."

The room was silent, every eye on him. "There's no point in getting ahead of ourselves. Take a break, get something to eat… we'll reconvene as soon as Captain Fritz is able to complete her tests."

And then we'll try to figure out what the hell is really going on out here…

Chapter Thirteen

The Promenade
Spacer's District
Port Royal City, Planet Dannith, Ventica III
315 AC

"Thank you for your assistance, Mr. Trencher. You may consider your debts paid in full."

Trencher nodded, clearly trying to avoid eye contact with Andi. "Thank you," he finally said, his voice weak, soft. Then he turned and walked away.

Andi sat silently, watching as Trencher slipped out of sight. He'd done what she needed him to do, led her right to the top of the Sector Nine presence on Dannith. Though, the circumstances of that discovery were far from ideal.

And, it wasn't going to stop her from putting a bloody hole in the treacherous bastard's head when she got back.

"What's this about?" She glared at Lille. She was in deep now, she knew that. But she still had to play the part.

"It's about employment, Captain Lafarge. You came here under the pretense of prospecting for old tech, but I'm afraid I don't believe that is the case. I think you were looking for us, at the behest of your friends from Confederation Intelligence." He paused and turned toward the man sitting next to Andi. "Have you found it yet?"

The man was holding an instrument of some kind, a probe with a cable connected to a small screen. "Yes, sir. It's in her left arm, approximately three centimeters below the elbow."

Andi was watching…and getting a very bad feeling.

"Do it." Lille's voice was calm, without anger. But she could hear menace in it nevertheless.

The man grabbed her arm. She pulled it back, but then another man, the one sitting across from her, punched her. She saw it coming too late, and managed to get partially out of the way, but it still hit her hard. She gasped for a breath as her assailant lunged out of his seat and grabbed her left arm, holding it like a vice.

She struggled, but both men were larger and stronger, and she was woozy from the punch. She felt fingers on her arm, feeling around for a few seconds…and then pain.

It was a blade of some kind, digging deep. She tried to hold back a scream, but it forced its way out. She could feel the blood pouring out onto her arm, and something metal digging into her flesh.

She gritted her teeth and struggled to get out of her assailant's grip, but to no avail. Finally, the man next to her said simply, "Got it." He was holding up a small piece of metal, just under a centimeter in length, and covered in blood and tiny bits of muscle tissue.

It was her tracker. The device that allowed Holsten and his people to follow where she was taken.

"Excellent." Lille's voice was unchanged. He reached out and took the capsule, handing it to a woman seated next to him. "See that this ends up in another vehicle, perhaps one heading downtown. We might as well give our friends at Confederation Intelligence an interesting ride while we have a…chat…with Captain Lafarge here."

Andi was hunched over, whimpering slightly at the pain despite her best efforts to hold it back.

"Here, Captain." Lille handed her a long strip of bandage. He turned toward the man next to her, the one who'd sliced open her arm. "Help her with this. The captain is our guest, after all." He angled his head back toward the front of the vehicle. "Let's get moving. We don't want to be at the last place Confed Intelligence got a reading from that thing."

The man grabbed her arm and began to wrap the strip of cloth around the wound. The material was bright white, but it quickly became soaked through with blood.

"I must apologize, Captain Lafarge, for our apparent lack of manners, but we couldn't allow your friends from Confederation Intelligence to crash our little party, not so soon. We have so much to discuss, and I'm afraid they would just spoil things."

"What do you want from me?" She took a deep breath, fighting to ignore the pain as much as she could, and she stared at him, making no effort to hide the hatred in her eyes.

"Confederation Intelligence sent you here to uncover our operation on the border. Frankly, I've been shocked at how freely we've been able to infiltrate the worlds along the Badlands all these years."

"I don't know what you're talking about. I'm just here to prospect for old tech."

"Captain Lafarge…we're going to get along much better if we respect each other's intelligence. I will confess, I wasn't sure you were working for Holsten's people, not until Trencher got you to the vehicle. My studies of your…adventures…suggest you're far too cautious to go along with something like that… unless you were trying to uncover our operatives."

Andi stayed focused on Lille, but she didn't say anything.

"Well, we can leave that unspoken. Any doubts you are working for Confederation Intelligence were eliminated the instant Sid here pulled that tracker out of your arm. Your people have been using those for far too long, I'm afraid. They might as well tattoo 'operative' on your forehead."

Andi remained silent, but any hope she'd still had of convincing Lille she was just on Dannith to make prospecting runs slipped away.

"I will be blunt, Captain. We want you to work for us instead. I assure you, we are more generous paymasters than Confederation Intelligence. And we would like to employ you in operations far closer to your expertise than the folly Gary Holsten lured you into."

She glared across the transport's small cabin toward Lille. "Yes, your 'incentive' program is quite clear." She held up her bloody arm, wincing from the pain as she moved it.

"That was an unfortunate necessity, Captain. Had it been possible to have, shall we say, more of a medical environment available, we might have been able to achieve it with less discomfort."

"Drop dead." Her words were cold.

Lille sighed. "Your friend, Mr. Trencher was far more reasonable. Once we'd taken over his debts, it was quite easy to secure his cooperation. I would advise you to follow his lead, Captain."

"Trencher is a foul pig. And, he's going to be short one head as soon as I can get out of here and blow it off." She felt defiance inside rising, bolstering her courage. Fear was there, too, of course, and she knew it would be a struggle to hold it back. She'd faced Sector Nine before, and the experience had not been pleasant…but Ricard Lille was something else entirely. She'd heard of him, shadowy rumors and stories always told by someone who said they'd been told by someone. She wasn't sure what was true and what wasn't, but she doubted there was anything he wouldn't do to get what he wanted, and that suggested the coming hours and days were likely to be very…challenging.

"Yes, I believe you will, Captain. And you'll have that chance…as long as you cooperate with us."

"That will never happen."

"Ah, Andi…may I call you Andi?"

She glared back, silent, unwilling to play Lille's little game.

"I'll take that as a yes. Anyway, Andi…many people have said that before, and they have suffered needlessly. Although Sector Nine no longer exists, my people have considerable… experience…in this area."

"Do what you're going to do, but don't treat me like a fool. You can call a bucket of maggots a vase full of flowers…it's still a bucket of maggots." There was venom in her tone. She was harnessing her rage to bolster her courage.

"You're as charming as I had heard, Andi. I'd like to say this is going to be a pleasure, but despite your obvious opinions of me, I'm not as sadistic as you imagine. I will admit, I do enjoy the excitement of the kill, but the exhilaration is in the hunt, the chase. Inflicting pain on a helpless captive...well, there are some in my employ I daresay derive a level of pleasure from that, but I assure you, I'm not one of them. You may believe me or not, but I would be just as happy rewarding you, enticing you to our service, rather than breaking you." He paused, and though his tone remained even, Andi could feel a new level of malevolence there. "You would also be more useful in such a scenario. We will, of course, break your will if we must, Andi, but I fear you will be a stubborn candidate, and it will take...aggressive... means to bring you around. Such methods are not without consequences. Or long-term effects."

Andi sat still, trying to keep herself from letting Lille know how scared she was. She wouldn't give the son of a bitch the satisfaction. She angled her head and looked right back at him. "Do whatever you're going to do. Anything would be better than listening to you talk me to death."

* * *

Holsten's eyes were fixed on the small dot on the screen. He was sitting in the back of a transport, not the kind of luxury vehicle to which he was accustomed, but one that appeared to be a non-descript delivery truck of some sort. The vehicle looked old and somewhat rundown, but it was actually almost new, and the special equipment inside cost twenty times what even the most high-end of transports did.

The vehicle was moving down the street through relatively light late-night traffic. That was good. Holsten's truck was following another transport, and it was crucial to stay close. The dot on the screen was Andi Lafarge's tracker, and his newly recruited agent was being taken somewhere.

Holsten was nervous, on the verge of ordering the half

dozen vehicles he had in play to converge on the transport and extricate Andi from whatever situation she was in. He'd held back, not wishing to interfere with any operation she might be conducting. He knew where she was because of her tracker, but he had no idea if she was there willingly, or if she was a captive.

"I want units four and five to move up. I don't want that transport out of sight."

"Yes, sir." The driver was one of his agents. Everyone involved was a Confederation Intelligence operative…except for the detachments of Marines, and, of course, Andi Lafarge. *No, Andi is one of yours now, too.* He had trouble thinking of Lafarge as a spy, but that was just what he'd made her.

Lafarge *was* an agent now, at least officially, but now he was worried about how she would handle the situation he'd put her in. Holsten had lured her to the operation, persuaded her to join Confederation Intelligence, but he knew she lacked experience in espionage, not to mention the assorted skillsets his people called tradecraft.

That didn't mean she was helpless, not by a longshot. She was a fierce and capable fighter, an accomplished spaceship pilot, and an expert on working the slime pit of the Confederation's Badlands border. Those last skills were not unlike intelligence work, but they weren't exactly the same, either. He'd done his best to bring her into this, but now guilt was preying on him. Andi had been bored, having some trouble adjusting to retirement, and he had used that to get to her, to convince her to come back to Dannith.

Andi Lafarge doesn't do anything she doesn't want to do…

He knew there was truth to the thought his mind had shoved forth in defense of his actions. Still, he was well aware that she wouldn't be on Dannith now, in some mysterious vehicle, possibly a prisoner—possibly facing imminent death—if he hadn't gone to Tellurus and lured her there.

The dot turned, moving onto the main street leaving the city. He'd been on the verge of ordering his people in for the last fifteen minutes, but now he decided. If he let the transport get too far out of the city, his talking units would stick out like flashing lights amid the lesser traffic.

"All units…move in and intercept. And remember, one of our people is in that vehicle, so stun guns only." He turned and looked to the front of the cabin, toward the driver. "We're moving in. Get us up there. Now."

He reached down to the seat, scooping up the weapon he'd set next to him. It was a stun gun, fully charged. Holsten couldn't remember the last time he'd been so close to the action in an operation, but he felt responsible for Andi, and he'd promised himself he would be in the field with her, close by, ready to come to her aid any time she needed it.

Like now.

The vehicle accelerated, moving to the side to pass several others. Holsten could see the transport carrying Andi just ahead. As he was watching, he saw three of his vehicles converge, one pulling in front, completely blocking the target's path.

He reached over and opened the hatch, climbing out, even as his peripheral vision caught almost two dozen of his people, armed agents, and—very heavily armed—Marines, moving up on the vehicle. He was expecting some kind of resistance, perhaps even a hostage situation as whoever was in the surrounded transport held Andi at gunpoint. But there was nothing, no activity at all, save his people advancing right up to the transport.

Then, the hatch opened, and a man came out, his hands high in the air. He was older, perhaps seventy, wearing a simple, nondescript outfit. And he was shaking, clearly terrified. Not at all what Holsten had expected.

He raced up toward the vehicle, and as he approached, one of his people turned and walked over to him. Isaac Stewart, the ranking agent on the op. "There's no one else in the transport, sir. This man claims he is the owner of a store on the Promenade. His documentation seems to check out, sir, and the vehicle is registered to the store."

Holsten's mind raced. "We picked up Andi Lafarge's tracker in that truck. I want it searched, completely." It was a needless command, he knew. His people were already well into the effort.

He moved up, looked over at where several agents were

questioning the clearly stunned driver. He was staring through the open hatch into the battered old truck when one of the agents said, "Found it, sir."

The man walked right up to Holsten and extended his arm. He was holding a small bit of metal, streaked with red marks, clearly half-dried blood.

Holsten looked at the tracker, and his stomach tightened as cold realization set in. Whoever had Andi had removed the device—painfully, he suspected—and planted it in this transport. *They hoodwinked me.*

He looked around, at the transport, at the driver. He was sure the man had nothing to do with any of this, though he intended to make absolutely sure. He'd been taken once, and he wasn't about to let it happen again.

He was angry, sick with worry. He was responsible for Andi being involved in any of this, and now he had no idea where she was. Her captors could be anywhere in Port Royal, even out beyond city limits by now. He'd lost her.

"Agent Stewart," he snapped.

"Yes, sir." Stewart had moved back toward the driver, but now he turned and rushed back to Holsten.

"I want a Priority Alpha alert declared, at once."

Stewart looked back, a stunned expression on his face. "Sir, we'll need the planetary governor to sign off on that order to sustain Alpha status."

"Then get it. I don't care if you have to shove a gun in his mouth to do it." He paused, then added. "This is all on my personal responsibility, Isaac. Just get it done now. I've got a naval task force in the system. Get the order to them. I want a complete blockade, in effect now. No ships land or take off from Dannith until further notice. Not even a garbage scow. Is that clear?"

Stewart nodded and then said, "Yes, sir." The agent was clearly nervous, but he snapped off a crisp nod and moved back toward his agents, blasting out orders.

Holsten sighed softly. He was stirring up a real hornets' nest, he was sure of that. He'd just ordered an entire planet embargoed. He had the authority, but only in the face of a grave threat to national security. He didn't imagine the Senate committee that would investigate his actions would consider one missing agent sufficient grounds for such sweeping action.

And he didn't give a shit. He was responsible for Andi Lafarge being there, and for whatever trouble she was in now… and he was going to find her, if he had to tear Dannith apart one building at a time to do it.

Damned the consequences. If the Senate wanted to take him down over it, he'd bring more than one of the pompous fools with him.

Chapter Fourteen

**CFS Dauntless
Zed-4 System
Year 315 AC**

"I'm as sure as I can be, sir. I've run half a dozen different tests. That thing's hull is an alloy we've never seen before, something beyond our science at present, and that means I can't be absolutely sure. But based on every data point we've been able to establish, my best guess is that the...artifact...is somewhere between one hundred and one hundred fifty years old."

"Thanks, Fritzie. I know your people have been working around the clock." Barron was tense. He'd reconvened his senior personnel now that Fritz and her people had run more tests. There were a number of potential implications from what his top engineer had just reported, but none he could think of were good.

"Of course, sir."

Barron looked out across the conference table. "Any thoughts? We're short on answers, so any ideas are welcome."

"It could be from some kind of automated production facility that's still operating...or that was still running a century ago." Sara Eaton didn't sound at all convinced, even as she made the suggestion.

"Without incoming raw materials...or other manufactured

parts? And how did it get here? Not to mention, whoever programmed it would have been scheduling routine production
more than two hundred years in advance." Atara Travis shook
her head as she spoke.

"We need to consider every possibility, no matter how bizarre
it sounds. Captain Fritz was clear that this alloy is new to her.
We haven't satisfactorily penetrated the hull yet with our scans,
and we haven't disassembled any parts of the device, so we don't
have the whole picture. Perhaps it has some kind of anti-aging
process, something that interferes with the tests we've done or
slows normal decay."

The likeliest explanation was simply that Fritz had somehow
miscalculated, and the device was older than she thought. Perhaps the artifact had been produced just before the Cataclysm.
That would make it something like three hundred seventy-five
years old. But Barron didn't believe it, not really. Fritz might not
be familiar with the metal, but it was normal matter, and she had
done intense subatomic scans. He'd seen her work for too long
to convince himself she had made an error.

"There is another possibility, one we have not discussed."

Barron looked across the table at Globus, and he knew just
what the Palatian was thinking.

"We have assumed there were no survivors of the Cataclysm
outside our own sector of space. But there has never been any
real evidence to that effect, has there?"

"Are you saying the empire is still out there?" Travis asked.
"Shrunken, but still inhabited?"

"Well, that is a possibility, albeit an unlikely one. Based on
what we do know of the Cataclysm, it is hard to imagine that
the ancient political entity survived." Globus turned and looked
over at Barron. "But isn't it possible that more than one pocket
of survivors remained? If our sector could escape extinction,
why not another? We don't even have reliable data on how big
the empire was. We have to accept that we really don't know *what*
is out there."

Barron found himself nodding gently. Globus surprised him
with the calm, studied nature of his statement. The Palatian was

the last one he'd expected to make such a suggestion. The Alliance was out beyond the Rim, and it had far less in the way of legends and histories of the old empire and the Cataclysm than its coreward neighbors…at least until the treaty with the Confederation opened up the exchange of information. Globus had apparently taken advantage of that fact and educated himself before the mission, and Barron had to admit to himself, he was surprised.

"Perhaps there's some remnant of the empire remaining, after all…or some other sector where elements of civilization survived." Barron paused. The entire idea was a bit overwhelming. "Or, maybe some undocumented group of explorers ventured out from our worlds, and pressed far more deeply into the Badlands than we'd previously suspected? They could have found enough old tech to establish themselves, at least temporarily. Perhaps we've found something they constructed. They might even have died out eventually, which would explain the lack of any contact in the intervening years. This could be something they left behind." Barron felt like he was babbling, but he had no idea what else to do. "It doesn't matter which of these possibilities is correct, if any of them are, but one thing is certain." He hesitated again, and when he continued, his voice was deeper, more somber. "Our mission just became exponentially more complex. And dangerous."

"Yes," Globus said, nodding. "There is no question about that."

* * *

"What do we know about that energy flash Captain Stockton saw? Could it have been some kind of communication beam? I fear we have to be concerned not only with what may be out there, but with whether or not they know *we* are here." Barron had sent Eaton and Globus back to their ships. The fleet was setting out in a few hours, and the two officers would be taking the lead, their ships the first to move through the transit point, and into whatever system lay beyond. He'd asked a few of his people, old *Dauntless* crew all, to come back to his office for one more discussion before he gave the final order to advance.

"We can't be sure what Captain Stockton saw, or thought he saw. His fighter's malfunction cost us any data he might have tried to record." Anya Fritz sat at the end of a small couch on the wall across from Barron's desk. "I did everything I could, but the banks were wiped clean."

"Data or no data, I'm telling you I saw an energy spike." Stockton turned his head, looking around the room. "I'm sure of it."

"Nobody doubts what you saw, Jake. We're just trying to figure out what it could have been. Perhaps the thing was scanning you again, or maybe it was searching a different area."

"I suppose that's possible, sir, but I don't think so. It was... different...the second time. I didn't have time to check the readings, but it wasn't like a scan."

"You think it was a communication of some kind, don't you?" Atara Travis was sitting next to Stockton, and she turned to face him as she spoke.

Stockton paused for a few seconds, looking uncomfortable. "Yes," he finally said. Then: "But I can't guess its purpose. My first thought was that there was something else in the system, but we've conducted a thorough search, and we haven't found a thing." Stockton had directed that operation himself, and he'd had almost three hundred fighters scouring what seemed like every cubic meter of the system. His people had scoured those areas far too closely to have missed anything.

"If there was some kind of force hidden somewhere, if that was a distress call you detected, it seems likely that whatever was out there would have responded in some detectable way by now."

"Could it have been an attempt to send a message through the transit point, to the next system? Or beyond?" Anya Fritz seemed to be deep in thought even as she spoke.

"How would that have been possible?" Barron looked over at the engineer. "There was no indication of any physical probe being launched." He turned his head toward Stockton. "You didn't get any readings on anything like that, did you, Jake?"

"No, sir. Just an energy surge. Nothing material. I was within eight hundred kilometers…I can't imagine something physical could have escaped detection at that range." Stockton shook his head. "And, our patrols would have detected any kind of relay station located near one of the transit points. There was nothing."

Barron glanced down, looking at the patrol reports on the tablet sitting on his desk. Transit points were poorly understood, a vestige of man's vastly more advanced past. No one knew if the empire had constructed them, or if they were the legacy of some totally unknown, earlier civilization. But in more than two centuries of usage during recorded post-Cataclysmic history, a few things had been discovered about the portals and how they functioned. And, one of those was that only physical objects could pass through. No signal beams, or any kind of pure energy, had ever passed through a transit point from one system to another.

At least not any known to Confederation science.

"Fritzie…" Barron looked over at his engineer, but he paused, uncertain how to phrase what he wanted to say. "…what can you tell us about experiments in sending communication signals through transit points? I know there have been research programs."

Fritz shook her head. "I can't tell you anything, sir, except that as far as I know, every attempt to push any kind of raw energy or signal through a point has been a complete failure. As far as our science knows, the only way to send a message through a transit point is to carry it on a ship, or at least a drone of some kind, and nothing we've ever been able to observe has suggested otherwise."

"But even though you feel this artifact is less advanced than something like the pulsar, you believe it's ahead of us, don't you?"

"Yes, sir. I am *sure* of that. The alloy the hull is constructed from alone is stronger and lighter than anything comparable we've ever developed."

"So, then it is possible?"

"Sir?"

"It's possible that the artifact sent some kind of communication beam through the transit point, using technology unknown to us."

Fritz sat for a moment, silent, looking uncomfortable. "I suppose it is possible, Admiral. We know far too little about the transit points to have any real idea what is or is not possible. All I can say is, every effort to do so in the past has been an utter failure."

"I understand that, Fritzie, and I'm inclined to agree it's unlikely." Barron turned toward the others. "But it *is* possible, and we cannot forget that."

"What are you suggesting, sir?" Travis asked the question, but even as he listened, he'd have bet she knew the answer. No one got inside his head like Atara Travis did. Not even Andi.

"I'm suggesting there's at least a possibility that there were not only survivors long after the Cataclysm, but that they may, in fact, still be out there...and that now, they may know we're coming."

He could feel the effect of his words, hitting those present like a sledgehammer. He had some of the best and brightest the Confederation had to offer in the room with him, and he was sure the same thought had nagged at each of them. But, he'd put it out there, brought the concern—the fear—to the forefront.

"Well, sir, as unlikely as that seems, it would explain a number of things, wouldn't it?" Stockton had been silent since Barron had asked him about the energy readings, but now he spoke up.

"Yes, Jake, I'm afraid it would." Barron leaned back, pausing for a moment, clearly deep in thought. "It also complicates our decisions now. This is an exploratory mission. Our primary purpose, other than gathering some historical data, is to find and recover any old tech we can. We discovered a few trinkets in some of the closer in systems, and the device we discovered here is certainly of great interest. But, now we have to decide whether to press on...or head back to Megara."

"Head back?" It was Stockton again. "How can we come all

this way and go back with just one significant piece of old tech? We have to press on." It was the brash pilot inside Stockton coming out, all bluster and bravado.

"And, what if we encounter more than an old, automated scanning device? What if we run into something like the planet killer, or the pulsar…and what if this time there's someone else there, operating it?"

Barron's words silenced the room. He'd put everyone's biggest fear right out on the table.

"Do you really think that's likely, sir?" Fritz asked.

"I don't know if I'd say 'likely,' Fritzie, but I think it's just become a fringe possibility we have to take a lot more seriously."

"It's your decision, of course, Admiral." Atara Travis sounded uncharacteristically uncertain. Barron realized she didn't know what she would do in his shoes. He found that unnerving. All the years they'd served together, the dangers they'd faced…and this was the first time he'd seen her paralyzed by indecision.

Barron had his own doubts as well, heavy ones. Concerns not only about what might happen to the fleet, but also what dangers he might provoke and where they might lead. He was never one to ignore problems and hope they would go away… but he'd never let fear rule his choices. His concerns were very real, but he'd already decided on a course of action.

"We're moving ahead." His tone was hard, a signal to all present that his decision was made…and final. He turned and looked toward Stockton. "Jake, I want to institute a number of new protocols, mostly extra security in fleet operations. First and foremost, I want a much heavier patrol rotation, including a substantial force of fighters well in advance of the fleet's lead elements. I want four squadrons on point at all times, except during transits. And I want a spread of drones put through each point before any ships follow."

"Yes, Admiral." Stockton's tone suggested he agreed fully. "I will see to it."

Barron turned and looked over at Stockton. "I'd like you to do more than that, Jake. I want you to transfer over to *Repulse*, just temporarily. That way, you'll be able to keep a close watch on things. You've got command authority over every fighter in the fleet, so feel free to rotate squadrons as you need. We don't want to wear the pilots in the advance guard down to a nub."

"Yes, Admiral...I agree completely. I will see to it."

"I know you will, Jake." He nodded. "Fritzie, I want you to keep your crews working on that artifact." His eyes moved toward Travis. "Atara, have one of the escorts to take the device aboard." He thought for a moment. "*Leopard*, I think. She's one of the smallest. And, I want her crew reduced down to a skeletal staff. Anyone not absolutely necessary for safe operation will be transferred to other ships."

"Yes, sir. I will see to it."

Barron looked back at Fritz. "Fritzie, I want your people shuttled on and off that ship for duty shifts. We still don't know for certain that the artifact is safe, and I'm not risking anyone who doesn't absolutely have to be there."

"Understood, sir."

"And Fritzie..." Barron stared intently at his engineer. "That includes you. Do what you can to research the thing...and manage your people. But when you're not doing that, I want you back on *Dauntless*." He turned toward Stara Sinclair. "Stara, I want you to make sure we've got enough shuttles doing runs back and forth to move personnel back and forth. And I want *all* engineering personnel off Leopard twenty minutes before each transit."

"Yes, Admiral. I'll put together a regular schedule to ferry Captain Fritz and her people back and forth between *Dauntless* and *Leopard*. It would help if Leopard could hold position within five thousand kilometers of *Dauntless*. That should be far enough to protect from any...problem that might occur, and keeping the range down will simplify shuttle operations."

"Very well." Barron turned toward Travis. "See to that flight plan, Atara. I want *Dauntless*'s navigational AI running both ships."

"Yes, sir. I'll see to it immediately."

Barron stood up. "Okay, we all know what we're doing, so let's get back to our stations. The advance guard will transit in…" He looked over at the chronometer on the far wall. "…one hour, forty-three minutes." He turned toward Stockton. "Jake, that should just give you time to get over to *Repulse* if you take your fighter. I'd like you to be ready to get those scouting patrols up and out as soon as we get through the point."

"Yes, sir. Consider it done."

"I'm sorry not to give you more time, but we will have send anything you want over after the fleet transits. Transmit a list of personal gear you need, and I'll have one of the stewards collect it and shuttle it over right after the jump."

"Thank you, sir." Stockton nodded as he answered.

Barron turned toward Travis. Like everyone else in the room, she had followed his lead and stood up. "Atara, send a communique to Commodore Eaton. She is to launch a spread of drones immediately to explore the other side of the transit point. Her forces are to proceed on schedule without further orders, unless the drones discover something she deems to be of concern."

"Yes, Admiral."

"Okay then…let's go see what the hell is out there."

Chapter Fifteen

Villieneuve read the report, and the further he got, the wider the smile on his face became. Part of him still couldn't believe the luck he'd had in his desperate grab for survival—and power. Ricard Lille's successful assassination of the Presidium had played a huge role, but he also credited himself with executing every subsequent step almost flawlessly. Still, he was not delusional enough to lose sight of the fact that fortune had played an enormous role, especially in the early stages. He knew just how easily he could have ended up under the boots of the mob rather than leading it.

Luck or not, he was even more impressed with the job Ricard Lille had done with the workers' councils. The first small revolutionary groups had sprung up on their own, but instead of crushing them, Villieneuve had seen an opportunity to use them to his advantage. He'd started that process himself, gaining control of most of the largest councils on Montmirail and the other close-in planets. But in just a few short weeks, Lille had put together hundreds of teams, and he'd dispatched agents to dozens of worlds, disguised as grassroots agitators and organizers to extend clandestine influence throughout the rest of the Union.

The cost had been high, at least in absolute terms, though many of the bribes to council leaders had come from the confiscated properties of former government members. The Union's economy was still too prostrate for Villieneuve to liquidate any significant amount of such property at any reasonable price. Those assets were far better used to extend his control, to lure those who'd loudly proclaimed the ideals of the revolution to sell themselves and become his cronies. A massive manor house he couldn't sell worked perfectly to entice a former revolutionary to corruption.

He was still stunned at how effective the whole campaign had been. To date, fewer than ten percent of the councils had resisted such infiltration, and the small number that had remained true to their stated ideals fell into the delicate hands of his trusted friend. Lille had accomplished every aspect of his mission, but it was in the handling of the most stubborn bodies that he had truly shined.

Death was Ricard Lille's business, and as far as Villieneuve was concerned, his friend was without peers in his chosen profession. He could have killed recalcitrant council members in a hundred ways, most of which would have been dangerous, and might have risked some kind of backlash. But Lille had avoided such pitfalls, and, for the most part, he'd manipulated the proscribed members into *killing each other*.

It looked easy enough—on paper—though Villieneuve knew it was far more difficult and delicate in practice. Lille and his teams had arranged for incriminating documents and other evidence, most of it faked, to fall into the hands of each target's rivals. The denouncements had gone on for weeks now, as had the subsequent killings. Often, Lille had used one problem member to denounce another, after which the first whistleblower was cast in turn to the mobs, condemned by "evidence" no less manufactured than that which they had used to denounce their own enemies.

The mobs were still enraged, at least in the cities on most of the Union's core worlds. Their fury was ready to be unleashed on anyone. It was always astonishing—and to Villieneuve reassuring—how little actual proof was required to turn people into wild throngs screaming for blood.

Lille had accomplished an amazing amount in just a few weeks. The assassin—and new head of the People's Protectorate—was on Dannith now, ready to begin the second assignment Villieneuve had given him. That planet was in every way the center of illicit exploration and black market activity for old tech.

Villieneuve wished he could have kept his friend back in the Union to continue to assist him with his final efforts to secure control. But crushing resistance in the Union was only one task he needed to accomplish. The events of the war, as frustratingly unsuccessful as they'd been, had made one other thing absolutely clear to him. The possession of old tech would be the key to dominance in the future.

He'd long been aided by the Confederation's foolish adherence to the treaties requiring nations to share any old tech items that came into their possession, regardless of where they had been discovered. Men like Van Striker and Gary Holsten had ignored such requirements, of course, at least when it had been vital to do so…and when they'd been able to get away with it. But the treaties had definitely hampered the Confederation's exploitation of old tech, and they had done so for almost a century.

He was concerned about whether that advantage would continue, however. Certainly, the Confederation Senate was as ineffectual and politically fractured as ever. But it was Striker and Holsten, and others like them in the Confederation's halls of power, that most concerned him. Not to mention Tyler Barron, and whatever his massive exploration fleet might find… hundreds of lightyears from the prying eyes of the Senate.

Confederation politicians were largely fools, far too worried about their petty bickering to look seriously to the future. But he couldn't afford to assume that Holsten and Striker, and the others like them, would just sit back as he moved to gain an unbeatable advantage in old tech for the new Union.

Unless they're preoccupied with something else.

Marieles...

Desiree Marieles was a gifted agent, one who combined unquestionable physical charms with a sharp incisive mind... and an absolute lack of hesitation to do whatever was necessary. Next to Ricard Lille, he imagined she was the least afflicted by conscience and regret of anyone he'd ever known.

She would be well on her way to Megara by now, assuming she managed to get through Confederation space undetected. It was dangerous enough for a Union agent to travel anywhere in the Confederation, but the capital world was a heavily-regulated place, with customs agents and law enforcement everywhere. Lille suspected that had as much to do with keeping out undesirables within the Confederation as it did guarding against foreign spies. Confed politicians prattled on endlessly about equality and egalitarianism, but they were as corrupt—and lived lives as luxurious as—any of their equivalents in the Union. Hypocrisy was an affliction that seemed to afflict all humanity with relentless intensity.

Despite his token worries, he was reasonably confident Marieles would make it to Megara. Her aliases were well-crafted, and the prep work had been completed to the highest standards. She would not only get there...she would cause trouble, he was sure of that. But her mission would be incredibly difficult to see to fruition.

He glanced down at the tablet sitting in the center of his desk. The screen was blank, save for a title in non-descript, white letters. *Plan Black.*

He'd written the document himself, and he'd shared it with no one, at least not in its entirely. It was a second effort to undermine the Confederation, to gain the dominance he'd sought, and failed to achieve, in the war. Discovering one or more dominant old tech artifacts was still the likeliest route to victory...and the vengeance he craved on those who had handed him his failures and defeats. But Plan Black was a backup, another route to total victory, to dominance over his hated enemies.

He didn't expect complete success, not really, but even a partial attainment of the plan's goals would be helpful. And, if Marieles somehow pulled the whole thing off, she'd go a long way toward erasing the defeat in the war…and moving the Union toward the uncontested dominance it had sought for a century.

* * *

Villieneuve sat quietly as the door opened and a tall man in a spotless naval uniform walked in. It had been a pleasant day so far, progress reports from both Marieles and Lille looking very good indeed. For the last hour he'd been with Admiral Turenne, discussing something that had been a painful thorn in his side for almost two years now.

He looked up at the new arrival. "Admiral Denisov, come in. Have a seat." Villieneuve gestured toward one of the chairs facing his desk. It was old, hard metal, blemished by irregular oval-shaped rust stains along the back. All part of the image the Union's leading Citizen wanted to portray.

"Thank you, sir…Citizen Villieneuve." Denisov paused, noticing the man sitting in the second chair facing Villieneuve. "And, Admiral Turenne." He was clearly surprised at the naval CO's presence, and he snapped to attention and saluted.

"There is no need for such formalities here, Andrei. I'm sure Admiral Turenne would agree."

"Of course, sir," the other admiral said. Actually, Villieneuve was fairly certain Turenne did *not* agree, not at all. Turenne was the closest thing to a hero the Union had seen in the battle at the Bottleneck, and for all he was somewhat of a maverick, he'd shown that he expected a certain amount of respect from subordinates.

Villieneuve had almost ordered the officer executed for failing to stop *Dauntless*. That would have been a terrible injustice to the one officer who'd come closest to safeguarding victory in the Bottleneck, but Villieneuve had been blind with rage, and ready to lash out at anyone. Fortunately, his reason had won out in the end. Turenne had actually detected *Dauntless*, or at least he'd gathered enough data to raise his suspicions that *something* was out there.

So Villieneuve had satisfied himself by executing that fool Admiral Bourbonne instead. And rather than having Turenne shot, he'd promoted him to the navy's top command. That had meant leapfrogging him over a legion of superior officers… many of whom complained loudly…and foolishly. Very few of those bypassed ultimately survived the revolutionary purges that followed.

Denisov walked across the room and pulled out the offered chair, sitting as he'd been instructed to do. Denisov was clearly nervous as well as uncomfortable, not only at being summoned to Villieneuve's office, but also by the presence of his commanding officer. Villieneuve was amused by the admiral's twitching, a natural effort to assume a comfortable seated position. It was something that did not seem possible on the old, battered chairs.

"I wanted to discuss a pending military operation with you, Admiral Denisov. Although we are at peace with the Confederation now, we have another matter, one which has gone on for far too long." He stared across the desk at the admiral, noting the surprise and anticipation in the officer's expression. He didn't doubt for an instant Denisov knew what he was talking about, or that the admiral would fail to see that the mission he was about to receive was the prime assignment in the navy…and that success in carrying it out would create a career trajectory directly to the very highest command echelons.

That was seductive for any ambitious officer, but Denisov had only been a captain when the war ended, which made attaining such heights so soon particularly dizzying. Villieneuve's rage—and the need to keep feeding scapegoats to the mob—had ravaged the flag ranks badly since the fight at the Bottleneck. Denisov was one of a group of formerly junior commanders who'd exhibited a level of skill and ability beyond that of his peers, and Villieneuve had responded by giving him a huge promotion, and putting him in charge of his own task force.

"Yes, sir…Citizen. I will be honored to accept any mission you give me."

"I think we all know we're talking about Barroux, Admiral."

"I suspected, sir."

"As you are aware, the traitors on Barroux have defeated two attempts to liberate the planet. Until now, we have been unable to assemble a force sufficient to overcome the planet's defenses and reestablish control. I believe we are now capable of doing just that."

Denisov was silent for a moment, seemingly uncertain if Villieneuve was going to continue. But then, after a quick glance at Turenne, he said, "The problem on Barroux has certainly gone on for far too long, sir. I couldn't agree more on the urgency of taking action as quickly as possible."

"I would like you to lead the assault force. Admiral Turenne had planned to do it himself, but I'm afraid he simply cannot be spared from the fleet's rebuilding efforts. We have a long way to go before we recover our prewar strength."

"I understand completely…and, I am honored to be given the chance to pacify Barroux at last." Denisov paused. "May I ask what forces will be available for the operation?"

"Admiral Turenne will go over all of that with you in detail in a few minutes. I just wanted to have a few words with you first. I want to be certain that you do not underestimate the Barroux forces. They may be vile traitors, but that doesn't mean they can't fight. Overconfidence has already caused two disastrous reconquest attempts. I do not want to see a third."

"No, sir." Denisov sounded confident…but Villieneuve could hear some edginess in his tone as well.

Good. We don't need another fool not taking this seriously enough.

"We have significant People's Army units available for the operation, however, transport is of greater concern. I believe we can send ten divisions to Barroux. More than that will be difficult, at least in the near term. Diverting additional vessels to carry more troops will damage our ability to keep your forces properly supplied, an endeavor which will be difficult enough without any added problems. I suspect it will take some time to truly pacify the planet, which puts an emphasis on our ability to keep your logistical line operating effectively."

"Understood, sir. I believe ten divisions of Foudre…of People's Army forces…will be sufficient." Denisov paused, clearly wanting to say something but unsure if he should.

"Please, Admiral…speak your mind."

"Well, sir, I'm more concerned with the orbital battle. Barroux is a heavily-defended planet, sir, and…" Another pause. "…well, sir…the previous assaults do not appear to have significantly degraded the defense network. I can't help but wonder if we will be able to concentrate sufficient forces for the attack, and I'm reluctant to proceed unless we are."

Villieneuve didn't answer immediately. He wasn't used to people questioning him, not even in the limited way Denisov just had. But he needed strong and capable subordinates now, not a pack of political appointees and cronies of the sort that had dominated the fleet before and during the war. "You are extremely insightful, Admiral," he finally said. "No doubt, your fleet will face significant resistance. We will give you every ship that can be spared, which I believe will be sufficient force…but it is up to you to find a way to take out the orbital forces, and establish total space superiority prior to launching the ground assault."

"Yes, sir. I understand." Villieneuve suspected the admiral did actually understand. Villieneuve was giving him every hull he could scrape up. The pacification of Barroux simply couldn't wait any longer. The nascent but growing People's Protectorate had done everything possible to prevent the rebellion there from spreading, but allowing a world to remain in open defiance of the new Union government was unsustainable. It would inspire other resistance, sooner or later…and at this point, more likely sooner. Unless Denisov made an example of them with such grim intensity that news of it spread farther and faster than word of the rebellion had.

"You must not only defeat them, Admiral, and retake the planet. You must do so in a way that leaves a lasting impression…on the citizens of Barroux, of course, but also on those throughout the Union. Treason will not be tolerated."

"Yes, sir. I will…ah…I will do my best."

Villieneuve had selected Denisov because he believed the admiral had the tactical skill to carry out the mission. Now, he wondered if the man had the brutality it would take to exploit that victory.

"I am sure you will, Admiral." He glanced down at his desk. "Now, if you will both excuse me, I have quite a backlog of other matters to address. Admiral Turenne will discuss tactics and logistics with you at greater length. And timing as well. I'm afraid you will probably not have the amount of lead time you'd like. The invasion fleet will depart in five days."

Chapter Sixteen

"We're about to complete orbital insertion, Admiral. The planet definitely looks habitable, and the ruins in orbit appear to be more extensive that we'd anticipated from initial scans. Our best guess is, we're looking at the remains of a series of space stations, destroyed long ago."

Barron sat and listened to Sara Eaton's report. It was more or less a one-sided communication. Eaton's advance guard was a full eight light minutes ahead of the main fleet, and sixteen minutes was one hell of an annoying lag time in any kind of a real conversation.

"I've launched twenty spreads of probes as part of a comprehensive scan of the planet's atmosphere and surface. Based on the debris in orbit and preliminary ground readings, it appears likely we've found a world that was once massively inhabited."

Eaton's words carried a heavy meaning that was not lost on Barron. Whatever space stations—or the remains of them—her ships had found, it was a far greater concentration than had been discovered around any world in the Badlands. Much greater. Debris, at least on the scale Eaton had reported, meant the stations hadn't been vaporized by massive nuclear and antimatter

122

bombardments, and that exponentially increased the chance of finding usable old tech amid the ruins.

It also meant this planet might have been a *real* imperial world, not just a fringe outpost. For all the post-Cataclysm success and prosperity of a planet like Megara, Barron didn't let himself lose sight of the fact that all the inhabited worlds he knew of had once been part of the Rim, distant outposts so insignificant, they weren't even worth the trouble to obliterate when humanity was destroying itself.

There were as many legends as facts about the empire, but the thought of glimpsing the heights of power and technology mankind had attained before they'd thrown it away, was beyond exciting to him.

"I've also ordered Captain Stockton to launch six squadrons to conduct sensor sweeps in orbit and around the planet, to back up the data from the drones. I will report in full as soon as I have additional findings. Eaton out."

Barron leaned back in his chair and rubbed his hand across his face. Eaton's ships had traversed the system from the transit point without incident, so he didn't see any reason for the rest of the fleet to hang back any longer. He turned toward Atara Travis. "Commander, let's get *Dauntless's* engines up and running, at 8g absolute thrust." That was a modest rate of acceleration, at least in terms of the dampeners' ability to absorb most of the resulting force.

"Yes, sir." Travis turned and leaned down over her own comm unit, passing Barron's order to her nav station. Barron remembered Travis relaying such commands without the comm unit before, but the new *Dauntless* was just too big for that, and the nav team was halfway across the cavernous control center.

"Captain Eaton…fleet order. All ships are to match *Dauntless's* course and velocity. Maintain fleet formation. We're going in." Barron had transferred Sara Eaton's sister to *Dauntless* to act as his primary aide. It was a move that had come with a significant promotion, and one that had been motivated primarily by his great respect for Sara, at least at first. But Barron had come to appreciate Sonya Eaton's abilities…and her even manner and cool demeanor. She'd adapted well to being a part of Barron's team, and she didn't seem to resent that, in many ways, Atara Travis already functioned as his aide, in addition to her duties as *Dauntless*'s captain. Eaton just filled in the blanks wherever she was needed, stepping aside when Barron and Travis worked together, as they did so fluidly, and taking the fleet duties onto herself when they fell to her.

"Yes, Admiral." Eaton tapped her headset, connecting her to the fleet comm line, and she relayed Barron's orders.

Barron sat quietly for a minute, his eyes fixed on the main display. Sara Eaton was relaying preliminary scanner information, and he was getting his first actual view of the planet, along with early readings on things like atmosphere, climate, geography. It looked like a hospitable world, right in the middle of the habitable range. In fact, based on what he could see, the planet seemed like it might be a virtual paradise.

He glanced over at the data on the orbital debris. There were some very large chunks, fifty meters or more in length, that looked very much like pieces of orbital platforms. In their own way, they were as exciting as the planet itself. Wind and weather were hard on artifacts on the ground, but items floating in space were likely to be well preserved. This planet was the true start of the fleet's mission, the first real find. But, even as he imagined how much farther his people could press on, he realized those chunks of floating debris alone could very well include enough old tech to radically advance civilization back home.

And, depending what the Confederation government decided to do, particularly regarding the interpretation of international law, what his people found here could radically alter the balance of power. Such a thing would be dire if the advantage fell to a power like the Union—or even, possibly, to his Alliance allies—but a Confederation with an overwhelming technological advantage could keep the peace, impose a Pax Confederica on the entire sector. He imagined a future without the wars that had plagued his people and their neighbors for centuries.

He shook his head. He wondered if the Senate would break the treaty, keep anything he found for the Confederation's use alone. They would have to do that if the Confederation was to safeguard the peace.

And then he wondered if he was being naïve, if a Confederation suddenly in possession of overwhelming strength would indeed be a force for good and peace. Or, if such power would corrupt all it touched, as history showed such things usually did.

* * *

"We're getting fresh readings now, Commodore."

Eaton turned her head toward the tactical officer's station. She expected data…a lot of it. She'd launched a massive number of drones—*too many*, she'd thought after the fact. Her overreaction was normal enough, considering that the fleet had encountered two more scanning devices on their way to the planet, both situated adjacent to transit points, but the expedition had limited supplies and no way to replenish them anytime soon. She'd have to be more careful in her logistics going forward.

"Feed it to the main display, Commander. And to my screen."

"Yes, Commodore."

Eaton watched as a wave of information scrolled down the screen, numbers, charts and tables, images. The planet looked pleasant enough, a blue globe streaked with stringy white clouds, not much different in appearance than Megara.

The display was showing various views of the planet, transmitted from the drones. The lead spread was just entering the atmosphere. The scanning devices were not equipped for atmospheric operations, which made descending somewhat of a suicide mission for the robotic probes.

The images on the screen were dark at first, but then there was light, a blue sky that looked inviting and hospitable. The transmission became a little less stable as the probes penetrated deeper into the atmosphere, and the heat began to affect their instrumentation.

The long-range cameras aboard were starting to pick up ground images. The probes were still fifteen kilometers from the ground, but now, Eaton and her people were looking at images of vast forests, and great oceans that extended out of sight.

The picture on the display became fuzzier. She knew the probes would disintegrate in a few seconds, and she focused, staring intently at the deteriorating image. She was still staring when the display went dark, but even after the transmission terminated, she sat dead still, her eyes fixed on the dark screen.

She'd seen something…

And, from the expressions she saw on the bridge, and the tense silence in the air, she wasn't the only one.

"I want that last few seconds replayed, Commander. Full AI enhancement…and run at one-tenth normal speed."

"Yes, Commodore."

She watched intently as the projection returned to the screen. The camera was moving over a large valley, and then up and over one of the flanking hillsides.

And there it was.

"Freeze projection."

"Yes, Commodore."

She stared at the screen. *Repulse*'s bridge was silent, every set of eyes fixed along with Eaton's.

It was a city…or, at least, what was left of one. There were chunks of metal jutting upward, and vast fields of rubble. It had once been a massive metropolis, that much was clear, even larger than Troyus City on Megara.

Much larger.

There were lines extending out from the perimeter, looking very much like the remains of some kind of monorail or other transit system. Nature had since encroached, and vines and other plant growth had wrapped around the ruins.

For an instant, she'd imagined that the city had simply been abandoned, perhaps even as part of an exodus from the entire planet. But, as she looked at the still image, the truth because all too apparent.

The city had been destroyed by some kind of attack, almost certainly one with thermonuclear—or even antimatter—weapons. All that remained were scattered remnants, and blasted and broken wreckage of buildings.

She glanced at the numbers on the screen below the images, the calculations the AI had made and displayed. The city had been immense. It must have been the home to tens of millions of people at one time.

And someone came here and obliterated it. Killed all those people.

She tried to imagine the attack. The sheer terror of the city's inhabitants. The fury and hatred that had driven someone to incinerate so many millions.

She'd heard the Cataclysm spoken of her entire life, but she'd never really considered what that word truly meant.

Until now.

* * *

Jake Stockton tapped his controls, altering his vector a few degrees to port. His fighters really didn't have much to do, and the situation certainly didn't call for his presence. But, he'd taken advantage of the monumental nature of the find to lead the patrol himself.

His fighters had done some recon duty earlier, but that had mostly been overkill on Commodore Eaton's part. The Lightnings were designed primarily for combat, and for routine scouting duties. The probes had scanners ten times as powerful, as well as the ability to detect all sorts of things a fighter couldn't.

The current mission was, if possible, even more useless. Eaton had dispatched search teams to comb through the orbital wreckage. There was a lot of excitement in the fleet about what kinds of old tech they would discover. Almost every spacer in the fleet had been at the Bottleneck, had faced death fighting against an old tech artifact. And, as far as anything had been documented, no one had ever found anything as extensive as the apparent remains of the planet's space stations.

He looked down at the tactical screen, checking on the rest of the patrol. He'd been running the rookies hard since the fleet left Megara, but now he had only veteran pilots with him. Flying around so close to a planet and in and out of orbit was tricky, and the last thing he wanted to see was some green flyer slam into one of the chunks of debris.

Everybody was where they were supposed to be. That was no surprise. The pilots on duty now had an average of six enemy kills in the war. They could handle a bunch of floating ruins.

Stockton twisted his body, trying to stretch as well as he could. Years of service had taught him the best ways to stay loose in a Lightning, but the hard truth was, there really weren't any *good* ways. That was a lesson he'd learned on the long-range probe missions he'd done. Pilots who complained to him about long scouting runs tended to get a lecture on just what it felt like to be in a cockpit for *days* without a break.

"This is team alpha, contacting command."

Stockton looked down at his control panel. *Repulse* was on the far side of the planet, and its orbit wouldn't bring it back around for another few minutes. That meant Stockton was "command," at least for the moment.

"This is fighter leader, team alpha. I'm the closest thing to 'command' you've got right now, so report." Sara Eaton was a cautious officer. She'd brought *Repulse* into orbit alone, leaving the rest of the advance guard about fifty thousand kilometers out. That wasn't far at all in terms of space travel, but it was a bit out of reach of a space suit's low-powered comm unit.

Of course, if she was really *cautious, she'd have kept her flagship back and sent in one of the other vessels…*

"Sir…something is strange here. These are definitely chunks of some kind of station, and they're in pretty decent shape too, but…"

"But what?"

"Well…there doesn't seem to be anything of, well, of value, sir."

"What do you mean?"

"We've been through three sections, and it's the same everywhere. There are places that seem like they were work areas. We've even found a few workstations with their chairs still in place." The voice went silent for a moment. "There's nothing in any of them, sir."

"In any of them?"

"No insides. There are workstations, but there's no circuitry inside, no computer equipment. Just what looks like empty cabinets where that stuff would be."

"Could it all have been destroyed? Something blew these stations apart after all."

"And left the cases intact? We've got whole panels and consoles, hardly damaged at all…but they're completely empty."

Stockton froze in his cockpit. "Are you saying someone *removed* them all? Manually?"

"It sure looks that way, sir. We've only been in three of these, but I'm awfully curious to see what the others have found. Maybe this section was under maintenance or something when it was destroyed."

"Maybe," Stockton said, not believing it for an instant. "Keep searching…and report back whatever you find."

"Yes, sir."

He reached out and punched up the data on *Repulse*'s location. Another fourteen minutes before the ship would be in direct line of sight.

No, that's too long. Commodore Eaton needs to hear this. Now.

He grabbed the throttle, firing up his thrusters, and tapped his finger against the small comm keypad. "Beta team, do you read?" He was going to get all the information he could…and get it to Eaton now.

"Beta team here, sir."

"I need a full report. What have you found?"

He hadn't expected to discover much on this journey, but now he didn't know. He had no idea what to expect.

No idea what they were up against out here.

Chapter Seventeen

"*Albaron* made it through, but I think that's going to be the last. Captain Higgs isn't even sure he wants to try to make the run back out."

If the fact that he had a crew of outlaws as unexpected long-term guests didn't stress things enough to him, Mike Hoover could tell all he needed to know from Silvia Breen's tone. He'd come to trust his number two, which was a rare thing in his trade.

"So, they've finally managed to tighten the blockade? I guess we should be thankful it took them as long as it did."

"It looks like the intel was right about that. They must have still been trying to finish repairs on their ships from the war. It does take a large force to mount an effective blockade." He could hear the scorn in Breen's voice. The Confederation's entire fleet had been totally refitted for months now, save for a few ships with truly extensive damage. It was a stark contrast to the Union's continued efforts to get its fleets back to something like full readiness.

Which is an ironic advantage, since so many of our ships were just fixed up so they could be decommissioned.

"Well, I guess it's not easy to conduct business as usual in the middle of a revolution." Hoover didn't know exactly what had happened in the rest of the Union since the end of the war. There had clearly been tremendous unrest…and yet, Gaston Villieneuve was still at the top. If anything, the Sector Nine chief had more power than he'd had before. That was a sobering thought, and one that fostered a less than optimistic view of the prospects for long-term peace.

It was also the main reason Hoover and his team were on Barroux. The planet was the sharpest thorn in Villieneuve's side, and the longer the revolutionaries there could hold out, the greater the drain on Union resources.

"No, I'm sure it's not. Unfortunately, from what little intel we can get here, Villieneuve has made great strides in quelling resistance on most of the old Union planets. He's gotten more industrial facilities and shipyards up and running again, which is probably why the blockade is finally closed."

Hoover forced a smile. "Which means we're stuck here, Silv."

"Yes," she replied, her own grin looking just as insincere. "Can't think of a nicer place. Still, we've got plenty of work left to do, so it's not like we were leaving anytime soon."

"True enough." He sighed softly. He'd gotten seven ships through, which represented far more in the way of supplies and logistics than he'd dared to hope for. And, for all the disorder still lingering from the revolution, the new defense network was coming along nicely. He'd put the simplest components into production first, the ones easiest to complete and deploy. That meant mostly laser satellites and disposable orbital insertion vehicles. There were forty of the laser units in orbit already, and within a week or two, he'd have that number up to one hundred. Combined with Barroux's already formidable fortresses, the planet would be a tough target for the Union.

Which is a good thing, because I'd just as soon not be gunned down by rampaging Foudre Rouge…or whatever the Union is calling its clone soldiers now. The People's Army, he thought he recalled from the last intel briefing before he'd left Megara.

"Mike…"

He could tell Breen was troubled about something, beyond the stress and danger of the mission. He knew what it was too. The same thing had been eating away at him for some time.

Ever since he'd met with Henri Bernard.

"I know, Silv...but our mission is clear, and to be brutally frank, it has nothing to do with what's best for Barroux."

"I know that, Mike, but..." She let her voice trail off. Hoover understood completely how she felt. He'd been inclined to believe Bernard from the minute he'd first met the man. Assessing people, deciding if they were trustworthy, was a huge part of his profession, and every instinct he had told him the resistance leader had told him the truth.

Now, months later, he only believed that more. Caron and his people had treated Hoover's party well, but they'd been clumsy in their attempts at subtlety and deception. The brutality of Barroux's new regime was all too obvious. Hoover had lost count on how many people had been killed since he'd arrived, and those were only the ones he knew about.

The planet had become divided, with Caron's people on one side, and those like Bernard on the other. The vast majority of the population was in the middle, their lives no better than they had been under the Union...and their fear of Caron's enforcers even greater than what they'd felt for Sector Nine. The Union had demanded obedience, but before the terrible shortages at the end of the war, workers who did their jobs could usually get by without too much trouble.

Many of those around Caron seemed to crave spilling blood for its own sake.

"What could we do, even if we wanted to?" It was an irrelevant question, one he knew he shouldn't even be asking. His mission was to protect Barroux, and undermining Caron's government, however repugnant and brutal it was, certainly wasn't going to strengthen the planet's defenses. Open rebellion would only make a Union invasion that much easier.

"I don't know. You know I've been on my share of missions, and some of those required doing things I didn't like... but I'm starting to hate myself, Mike. Caron and Delacorte...

they're what we fight against. For all the lying and deceit we use on our missions, I never doubted that we were the good guys." She looked up at Hoover. "Until now."

Her words hit him hard. He'd never heard her say anything quite like what she just had, and he'd served alongside her on many missions.

But mostly, he realized he agreed with her completely. He was carrying out his mission, following his orders…and he was beginning to despise himself for it.

* * *

"I'm worried, Remy. The resistance has been harder to finish off than I expected. They've got cells all across the planet, even in the capital city. And, I'm certain they've made contact with our Confederation…guests."

Caron had rolled over, intending to get some sleep. But it was clear that wasn't going to happen, at least not until Ami had expressed her concerns.

He looked at her, naked, covered only by a fine, white silk sheet. He'd always resented the privileges the government officials had enjoyed while he and his peers worked twelve-hour shifts and wore coarse old rags. Now, he'd come to enjoy such things, and he'd quickly learned to appreciate the luxuries taken from the homes of the now-dead Union officials.

He'd come to appreciate Ami Delacorte, as well. She'd been a follower at first, and then a close confidante, one who shared his secrets…and eventually his bed. He'd resisted her seductions at first, remained devoted to his wife and child, but his resistance had quickly waned. Now, the two practically lived together in a palatial villa taken from the old planetary governor…and Elisa Caron and her daughter remained in the tiny, drafty room where she and Remy had lived before the revolution. Remy had visited a few times, mostly to see his daughter, Zoe, but he hadn't been to see her for months now either.

"I'd like to see Bernard and his troublemakers crushed as much as you, but we're doing everything we can. And the Confederation envoys have helped us triple our orbital defense capability. You know as well as I do, the Union will be back, and with more strength than last time."

"You misunderstand me, Remy..." She reached out and stroked her fingers gently down his face. "I'm not saying the Confederation visitors weren't useful or that they didn't help us considerably. But Hoover himself said there was very little chance of getting any new ships through the blockade. And, we have all the specifications they brought with them. The factories have been modified and producing for several months now."

A cold feeling moved through Caron's gut. "What are you saying, Ami?"

"I'm just wondering if we need to take the risk of our Confederation...friends...misinterpreting Henri Bernard's lies and propaganda."

"You aren't suggesting we..." He couldn't even finish what he was thinking.

"Who would know?" She grinned at him playfully. Even as deeply under her spell as he was, he was still unnerved at the casual way she could suggest murder.

"We need the Confederation, Ami."

"Do we?"

"Come on...you're not being serious."

"I'm very serious. The Confederation is far away. They were able to take advantage of the Union's disorder to get us some supplies and advisers, but it's unlikely they'll be able to contact us any time in the foreseeable future. For that matter, Agent Hoover and his people have no way to return home...and little more they can do for us here. They're a liability now, Remy."

Caron inhaled deeply. He'd listened to virtually every piece of advice Delacorte had given him, but he was uncertain about this one. He understood her concern, of course, but killing Confederation personnel seemed dangerous. Hell, it *was* dangerous. Barroux would need the Confederation again, someday. Delacorte was right that there was little more they could expect from the Confeds in the immediate future, but Barroux could never survive for the long term without some aid from the Confederation…perhaps even some pressure on the Union government to accept a negotiated resolution.

"We can't, Ami. I understand your concern, but it's not just Hoover." One death could possibly be explained away. But if they moved against the Confeds, they'd have to kill them all. "He's got a whole group with him, other agents, and all the experts who helped retool the factories. Not to mention the crew of the last supply ship who couldn't get away. You're taking about killing dozens of people…and eventually explaining their deaths to the Confederation. Without Confederation help and recognition, we've got no chance the Union will ever recognize our independence."

She slid closer to him on the bed, moving her lips close to his ear. "It's true, my love, that we can't seem to be responsible for their deaths. But what if they were killed by a splinter group, by that rodent Bernard and his rabble? Perhaps they're even under the influence of Union agents…or better still, what if Bernard and his people are Sector Nine, agents left behind to infiltrate and destroy the revolution? We might even report those deaths to the Confederation if we're ever able to get a message through. Such an outrageous atrocity by Union agents might even provoke a renewal of hostilities between the two powers. What could serve our needs more than that?"

Caron listened to everything she said, and as he did, a new thought materialized, one he found unsettling. Ami Delacorte was insane.

He quivered with pleasure as she moved even closer, pressing her lips against his neck. Rationality slipped from his mind, replaced only by desire. He'd never been able to resist her, and this moment proved no different.

Still, the more he thought about it, the more he was certain she was crazy.

He just didn't care.

Chapter Eighteen

**Confederation Intelligence Headquarters
Port Royal City, Planet Dannith, Ventica III
315 AC**

"Mr. Holsten, Colonel Peterson is here to see you, sir." The aide stood by the door, poking his head inside the small office. Confederation Intelligence's headquarters in Port Royal City was an underwhelming facility—small, cramped, and lacking modern equipment. Holsten had realized all of this shortly after he made the office his command center, and he immediately understood one reason, at least, that Sector Nine had kicked his tail for so long in pursuit of old tech.

He also realized it was his fault, at least on some level. He *was* the head of Confederation Intelligence. He'd always known he needed to pour greater resources into Dannith and the others border planets, but there had always been another crisis, a problem with a higher priority...and then there was the war.

"Show him in." Holsten didn't address the aide personally... mostly because he'd forgotten the man's name. He wasn't part of the team Holsten had brought, just some career Intelligence hack who'd been mediocre enough to get posted to the tiny, ineffective office.

"Mr. Holsten, it's good to see you again." Peterson walked into the room almost immediately. Clearly, he'd been standing right behind the aide. The Marine was a big man, nearly two full meters, and muscular to match. His steel gray hair was neatly clipped, and a massive cigar hung out from the side of his mouth.

"It's good to see you, too, Colonel. I wish the circumstances were more cheerful."

"My people don't get called very often when the circumstances are cheerful." Peterson reached up and pulled the cigar from his mouth. Technically, there was no smoking allowed in the office, but Holsten didn't really care, and, by all appearances, Peterson didn't give a shit either. "So, tell me…can we drop the 'Mr. Holsten, Colonel Peterson' shit, or are we performing for your people here?"

"No, Jon, there's no need for formality." Holsten almost overcame his grim mood and laughed. Almost.

"All right, Gary…then tell me what you called me here for. And, for God's sake, let me know what you need with a division of crack Marines on a Confederation planet in peacetime." Peterson dragged out one of the chairs facing Holsten's desk, and he sat down, dropping his bulk hard into the seat.

"I've got an operative missing, Jon, and I intend to find her… if I've got to tear apart every building on Dannith to do it."

"Well, I saw the naval task force in orbit, and you've quarantined the entire planet…so, I'm guessing this isn't just any agent."

Holsten sighed. "No, Jon, she's not. She's a friend…and she's very close to another friend. But that's not it, not really. She's wealthy. She was retired from a difficult and dangerous career. And, the Confederation owes her a debt, one few people will ever know about. She only came back here because I asked her to…and she'd barely gotten started when she got snatched under my nose."

"So, you feel responsible. Like you sucked her in and failed her."

Holsten wasn't very sensitive most of the time, but Peterson's words made him wince. The Marine had a reputation for cutting the crap and getting right to the point. A well-deserved relationship.

"Yes, I feel responsible…mostly because I *am* responsible."

"Okay, Gary, let's forget for a minute that whoever this is, it sounds like she was experienced, tough…hardcore in her own right. Am I far from the mark?"

Holsten shook his head.

"All right, so she might have come back because you asked her, but I'll bet she was perfectly capable of making her own decisions. Still, I know none of that matters. You're going to blame yourself, and I understand that." The Marine paused. "So, let's talk about the real problem. You've got the statutory authority to shut down ingress and egress from a planet—at least, it's a gray area and you've got a good case to claim you do. You've even got the power to order my division here, and put us to work bashing down the doors of Confederation citizens. But it's all subject to review, my old friend, and I know *you* know it won't be long before you're called before a Senate committee to justify your actions. I've been blissfully removed from the fetid swamp of politics most of my life, but I know enough about it to guess that a lot of the gasbags on that committee are not going to agree that a lost agent was sufficient justification for what you're doing." He paused again. "You're putting yourself on the line here, old friend. You've got to realize that." Peterson's voice was soft, sincere.

"Yes, Jon…I realize that. But no more on the line than Andi put herself. Getting blasted by a bunch of politicians doesn't seem like much compared to being tortured or killed. Hell, if they want to fire me, let them fire me. Who the hell else would want this damned job anyway?"

"You've got a lot of enemies in the Capitol. Don't forget that. You've run roughshod over them more than once." Holsten was about to argue when Peterson raised his hand. "Don't worry…I know you only did what had to be done. Odds are, we'd be fighting Foudre Rouge on the streets of Megara if you hadn't, but that doesn't change the fact that there are resentful politicians there. Powerful ones. They may try to do more than fire you…and they'll have crowds of angry citizens and business owners on Dannith screaming about what you did, demanding restitution for their losses."

"You think after all I've seen, I'm scared of a bunch of Senators trying to put me in prison? They're welcome to try. I've got so much foul dirt on half of them...if they want to start a war with me, they're going to find it's *very* two-sided."

"That may be, Gary...but the fact is, a lot of these guys know how to play dirty. You may be the master, but don't underestimate the political enemies you've got."

"I don't, Jon. I know this is risky. But I just can't abandon Andi. She's here because of me, and whatever it takes—whatever the risk to me—I've got to get her out."

The big Marine nodded. "All right...that's enough for me. I just hope my helping you doesn't end with you on some prison planet a year from now."

"Let's hope. If I am, I can guarantee you, I won't be alone."

"So much for caution and 'are you sures.' I knew you wouldn't listen to my warnings, so I've got one of my regiments on the way down already. I just hope people don't see the landers coming in and panic. I'm afraid it probably looks a lot like an invasion."

"That's a chance we'll have to take. It's bad enough whoever's got Andi might see those landers too...I'm damned sure not going to make any public announcements until we've got your people in place."

"I understand." Peterson nodded. "So, where do you want my people, Gary? What are the top priorities?"

* * *

"Minister Lille, I'm sorry to interrupt."

Lille glanced back quickly toward the aide, almost correcting the woman's nomenclature again, but then deciding it was pointless. He understood Villieneuve's purposes in instituting the new system, but just calling everyone "Citizen" wasn't very useful in most situations. His people were all Sector Nine veterans, agents who were clever enough, or who'd maintained a low enough profile, to escape the bloodletting that had cleared the way for Gaston Villieneuve to become the hero of the revolution. They were *good*, all of them, but they were also used to a hierarchal system, and he was accustomed to being close to the top of such a pyramid.

"Yes, what is it?" His impatience was clear in his tone. It wasn't directed at the operative—though he doubted she'd come with good news. Andi Lafarge was proving much harder to break than he'd expected. He'd held back from the harshest treatments, anything that would cause permanent damage. Lafarge had spent her life as an outlaw in the eyes of the Confederation, and, in his view, she had no cause to exhibit loyalty to a government that had condemned and hassled her all her life. He'd allowed himself to hope he could win her over eventually, convince her to join forces with him…and to reap the true benefits of her extraordinary—and unorthodox—skillset.

She was stubborn, he'd known that much going in, but she was a survivor, too. She *had* to know the only way she was going to get out alive was to agree to work with him. He'd heard rumors that she'd had an extraordinary windfall, one which had made her breathtakingly wealthy…and, consequently, immune to bribery. But if those whispers were true, what the hell was she doing on Dannith, poking around the seedy adventurers' bars that dotted the Promenade?

"Sir…" The aide had hesitated, clearly aware that he was distracted.

"Go on." He turned and looked toward the agent, still only half paying attention.

"We have confirmed that Dannith is under quarantine. All ship traffic, both in and out, has been halted. The spaceports are closed down, and we have multiple sources confirming that a naval squadron is in position around the planet."

Ricard's distractions slipped away. He'd heard several reports of the sort the aide was giving him, but none of them had been confirmed until now. But the Confeds *had* closed down Dannith…and that *was* a problem. First, it meant he was trapped there. He might have made a run past a quarantine order, but if the Confed navy was up there enforcing it…that pretty much removed that option.

Perhaps the more dangerous question was, why had they taken such action? It couldn't be just because he'd grabbed Lafarge. He knew she'd had some interactions with the navy in recent years—and that she'd had a sporadic dalliance with Tyler Barron—but he hadn't considered any serious implications. Could that be it? Is she closer to Barron than I thought?

He shook his head. Any serious connection between Barron and Lafarge changed things dramatically. If she was truly involved with the admiral, his chances of winning her over to his side were far less than he'd hoped. It might mean that Lafarge was truly committed to Confederation Intelligence— and his plans would have to change. If he couldn't win her over, he had to find out everything she knew, and her true purpose on Dannith.

He wasn't ready to give up on her entirely, not yet, at least. But he was far closer to doing so than he'd been a few minutes ago. The loss of Lafarge as a potential asset would hurt his plans. She'd have been invaluable as one of his operatives. But giving up on recruiting her would have its advantages. He could focus entirely on getting information out of her.

And he could use more…aggressive…means to extract what he needed. He'd no longer have to be concerned about causing permanent damage, especially since he'd be putting a pair of bullets in her head when he was done with her anyway.

Chapter Nineteen

"Yes, Commodore, I had three separate reports, each from a different team. Every section of debris they've searched is completely cleaned out, all the equipment—or what was left of it— removed, nothing but the main structures remaining. I thought that was something you needed to know as soon as possible."

"*Removed? Are they certain?*" Eaton sat in the center of *Repulse*'s bridge, the huge space suddenly devoid of the normal chatter and background noise. If she'd known what Stockton was going to report, she'd have had him piped directly to her headset instead of broadcasting on the main speakers.

"That was my perception, Commodore. We didn't discuss it at length, but all three groups reported similar findings."

"Very well, Captain." Eaton sat for a few seconds, silent. The truth was, she didn't know what to say, or what to do. The news was unsettling, but far from conclusive. Was it possible some border adventurers had made it out this far some time over the last century? It seemed unlikely...impossible, she'd almost call it. Yet, that would explain Stockton's report...in a far less unsettling manner than anything else bouncing around in her mind. "You made the right decision to expedite the report, Captain

142

Stockton," she added abruptly. "*Repulse* should reestablish communications with the teams in ten minutes. As soon as we're in position, land your fighters and send out fresh ones. I want the orbital areas patrolled constantly, Captain."

"Understood, Commodore. I'll see to it. Stockton out."

Eaton leaned back in her chair. She could feel every eye on the bridge boring into her. Her people had been on edge, if not since the mission began, certainly since the fleet had discovered the first active scanning device. Individual tolerances varied for feeling far from home, lost in the endless dark…but by now, pretty much everyone in the fleet was dealing with a heavy dose of stress. Stockton's report only made that worse.

"All right, I want all stations ready. As soon as we come about, we're launching shuttles to retrieve the teams. I want them brought aboard *Repulse* for debriefing at once. And I want twice as many fresh teams sent out. We're going to examine every piece of orbital debris out there, one at a time, and we're going to see if they're all in the same condition."

"Yes, Commodore."

Her order spurred some activity, a bit of chatter going back and forth between stations. But the activity level was subdued, her people still distracted by what they'd heard.

"That wasn't a request, people," she said, her voice stern and loud. "We've got shuttles to prepare and exploration teams to get ready, and not much time. Move it!"

The bridge erupted into a nervous beehive of activity, half a dozen voices suddenly speaking into comm units, and most of the other officers busy at their workstations. That was good. Better for them to be thinking about work than wondering who—or what—had taken the equipment from those space station segments.

"Bay command reports shuttles will be ready to launch in sixteen minutes, Commodore."

"No," she said coldly. "I want them ready in ten minutes."

"Yes, Commodore."

She listened as the officer repeated the order. She suspected whoever was on duty in launch control was arguing that ten minutes wasn't enough time, but she didn't care. Her people were good, but there wasn't a doubt in her mind that their performance had slipped a notch since the war. Nothing matched the threat of impending death and destruction to inspire the best possible performance.

At least nothing but a commodore and hardcore combat veteran breathing down their necks.

Eaton didn't let herself get carried away with her thoughts, imagining there was any combat imminent, or anything like that...but she'd been edgy since the fleet left Confederation space, and now she was as tense as she'd been since the ceasefire had ended combat and sent her ships back to friendly territory.

"Launch control acknowledges, Commodore. Shuttles will be ready in ten minutes."

"Very well." Eaton nodded, feeling a touch of satisfaction... and wondering if the new exploration teams would be ready and mounted up as quickly as the shuttles themselves.

She glanced at the main display, watching as the oval that represented *Repulse* moved slowly around the large sphere of the planet. Then, she stood up abruptly. "I'll be in my office. Report anything at all out of the ordinary to me immediately."

"Yes, Commodore."

She took a few steps toward the back of the bridge, to the small corridor that led to her private office. She *had* to report this to Tyler Barron, and the sooner the better. *Dauntless* was still a good fifteen light seconds away, which made a two-sided communication possible, if frustrating. She wasn't sure how Barron would react, or what orders he might give her...but she was damned sure she wanted to have that conversation in private.

She stopped just outside the hallway and turned back. "And bring Captain Stockton to me the instant he lands."

"Yes, Commodore."

She hesitated for a few seconds, and then she walked down the corridor and into her office.

*   *   *

The shuttle shook hard, skipping off the atmosphere as it continued its descent from orbit. The planet's air was a bit heavier than Megara's, and that made for a rougher ride, and a tougher workout for the heat shields.

Bryan Rogan had seen worse, of course. Serving seven years under Tyler Barron had been many things, but one thing they hadn't been was quiet. Rogan still had nightmares from the battle his Marines had fought with Alliance stormtroopers on Santis. That had been a small engagement—insignificant, perhaps, by historical standards—but it was a near certainty that no one who'd fought there would ever forget any of it.

Rogan had worn a captain's insignia then, and his command had consisted of approximately two hundred men and women, *Dauntless*'s Marine contingent plus a few survivors from the Santis garrison. Now, a pair of stars sat in the place those captain's bars had occupied, and the two companies he commanded had grown to a reinforced brigade of over four thousand Marines, every one of them a veteran from the Union War.

Rogan had been based on the new *Dauntless*—no one who'd served on the first ship to bear that name could think of the massive new battleship of anything other than the "new" or "second" one—but he'd transferred temporarily to *Repulse* when Commodore Eaton took her force to the advanced guard position. He hadn't particularly expected his Marines to be needed for anything beyond routine duty guarding the landing party camps on any planets worth exploring, but now he wasn't so sure. He'd heard enough of the reports from the orbital search parties to reignite his Marine's suspicion. He didn't know if the search teams would run into old tech systems that were still operational, or some kind of rogue adventurers farther out than anyone had imagined possible...but he was damned sure of one thing. It was his job to make sure everyone Eaton or Barron sent down was protected.

And Bryan Rogan took his job very seriously.

He shifted in his seat, feeling every minute of the year or more since he'd been fully armored for battle. It was probably overkill—from the complaints he'd heard from his Marines, they clearly thought it was—but he wasn't taking chances. His people would be the first ones out of the shuttles…and they would be setting foot on a world vastly distant from home, from anything familiar. Rogan wasn't taking chances.

"We'll be down in about three minutes, General."

Rogan nodded, though he realized, of course, the pilot up in the cockpit couldn't see him. "Acknowledged," he finally said. He sucked in a deep breath immediately after, doing what he could to hold back the nausea. Rogan had done his share of combat landings, but he'd never gotten quite completely used to the stomach churning aspects of the whole enterprise.

He flipped on his comm unit, activating the main channel. "All right, Marines, we'll be on the ground in a few minutes. I want everybody sharp. You know the procedures, and I don't want to see any sloppiness just because there aren't any Foudre Rouge out there waiting to blow your brains out. Every one of you knows where you're supposed to be, so stay sharp and get it done."

Rogan felt a small grin forming on his face. He had about seventy Marines with the landing group, two platoons. He remembered his days as a young Marine, and how nervous it would have made him to have a general in direct command of the force. Rogan knew he probably should have delegated the duty to one of his junior officers, but rank did have its privileges, after all.

And, after almost two years of quiet, routine post-war duty, he wasn't about to miss out on the first landing on an ancient imperial world.

"Keep your eyes open, and report anything that seems strange. Even if it's just a tightness in your gut you think is this morning's breakfast. No one is to take any chances." He paused, then added, "And, keep those breathers on until you get orders to the contrary."

The probes had confirmed the atmosphere was breathable, and preliminary scans hadn't detected any unusual pathogens. That made sense, since it appeared that millions of people had once lived on the planet. Still, Commodore Eaton had ordered full precautions to be taken until the ground teams could confirm the drones' analysis.

He reached down and grabbed the mask hanging down at his side, strapping it across his head and tucking the strap under the back of his helmet. He tapped the small switch on his side, and he felt the cool, oxygen-heavy air begin to flow.

There was an immediate rush, a burst of energy and awareness as the oxygen-heavy gas filled his lungs. His eyes darted around the cabin, noting every detail as the nineteen other Marines present more or less copied his actions. He looked up at the main screen. Less than thirty seconds to landing.

His stomach tightened, his whole body tensing up. This mission would likely be nothing more than routine security for the landing parties, but his combat reflexes had been hardwired by all the action he'd seen, and his instincts reacted as they would for a combat drop.

He reached around for the assault rifle he realized wasn't there. He had a sidearm, but he'd advanced well into the ranks that rarely carried weapons heavier than pistols, especially when it wasn't a combat assault. Still, his reflexes remembered his earlier days, and his hands felt empty without the feel of his old Mark IX rifle.

The shuttle shook as the landing thrusters fired and lowered the ship gently—fairly gently, at least—onto the ground. *We're here. On a planet no one has visited since the Cataclysm.*

He felt exhilarated...and nervous too. This was something new.

"Let's go," he roared, slapping his hands down on the harness release and jumping to his feet the instant the ready light turned green. Even as he turned toward the rear of the shuttle, the back ramp began to open, dropping hard into place.

He raced toward the opening, his eyes catching the rays of sunlight pouring in, reflecting off the metal of the ramp. He knew a general should wait, allow his Marines to exit first and secure the area, but Rogan hadn't led from behind when he'd been heading toward thousands of Foudre Rouge, dug in and supported by heavy weapons. He wasn't about to hang back and hide behind his Marines on a dead and empty world. Besides, his curiosity was almost overpowering. He was about to see something humanity hadn't seen for centuries.

He ran out into the bright sunshine, feeling the gentle warmth of the day, an almost perfect temperature. There was a light breeze, and above, he gazed at a bright blue sky, with just a few puffy white clouds. It was as pleasant a sight as he'd seen on Megara, or any other world of the Confederation.

But the euphoria didn't last.

He turned his head and looked off to the north. The shuttle had landed on a large rise overlooking a long valley, and he froze as he saw it. A city, one the probes had located from the air. A vast metropolis that stretched almost as far as the eye could see.

And one that was nothing but shattered remains of steel girders covered with overgrown rubble.

He'd known it was there, of course—he'd come looking for it—and yet he was stunned at the actual sight of the thing.

There were a few shadowy structures, low buildings that had at least partially survived whatever had destroyed the city…but most of what he saw was rubble, fields of debris extending to the horizon. Shattered masonry and twisted girders of steel, melted and reformed, protruded from the ground at all angles.

He'd been to Troyus City, the Confederation's capital, a dozen times, and each time he'd walked away amazed at the magnificence of what his people had built. But Troyus was scarcely a rural village compared to what this immense metropolis had been.

Rogan tried to imagine the magnificent skyline of vast buildings that had once stood there, but nothing now reached more than ten or twenty meters from the tortured ground. All around, plant growth had encroached on what had once been humanity's domain, and even in the dead city's center, vines climbed and twisted all around the blackened, skeletal remains of buildings.

He turned and glanced back at his people. The Marines from his own shuttle had formed a rough circle around the craft, their weapons drawn and ready, but their eyes all focused on the remains of the ancient city.

The scientists and others on the shuttle were coming out now, moving up behind the Marines. They were just as mesmerized by the sight laying before them. Half a dozen shuttles were down now, their passengers beginning to stream out as the other ships of the expedition continued to land.

Rogan pulled his attention away from the city, checking on the Marine contingents deploying all around the hill. "Let's go, Marines," he snapped into his comm. "The city is interesting, but you've all got jobs to do...so let's get to it."

He turned back and walked toward a trio of technicians who were setting up a portable comm station. "Status?"

"We'll have it up and running in a minute, sir."

Rogan nodded. As soon as the station was working, he had to report back to Commodore Eaton. Rogan had no problem commanding the Marine detachment and handling security for the landing parties, but for reasons that escaped him, Eaton had put him in command of the entire expedition. It wasn't unreasonable, considering his rank, but he couldn't help but feel he had no place ordering the scientists and engineers around, not to mention archeologists, medical teams, and a dozen other types of experts.

The med team had set up their equipment right next to the comm station, and they were already running their tests. Once they gave the clearance, he could issue the go ahead to ditch the breathing gear, which would make everyone a lot more comfortable.

"We should have a direct line on *Repulse* in another ninety seconds, sir."

"Very well." Rogan took a deep breath, feeling almost lightheaded for a second from the oxygen-rich mixture he was inhaling. He watched as the comm technicians finished their setup, and then he waited for *Repulse* to come around in its orbit far enough to establish a connection.

He'd counted down to twenty-four when he heard it.

"General Rogan!" The voice was wild, out of control, thick with every emotion from excitement to stark terror.

"What is it?" He spun around, pulling out a small tablet and pulling up a location on the caller.

"Sir, you need to get here. Now!"

He turned his head, looking off to the southwest. The lieutenant on the comm was about sixty meters from his current location, hidden right now by the crest of the hill.

He jogged over toward the designated location, and as he did, he saw a crowd forming, Marines and technicians alike standing in a rough line, all of them focused on...

Rogan stopped, frozen, his eyes fixed on a small cluster of... people?

They were very short, and they seemed to be hunched over. Long brown hair hung down from their heads.

Then Rogan realized they weren't as short as he'd thought at first...they were bent over. No, they were on their knees...right before the cluster of Marines at the front of the growing crowd.

My God...people...

Rogan swallowed hard, still trying to convince himself he wasn't hallucinating.

They had come looking for old tech.

But they had found...*is it even possible?*

Could they really be...descendants from survivors of the Cataclysm?

Chapter Twenty

Hall of the People
Liberte City
Planet Montmirail, Ghassara IV
Union Year 219 (315 AC)

"I want to thank you again for accepting our invitation. It's an honor and a pleasure to host our neighbors as friends." Villieneuve stood in the vast reception room, smiling at the half dozen emissaries from the Collective. The cavernous chamber was one of the few of such magnificence to survive the orgy of destruction that had accompanied the revolution and Villieneuve's march back to power.

He was clad, as he always was in public, in a factory worker's drab garb, but he'd donned a fresh set for the occasion, new and clean and devoid of the tears and stains that scarred so many the outfits he'd worn since the revolution.

"We are equally honored, Minister Villieneuve…" The ambassador, dressed in significantly more opulent formal attire, paused. "…though I must say that we were somewhat surprised at the invitation."

Villieneuve maintained his smile. He understood the diplomat's hesitation, and the meaning behind the man's restrained words. The Union had bullied its weaker neighbors, imposing harsh trade terms on them or conquering them outright. The

Collective was the largest and strongest of the remaining entities, with about thirty inhabited worlds…though habitation along the Periphery tended to be modest, and the Collective's capital world had fewer than two hundred million inhabitants. That was miniscule by comparison with Union planets like Montmirail.

"Mr. Ambassador, I can only apologize profusely and with all sincerity for the actions of the old government. The Union was founded with the purest of intentions, but I fear it fell from its path long ago and, I daresay, became a bully in international relations. I can assure you, the People's Union will in no way follow in the footsteps of its predecessor. We seek only harmony with peaceful neighbors…and the strength to resist those who would threaten us." A pause, then: "And, I'm just 'Citizen' Villieneuve, Your Excellency. We've dispensed with the structure and titles of elitism in the new Union."

The ambassador had an uncertain look on his face. It was no secret that Villieneuve had been a high-ranking member of the old government of which he spoke—though he was pretty certain the ambassador couldn't know just how at the center of things he'd truly been.

"I work now," Villieneuve continued, "to build a new future for my people…and to wash away the guilt and pain I bear from my participation in the old government. I fear I wasn't in a position to change the Union's ways, yet I was also too weak to take a stand by resigning my posts. I shall take that shame to my grave." He cast his eyes down as he spoke, impressing himself with the intensity of his false remorse.

Villieneuve watched as the ambassador's expression softened. He felt a rush of satisfaction. It never ceased to amaze him the degree to which people could convince themselves to believe what they wanted to believe. The Collective had long lived in fear of its larger neighbor. The thought of a friendly relationship was a seductive one, and clearly the ambassador had allowed that to cloud his judgment.

"We are very pleased at the prospect of improved relations…Citizen Villieneuve. I congratulate you, and your people, on the steps you have taken. You are to be praised. The unrest in your nation could have led in a much darker direction."

"Indeed, it could have, Mr. Ambassador. I can only hope that our continued efforts will keep us on the path to peace and prosperity, for our billions of workers, and for our neighbors and friends."

"We of the Collective certainly share that hope with you, Citizen Villieneuve, and I can state our sincere and fervent hope that our future is one of friendship."

Villieneuve smiled and nodded. A few seconds later, he allowed his expression to shift to one of concern. "There are many challenges ahead of us, I fear…"

"Challenges?"

"Yes, Ambassador. It's a travesty that past Union governments have behaved badly toward the Collective and the other nations on the Periphery. We all face the same threat, after all. We should have been natural allies rather than cold war adversaries." Villieneuve didn't mention the fact that the Union's "cold" war on its frontier neighbors had gone hot several times, resulting in more than two dozen systems being annexed over the past two decades.

"What threat do we share, Citizen Villieneuve? Without any intent to offend, I must state that we have long considered the Union itself to be the greatest danger to our sovereignty."

"That's understandable, Ambassador. As I've said, the actions of the government of the old Union were indefensible. Yet, I fear the rational concern Union actions may have caused your nation helped to hide the true danger posed not by us— certainly not now, at least—but by the Confederation."

"The Confederation?" The Ambassador seemed surprised at Villieneuve's words.

"Of course, Ambassador. Even in the dark years, when the Union was perceived as a menace to you, it also insulated you from the Confederation's expansion. They are a nation that exports propaganda, stories of prosperity and peaceful intentions, but the reality is quite different. Their prosperity is built on their utter disregard for their workforces. Billions of workers toil in unsafe factories, living in abject poverty as their labors help to build the vast wealth of the industrial princes and the oligarchical families that rule through the sham of their Senate."

"We have had limited contact with the Confederation. They are far from us, and the Union lies astride almost every route to their space. We have never considered them a threat."

"For the very reasons you just stated, Ambassador. Because the Union always lay between you and them. But, it's no secret that the Union has been weakened, that we are more vulnerable to Confederation aggression than ever in our history…and, if the People's Union is conquered by the Confederation, how long do you think the Collective and the other Periphery nations would remain independent? If we're defeated, your fates will be sealed. You will all fall under Confederation control, sooner or later."

The ambassador looked back, a puzzled look on his face. Villieneuve knew he wouldn't bring the Collective, or any of the other Periphery nations, over to his side immediately. There was too much history of Union aggression. But he was sure he'd get there. He could feel movement even now, doubts in the ambassador's mind that hadn't been there moments before.

He had time, some at least. But when the moment came for the next phase of the struggle, he intended to have the entire Periphery behind him…and, with any luck, they would face a Confederation riven by internal dissension. The Union had always relied on brute force against the Confeds, but now it was time for finesse.

Time to end this century-long conflict once and for all.

*   *   *

Villieneuve read the report for the second time. Lille had been aggressive from the instant he'd arrived on Dannith…very aggressive. He'd grabbed a suspected Confederation operative, one he seemed to believe he had a chance to subvert. Villieneuve wasn't so sure about that, but Lille was no fool. If he couldn't entice the captured agent to support Sector Nine…

The People's Protectorate, you fool…you have to remember that.

If he couldn't get the agent to switch allegiances, he'd still get useful information out of her. And no one matched Ricard Lille's ability to dispose of an asset that had no further value.

He reached over and tapped a few keys on his keyboard, bringing up another, highly classified, report. His intel from inside the Confederation was spotty, and only partially reliable. His resources were fewer than they'd been in the days of Sector Nine, and he'd deployed almost all of what he did have to Lille's and Marieles's operations. But the report seemed reliable, and it concerned him greatly. There was a naval task force in Dannith's system, far larger and more powerful than anything he'd expected to be there, especially since the post-war demobilizations.

The Confeds had decommissioned dozens of ships since the war ended...just as he'd suspected they would...as he'd counted on them doing. The peace party in the Confederation was strong and energetic even without his assistance, and despite his own troubles, he'd managed to continue to exert influence in the Senate. It was difficult to bully or entice Senators to undertake actions viewed as disloyal or treasonous, but it was relatively easy to encourage them to be more aggressive about things they wanted to do anyway. The Confederation navy's budget had been slashed on three separate occasions, and it was now barely eighty percent of what it had been *before* the war. Thousands of veteran spacers had been retired on half-pensions, and their return to the civilian workforce, coupled with the millions of workers laid off as military production fell from a breakneck pace to almost nothing, had impacted planetary economies throughout the Confederation.

The Confeds didn't face an economic depression anywhere near as severe as the one he was still struggling to overcome in the Union, but Confed citizens weren't as used to deprivation either, and there had been unrest on a number of worlds. That all played into his hand perfectly, making it easier for his creatures in the Senate to push for yet more diversion of funds from the military budgets to social programs and civil spending designed to boost the economy...and quell the angry population.

Villieneuve had spent the year after the ceasefire concerned that the Confeds would reinstate hostilities. Though he knew the Confederation well enough that he wasn't surprised at their willingness to stop the war as they had, he was still relieved when the ceasefire turned into a treaty, and the Confed forces pulled back into their own space.

Tactically, it had been a huge mistake, and in terms of long-term strategy, it was even more foolish. The Confeds had thrown away a chance to establish a level of dominance that would have eliminated the prospect of future wars. They could have made themselves almost invulnerable, but instead they had given him a chance to salvage the Union, to rebuild its strength and continue to scheme…and to prepare for a day when he could seek vengeance for what he knew perfectly well had been a defeat, however much his propaganda specialists might call it a draw that the Union had accepted to achieve peace.

Now, his concerns of renewed war before he could have the Union ready had faded away. The greatly-reduced Confed navy was still stronger than his battered forces, but not by enough of a margin to mount a credible invasion threat. And the Alliance, now allied with the Confederation, had seen its own forces devastated, first by civil war, then in combat at the Bottleneck…and finally in their vengeance-driven conflict with the Krillians. In the long-term, the Alliance, bolstered by the annexation of the Krillian systems, would be more powerful than ever, but for the immediate future, they had significant rebuilding to do before they could project meaningful offensive power far beyond their own borders.

He had time…but not an unlimited amount of it. He had to make things happen before his adversaries became too powerful to match. A league between the Union and the nations of the Periphery would help. If he could bring the Collective in, he was sure the others would eventually follow. The entities on the edge of human habitation were small and weak by the standards of nations like the Union and the Confederation, but combined together, they would be a significant factor in any future conflict.

Still, that wouldn't be enough. League forces might just offset the Alliance, but there was little chance of the Union regaining its advantage over the Confeds. He had to do everything possible to weaken the Confederation, even to destabilize it. It has been months since he'd sent Marieles to Megara, and the reports he'd received suggested she had made some progress expanding on the influence he'd established in the Senate. But her mission was a colossal one, and he knew he'd have to give her all the support he could if she was to have any real chance of pulling it off.

Perhaps Dannith is a start on that...

The fleet concentration in the system was out of the ordinary, and Villieneuve doubted the Confederation Senate knew what was going on there. Most likely, it was Confederation Intelligence...possibly overstepping their authority, and very likely trying to keep it as quiet as so massive an operation could be.

It seemed odd to him, coming as he did from a system where the intel agencies had almost free rein, but the Confeds didn't operate that way. Gary Holsten had been continually hampered by Senatorial oversight and other restrictions that had handicapped his agency's efforts to match Sector Nine. It was an unavoidable aspect of republican government, one he fortunately didn't have to deal with in his own operations. Still, it told him Holsten must have a good reason for taking such a risk.

They must be on to Ricard...

That greatly increased the danger his friend faced. Lille was a survivor, but if Confederation Intelligence had sent an entire naval task force to the system, it didn't bode well for Lille getting very far on his mission. He'd be spending most of his time avoiding capture, and trying to preserve his operation from Confed attempts to crush it. That would interfere with expanded efforts to locate old tech artifacts.

But, maybe we can still gain an edge from this...

His fingers moved across the keyboard, pulling up a blank screen and then typing a set of new orders. Orders for Desiree Marieles.

Villieneuve understood the Confeds...he'd spent his entire adult life trying to devise ways to defeat them. Whoever sent a naval task force to Dannith had to be highly-ranked, probably

Gary Holsten himself.

If it *was* Holsten, he'd pushed his authority to the absolute limits. The Confederation Intelligence head had stuck his neck out on this one...and Villieneuve was more than ready to chop it off if he could.

He finished typing the orders, and then he hit the send button. His system was highly secure, and no one but his personal AI would see what he'd written. The computer would encrypt the message, and see that it was sent to Marieles, looking very much like normal diplomatic comm traffic or personal correspondence...anything but what it was, instructions to see that the right Senators found out about the naval concentration at Dannith, and that they responded as he knew they would.

Holsten had been a worthy opponent over the years, especially considering the difficulties he'd had to bear working in the Confederation's system. But now, he'd made a rare mistake, he'd exposed himself.

And Gaston Villieneuve had every intention of taking advantage of that fact to destroy his rival.

Chapter Twenty-One

CFS Repulse
Zed-11 System
Year 315 AC

"Commodore!" The officer's voice was shrill, uncontrolled, not at all what Sara Eaton had come to expect from her crew.

"What is it, Lieutenant?" Eaton's voice was hard, expressing her displeasure with the lack of discipline in the officer's voice without actually saying anything about it.

"Commodore…General Rogan reports the landing party has encountered…" The officer paused.

"Encountered what?" Eaton was getting very impatient.

"People, Commodore. They've found people."

Eaton was taken aback by the report. Her mind raced to accept what she'd just been told. She'd been ready to find every manner of artifact, even some still active and attacking her people, but encountering live humans…

"Put General Rogan on my line, Lieutenant. Immediately."

"Yes, Commodore." A short pause. "The general is coming, sir. He stepped away from the comm station for a moment."

A few seconds passed, then: "Commodore?" It was Rogan, and as soon as she heard his tone, she knew something significant had happened.

"What's going on down there, Bryan?"

"We found live survivors." It was a matter-of-fact statement, but it hit her like a hammer.

"Survivors of what? Some forgotten expedition? Have we actually encountered some smuggler traffic out this far?"

"Negative, Commodore. They appear to be actual survivors. Of the Cataclysm." A short pause. "Or, at least, their descendants."

Eaton just sat in her chair, silent for a moment, trying to accept what the Marine officer had told her. She'd probably have written the words off to space-fever or delusions if they'd come from almost anyone else. But Bryan Rogan was the coolest, most controlled person she'd ever met.

"Are you sure, Bryan?" It was a stupid question, and she realized that the instant it escaped her lips. It was hard to believe they'd found people living out this far, but unless the entire landing party was suffering from hallucinations, there didn't seem to be any doubt.

"Yes, Commodore. There's no question." The general paused. "They're...different. We're trying to communicate, but we can't understand them...and it doesn't seem they know what we're saying either." Another hesitation. "And, they're..." She could tell Rogan was struggling for words. "...altered."

"Altered?" She wasn't sure what he was trying to say.

"They seem to have a variety of physical...defects. Many of them seem unable to stand completely upright, and others seem to have partially withered arms or legs or strange lesions on their faces or extremities."

"Could they be injured? Crash victims, perhaps?"

"That was my first thought, too...but, I don't think so, Commodore. It seems almost like they're suffering from mutations of some kind, possibly from the atomic bombardments that obviously occurred here, and maybe also from chemical or biological agents used. They also appear to be members of a primitive culture of some sort."

Eaton leaned back in her chair, trying to understand the implications of Rogan's statement. She knew that some of the outer worlds, planets in systems now part of the Confederation or one of the other powers, had fallen into primitive barbarism of a sort after the Cataclysm. Some planets had lost more technology than others, barely hanging onto basic civilization. It was the retention of a significant knowledge base that gave worlds like Megara and Montmirail an advantage over their neighbors and led to the formations of the Confederation and the Union. But, she'd never heard of a civilization fallen as low as the one Rogan seemed to be describing.

"Do the best you can to try to establish some kind of communication, Bryan. I'm sending down another wave of landing parties. I'll get you every expert we've got…and, we'll go from there."

"Very well, Commodore. We'll do our best down here."

"Good luck, Bryan." Eaton cut the line, and then she turned toward the comm station. Before she did anything, she had to report this to Admiral Barron.

"Get me *Dauntless*. Now."

*   *   *

Rogan walked back toward the front of the group facing the—he wasn't sure if "natives" was the right word, though he no longer doubted the people standing and watching the landing parties had been born on this world. His own people were mostly quiet, staring back in stunned shock, but the Marines had their weapons out and at the ready. He almost ordered them to sling their rifles, but he was a Marine himself, and he couldn't help but think of the visitors as a potential threat.

They didn't look terribly dangerous. In fact, when he got back from the comm post, they were laying prostrate in front of his people, almost as though they were kneeling…or paying homage of some kind.

He almost told them to get up…but they wouldn't understand his words anyway. He turned and looked back behind him, toward the shuttles and the stunned crowd of Marines and scientists. "Where the hell is that thing?"

"Coming, sir." The answer came from behind the crowd,

and few seconds later, three Marines came running forward, carrying a large piece of equipment. It looked a bit like a portable workstation, but Rogan knew it was the mobile translation AI he'd ordered his people to retrieve. "Sorry, General. We had a tough time finding it. For a minute, I thought it got left behind."

Rogan wouldn't have been surprised. The shuttles had been stripped of most of their normal gear to make room for weapons and scanning equipment. The last thing anyone had expected was the need to translate between different tongues so deep in the long-dead empire. It was just dumb luck one of the units had remained aboard a shuttle and not gotten pulled out and thrown on the deck of a launch bay.

It was still a long shot at best anyway. He doubted it would be of any help. It was only programmed with known languages, and it was clear to Rogan that whoever these people were, they hadn't come from the Confederation, or anywhere near it.

"Get that set up as quickly as possible." He turned back toward the visitors, looking at them intently, panning his eyes across the group. There were ten of them, and every one was down on his or her hands and knees. Rogan wondered if it could be some kind of normal greeting…but it seemed very degrading for that. They almost looked like worshippers lying prostrate before a deity.

There were small piles in front of each of them. At first, Rogan couldn't tell what they were, but now he realized they were polished stones and similar trinkets. Gifts? Perhaps a way to greet visitors?

But how would they have ever had visitors?

It didn't make sense. Even if some small vestige of a civilization had survived on this world, bereft of the technology their ancestors had once possessed, it didn't explain their apparent lack of astonishment at people landing on their planet in spaceships. They were respectful, even obsequious, but they didn't seem surprised. *Almost as if having visitors is a common occurrence…*

Barron looked intently at the natives closest to him. They wore strange clothing, old and worn, and very simple—but clearly of some type of manufacture and not the kinds of skins or simple garments a truly primitive culture might wear. The men and women seemed to be dressed identically, each of them wearing a pair of brown pants and a tunic that looked like a cross between a shirt and a jacket. They were all filthy, their clothes torn in places and covered in some kind of thick, gray dust.

Rogan wished he had a cultural expert with him, but the landing party had been assembled to examine ancient technology...not some kind of civilization. He wondered if the fleet even had a decent cadre of anthropologists and language experts among its complement. He suspected if such personnel were there, Commodore Eaton and Admiral Barron were looking for them now.

"The AI is set up, General." The lieutenant was standing next to the apparatus, looking at it like he was far from certain he'd know whether it was ready or not. But the landing party had its share of electronics and computer experts, and Rogan could see several of them nodding.

"Just bring this unit with you, General," one of the engineers said. He handed Rogan a small device that looked like a microphone. After the general took it, the engineer gave him a headset. "The unit will translate anything picked up by the microphone and relay it to your headset. Assuming, of course, it is identifiable. The AI will estimate if it cannot positively identify any language, and it will provide a projected percentage chance of accuracy." The engineer paused. "Once the unit has gained some data on the language in use, it will be able to convert your own speech as well."

Rogan just nodded. He'd led desperate assaults, and faced almost certain death more than once, but this was a situation he'd never imagined. One all his years of training and experience had done nothing to prepare him to handle.

He walked toward the closest native, slowly, not wanting to appear threatening. He knelt down slowly, edged closer, and he reached out and touched the man's shoulder.

The native jumped up and back from Rogan, shouting a series of words the Marine didn't understand. *No*, Rogan thought, *not shouting.* The man's tone was respectful, almost…reverential.

"The subject is professing his loyalty to you, General." The AI's voice was loud in the headset. "Perhaps more than loyalty. The tongue appears to be a variant of the ancient imperial language, though the version in use by the subject is severely degraded. It is too early to make definitive assumptions, but the choice of words suggests a sharply limited vocabulary. Preliminary analysis indicates findings consistent with an ex-imperial culture that has regressed considerably."

That made perfect sense to Rogan. It was clear the people standing in front of his Marines had fallen considerably in technology and knowledge. And they had to be the descendants of survivors of the Cataclysm. Where else could they have come from?

"Can you translate into their dialect?"

"Yes," the AI responded. "Partially, at least. I do not have a sufficient pool of colloquialisms nor a firm idea of the limitations on vocabulary, but I do have a full database of all known variants of imperial languages."

"Translate what I say." Rogan took a deep breath. He hated being the point man in this contact. He felt out of his depth and far from his areas of expertise. But the natives were there, right in front of his people. He couldn't exactly tell them to wait until Eaton got another wave of shuttles to the surface…and he *was* in command on the planet.

If they even understand what a shuttle is…

"Yes, General."

Rogan looked toward the man closest to him. He had no real idea, but his gut told him that was the leader. "We have come in peace. We mean you no harm."

Rogan paused as the AI's emotionless voice broadcast from the unit's speakers. He could make out some of what it was saying—the Prime Tongue used throughout most of the Rim was also based on ancient imperial, though it had evolved and changed considerably over the centuries. Still, many words were the same, or at least similar.

The man looked confused at first, his eyes darting around,

trying to identify the source of what he was hearing. Finally, he turned toward Rogan, his head still downcast, and he spoke.

Rogan tried to follow what the man was saying, and he managed to pick up a few words, but the guttural nature of the speech made it difficult to pick out even recognizable words. Before he could make anything of it, the AI's voice filled his headset. "I have been able to translate a portion of the subject's speech. The grammar and structure differ considerably from any imperial norms in my database, but I was able to identify a sufficient sampling to decipher basic meanings. The response was almost certainly a greeting, though not one between equals. The subject is speaking to you as though you are a higher being."

"You mean a superior rank?"

"No, not precisely. A better. A superior being. Not a deity, but something on that order. One term that has been repeated translates as 'higher one' or 'master.'"

"Master? As in master and slave?" Slavery wasn't an unknown concept among the Rimward nations, but no world in the Confederation had seen it for a century or more.

"There is a level of analytical speculation required to answer your question. I do not perceive a representation of literal ownership as much as a term of grave respect. There are definite indications of fear in the subject's voice."

"Respect? Like a peasant-lord relationship?"

"I do not believe your comparison is entirely accurate. There is a ninety-four percent probability that the subject considers himself an inferior being to you and the other members of the landing party. However, no indication has been given as to the source of such an assertion. It is possible the being's deference is simply the result of seeing the technology on display, but I also detect signs of familiarity and ritual in the speech and actions of the natives."

Rogan was really uncomfortable now. His entire life had been one subject to the rigidity of rank, and he'd seen his share of such things from both the bottom and the top. But that wasn't what the AI was describing. The Confederation was a republic, and in theory, at least, its people were equal. There were other cultures, of course, with such hierarchies imposed by law. He didn't have to look any farther than his Alliance allies to find an inflexible caste system enforcing institutional inequality. But, again, that wasn't what the AI was telling him. Not exactly.

"Are you saying this person considers us gods?"

"Your terminology is too broad to acknowledge without qualifiers...yet, you are closer to the truth here. These people apparently consider you and the others to be higher order beings of some kind. They regard you with a combination of awe and fear."

Rogan sighed, unsure how to proceed. He'd signed onto the mission, fully prepared to do his duty, to defend the members of the expedition from any dangerous old tech that might be active enough to cause a threat. But he'd never imagined finding survivors, and certainly not having them crawl before him as though he were some kind of god.

He glanced down at his chronometer. It would be at least another thirty minutes before the new wave of shuttles landed... and he wondered how his visitors would react to watching a whole flight of ships blasting their way down. Would they run in terror...or would it just reaffirm their belief that he and the others from the fleet were gods come down to them from the heavens?

"Shit," he muttered softly, hoping the AI didn't pick it up and translate it. *I didn't sign up for this...*

Chapter Twenty-Two

CFS Repulse
Zed-11 System
Year 315 AC

Rogan walked through the sparse woods, following the group of natives. He'd managed to communicate to a certain extent, and while he was talking, he noticed the differences in the men and women who appeared to call the planet home. They were humans, of course, that much was clear, though they were... different...from his own people, and not just in language and knowledge. Most of them displayed physical variations beyond those typical of human beings. Some were completely hairless, others seemed to have misshapen limbs. A few appeared to have larger than normal heads or protruding foreheads.

Most of them seemed weaker than normal humans as well, and they moved slowly as they led the landing party to...wherever they were going. So slowly, he'd had to tell his people to slow down half a dozen times so as not to overtake their... hosts.

Rogan had no idea where they were being taken. He'd breathed a sigh of relief when the second wave of shuttles finally landed, and every expert or semi-expert Sara Eaton could find debarked and relieved him from his unwanted duties as primary ambassador to the residents of the planet. He gratefully fell back from the forefront of the exchanges and focused on organizing his Marines into security details to accompany the landing teams. The natives didn't seem particularly threatening, but he wasn't one to take chances. And, whatever was going on, it was certainly strange enough to warrant caution.

The natives did view his people as something close to gods. He'd managed to verify that much. From what the linguistics AI and the newly arrived experts had told him, they were being taken to a place where some kind of offering awaited them. That word gave him the willies. He didn't know what it meant—other than something beyond the polished stones they'd been given earlier—but the whole situation was just to strange and unexpected for his tastes. Thoughts of all sorts of things drifted into his mind...baskets of grain, butchered animals, even human sacrifice. Anything seemed possible.

The group followed a rough path through the woods. They were moving south, away from the ruins of the great city. That, at least, was good news. Admiral Barron would want the city explored, almost certainly, but the radiation readings were quite high, even from almost ten kilometers distance, and any team planning to move closer or to explore the ruins themselves would need heavy protective gear. It would take time to shuttle down the equipment required, along with another group of experts to carry out the exploration. Meanwhile, everyone in the landing party had strict orders not to approach the dead city.

You assume it's dead...but we thought the whole planet was dead...

Still, the radiation readings suggested nothing human, at least, could have survived long in the city. He imagined things like immense, mutated cockroaches, but then he scolded himself for foolishness.

He reached down to his belt and pulled off a small canister, replacing it with a fresh one from his pack. He was down to his last oxygen tank, and that meant he'd either have to get back to basecamp in another hour, or he'd have to risk breathing the native air.

The medical teams had already cleared the landing party to discard their breathing gear, but Rogan—still technically in command on the ground—had overruled them. He was cautious by nature, and too much had already happened far outside the parameters of what was expected. He suspected his people had moaned about the order, but he didn't give any of it a second thought. They'd manage to endure the discomfort a while longer.

He slid the empty canister into his pack and slung it back over his shoulder. He supposed a general could delegate someone to carry his gear, but that wasn't the way Rogan operated. He'd worked his way up from the bottom, and he'd never forgotten those days, not even after Tyler Barron had placed stars on his shoulders.

He twitched a little, feeling something strange on his arm. He reached around and scratched it, and then he continued forward, jogging a bit to catch up. There were buildings around now, on both sides of the rough path. They were huts—that was the kindest word he could think of to call them—small, ramshackle structures built of wood and what looked like dried mud. There were a few made of metal, what appeared to be old, repurposed sheets of thin aluminum or something similar. He wondered if the natives had salvaged them from the city, and he turned to order one of the technicians to take radiation readings…but he saw that he was too late. Three or four of those near him were already looking down at tablets, running a whole battery of tests, he assumed. They'd warn him if they detected anything dangerous. But, even without their warnings, Rogan was on edge. He didn't like this place, he'd decided, and for reasons he couldn't completely comprehend, he was sure nothing good would come of the fleet's visit.

Masters…

That was what the AI had decided the natives were calling the landing party. The computer had finally refined its guidance, and it had assigned a seventy percent probability to the determination that the subjects were not calling his people masters, but rather they were asking if they *were* masters. That was an oversimplification of the elaborate scenario the AI had laid out for him, but it left him with an uncomfortable feeling, and one thought, haunting him since he'd listened to the computer's words.

What is a master? Is it something they've seen before?

He snapped back from his thoughts...abruptly. There was activity at the front of the group, chatter from the scientists and Marines alike, and they had stopped moving. He quickened his pace and moved forward, stopping suddenly as he saw what had caused the column to halt.

It was a building, large and vaguely pyramidal, constructed from a strange material that looked a bit like polished metal or glass.

"What is that?" Rogan walked over to one of the civilian experts, or at least what passed for a linguistics pro among the advance guard's limited staff. The fleet had been prepared to decipher any old data systems or records that were found, but no one had expected to end up talking to actual people.

"I don't know, sir. I'll ask." The man turned toward the closest native, the one Rogan had assumed was the leader, and he spoke. The Marine could follow some of what was said, perhaps a quarter of it, based on similarities between ancient imperial and the Prime Tongue.

"He says it's a...I think 'temple' would be the closest thing to the term he used. He seems to think we wanted to come here. If I had to guess, I'd say these people think we have something to do with..."

The man never finished. He fell silent, spinning around as Rogan did...and watching as several hatches on the sides of the structure slid open. The Marine's eyes were fixed on the building, and on the openings that had just appeared. His instincts were on fire, and he was bringing his rifle up even as he tapped at his headset, activating the comm unit.

But he was too late. He saw a flash, and then another. The man next to him, the one who'd been translating until just a second or two earlier, fell to the ground. Rogan's eyes followed him down, focusing on the blackened, gaping wound that had taken off most of his shoulder and a good part of his chest.

If Rogan had been anything but a Marine, a veteran with

years of combat experience, he would have died an instant later. But his instincts took control, and without even knowing how he'd gotten down, he was prone, tucked behind the partial cover of one of the huts.

He was on his comm, shouting orders to his Marines, calling reserves forward. His finger tightened on the trigger, and his rifle fired on full auto. He could see the attackers now, large shadowy figures emerging from the structure. They were humanoid in shape, but larger, bulkier. They were firing as they poured out.

And he could see his Marines, falling, dropping to the ground one after another, as the attackers moved forward.

*　*　*

"Commodore, I've got Captain Stockton calling for you." There was urgency in the comm officer's voice.

"Put him on my line, Lieutenant."

"Commodore?" She could hear immediately something was wrong. Stockton was a cool customer, one who rarely let on when he was unnerved by something, but even he couldn't hide the concern in his voice.

"Yes, Captain? Any status updates?" She wondered what Stockton could have found. She'd been receiving constant reports from the search teams. They all had the same story. The blasted sections definitely appeared to be parts of some kind of space stations or orbital platforms. And, every one they'd examined so far had been picked clean of any old tech that had been there. But she could tell from Stockton's tone, there was something else happening.

"Commodore...I'm picking up strange signals. Very powerful."

"Signals? From where?"

"From the debris fields. I got partial locks on a couple, and I managed to trace one. There seem to be a number of satellites in orbit...and they're fully functional. My guess is they were powered down to minimum output to make detection difficult, and to appear like part of the debris field. But *something* activated them. I identified the power surges. They're comm beams, strong ones. I managed to get a vector on one."

Eaton could *feel* what the pilot was going to say next.

"It was a direct line to one of the transit points, Commodore. On the far side of the system."

A wave of coldness ran through Eaton's body. Random old tech that still functioned, unexplained survivors on the planet… the strange, seemingly unrelated events were piling up, far too quickly. Something *was* happening, something very disturbing.

The fleet's mission had just gotten a whole lot more complicated. And dangerous.

"Captain…do what you can to track any more comm beams…and find all those satellites. Launch as many squadrons as you need for backup…and as many drones, too. Just find anything that's out there."

"Yes, Commodore. I'll report back as soon as I have anything new."

Eaton took a deep breath. Then, she turned toward the comm station. "Get me a line to Admiral…"

"Commodore, I've got General Rogan. He says it's urgent."

"On my line."

"Commodore, we've had a problem down here. I need additional medical teams dispatched at once. And my reserve units as well."

Eaton turned toward the tactical station. "I want three med teams sent down immediately, Lieutenant. And all remaining Marine units are to prepare to debark for the surface at once."

"Yes, Commodore."

Eaton turned her gaze from the tactical officer, staring down at the floor in front of her as she put her hand on her headset. "Med teams on the way, Bryan. Your Marines will be right behind. What happened?"

"The natives brought us to their village. The whole thing was primitive, rough huts and the like…except for one building in the center. It was modern…very modern. Maybe more advanced than anything on Megara. Then…well, there was a firefight down here, Commodore."

"A what?" Eaton almost shouted her response. She'd expected the Marine would report something strange, and almost certainly bad, but actual combat had never entered her mind. Initial reports on the natives suggested they were not only passive, but also utterly incapable of fighting Rogan's Marines in any real way.

"A firefight, Commodore...a nasty one." As she listened, she realized that Rogan was still out of breath. Whatever had happened down there, the general had been in the thick of it. "The building opened up, armed soldiers came out, and they attacked. No attempts at communication, they just came out shooting."

"By armed, you mean…"

"Armed and armored, Commodore. High tech all the way. They had some kind of energy weapons, years ahead of anything we've got. They looked human...sort of…"

"What do you mean, 'sort of?'"

"Well, they seemed part human...and part machine. They had some kind of partial exoskeletons, sections of dark metal that seemed to be...implanted...in their flesh. They were fast, Commodore, agile. And their weapons were powerful. They sliced right through our front line." A pause. "I'm afraid we suffered heavy losses. I don't have a final count yet, but it's at least twenty...including some of the technicians and engineers who were caught up front and couldn't get out of the way in time.

"Do you need orbital bombardment support?" Eaton didn't let herself think too deeply about what the Marine general had just told her. The implications were staggering, and right now her focus was on making sure her people had what they needed.

"I don't think so, Commodore. There were only ten attackers and they're all dead now. They put up one hell of a fight, but there are no signs of any others right now. I think we'll be okay until the reserves land. Our scans can't penetrate the structure. We've got it surrounded, and we're about to go in."

"Hold on that Bryan...I'd feel better if you waited until you had more reserves down there." She hesitated. Barron and the rest of the fleet were still on the way to the planet...and Rogan already had most of the advance guard's Marine strength with him. "We've got another company prepping to come down now, maybe a bit more, but that's all we've got. Stay where you are until they arrive, at least…and do not proceed without further authorization."

"Yes, Commodore." She couldn't tell if Rogan agreed with her or not. She suspected his blood was up, and he was anxious to get into that building and see if there was someone there responsible for the losses his Marines had suffered. He might understand waiting for reinforcements, but she suspected he would resent her order to stand down until she gave the specific go ahead to move. Especially if she held him back again after the extra company had landed.

Eaton had a cautious mindset. She wasn't one to jump to conclusions, but there was no escaping the realization that the fleet had discovered far more than a cache of old tech, more than traces of the old empire.

It had found survivors—more accurately, the descendants of survivors. The Confederation, and every other civilization in the sector, had long assumed they were the only ones to endure past the Cataclysm. She closed her eyes and shook her head, struggling to face what her mind was telling her.

The primitives the landing party had found were a shocking enough discovery, but this was stunning. They had found another civilization…and from what little information she possessed, it seemed clear it was one significantly ahead of the Confederation's technology.

Chapter Twenty-Three

Cellar of a Non-Descript Warehouse
Spacer District, Just Off the Promenade
Port Royal City, Planet Dannith, Ventica III
315 AC

Andi Lafarge took a breath, forcing the cool, damp air into her lungs despite the pain in her chest. She had a broken rib, at least, maybe two or three, and she was covered in bruises from head to toe. Her captors had restricted their interrogations to emotional and mental pressure for the first week or more that she'd been their prisoner. In between sessions, they'd dangled rewards: wealth, power, a place of rank and respect in the Union. They'd mocked her for loyalty to a Confederation that treated her and those of her profession as outlaws. They'd offered her a place with people who respected what she did, who valued her skill and experience.

She knew things would probably go easier on her if she feigned some interest in their entreaties, if she fed them enough to convince them they were making progress convincing her. But her rage and spite were too strong, and instead of playing along, she'd hit them with every vile curse she knew, the foulest and nastiest things she'd heard in filthy spacer's dives, even a few swear words in old imperial that she'd picked up somewhere. She didn't know exactly what those meant, but she was sure they were insulting and vulgar.

Still, for all her anger and resistance, her captors—Sector Nine, she knew—had refrained from really hurting her, no matter how viciously she provoked them. Until three days earlier.

She'd had no warning about the change, not until the interrogators came into the reasonably comfortable room where they'd kept her…and beat the hell out of her without so much as asking her a question. She'd stood up, as she had every day since they'd brought her there, but this time she rose to a hard punch in the face, one that almost knocked her back on the bed. She staggered, but she managed to maintain her footing, as much through sheer stubbornness and the refusal to give her assailants the satisfaction of seeing her fall.

It was a short-lived bit of spite. The two interrogators had begun pummeling her, one of them with huge, balled up fists, and the other with a hard rubber club. She felt pain everywhere, up and down her body as the blows landed, and despite all her tenacity and grit, she fell, first to her knees, and then face down to the floor.

They'd dragged her from the room then, and taken her down to a cellar, somewhere at least two levels below ground. There, they threw her into what seemed to be some kind of cell. It was dark, and damp—hell, it was wet—and she landed hard on the cold cement floor.

She'd sat on that same floor, ate there when they'd deigned to feed her, and even slept there, shivering in her half-wet clothes, soaked through from the seemingly perpetual puddles on the ground. She'd reacted at first with her usual fiery rage and determination, but deep down, she knew her strength was faltering. She hated her own weakness, but she was aware that she was getting closer to telling them whatever they wanted to know, anything if they'd just bring her back to her room, stop the beatings.

Her thoughts had turned from escape—which seemed hopeless—to thoughts of suicide, assuming she could find a way to do it. It was counter to every impulse inside of her, every urge that drove her to fight to the end. But this wasn't that kind of situation. Sooner or later, her captors would break her...and she would tell them everything she knew.

Still, she wasn't sure that would matter much. After all, Lille clearly knew already that Confederation Intelligence was making a move against his operations. She didn't really know much more than that. She could give the names of her crew, all operatives, of course, but she couldn't imagine Holsten hadn't already assumed that their covers were blown and pulled them out. It wouldn't exactly be an intelligence coup for Sector Nine to discover that Confederation Intelligence was sick of being made into fools on their own border worlds.

If she'd known anything truly sensitive, she probably would have taken her own life, assuming her captors gave her the chance in some way. She wouldn't want to live knowing she'd given her enemies what they needed. But, she knew her interrogations would be fruitless. Whatever they thought she might know, whatever information they expected to get from her... that was all that was keeping her alive.

And, despite the thoughts that had plagued her weaker moments, Andi resolved she would not kill herself. It just wasn't in her DNA to do something like that. She would resist to the last, and if they wanted to break her, she would make it as difficult as she possibly could.

And if one of them gets careless, gives me an opening...

Killing one of the bastards...now, that might be something worth dying for.

She was tired, and her entire body was wracked with pain... but there was something else, too. An old friend. Defiance. And, it was still there—a warmth inside, keeping her going despite the fear and growing hopelessness.

Yes, they would break her.

But not today.

*   *   *

"Confederation Marines...open this door right now, or we'll break it down." The sergeant had barely finished his threat when he gestured to the private standing next to him with the hand-held battering ram. The armored Marine hurled himself at the door, holding the heavy metal cylinder in front of him, and his momentum carried him straight through into the room beyond. The old wooden door didn't so much open as shatter into hundreds of tiny shards.

The sergeant followed right behind, flanked by three other privates, all with assault rifles drawn and pointing toward the room's occupants. There were two men and a woman, and they were sitting at a table covered with boxes containing some kind of small electronic components. They leapt up, moving their bodies in an almost comically ineffective effort to hide the items from the Marines.

The sergeant held back a sigh, but only through pure discipline. Bashing down doors in a Confederation city wasn't usually part of his duty roster. Sergeant Malcolm Jones was a veteran of the Union War, and he'd seen service in two significant battles in that conflict, as well as half a dozen skirmishes. He'd been wounded twice, once superficially, the other time seriously enough that he'd spent the first day unsure if he'd make it.

He knew orders when he heard them, and he damned sure obeyed them without question, but he had no idea what was actually going on. Command HQ just sent lead after lead, addresses around the city that had triggered the suspicions of someone substantially higher in rank than Jones himself, and each time, his people interrupted one more sex worker plying his or her trade, or a group of petty thieves divvying up their haul.

He knew Border worlds like Dannith had more than their share of lowlifes and crime, though he'd still been surprised at the sheer number of jailable offenses his people had uncovered in a few nights' work. He'd wondered what the local police did, and then he came to the startling conclusion that all the crimes his people had seen were the crumbs—offenses that didn't even rise to a sufficient level to provoke a reaction from Dannith's overworked, and likely corrupt, law enforcement agencies.

He still had no idea what Marines were doing on the planet, a hundred teams like his raiding criminal enterprises the local

police didn't even bother with. Jones knew his people were looking for someone specific—a woman, one of the dispatchers had
told him, not sounding entirely sure of himself when he did.
Neither Marine command nor the local authorities were very
interested in the routine illicit activity they'd uncovered, and for
the most part, after searching and finding nothing of note, the
Marines moved on, leaving the terrorized criminals no doubt
breathing hard, but otherwise unmolested.

Jones walked toward the table as his Marines moved the
room's occupants against the wall, relieving two of them of guns
that looked ancient enough to predate the Confederation. He
looked down at the boxes, reaching out and tilting one toward
him to get a better look at its contents. It looked like a collection
of small circuit boards of some kind, or, more accurately, broken shards of larger boards. As far as he could tell, the stuff was
old tech of some kind, but it was in terrible condition, damaged
by acid and clearly missing components. He guessed it still had
some value, but not enough to worry about. Still, he'd check. He
didn't want the responsibility of making that decision himself.

He grabbed his comm unit and hit the switch to activate it.
"Base, this is team Gamma-7. We're at location A4-C37B. We've
searched the place. There are three people here, suspected traf-
fickers in old tech from the looks of things. They've got some
contraband here, but it looks like pretty low-level stuff, and in
poor condition. Should we bring the suspects and the materials
in?"

"Negative, Gamma-7. Release the suspects and proceed to
location A5-D11A. Enter and search…and, as always, exert
extreme caution."

Jones held back another sigh, burning through more of his
precious discipline to do it. It had been the same for more than
a week now. One location after another. No report on what to
expect, no details on what his people were looking for.

"Let 'em go, Marines…we've got another stop to make." He
stood where he was, his eyes fixed on the room's occupants.
They looked too scared to move, but Jones's Marine training and
his experience held him firm. He wasn't going to chance some

petty crook grabbing a weapon and shooting one of his people as they left. Then, a few seconds later, he backed out the door, following the last of his Marines through and into the street.

Somebody's got a bug up his ass about something, that much is for sure, he thought.

Someone damned high up.

* * *

"This is outrageous. I demand this unjustified embargo be lifted at once, and that free communications be restored immediately." The man was dressed in civilian clothes, a suit that looked expensive enough, but something that would have been out of style on a world less provincial than Dannith.

Gary Holsten sat in a small office, staring at a screen, watching one of his people dealing with Dannith's planetary administrator. The local politician was almost apoplectic, and the more Holsten's agent politely listened without response, the angrier the man seemed to get. Holsten understood. He was causing all sorts of damage to Dannith's economy, not to mention monstrous inconvenience to many of its citizens. And, if the situation continued much longer, he knew there would be shortages of many things. Already, if he could take the administrator's complaints at face value, certain electronic components were changing hands at three times the pre-embargo price. That kind of thing was only going to get worse.

He could scarcely imagine the complaints flying around elsewhere as well—and probably getting all the way back to Megara by now—the freight lines disrupted, people unable to reach relatives on Dannith, natives barred from returning home from trips to other worlds. The whole thing was a mess, one that was rapidly approaching debacle status. But Holsten didn't care.

The thought of letting Andi go had crossed his mind, of course. He knew he could call off the whole mad search and give her up for dead. Holsten liked to think he was loyal to his people, but he was honest enough to acknowledge that he'd sacrificed more than one operative before when the cost of rescue was too high in one way or another. But he couldn't reduce Andi Lafarge to that kind of cold equation. She was only there because of him, and this time, he just couldn't let go, whatever the cost. He was going to find her—alive or dead—if he had to tear down every building on the godforsaken planet.

The reports were coming in constantly, the Marine teams in the streets checking in after every assigned search. Every establishment on the Promenade had been inspected, most of them twice. But Dannith's capital city was quite large, and its Spacer's District alone stretched for more than five kilometers along the outskirts of the now-closed spaceport. The reports had all been the same. Nothing, at least not yet. No sign of Andi, nor even the slightest clue leading to where she was being held. His people had turned up several Sector Nine operatives—the People's Protectorate, they were calling themselves now—and they were being held secretly in the very building he now occupied.

The prisoners had been interrogated aggressively, though he knew such a description had a significantly different meaning in the Confederation than it did in the Union. He knew from experience that Sector Nine operatives were well trained to resist the kinds of things the Confederation did to get information from captives. Even when his people got rough, that usually meant sleep deprivation or mental and emotional games. The Confederation didn't torture prisoners, and while in his heart Holsten agreed with that policy, right now he was feeling the absence of a Sector Nine inquisitor's toolbox.

He'd even considered crossing that line. It would be a crime, one almost guaranteed to end his career and result in jail time if he was caught. Even with his vast wealth, he'd be hard-pressed to save himself if such a thing were discovered. Still, he suspected some of his people would follow the orders if he gave them, and, afterward, they'd certainly have every incentive to remain silent about what they'd done.

He'd held himself back…so far. He told himself the searches would pay off eventually, that he had whoever had kidnapped Andi trapped on Dannith, and probably in Port Royal City. But each hour that passed wore away at his patience and his restraint.

He didn't know if the Sector Nine prisoners had the information he needed, but they were, without a doubt, the best leads he had.

He tried to push the thoughts aside again, to no avail. *Bergen*, he thought, trying as he did to stop even as the images flooded into his mind. *Bergen will do it if I ask him to…and I'd wager he'd do a damned good job, too.*

Chapter Twenty-Four

Planet Zero
Zed-11 System
Year 315 AC

Rogan moved forward cautiously. He knew he had no place at the head of the team infiltrating the pyramid, a thought more than one of his junior officers had tried to express to him with as much oomph as they dared to direct at a Marine general. But this wasn't any standard ground combat situation. It was possibly the most crucial mission Confederation Marines had ever undertaken. What would they find? Would there be more soldiers inside? Would another combat take place? And, if so, were Rogan and his people about to start a new war, this one against an enemy that seemed to have a significant technological edge on the Confederation?

He'd come because he didn't want his Marines facing a new enemy without him there, because he had no idea what to expect and felt he had to lead from the front to make decisions on site. But, mostly, he realized he was there to do the one thing his simmering anger railed against. To prevent another fight if there was any possible way to avoid one.

He'd landed with only a sidearm hanging from his belt, but now he clutched an assault rifle, and he'd strapped a belt over his shoulder, studded with grenades and extra clips. Had it not been for the small stars on the collar that protruded from his armor, he'd have looked like any other private ready for action.

His people were silent. He'd forbidden any communications save for warning of enemies or other danger. Combat was always serious business, but the company of Marines moving into the pyramid carried an immense weight with them as they advanced. Billions could die as a result of what happened in the next few minutes.

It had taken longer than he'd expected to force open one of the hatches, to allow his people to get inside. Whatever material the structure was made of, it was tough. In the end, it had taken a combination of powerful explosives and plasma torches to force an opening, and even that had been barely large enough for armored Marines to penetrate in single file. If his people had to retreat in a hurry, it was going to be a bloodbath trying to get out.

They were moving down a corridor now, about five meters wide, and stretching as far as the electric torches could illuminate. That wasn't as far as he'd have liked, but the strange material of the walls absorbed most of the light, reducing the effectiveness of the lamps. The floor was pitched, slanting steadily downward, and Rogan realized his people were well below grade now, advancing into some kind of subterranean complex that seemed to extend considerably farther than the structure above.

After another ten meters or so, the corridor ended at a "T," with narrower hallways continuing to the left and the right. He signaled the force to stop, while he peered cautiously around the corner in both directions. They seemed identical. He didn't want to split his force, especially since he was fairly certain the comm units couldn't penetrate the material on the walls. He'd lost contact with the surface not long into the mission. That was bad enough. But having groups of his Marines wandering around, unable to warn each other or call for help…it went against every instinct he had. But if he chose one direction and took everyone with him, he'd leave the other unexplored and his rear open to attack.

He leaned back suddenly, pressing himself against the wall,

trying to rub his back against the inside of his armor. He'd been ignoring the itchiness for as long as he could, but it was starting to drive him mad. It had gone from occasional discomfort to full on pain, and as much as he tried to focus on the situation, he had a hard time getting past the distraction. He'd been in full armor more times than he could count, but now his skin was irritated in a way it never had been before...almost on fire.

He took a deep breath and tried again to ignore the growing discomfort. "All right, we're going to divide up into two groups." He could almost hear the groans from the Marines. "I know nobody likes that idea, but we can't leave our rear undefended, so there's no choice. Major O'Toole, you've got the left. I'll take the right. Odd squads with me, evens with the major."

Rogan took one last look around the corner, and then he set off down the corridor. He stopped after about ten meters. There were doors on both sides of the hall. There were small panels next to each, but his efforts to operate the controls were unsuccessful. Both doors remained closed.

"Horn, Balder...get up here with that plasma torch." He paused an instant, looking at one door and then the other. They were identical. Finally, he just tossed a coin in his head. "This one," he said, gesturing toward the door on the right.

He stepped back as the two Marines moved forward, hauling the heavy plasma torch with them. They set it down and angled the cutting blade toward the door. Then, they activated the power source.

Rogan could hear the loud hum as the portable reactor roared to life. He'd never been comfortable standing next to a barely contained fusion reaction, though he'd spent most of his life flying around in spacecraft powered by larger versions of the very same thing. He guessed it was the compact size of the torch that got to him. Dauntless's massive reactors seemed more substantial by comparison, but Rogan didn't have any real idea of the comparative safety of the two systems.

He took a few extra steps back as the two Marines began cutting their way through the door. It was tough, apparently the same material as the outside veneer of the building, though it looked like it was thinner down here. The torch cut through more quickly than it had on the exterior, and about five minutes after they'd started, the Marines gave the door a hard kick, and the cut out section fell into the adjoining room, landing with a loud clang.

Rogan had been standing ready with four Marines next to him, weapons drawn, waiting to see what was inside. He hesitated for a moment, half expecting more of the armored soldiers to come pouring out or hose down the doorway with fire. But there was nothing.

He leapt forward into the room, followed by the Marines standing with him. His eyes moved quickly from one end of the room to the other. It was a large space, and he could see racks on the far wall. Some were empty, and others held what appeared to be weapons and various components of body armor.

"The other door," he snapped back toward the hall. "Get that door open now." He turned back and panned his eyes all around. There was no one in the room except his Marines, but it was clearly an armory of some kind. Whatever the people on the surface thought the pyramid was—a temple they had called it—Rogan knew a barracks when he saw one. The primitives above might call whoever lived down here "gods" or something to that effect, but he knew damned well they were just soldiers, most likely deployed to watch the primitives, and probably to keep them in line.

But for what? How could it be worth the cost of this to watch those people?

"General!"

He heard the voice shouting from out in the corridor, and he raced back out of the room. He turned and looked back at the Marines stacked up behind him. They were passing a message forward.

"General Rogan…the other group has found something."

Rogan cursed under his breath. He had no idea how the material used in the pyramid blocked their comm, but he was pissed as hell that he couldn't reach the rest of his Marines.

He made his way back, squeezing past the Marines lined up

in the corridor. He'd gotten about halfway toward the "T" when he heard an unmistakable sound.

Gunfire.

He picked up his pace, shoving hard to clear his path through the reacting Marines. His hand tightened around the assault rifle, and he could feel the sweat pouring down his neck, the thunderous beating of his heart. His people were in some kind of fight against...he had no idea what they were up against. But however many enemy troops they were fighting—and he absolutely thought of whoever these people were as enemies now—he was sure they were better equipped than his Marines.

And he knew any fight with them would cost.

It would cost heavy.

* * *

"We found trouble, that's what we found." Tyler Barron was sitting at the head of the conference table. Like everything else on the new *Dauntless*, it was oversized, a gargantuan metal oval that seated twenty comfortably. He'd wondered more than once what architect had decided such a thing was worth the space and resources on a warship. His old vessel had been considerably smaller, and her power plants and weapons hadn't held a candle to those of his new command. The first *Dauntless* had been cramped, in a way he found comfortable, a way he felt a warship should be. But none of that was on his mind now. He had far more pressing matters to worry about.

"General Rogan's people have penetrated the pyramid, Admiral. Hopefully, they'll be able to gather some more information." Travis was sitting next to Barron, the two of them alone in the huge room. Barron had dismissed *Dauntless*'s section heads twenty minutes before, but she had remained. The conference had not been productive, to put it delicately. No one seemed to have a fix on what they were up against, or how to deal with it. Travis's eyes moved from the screen toward the admiral, and back again, but she didn't add anything to her statement about Rogan.

"General Rogan and his people might run into a legion of soldiers whose weapons make their assault rifles look like popguns." Barron's mind had been racing ever since he'd gotten the first reports from Sara Eaton. He'd increased *Dauntless*'s acceleration immediately, and brought his ship to the planet at flank speed, ordering every vessel in the main fleet to do the same. Among other resources, those ships carried thousands of Marines and with no real idea of what was actually down on the planet, Barron didn't know what kind of reinforcements Rogan might need. He had a full battalion, seven hundred strong, boarding landing craft on a dozen ships of the fleet even then, and he was ready to send more if the situation warranted.

Barron was edgy about the tactical problem, and worried about his ground teams…but in a way, that tension was a relief. The more he could focus on the pressing situation and the specific details, the less thought he had for the larger fact that his White Fleet hadn't found great caches of ancient technology, it hadn't uncovered the mysteries of the empire and the Cataclysm. It *had* found what was rapidly beginning to look like a new enemy, and worse, one that seemed to have superior technology and weapons. The implications of that line of thinking were overwhelming…and unproductive at present, since there wasn't much he could do about it that he wasn't already doing.

"Tyler…I know you're worried about Bryan and his Marines, but there can't be too large a force in that pyramid. We've sent almost a thousand drones down to the planet, and burned half of them getting close-in shots from within the atmosphere. We've found more ruins of cities on half a dozen continents, but we've only seen inhabited villages within a few hundred kilometers of the one the landing party found, all clustered around a mountain range. Everywhere else, the planet seems to be completely dead, or devoid of intelligent life." She paused. "And, there's only the one pyramid."

He nodded. "I realize that, Atara. But we don't know what the hell is actually going on down there, we have no idea what other high-tech installations may exist underground or obscured under cover. What is happening? How can we explain any of it?

We've seen no signs of infrastructure to support a technologically advanced society, certainly nothing that explains the equipment those soldiers appear to possess. Are they even from this planet, or…" He stopped, not wanting to finish the thought.

"We're just going to have to take this one step at a time."

Barron nodded. He didn't like the fact that he kept coming up blank when he tried to think of a course of action, but somehow, the fact that Travis also seemed to be at a dead end troubled him more. He'd come to rely on her in many ways since they'd first served together, and he hadn't realized how much he expected her to fill the gaps, to have the answers when he didn't. But now, they were both at a loss.

"Admiral…" It was Sonya Eaton. Barron had given his aide direct access to the conference room's comm.

"Yes, Captain?" It had to be important. He'd told her to interrupt him any time she needed to, but he knew she'd never do it unless she had no choice.

"General Rogan just reported, sir. His people have secured the pyramid. They engaged approximately fifteen more of the enem…unidentified fighters." Eaton paused. Barron shook his head slowly. The word "enemy" came so easily to the lips of his people, and yet most of them were trying to hold it back, not ready to jump right to the conclusion that the Confederation had another adversary. Another war.

Barron almost told her to continue, but she did before the words came from his mouth.

"They suffered heavy losses, sir. General Rogan reports thirty-four confirmed dead and at least forty wounded. He reports massive damage to the internal areas of the structure…" Another pause. "…and he reports his people have taken a prisoner."

"A prisoner?" Barron tried to hide the shock in his tone, but it was too late.

"Yes, Admiral."

"One of the…unidentified…soldiers?"

"Negative, sir. Apparently, they all fought to the death."

"A villager?"

"No, sir. He says the captive is…different."

Barron almost asked another question, but he realized Eaton didn't know anything more, not yet. He almost ordered her to get Rogan on the line, but then he said, "Get a shuttle ready, Captain. I'm going down to the surface to see this for myself."

"Sir…" He could hear the doubt in her tone, and he was about to tell her just to obey his orders when Travis spoke up.

"You can't go down there, Tyler. You're the commander of the entire fleet, and the only one with anything resembling authority to speak…or negotiate…on behalf of the Confederation. It's too unsettled down there. I know how you think, and I know how prone you are to disregarding your own safety, but now is not the time. There's too much depending on you."

Barron was going to argue, but he held it back. He wouldn't have listened to anyone but Travis, but he knew she was right. Still, he had to deal with whatever was happening on the surface. "I understand what you're saying, Atara, but I need to see what we're dealing with. We've got to cut some levels out of this chain of command and get closer to the scene."

"Let me go."

"What?"

"You trust me to go in your place, don't you? I'll report directly to you. How much does *Dauntless* really need me when you're sitting a meter away?"

Barron wanted to refuse. He almost did. But she was right, and he knew it. "Okay, Atara…but I want you to be careful. We have no idea what we've stumbled on here. You're not expendable."

"Well, we agree on that, Tyler. I'll be careful. You know me."

He did know her…and that didn't make him feel any better.

Chapter Twenty-Five

Planet Zero
Zed-11 System
Year 315 AC

"He's human, Captain. In fact, as far as the med teams can tell, he's pretty close to a perfect human specimen. They haven't done any blood or DNA testing yet. The subject is…less than cooperative, and we didn't want to restrain him any more than necessary until you got here."

Travis was standing next to Bryan Rogan as the Marine updated her on the captive. According to Rogan, he was different from the villagers or the dead soldiers. The natives were the descendants of survivors of the Cataclysm, that much had been pretty well ascertained. Their physical deformities were the effects of mutations, probably passed down through the generations from those who'd survived the nuclear assaults but had suffered genetic damage from the intense radiation. Travis found the whole thing depressing, the idea of generation after generation of humans being born, and perpetuating the terrible damage done to their ancestors. But she had other problems on her mind now.

The soldiers were different from the villagers. They seemed to have less in the way of mutations, though still some, but they were so…altered…they barely looked human. Travis had seen

Marines in heavy combat gear, but the corpses she'd seen here hadn't been *wearing* all of their armor. Some parts of it had been implanted in their bodies, and they were a terrifying combination of man and machine, with a partial exoskeleton of some kind.

But the single prisoner was supposedly different. The image Rogan had showed her could have been of a member of *Dauntless*'s crew, and he was distinct from a normal person only in the seeming perfection of his physical characteristics. He was tall, his proportions close to the human ideal, and his posture was almost perfect. His teeth were utterly straight, his skin clear and blemish-free, and his eyes a clear bright blue. Travis didn't doubt the reports that said he seemed to be extremely intelligent.

"Well, Bryan, I guess there are a hundred things we need to deal with down here, but why don't we start with the prisoner?" She looked up at the Marine. "Do we have a translation AI and a linguistics expert up there?" It was redundant to have both a live and AI interpreter, of course, but the occasion was a momentous one, and she figured it made sense to have every resource available.

"Yes, Captain." Rogan hesitated, just for a few seconds. Then, he extended his arm, gesturing down the path. "This way. He's in one of the huts."

Travis nodded, and she waved her own arm forward, a signal for Rogan to lead the way. The two walked a short distance along a rough dirt road, passing between rows of the small, primitive shacks that seemed to be home to most of the natives. After sixty meters or so, Rogan slowed. There was a hut ahead, with a cordon of Marines holding back a crowd of the locals. The natives seemed restless…perhaps scared, she realized as she looked more closely. Some were on their hands and knees, crouched with their faces down to the ground, the tops of their heads angled toward the hut.

She shook her head. She'd read the reports about the primitives the landing party had found, but it still came as a surprise to her. Whoever these people were, they were the descendants of a technologically-advanced civilization, one that had colonized thousands of worlds. How could they have fallen so far, lost nearly all the knowledge and technology they'd once possessed?

She'd come up from the very bottom rungs of society herself, a penniless orphan on one of the worst industrial hellworlds in the Confederation. But, for all the vermin she'd known, rogues that would slit a child's throat to steal a half-eaten candy bar, she'd never seen anything like the people of this world. They looked like something from the distant past, from legends of man's pre-technology days on his long forgotten homeworld. Even beyond that, they looked…wrong…sick or injured in some way, though she knew that was their natural state, the inevitable result of their scarred and damaged DNA.

Rogan shouted a series of commands to the Marines up ahead, and four of them moved back toward Travis, positioning themselves between her and the crowd of locals. She glanced up at Rogan and nodded, and then she walked forward to the hut and slipped through the opening, pushing aside what seemed to be some type of animal skin acting as a makeshift door.

She stopped and looked across the room. Standing there, surrounded by several of the fleet's doctors and another four Marine guards, was a man. He looked like anyone on the fleet, at least to an extent, though there was something vaguely different about him. He appeared to be extremely fit, and his physical proportions were almost textbook. He was wearing what appeared to be a baggy pair of pants and a loose-fitting tunic, all apparently made of extremely fine fabric. He had been facing the nearest of her people, but as soon as she walked in, he turned to face her.

She returned his gaze and nodded, wondering if the gesture meant anything to her…guest. Then, she walked forward toward the translation AI, grabbing the headset and pulling it over her head. As she was still adjusting it, the man spoke.

She didn't know what he was saying, but the difference in his tone from that of the natives was astonishingly clear. His enunciation was far superior, and she could discern the haughtiness in his voice even while catching the meaning of only a few words.

She pulled out the small microphone extension from the headset and spoke to the AI. "What language is that? And translate what the subject just said."

"The language is almost flawless high imperial, Captain. The subject said, 'You will release me at once'…the final term is ambiguous. Creature, or worm. Or perhaps a variant on 'inferior.' An uncomplimentary term, certainly, one meant to show extreme disrespect."

Travis took a deep breath, holding back the anger she felt. She'd slapped down more than her share of arrogant fools in her life, and putting up with that kind of attitude was not something she considered among her primary skills. Still, there was too much at stake here, and she resolved to hold her temper.

Patience, Atara…patience…

"Translate," she said to the AI, then, "My name is Atara Travis. We mean you no harm. We just want to know who you are and where you are from."

The man glared back at her, and when he responded, his voice sounded, if anything, even more arrogant.

"I am a Master," the AI translated. "Why are you not on your knees, vermin? Do you wish death?"

This isn't going to be easy…

"We are not from here. I cannot speak to your customs, but my people do not prostrate themselves to anyone, regardless of rank or stature."

She waited as the AI translated her words, and then as the man responded and the unit repeated what he said.

"You are not Defekt. You are not Kriegeri or Arbeiter either. What are you? Where are you from? What is your purpose here?" A brief pause. "You are an invader. You will be destroyed unless you yield at once and accept the suzerainty of the Masters."

Travis shook her head, wishing for a moment she hadn't volunteered to come down in Barron's place. Her head was pounding. The captive was impossible, and his arrogance was overwhelming. He seemed to utterly ignore the fact that, whatever courtesies had been extended to him, he was, in actuality, a prisoner. Her prisoner. One she could shoot if she wanted to…

or, more easily, give the order to a dozen nearby Marines she imagined would be only too happy to obey after the losses they had suffered. But she wasn't here to pick fights, and certainly not to kill the only...Master...the landing party had found.

But it enraged her that the prisoner didn't even seem to consider the possibility that she would dare to take such an action.

"We are not invaders. We are explorers. If this world is yours, we will leave it peacefully. We did not intend to trespass."

"None of that matters, Inferior. I am a Master. Yet you presume to hold me captive, and you do not prostrate yourself before me. I will have you flayed alive for your insolence."

Travis *did* sigh this time. The conversation was going nowhere. *Whatever this...person...is, if he's representative of whoever is in charge out here...*

She felt her stomach clench. This wasn't going to go anywhere good.

"Captain Travis!"

She spun around. The voice was from one of the Marines outside the hut. "I'll be right back," she said hurriedly into the microphone, grabbing the headset as soon as she did and handing it to the Marine standing next to her.

She raced outside, her eyes darting back and forth, trying to see what was wrong. Then, she saw.

It was Bryan Rogan...on the ground, lying on his side and convulsing with some kind of seizure.

"Get a medic over here...now!" But even as she shouted, she saw one of the landing party's doctors rushing down the path toward the stricken Marine.

*   *   *

"We need more medpods, Admiral. We're up to twenty-one cases now, each with the same symptoms as Bryan."

Barron sat quietly in his office, listening to Travis over the comm. He'd been worried enough about the discovery, not only of survivors of the Cataclysm, but also of their markedly superior technology. And now his people on the surface were getting sick. The first report he'd received mentioned only Bryan Rogan, but it hadn't taken long for the follow ups to arrive, and for him to realize there was some kind of pathogen down on the surface, one that eluded all scans and analysis…and that had somehow affected Rogan and a number of others despite the fact that they'd remained on canned air the entire time they were on the planet.

"I'm sending another twenty immediately." The fleet had some provisions for supporting landing parties and ground teams, but he was already pulling units out of ships' sickbays to supplement the spare pods in the cargo holds. "I've ordered more taken from deep storage, and I think I can get at least another two dozen from the sickbays of the battleships…but that will take longer." He was talking about more pods than his people needed right now, he knew…several times as many. Neither Travis nor Barron had spoken the words, but they both knew they were dealing with an unfolding epidemic of some kind. He didn't have a doubt they'd need however many of the medpods he could get down there, and as quickly as he could land them.

There were more unsettling implications to that realization than Barron cared to think about. First among them was the plight of his people down there. With no details on contagion or concrete evidence on containing the spread of the—virus, bacteria, whatever it was…he didn't even know what was at play. He realized he couldn't allow any of the landing party personnel to come back aboard any of the fleet's ships, and that knowledge preyed on his thoughts. They were all trapped down there…at least until his med teams could get a concrete idea of what they were dealing with.

Atara was down on the surface. The thought of his friend trapped on the planet, at the mercy of some deadly disease, was eating at his control, a wave of despair trying to overcome the cold reason dictating his actions and decisions. He was worried about all his people, as he always was. But Atara had gone down in his place…and he'd allowed her to do it. It was his fault she was there, that she might end up dying of some horrible disease, even more than it was his fault all the others were there too.

"The med teams have requested more equipment to aid their research, as well. If you could expedite that, I'm sure it would be helpful."

"Of course. I'll see that it gets down on the next flight of shuttles. Anything else you need, call me directly, Atara. I don't want the research teams hampered by lack of resources."

"I will, Admiral." There was a short pause. Travis's tone was cool, professional, with no sign of the fear he knew she had to be feeling. It was typical of her, the inner strength that had made her such a capable officer, and the one person on *Dauntless* he'd always truly considered a replacement for himself. "We need to discuss the prisoner...and these dead soldiers. I don't know what it all means, but it's pretty clear we've stumbled onto something well beyond anything we expected." Another pause. "We need to be ready, Tyler...for whatever happens."

Barron took a deep breath and nodded, an ineffectual gesture since the connection was audio only and he was alone in the room. "What have you managed to get from the prisoner?"

"Nothing concrete. He's resisted any kind of comprehensive physical examination...and I've been hesitant to force him. If he resists, we might end up injuring him."

Barron nodded again, expressing his agreement with Travis's caution. They had no idea who their sole captive was, but it seemed likely he was a representative from a technologically advanced culture of some kind, one that had somehow survived the Cataclysm, or risen from its ashes...and the initial contact had, to that moment, been little short of disastrous. The fleet had not come all this way to find a new enemy, and rough treatment of the captive could only make things worse than they already were.

"No, don't force him. Not yet, at least. What have we been able to discern without his cooperation?"

"Well, he's human, of course...but there was never any doubt of that. We did manage to run some DNA scans, using a hair sample we recovered from his cell." She hesitated. "He's human, as I said, but..." Another silence. Barron suspected she was struggling to choose her words. "He's as close to genetically perfect as any specimen the med team has ever seen."

"Perfect?" Barron felt a discomfort he couldn't fully explain. It seemed a difficult word to assign to a human being's DNA, at least from a perspective of prevailing Confederation ethics and morality.

"Yes…our best guess, without examining him more closely, is that he's perhaps twice as strong as a normal man his size, possibly even stronger. His DNA profile appears to be absent almost every genetically-transmitted disease or weakness. Treading a bit further into speculation at this point, the team hypothesizes that he's extremely resistant to normal pathogens, that his vision and other senses are considerably keener than what we consider human norms, and that his muscle tissue is denser and more efficient than in a…normal…person."

"Are you saying he's some kind of superman?"

There was silence for a moment. Then, Travis said, "I wouldn't want to go there. Not yet, at least. But, it seems likely he's a very highly-functioning human being, free of many of the weaknesses that plague the rest of us. If we want to go a bit further, into the realm of wild guesses, the team feels he would likely have a life span considerably longer than what we perceive as a standard human range. Perhaps twice as long…or longer."

Barron sat quietly for a moment, considering what Travis was saying. Finally, he asked, "Is it possible he was the subject of some sort of genetic engineering?"

"That was my initial thought as well…but the team says no, at least not to the extent they can detect it. His DNA sequences appear to be completely natural. He just has most of the best and strongest gene combinations. More like…" She fell silent again.

"More like what, Atara?"

"More like an animal from a breeding program that utilizes optimal genetic matches…a racehorse bred from nothing but champions, for example."

"Eugenics. You're saying that wherever this…person…is from, his people manipulate human bloodlines to…improve…

the species." Barron was uncomfortable with the words even as
he said them. There was an undeniable logic to restricting repro-
duction to the most genetically ideal subjects, but it also went
against every principle of Confederation society and morality. It
was even difficult for him to think of people as genetically superior or inferior. He couldn't imagine the government, as little as
he cared for it or the politicians who ran it, telling ninety percent
of the population they couldn't have children because they were
genetically inferior.

But that didn't mean whatever civilization the fleet had just
found shared those belief systems. There was an arrogance that
made it easy to measure others based on one's own standards,
and Barron knew it affected him as much as anyone else. As
difficult as it was to escape his own prejudices, it wasn't really
that difficult to imagine a culture, very different from his own,
building a system of ethics around their own quest to improve
lifespans, eliminate disease, increase strength and intellect. Especially if their history was one of surviving an apocalypse that
nearly destroyed humanity and left most of those who remained
deeply scarred.

*If that's what we've found, it's going to complicate the prospect of peace-
ful relations, to say the least.* The Confederation and the Union, and
most of their neighbors, had spent at least half of the past century fighting each other, seeing each other as hateful enemies…
and *they* shared much of the same culture. A society based on
eugenics would be almost alien to the Rim nations…and no
doubt such people would feel the same about the Confederation, or the Alliance.

"It certainly looks that way, Tyler. What little communication I've been able to have with the captive, it's clear he considers himself superior to everyone else present, us included. And,
you have to see these soldiers. They're normal people, at least it
looks like they were, if tending to be a bit larger and stronger
than most, but what was done to them is…" She let the words
trail off.

"I've read the reports." He'd gotten a stack of updates on
the analyses of the soldiers killed in the fighting, from the medi-

cal teams and Rogan's people. The Marines liked to think of themselves as the best, but they'd suffered a loss ratio of more than two to one in their fights with the still-unidentified troopers, and that was in spite of having significant numerical superiority. "It's hard to imagine anyone letting someone…do that to them." The soldiers were human, or at least they had been at one time, but they had so much equipment attached to their bodies and implanted inside them, Barron would almost call them cyborgs.

"And the people who seem to be native to this world… clearly, they're the descendants of survivors who suffered mutations and genetic damage. From radiation certainly, but perhaps also from biological and chemical agents. The strange thing is…" She was silent for a moment. "…well, they seem to be familiar with the prisoner, and with the soldiers. They appear to be very concerned that we're holding the captive against his will, and there hasn't been a minute when there wasn't a crowd of them outside the hut, chanting, bowing, crawling around almost like…"

"Almost like they were worshipping the prisoner?" The intel Barron had seen all pointed to some kind of relationship between the villagers and the captive. He'd come up with a few thoughts on what that could be, and he didn't like any of them.

"Yes. Like they think he's a god…or something close to that."

Barron leaned back and rubbed his forehead. He'd faced death in battle more times than he could easily count, and he remembered the fear, the difficulty in deciding how to proceed in combat situations. But he'd never felt as unsure of what to do as he did now. He had his people on the surface analyzing everything possible, getting what little they could from the prisoner… but he knew they were all distracted now, worried that the mysterious illness spreading through the ranks would hit them next. Barron knew he had inadvertently inflamed their fears—and signaled that the problem was a very serious one—by terminating all return flights to the fleet. He'd even put the flight crews who'd piloted shuttles back and forth into quarantine, and ordered all future flights to drop cargo on one-way automated landing sleds instead of touching down. Whatever was ravaging his people down there, he couldn't let it spread to the fleet.

"Do what you can, Atara…and let me know how I can help. Anything you need. I mean *anything*." He felt the urge to call her back to *Dauntless*, to make an exception to the orders he'd imposed on the landing parties. But he knew he couldn't. He had to keep her there with the others, even watch her die if the med teams didn't find a way to defeat this new disease. He couldn't risk losing the entire fleet…or take the slightest chance of bringing a deadly plague back to the Confederation.

Chapter Twenty-Six

"You can see now, what I have told you is one hundred percent true, Senator. I don't know why Mr. Holsten has taken the action he has, but there's no doubt he has done it. Apart from the enormous costs of deploying a naval task force and a Marine division, the damage being done to Dannith's economy is staggering." Marieles stood with one hand on the railing, taking turns between looking at Senator Farrell and staring out over the pristine waters of the Crystal River. She suspected the waterway had been far less appealing a century and a half earlier, as Megara clawed its way out of the short dark age it had experienced after the Cataclysm. The planet had been an industrialist's dream then, with a focused obsession on production at all costs, and little regard for anything else.

Things had changed significantly, thanks to one hundred years of being the central hub of a prosperous and growing Confederation. She wondered how the factory workers on polluted Vespas or the indentured servants of Rogaloth would react if they could see what their sweat and toil supported. Troyus was a virtual paradise now, freed of the need to manufacture anything—save carbon dioxide from the endless chatter of Senators and other government officials.

"I understand your frustration, Desiree, and I assure you, I share it. I can also promise you that the Senate will not sit by and allow such a flagrant abuse of power go unchallenged. Confederation Intelligence has been far too unregulated for years now. That agency is, in my opinion, an ongoing threat to the liberty of our great Confederation, and the time has come to do something about it. We simply cannot allow…"

She reminded herself to listen…or at least to look like she was listening. She'd caught her mind wandering more than once in conversations with the longwinded Senator. It was all the more potent a reminder of how intensely boring the man was, since she was not the high-powered lobbyist she pretended to be, but a Sector Nine—*no, People's Protectorate*—agent. Her entire life had been spent humoring assets and marks, and the difficultly she'd experienced with Farrell spoke volumes of the inanity of the man's seemingly endless drivel.

"…tried for years to organize my colleagues to deal with…"

"Excuse me, Senator…I'm sorry to interrupt…" *But, if I don't, odds are I'm going to kill you and throw your body in the river.* "…but I'm afraid I have a rather pressing engagement elsewhere, one I cannot miss, as much as I wish we could continue this discussion."

"That's a pity, Desiree. I was about to suggest we might extend our conversation over dinner. I know of a very quiet spot not far from here. They have the most amazing…"

"I'm devastated that I must decline for now, Senator. As much as I would prefer to continue enjoying your company, sadly, work calls. I just wanted to get this latest…package…to you today, and I felt I needed to hand it to you directly."

"Thank you, Desiree. You are most kind…and conscientious. I understand the plight of your clients on Dannith, and I can promise you action. Quickly."

She smiled and nodded, though she suspected her definition of "quickly" and Farrell's differed significantly. She reached out, putting her hand on the Senator's arm and holding it there for a moment. The gesture wasn't overtly seductive, but was enough to make the politician think about it. "I trust we will find time for a more...productive...discussion soon, Barton."

"Soon, indeed, Desiree." The Senator leaned in toward her, but she pulled away first, somehow managing to look like she was driven by haste, and not pure revulsion for the Confed politician. Marieles was willing to do whatever was necessary to complete the mission, but if things went that way, she'd need to make sure she had an antiemetic on hand. She wasn't sure how much of her disgust was a reaction to Ferrell's physical unat-tractiveness and how much to the sheer idiocy he spewed every time his mouth opened. For now, she would get what she could through pure verbal manipulation. She'd worry about taking things further later, if and when it became absolutely necessary.

She turned and walked down the path parallel to the river. She *did* have other work to do—that, at least, was the truth. Farrell wasn't even a significant part of her original mission, but his position as vice-chairman of the committee overseeing Confederation Intelligence made him an ideal asset for her new secondary operation.

Her efforts to subvert the Confederation government had been going well, but by any measure, it was still a long-term plan, one of gradual destabilization. Turning the Senate on Gary Holsten...that was child's play by comparison, especially since half the sitting members of the body had engaged in past tiffs with the spy.

She knew Holsten had his own ways of keeping the Senate off his back, and after meeting so many of the august body's members, she could only imagine the grotesqueries which had ended up in the Confed Intelligence chief's private files. The list of those in that dossier included Ferrell, no doubt, and over-coming the Senator's fear of blowback from Holsten was the trickiest part of her assignment. She was working Ferrell, push-ing him as hard as she dared—and supplying him with writ-ten complaints from business owners and citizens on Dannith. Most of those were forged, but that was only because Holsten had been smart enough to cut off most communication from the embargoed planet. That was a short-term game for Holsten. It wouldn't keep things quiet long, and it only added to the actions that could be called abuse of power, but it would buy him some time.

Marieles had never minded lying to complete a mission. In fact, she didn't particularly differentiate between the truth and falsehoods. She thought more in terms of what those involved needed to hear, and she gave them that. She'd learned realities in her career that most people never managed to completely understand. A well-crafted, believable lie, for example, could be far safer and more useful than an unprovable truth. People constantly ruined themselves chasing after concepts of fairness and justice that didn't exist. She had long ago promised herself she would never be one of them.

She had an insurance policy on the Dannith operation, as well, a backup for the unreliable Senator's efforts. She'd assured Ferrell that everything she'd given him was confidential, and she'd promised to wait, to hold it all and let him proceed in his own way. Then, she'd almost immediately made sure all the information was leaked to the media and to half the other Senators in Troyus City. None of it could be traced to her, of course...at least she was pretty sure of that. But if Ferrell didn't move quickly, or if he allowed Holsten's dirty little file to deter him, he would be forced to take action when he started seeing news reports on the vid about the Dannith blockade. She'd even managed to line up some protests to start the next day, mostly professional rabble rousers who'd turned out to be quite a bit cheaper and easier to find on Megara than she'd expected.

The events on Dannith were unrelated to her Operation Black Dawn, but there *was* some potential crossover. If she could get Holsten in real trouble, perhaps even suspended from his role as head of the intelligence agency, it would wreak havoc on Confed counterintelligence efforts...just as she was putting Black Dawn into its final stages. And, if Holsten fought back as aggressively as she suspected he would, the Confederation's Senate would descend into an orgy of scandal and infighting... the perfect setting for Black Dawn.

The plan to destabilize the Confederation was enormously

complex, and there were countless ways it could be thwarted. Holsten in prison and his closest operatives scrambling for cover would create the perfect opportunity, and eliminate a good number of the potential sources of failure. Marieles knew quite well the rewards that would await her back on Montmirail if she succeeded.

She looked behind her, just a quick check to make sure she was out of Ferrell's sight, and then she stopped, turning again toward the river. It meandered from the government district through a neighborhood of exclusive shops, and, finally, to the base of Lantern Hill, where most of the Senators and the highly-paid lobbyists—including at least one fake one, herself—kept apartments. She'd come to Troyus City on a mission, but she still found herself surprised by its pleasantness and beauty. The metropolis outshone even Liberte City on Montmirail, and by several orders of magnitude.

She knew the capital was where the highest ranked of the elites were, and that the average Confed citizen never saw anything even remotely comparable to the wonders of Troyus. She was also well aware that many of the worlds of the Confederation's Iron Belt were industrial hells, populated by workers little better off than those of the Union. But, still, there was little doubt in her mind now that the average Confed lived a much better life than the near-sustenance level existence of vast majority of the Union's citizens. And, she understood even more acutely the importance of the propaganda machine that kept that information from the masses back home.

The same reality was one big reason why the Union had been unable to defeat its foe, she realized. For all the corruption and the poverty she knew existed on many worlds, most Confederation citizens felt some level of genuine patriotism. They believed their lives were better than they would be in another nation, and certainly in a place like the Union. The equivalent sentiment in the Union was a pale imitation, driven by blatant and repeated propaganda, and enforced by the deaths squads of Sector Nine…now, the People's Protectorate.

Another person might have come to the conclusion that she

was on the wrong side, that the Union was evil, and the Confederation good. Perhaps, for just a few seconds, something of the sort danced on the outskirts of her thoughts. But she was a creature of the Union, and she recognized where her path to wealth and power lay. She'd been a successful operative, and save for the past year and a half, she'd lived quite well on the fruits of her victories. She had long ago eradicated any weakness or moral quandaries that could interfere with the ruthlessness her own success required, and she recognized the importance of her current work. This was the true opportunity, the one that would lead her to the upper levels of the People's Protectorate, and potentially farther, perhaps to whatever body eventually replaced the old Presidium.

She smiled as she panned her eyes down the river banks, scanning one magnificent building after another. The Confederation was strong, there was no doubt about that. It had proven to be too mighty to defeat economically or militarily. But there were more ways to gain a victory, to destroy an enemy. Now she was going to kill it from the inside like a deadly cancer, invading its vital areas and destroying them one by one.

She would exploit their political divisions, use their corruption and decadence against them. She would turn them in on each other and watch them topple their own institutions in a mad frenzy to destroy each other. The Confederation's weakness was arrogance. They saw the troubles of nations all around them, civil war in the Alliance, revolution in the Union, and they believed such things couldn't happen to them.

She would show them they were wrong, that they were not immune to the sorts of upheavals that shook the other nations.

She would bring them the Black Dawn.

Chapter Twenty-Seven

"I need more samples. I don't care if you have to chase the locals through the woods and hold them down, but it has to be now." Stu Weldon was *Dauntless*'s chief medical officer, a position he'd held since the day Tyler Barron had taken command of the old *Dauntless*, and one he'd refused to give up, even when it had moved to a new ship bearing the name. Even when Barron had bumped him up in rank and gave him the added post of top sawbones of the entire fleet.

"Yes, Doctor Weldon." The assistant turned and raced off, away from the medpod Weldon was leaning over and out the small doorway of the hut. The shacks were filthy and dark, extremely poor raw material for a makeshift hospital, but they were all Weldon had, at least until the Marines finished putting up the prefab structures Barron had sent down from the fleet.

Weldon didn't like the readings on the pod…he didn't like them at all. Whatever was afflicting the landing party—and the number of victims had grown to over seventy now—nothing he'd tried had been even partially effective in slowing the progression of the disease. He'd started reviewing readings and data transmitted up to the fleet, until he'd thrown his hands in the air

208

at the difficulty of long-range analysis and stated unequivocally that he was going to the surface, and that no one was going to stop him. Barron tried, at least, but the admiral's legendary stubbornness had once more met its match in that of his chief surgeon. In the end, Barron had relented. Mostly, Weldon suspected, because Barron knew it was the best chance of getting somewhere on addressing the growing epidemic.

He hadn't lost any of the patients yet, but that was just because he'd put the worst of them in partial cryo-stasis. That number had risen to more than two dozen, and it had challenged the Marines and fleet support personnel hastily building infrastructure to keep up with his needs. The medpods used a fair amount of energy under normal circumstances, but activating the cryo systems really turned them into electricity hogs. The landing party was still on battery power, and it was going through fresh units as quickly as Barron could get more down to the surface.

The admiral had finally sent a portable fusion reactor, but moving something like that with shuttles required massive disassembly, and the corresponding need to put the thing back together. That was a complex job, especially when it was mostly a bunch of Marines working on it, following directions sent down from the engineering team on *Dauntless*. Weldon suspected many of the fleet's experts had volunteered to come to the surface, but he was just as certain Barron wasn't going to let anyone else down, not unless it was absolutely vital.

Weldon had managed to come to a few conclusions. First, whatever was afflicting the landing party, it was highly contagious, far more than any disease he'd ever seen. It could be transmitted by contact with the skin, even through clothing of a moderately protective nature. Anything short of sealed spacesuits did little to prevent the disease from infecting another host.

He'd come to a related conclusion, one he'd kept to himself, mostly because it would serve no purpose to pass it on. Its dissemination would only cause a panic, and cripple the ongoing work to get the landing party's infrastructure in place. But he was sure now, at least as certain as he could be. The pathogen at work was not natural. It had been engineered. It was a weapon.

"Doctor Weldon…"

He turned his head and looked back toward the doorway. It was one of the other doctors, and he knew immediately from her tone what she was going to say.

We've had our first fatality…

* * *

"Jake, thank you for coming. I imagine you're tired, and I'm sure another debriefing of sorts is the last thing you wanted to deal with right now." Barron stood up and walked around his desk, reaching out and shaking his chief pilot's hand.

"Of course, Admiral. I've never been the best at obeying orders, I guess, but there isn't a man or woman in uniform I respect more than you." It seemed odd to Stockton that Barron would thank him for coming, but then he caught the creases on the admiral's face, the dark circles around his eyes. He was sure he wasn't privy to everything that was going on, though he'd picked up enough to know the landing parties were stuck down on the planet, that Barron wasn't even allowing the resupply ships to land. He didn't know exactly what was happening, but he was sure it wasn't good. Now that he saw Barron's face up close, he understood just how much pressure the admiral was carrying around…and that meant things were even worse than he'd thought. Probably much worse.

"I appreciate that, Jake. It's a great comfort to me to have you in charge of our squadrons. You've fought it at times, but the truth is, you're a natural leader…and no one I've ever met knows better than you just what a pack of Lightnings can do."

"Thank you, sir." Jake forced a smile, but he found that Barron's stress was contagious. He'd seen the admiral face impossible situations before, but he'd never seen him look as lost as he did just then.

"Please, Jake…sit." Barron gestured toward one of the chairs, and he moved back around the desk, dropping hard into his seat. Stockton nodded and did the same, but he remained silent, looking across at Barron, waiting to see what he had to say. Why he'd been called to the admiral's office.

"Jake, I wanted to talk with you about those satellites. I read your report, and the reports of the other pilots involved in the operations. But, I wanted to be sure I understood everything." A pause. "It's important we have a good idea of what's happening. What may be coming."

"Well, sir…I don't know what I can tell you that wasn't in the reports. I picked up the signals, and the best I could get reads on them, they were heading to one of the transit points, the one we've designated Point Delta."

"Everyone seems convinced it was some kind of comm signal." Barron leaned back in his chair. "The prevailing guess is those things were part of some kind of still-functioning ancient imperial communications system. Much the same as the thoughts on the satellites we found in the previous systems."

Stockton could tell from Barron's tone, the admiral was far from convinced the "prevailing" wisdom was correct. Which was good, because Stockton didn't believe for a second those devices were old tech artifacts. The positioning was highly suspect, for one thing, the locations almost too perfect within the debris fields…debris fields that didn't exist when imperials would have placed them in orbit.

"I don't especially agree with those findings, sir."

"You think someone else put them there?"

"Yes, Admiral. But I have no idea who it could have been."

"I believe I do, Jake." Barron stared across the desk, his eyes fixed on Stockton's.

"Admiral?" The pilot returned the gaze, but he doubted he'd kept the confusion out of his expression.

"I'm going to tell you some things, Jake. What's going on down on the surface. What I tell you here is not to leave this room." Barron paused. "I'm afraid I'm going to need the best everyone has to offer in the coming days and weeks, and that includes you and your pilots. We came here as explorers, but I'm afraid we've found something far more dangerous than we'd expected. And, I'm not sure what to do."

Barron hesitated again, and then he filled Stockton in on everything that had happened on the planet.

* * *

"I want some answers from you." Weldon stared at the captive, his determination fueled by frustration over his inability to make any real progress on treating those afflicted by the epidemic.

"You are a medical *professional*, are you not?" The prisoner's every word dripped with arrogance. The emphasis he'd placed on the word "professional" was clearly derisive, something even the translation AI had managed to reconstruct as it repeated the Master's response for Weldon.

"Yes, I am," Weldon replied, keeping his voice even.

"You are, no doubt, among the most capable and intelligent of your expedition. You are clearly at a high range of capabilities among the Inferiors. Why don't you tell me what you believe is happening to your people?" The Master seemed calmer than he had before, as though he'd adapted to his situation. He still showed no signs of fear, but he seemed more…amused…than he had before.

"Okay…I'll play your game. Obviously, there is a pathogen on this world, one my people have never been exposed to, and for which they have little resistance."

"It is indeed a display of your weakness, of the inferiority of your people."

"Disease affects all people, especially a virulent agent like this one." Weldon found himself more affected by the prisoner's barbs than he'd expected to be.

"Does it? I am sixty-three imperial years old…" The AI couldn't translate the next term the Master used precisely. It offered "dog" and "vermin" as close substitutes. "I have never been what you would call…sick. Such is the fate of Inferiors, the Kriegeri and Arbeiter, and, of course, those who inhabit this world." He paused, clearly finding the whole thing amusing. "Yet, even the Defekts who work the mines here are immune from that which is destroying your people."

Weldon felt another angry response to the man's words, but it was deflected by the Master's disclosure of his age. He didn't look a day over thirty, and none of the scans the med teams had managed to conduct without actually examining the subject suggested anything different. He'd known the Master's genetic makeup showed few weaknesses, but he still found himself shocked at the practical effects of the man's DNA, in terms of apparent intellect, and now, aging as well.

"I need you to tell me everything you know about this disease. Is it familiar to you?" Weldon tried to push the revelation about the Master's age from his mind and focus on what he needed to know. Controlling the epidemic was the most important problem he faced.

"Why would I do that, Inferior? You have taken me prisoner, exhibited the audacity to treat with me without asking permission, denied me the respect one of your level owes to one of mine. I need only wait here until all of you are dead, and then I will again be free. The Defekts would not dare to hold me against my will, even though you have slain all my Kriegeri."

"We have an entire fleet in orbit, with…" Weldon caught himself. He was far from sure he should be sharing any information about the fleet with the prisoner. The Master was captive, of course, but it was beginning to look very much like his people would become enemies. "…with enough resources to send more people down to the surface."

"Unlikely. You have discovered, I suspect, despite your primitive science and limited analytical capacity…" The Master managed to make the insult sound matter-of-fact, like the declaration of an inarguable reality. "…that the agent at work is quite difficult to keep at bay, even with protective clothing and life support. Would your fleet, and whoever is in command, risk sending more of your people to the surface? Even fully-contained environmental suits would pose tremendous risks. The virus…and yes, it is a highly-engineered virus you are facing… was designed to facilitate contagion. It is capable of surviving considerable periods in space, even radiation-based decontamination procedures. And, it reproduces rapidly. A very small number, even a single virus surviving on an environmental suit, is likely to kill everyone on whatever ship it is brought aboard."

The Master paused and looked at Weldon, his expression something akin to a smile. "No, your commander will not dare to land more people to the surface, nor allow any of you already here to leave. So, all I need do is wait."

"Are you suggesting all of us will die?" Weldon wasn't as surprised as he imagined he sounded. He'd already considered the possibility of one hundred percent infection. He could call Barron for space suits, for life support habitats, but it wouldn't do much good. Everyone on the surface had already been exposed.

"Ah…you come to face the inevitable consequences of your own inferiority. You do seem to have some rudimentary intelligence, and some familiarity with tools and weapons of moderate technological complexity, but you lack the ability to resist the disease. It is called the Plague, by the way, and it was employed during the Troubles."

Weldon wasn't sure what the Master meant by "Troubles," but he suspected it was what was known at the Cataclysm among the Rim nations.

"You consider that an inferiority? Vulnerability to a disease designed to kill billions?"

"Do I appear to be infected, or even concerned? I am wearing no protective gear." The Master smiled, a grin that unsettled Weldon. "Even the Defekts, near-animals that they are—are immune. Yet, your people are dying. Such is the curse of your genetic frailty. Of course, that is inferiority. Nothing measures a being more than his or her genetic makeup. Your DNA has allowed you to master limited levels of technology, to imagine yourselves as something special in the universe—the top of your own small hill, so to speak—but now you see the true weakness of your people…and you have found your betters. Your masters."

Weldon struggled to hold back a burst of rage. He was astonished how effortlessly the Master could provoke him, without so much as raising his voice. But the discussion, frustrating as the prisoner could be, had not been in vain. Weldon knew he faced an uphill struggle in defeating the weaponized disease, but there was something useful in what the prisoner had said. Even the people he referred to as Defekts, clearly the unfortunate descendants of people who'd suffered terrible mutations, seemed to be immune.

Of course...they're all the descendants of survivors. All those who weren't naturally immune died out long ago...

He stood up, turning to leave the small hut.

"I will pity your death, Inferior. Among your rabble, you seem to be among the most capable. You would have made a fitting servant."

Weldon ignored the taunt. He didn't have time to argue with the prisoner. He could feel the itchiness, the discomfort on his arms and legs. The first symptoms of the disease.

He'd have to confirm it with a medical scan, but he didn't have the slightest doubt it would confirm he was infected.

He had work to do...and not much time left.

* * *

Barron sat on *Dauntless*'s bridge, which was what he still called the battleship's immense fleet control center. He was watching the members of his command crew at their posts, but his thoughts were with his people on the surface, with the prisoner and the strange natives of the planet...and with fruitless imaginings of what his fleet had found in the system. What lay out there, closer to the empire's old core. The expectations when the fleet left Megara had been based on finding old tech, and perhaps better information on the history of the Cataclysm. Now, he knew that history included other survivors, and that some of those, at least, were dangerous. He didn't know where that would lead, but the tightness he'd had in his gut for two straight days told him his instincts didn't expect anything good to come of it all.

He hadn't spent much time at the command station over the past few days. He'd classified everything that was happening on the surface at the highest levels, tried to keep as much as he could from spreading through the fleet. That had relegated him to his office, where he could have a degree of privacy unavailable in the control center, but now he realized most of those efforts had been pointless. It was hard to keep secrets in an outfit like the White Fleet, and even more so when he was stripping ships of medpods and imposing seemingly bizarre rules on the shuttles supplying the surface. He knew his people probably didn't know everything he did, but he was damned sure they knew something was wrong.

He was thinking about making a fleet-wide announcement, one that would explain all that had happened. He was about to order the comm officer to set up a line when Sonya Eaton turned toward him.

"Admiral, we're getting a transmission from the probes at transit point delta."

He turned and looked at his aide. "What is it, Captain?"

"Energy spikes, sir. It looks like we have ships transiting… and about to enter the system."

Barron felt as though he'd had the wind knocked out of him. There was no chance any Confederation vessels were coming through that point…none at all. And that meant…

"Bring the fleet to battle stations, Captain. Prepare to scramble fighter squadrons on my order."

"Yes, Admiral." Eaton was one of the very few privy to everything that was happening on the planet. She seemed calm, though Barron suspected that was an exercise in self-control and not any absence of fear and tension she was feeling.

He looked at the display, watching, waiting, even as *Dauntless*'s battle stations lamps bathed the entirety of the great control center in a soft red glow.

He was still focused on the display when ships started coming through the point, one after the other.

Chapter Twenty-Eight

"No further transits, Admiral. Fourteen ships total. The four in the front appear to have greater masses and densities, as well as significantly higher energy outputs. If I had to guess, I'd say they were warships of some kind, probably escorts for the others."

Barron nodded, but didn't respond. Sonya Eaton was serving her own role, and shouldering much of the burden of commanding *Dauntless*, and she was doing a magnificent job, by any objective standard. But she failed in one critical area. She wasn't Atara Travis.

He knew he did Eaton a disservice by comparing her to Atara Travis, but he couldn't help it. Travis had been at his side in every desperate battle he'd fought, and the two had long been synced together as a team. He'd have sworn they'd communicated telepathically during those terrible fights, and he felt naked going into a situation as crucial and dangerous as this one without her on the bridge.

"All ships are to remain at battle stations and hold their positions. No one is to fire or launch fighters without my express orders."

"Yes, Admiral."

The warrior inside Barron was screaming to deploy his ships for battle, to advance until his primaries were in range…and certainly to get his squadrons launched and ready for battle. But he wasn't just Admiral Barron now. He was the Confederation's ambassador to a new and mysterious power. His actions—or inactions—could prevent a war. Or start one, against an enemy that was almost a total mystery. About the only thing he knew was they had superior technology. Were they as big as the Confederation? Just a few systems? Or ten times the size of all the Rim nations combined?

His nerves were raw, and his thoughts drifted to the reports on the interrogation of the prisoner. The man's attitude didn't support a conclusion that whoever was in those approaching ships was friendly. But whatever chance there was to prevent hostilities, he knew he had to take it.

"Updated scans, Admiral. It definitely appears the lead vessels are warships. The AI has identified the other ten as freighters of some kind."

"Very well, Captain."

Of course. It all started to make sense, and to match the reports he'd gotten from the surface.

Those people on the ground, the ones they call Defekts…they work the mines. And these ships are here to pick up the ore, and drop off some token goods in return. That's how the natives have clothing that's manufactured.

Barron thought about it as trade, but only for a few seconds. It wasn't anything close to legitimate commerce. The Masters, whoever they were, ruled over the inhabitants of the planet, using technology to set themselves up almost as gods to be worshipped and obeyed. And they sent the locals into the mines without proper equipment or protective gear, giving them tokens like cheap clothing and manufactured food products in return for the priceless ores their sweat and blood produced.

The Defekts are expendable to them. They don't care how many die in the mines, as long as the ore flows.

He shook his head. He found the whole thing to be reprehensible…but the more he thought of the prisoner's attitude, of his casual, almost natural, feelings of superiority, he began to see the perverse logic in it all.

They think of these people as animals…or at least something very close to that.

He took a deep breath. That explained everything. The pyramid was a command post of sorts, to keep an eye on the locals and make sure they were keeping up with their production quotas. Any failure, any resistance, could be easily punished by sending out a few of the soldier types, the Kriegeri, and massacring as many as it took to restore obedience.

They probably didn't have to do even that very often. A light show or something around the pyramid would probably be enough to dazzle and terrify the locals.

His realizations only dragged down his mood. The people he was describing to himself didn't seem to be good material for likely allies, or even benevolent neighbors. Deep down, Barron knew his people faced a fight…but, still, he couldn't start it. He had to stay the course, hope beyond hope for a peaceful solution.

"Put me on a line to the lead enem…unidentified…ship. Patch in translation AI set for high Imperial." Barron actually spoke a little of the ancient imperial tongue, a benefit of the eclectic education he'd received as the scion of a wealthy and powerful family. But he didn't think his patchy and rough attempts at getting a message across in the old language were likely to aid the cause of diplomacy.

"You're live, Admiral. AI active."

"Attention approaching vessels…" He second-guessed himself, wondered if his tone was too hard-sounding. "This is Admiral Tyler Barron, commander of the White Fleet. We are representatives of the Stellar Confederation and the Palatian Alliance, on a peaceful mission of exploration. We have no hostile intent, and if we have encroached on your space, it was purely by accident."

He sat in his chair, bolt upright and as tense as he'd ever been. A response now could open the road to peace…or start a war right then and there.

There was nothing. Silence. *This is not good…*

Barron sat still, his eyes darting from one side to the other, watching the crew of the control center at their posts. There was no chatter, no sounds save those from the equipment. He felt as though he were falling, as if a darkness had come to take him. His grandfather was the hero of the Second Union War, the man the history texts say saved the Confederation. *And I will go down in history as the one who went out and found a deadly new enemy…another war and countless more dead…*

Suddenly, the comm unit crackled. A voice blared out, firm, cold.

"Attention, invaders. You have entered the space of the Hegemony. This is an Act of War. You will yield at once, power down your ships, and prepare to be boarded…or you will be destroyed."

Barron was struck by the casual sense of superiority evident in every syllable uttered by the speaker. He was stunned as well by the sheer audacity on display. These people—the Hegemony, apparently—did seem to possess superior technology, but could they possibly think their four warships could take on the entire White Fleet? It seemed absurd.

Could they be so certain of their own superiority?

Barron couldn't imagine the kind of confidence run wild that could fuel such an attitude. But, he knew if these people wanted a fight, they would get one. Almost every man and woman in his fleet was a veteran of six bloody years of war. They had seen friends die, stood to their posts in the midst of battle, faced enemy forces that outnumbered and outgunned them. To Barron's way of thinking, no four ships in the universe could defeat his fleet.

He reached up to his headset and flipped the small switch, activating the transmitter. "I repeat," he said, knowing in his gut there was no point. "We are not invaders. We are peaceful explorers, and our encroachment into your space was accidental."

"You have thirty seconds to surrender, Inferior. Then, you will be destroyed." There wasn't a bit of hesitation in the voice.

Barron turned toward Eaton. "All ships are to hold position. If there's going to be a fight here, we're not going to start it. All squadrons are to prepare for launch...but they will remain in the tubes until I give the order...understood?"

"Yes, Admiral." Eaton activated her own headset and transmitted Barron's orders.

He looked up at the display, wondering if the Hegemony commander was bluffing...or if he'd so casually start a war against people that had to be as much a mystery to him as he and his were to Barron. He wanted to believe it was posturing, that a commander of such a small force wouldn't take that kind of step against a superior force that offered peace.

He wanted to believe that. But he didn't.

His eyes were fixed on the approaching ships. They were still several light seconds away, a good bit out of range, even of Barron's primaries. They hadn't launched any fighters yet, and he wondered how they would make good on their threat when they were still so far out.

He didn't have to wait long for his answer.

His eyes were fixed on the chronometer, and the thirty second countdown Eaton had activated when the Hegemony officer made his threat. It was moving down. Three...two...one...

Nothing happened, not for a few seconds. Then the screen lit up, energy readings from the approaching ships, almost off the chart.

Eaton spun around, and Barron could see in her eyes what he'd just caught on his screen.

"It's *Formidable*, sir...she's been hit by some kind of beam. Captain Fitzgerald reports heavy damage."

Barron's eyes were still on the screen. Even as Eaton reported on *Formidable*, two more of his ships took hits.

Two things hit Barron like a sledgehammer. First, his people were at war again.

And, second...the enemy's guns massively outranged his own fleet's weaponry.

* * *

Atara Travis walked across the open space in the center of the village. It was a common of some sort, she imagined, though exactly what the small, muddy section of ground was good for eluded her. She'd found it difficult to accept that people actually lived the way the natives did, without any technology, save for the mining tools and rough clothes the Masters deigned to supply to their…she didn't finish the thought, but her anger flared anyway. She'd come from the bottom rungs of society, and she'd known poverty so intense that she'd rummaged through garbage for something to eat…but the idea of allowing people, victims of a war fought centuries before, to exist in such a primitive state, digging with hand tools through radioactive mines until the exposure killed them, fueled her growing anger, even hatred, for the people who called themselves *Masters*.

She turned and glanced back to the hut where their prisoner from that group sat quietly, engaging in short discussions with the various experts trying to learn more about him. She tried to imagine a ship full of such people. And entire fleet.

Travis was frustrated. She understood Barron's orders and the reasons for them, but part of her wanted to grab the obnoxious fool and beat all the information they needed from him. He'd been rude and arrogant in verbal exchanges, but he hadn't given up any information the teams hadn't already known. She wondered how someone with such a high opinion of his standing would hold up under a real interrogation. She'd fought the Union for years, learned to hate them with a passion…but she occasionally envied them the unrestrained tools at their disposal. Sector Nine wouldn't put up with this piece of shit and his nonsense. They'd throw him on a rack…and he'd be lucky if his refusals to submit to a medical exam didn't get him dissected.

The usual crowd of villagers was gathered around the hut. They hadn't dared to try to rescue the Master—*no doubt, they think we're some kind of rival gods, and they're afraid to provoke us, too*—but they remained outside the makeshift prison, chanting and singing and in between, looking generally mournful.

Watching the people practically worshipping beings who left them in such a pathetic state was throwing fuel on the fire of her anger. She'd have called Barron and done her best to argue for more aggressive methods…except she understood the same thing he did. Any wrong move could easily drag the Confederation into a new war, against an unknown and apparently very advanced enemy.

If there's any way to avoid that now…

Travis tended toward the pessimistic, and as she thought about it, she realized she'd already decided war was inevitable. She just wasn't sure she'd last long enough to fight it.

The infection rate from the virus seemed to be one hundred percent, or something very close to it. Most of the landing party was showing symptoms, and she figured she had two days, maybe three, before she wouldn't have any Marines left standing to guard the prisoner or the shuttles.

She'd watched helplessly as everyone around her fell sick, first with the relatively minor early symptoms, and then fever and delirium, before they finally ended up in cryostasis…and, for thirty-seven of them so far, death.

But *she* was fine, at least so far. She hadn't had a sign of the disease, and except for some fatigue and stress, she felt great. She suspected it was a matter of time, and each day she expected the onset of symptoms. But the days passed, and she remained healthy, even as the people around her got sicker and sicker.

Doc Weldon was still on his feet, though she knew he shouldn't be. Weldon was sick, his body ravaged by the deadly disease. She didn't dare to think about what variety of drugs—and in what massive doses—he injected himself to keep moving. The long-term effects of such heavy dosing had to be considerable, but she supposed that didn't matter if there *was* no long-term. Weldon was the best candidate to find a cure, and when he finally lapsed into the coma that had taken so many others, it would pretty much seal the fate of the rest of the landing party. The scientists on the fleet were working around the clock too, but Weldon was incredibly gifted, and he was on site. If he couldn't find a solution, it was doubtful anyone else would, at least not quickly enough. The doctors still aboard ships might figure the whole thing out eventually, but that would be far, far too late.

"Captain Travis…we just got a communique from *Dauntless*." The officer's voice was shrill, and it didn't take much listening for Travis to realize the news wasn't good.

"What is it?" she said, letting more of her frustration slip into her tone than she'd intended.

"There are ships entering the system from transit point delta. They've attacked the fleet."

Travis moved toward the officer, and the hut the landing party had turned into a makeshift comm center. She had to get as many details as she could.

Not that she could do anything about…anything.

Travis was a fighter, and her place was on *Dauntless* as the ship—*her* ship—went into a fight. The frustration hitting her was intense, almost overwhelming.

The war she'd expected had come…and she was stuck down on a shithole planet, wallowing in the mud and waiting for a deadly plague to take her…while her people, her ship—Tyler—went into battle.

* * *

"All ships are to advance at maximum thrust." Barron snapped out the order, almost instinctively. The enemy weapons were longer ranged than his own, and they had surprising hitting power, even so far out. His ships were sitting ducks at this distance. He was used to having the range advantage, and he knew exactly how well it could be used, even by an outnumbered force. He had to get them into primary range…now.

"Yes, Admiral. All ships, maximum thrust."

He leaned back, expecting the usual hard push from the thrusters. He was still surprised every time *Dauntless*'s upgraded force dampeners kicked in and absorbed most of even the ship's massive maximum thrust. The new units were not only stronger than the old ones, cutting out as much as 12g of force, they were faster, too. The old ones always kicked in late, which meant a couple seconds of enduring the full force of the engines. Now, it was an almost imperceptible delay, one that manifested as a strange feeling that was already gone by the time the brain processed it.

His eyes darted to the display every few seconds. The enemy ships—he'd been correcting himself every time he'd called them that, but there seemed little point now—had fired only their first volley. That gave him some hope. Their weapons were longer ranged than his, and they seemed to have more hitting power, too, a problem that would probably become more severe once the ships were closer. But, it also looked like they needed time to recharge before firing again.

"Fleet order…all squadrons, launch."

"Acknowledged, Admiral. All squadrons launch." Eaton repeated his order on the fleet comm, and no more than a few seconds later, *Dauntless* shook gently, the effect of the distant launch catapults sending his ship's fighters into space. He imagined Stockton had been the first one out, or damned close to it, and he would have bet his fighter commander was already on the comm, badgering the launch crews on the other ships to pick up the pace. Commanding Stockton hadn't always been an easy job, but Barron was pleased to see how his wild fighter jock had matured into his command position. He knew Stockton hated it, at least on some levels, but he was certain the legendary Raptor would get better performance from his fighters than anyone else could. He was legend, to young pilots and veterans, and Barron knew they would follow him anywhere.

Even into the unknown, to fight a new enemy.

"All ships report launch operations underway, sir." A short pause. "*Dauntless* launch control reports all squadrons launched, Admiral."

Barron turned toward the display, just as the enemy ships opened up with their second barrage. *Formidable* took another hit, and he could see from the reports streaming down his screen that the battleship had taken considerable damage. Her thrust was down to sixty percent, and it looked like she was experiencing sporadic power outages. Another two of his ships had also been impacted by the long-range beams. The enemy was scoring hits with roughly half their shots, which was an astonishing rate at such a long range.

"All ships, increase evasive maneuvering. Institute nav plan beta-2."

"Nav plan beta-2, sir."

He'd designed beta-2 himself. It cut the effective forward acceleration of his ships somewhat, but it would give the enemy AIs something to think about, and maybe reduce the effectiveness of their targeting.

He watched as the range counted down. The enemy fired a third time, and then a fourth. His evasive maneuvers had helped, cutting the enemy's accuracy to less than twenty-five percent. He wondered if that would last...or if the targeting computers out there were sophisticated enough to adjust. He wasn't going to take that chance.

"All ships...switch to nav plan beta-2."

"Yes, Admiral."

Barron felt *Dauntless* lurch hard as the new nav plan took effect. He didn't have many rookies aboard *Dauntless*, or the anywhere in the fleet for that matter, but he suspected the ones he did have would see their stomachs put to the test by the wild gyrations. Possibly some of the old timers, too.

He reached out and put his hands on his chair's armrests, an instinctive reaction to the ship's hard bouncing. His eyes remained focused on the range counter.

"All ships, reduce forward thrust to thirty percent. Arm primaries."

"Yes, sir."

The fleet was almost in range. The primary batteries were energy hogs, and he had to cut thrust to get them charged. The guns were potent—perhaps not quite as strong as the enemy's weapons appeared to be, but they would send the message they were intended to send.

Whoever was out there might call themselves Masters...but they weren't the only ones who knew how to fight.

And they didn't have any monopoly on deadly weapons either.

Barron watched the chronometer and the range finder. One by one the comms came in from the fleet, his ships reporting their primaries were armed and ready.

Barron's eyes were fixed on the display, watching as the range dropped. He waited as the numbers slipped into the range band of the primaries. He paused few more seconds, counting down from the last enemy shot, getting as close as he could before the attackers fired again. Then, he turned toward Eaton and nodded.

"Captain…all ships, fire."

Chapter Twenty-Nine

PUV Carcajou
Approaching Barroux
Rhian System
Union Year 219 (315 AC)

"All ships report weapons fully-charged and ready to engage, Admiral."

Andrei Denisov sat in his command chair, trying with all his ability to look calm, ready. He was a veteran, one of the few Union officers who'd distinguished himself in the disastrous war against the Confederation. He'd always been a confident commander, cool and professional under fire. But he'd never led more than a single ship in battle. He appreciated the massive promotion Gaston Villieneuve had given him, but now he was worried it had taken him too far, too fast. He had two-dozen vessels under his command, about to go into what he knew would be a vicious fight. And that didn't count the huge armada of transports on the other side of the transit point, waiting to invade Barroux after his fleet blasted the orbital defenses to scrap.

He stared at the screen in front of him, at the scanning data scrolling slowly by. He'd sent in a cloud of probes to back up his ships' sensors, and now he was getting his first good read on the planet's defenses. The fortresses were there, as he knew they

228

would be. And something else, too. Small contacts, clustered between the orbital forts.

It took a while to get a solid read on what they were. Some kind of laser platforms or buoys. That was unexpected, and it meant Barroux had a lot more firepower than he'd expected… and he'd already been worried about the forts.

He felt the urge to withdraw, to return to Montmirail and report that the rebels had somehow increased the planet's fortifications, and they were now too strong to assault without a much stronger force. But no stronger force was available, nor would they be for quite some time. And Gaston Villieneuve wanted Barroux pacified, now. It was likely just as dangerous— and maybe more so—to return home empty handed as to take a chance and assault the planet's defenses.

"The fleet is to institute maximum evasive maneuvers, starting now." His ships were still out of range of the fortress guns, and a quick review of the mass of the laser buoys suggested they would have a somewhat shorter target zone. But he wasn't taking any chances. Any way he looked at it, his fleet was going to pay a heavy price, and whatever he could do to lessen the damage until his ships were in range was worthwhile.

There was no choice. They had to go in…and that meant there was no point worrying about anything but attacking with all the skill and ferocity he could dredge up.

"All ships, increase thrust to maximum. We're going in."

*   *   *

"We've got to do something, Mike. We can't be a part of this. These people are worse than the Union. My God, they're more brutal than Sector Nine."

Mike Hoover sat quietly, listening to Silvia Breen. She was upset, and he thought it might help her to get it all off her chest. It was the least he could do, because he knew what she truly wanted was out of reach.

"Sil," he finally said, his voice as calm as he could manage, "you know our orders, and you know why we're here. Caron and his people are reprehensible, but we didn't come to liberate the workers of Barroux. We're here to put a thorn in the Union's side, and that's our only concern." He didn't feel good about what he was saying. He was as torn and guilty about aiding such ruthless totalitarians as Breen. But that didn't change their orders. Or the fact that there was little or nothing they could do to interfere, even if they wanted to.

"So that's it? We're just following orders? Do you think Director Holsten would even want us to prop up such a horrific regime if he knew the truth?"

Hoover didn't answer the question. He knew Holsten better than Breen did, and he'd served him for longer. He didn't know what the director of Confederation Intelligence would do or say if he'd been there, but he was far from sure Holsten would have changed anything. The Confederation had been fighting the Union for a century, and millions had died in those recurring conflicts. It was hard to see the workers of Barroux so victimized…but Hoover knew his allegiance—and Breen's—belonged to the Confederation and its people, first and foremost. And, he was sure that was exactly what Gary Holsten would have told them if he'd been there.

Finally, Hoover looked over at his number two. "Sil, I understand how you feel. I feel that way, too. But what, exactly, do you think we could do for these splinter rebels, even if we wanted to? Assisting Caron and his killers with holding Barroux helps the Confederation—it preserves the peace, or at least extends it. Nothing we can do for Bernard and his people is going to change a thing here. We don't have troops, we don't have any significant cache of weapons…we don't even have enough agents to conduct proper intelligence operations. If we tried to help the resistance, we'd only weaken the planet's defenses…and blow our mission."

Breen looked like she was going to argue again, but she just slouched backward and let out a long, loud breath. "I know you're right, Mike…but this is the first time I've thought of myself as one of the bad guys."

Hoover didn't know what to say. She wasn't wrong, though

perhaps her view was a bit naïve. War was a deadly business, and, while he knew Caron and his minions were evil to the core, he also had an idea how many of his own people had died in four wars against the Union. If helping Caron hold onto Barroux a little longer did the Confederation some good, so be it. He felt sorry for the workers of Barroux, but his own people came first. Always.

Besides, Barroux wouldn't hold out forever, no matter what he and his people did. One day, the Foudre Rouge and Sector Nine would land…and Remy Caron—and Ami Delacorte and the rest of his bloodthirsty mob—would get theirs.

Oh yes…if he knew anything about Sector Nine, or whatever they were calling themselves now, Caron and his cronies would get every bit of what was coming to them.

* * *

Rene Valours moved slowly around the outside of the building, pressed against the cold, masonry walls. He was one of Ami Delacorte's people, one of the first agents in her Protectors of the Revolution. He'd distinguished himself early, hunting down and disposing of more of the revolutionaries on the proscribed list than anyone else. Remy Caron had given the actual orders, but Valours had seen Delacorte's fingerprints all over the plan, even as he did his part to see it executed. And he saw her influence on Caron in this operation as well.

He turned and glanced back behind him. He had a dozen and a half Protectors with him, some experienced, others less so. The agency was still in its early stages, and the repeated purges to remove…unreliables…had slowed its growth. There were maybe three of the eighteen he'd have chosen, given better selection.

Ideally, he'd have worked alone, but that wasn't possible here. He knew that well enough. This job had to be done quickly… and completely. He was here to kill the Confeds, all of them, and he didn't want to think of the consequences of failure, or even partial success. There couldn't be any survivors, Delacorte had been extremely clear about that, and he also had to make sure it looked like the fringe rebel groups had done it. Valours tended not to think about the politics behind the killings he handled, but it was impossible not to grasp the sensitivity of murdering a couple dozen Confeds.

He reached down and pulled the small comm unit from his belt. He'd already signaled base, advising them his people were in position. Now, he was waiting for the final go-ahead.

He tightened the grip of his other hand around the old, battered rifle. He had far better weapons back at headquarters, inheritances from the Union forces that had once ruled the planet, but he wasn't taking any chances on this mission. The splinter groups he intended to blame for the killings—at least for Confederation consumption once contact was reestablished—generally had to make due with far less advanced weaponry. That meant his team had to make do with the junky garbage their intended scapegoats used.

He moved forward a few steps, standing near an air vent. He could hear talking—the Confeds, he was sure—but he couldn't make out what anyone was saying. His general opinion on questions of whether to kill someone was, why not? There was no reason to take chances, and letting some go was always a chance. If a mistake was made, better to kill a few innocents than allow one problem to escape...and become larger, more dangerous. But killing Confeds made even a stone-cold killer like him nervous.

It was time...no, it was past time. He looked down at the small comm unit, raised the hand that held it up to his head, tapping his earpiece. There was a burst of static, but still nothing.

On any other mission, he would have gone in anyway, without confirmation...but taking out the Confeds was a heavier load than he wanted on his shoulders alone. He would wait.

Another minute passed, then two. He started to get edgy. *Something is wrong...*

He turned again, looking back at his team. They were impatient, too. They were in a back alley, but the delay was endangering the mission badly. All it would take was one drunk wandering into the alley, looking for a place to take a leak or sleep off a bender. Any noise could tip off the Confeds, and Valours didn't have the slightest doubt they could defend themselves given any warning at all. He was here for a quick mass execution, not to start a firefight. One Confed escaping and eluding pursuit long enough to get a message back home…and the consequences could be dire.

He was about to give the order without confirmation, to wave his people forward and get the job done. Just as he extended his arm, his earpiece crackled loudly, and Ami Delacorte's voice filled his ears.

"Abort. Repeat, abort. We're under attack by a Union fleet. Return to base at once. I repeat, abort…"

* * *

"Open fire, all ships." Denisov glared forward, eyes fixed on *Carcajou*'s main screen. There was a smoky haze floating across the bridge, and his eyes were red, stinging. The orbital defenses had outranged his ships—that hadn't been a surprise. What had been unexpected was the strength of those installations. There were over a hundred laser buoys supporting the bases, and they were tearing his ships apart.

He watched as his vessels finally got to return fire. He'd ordered all batteries to focus on the forts…the lasers were just too small to effectively target at long range. But the buoys were ripping into his ships, doing as much damage as the fortresses. Possibly more.

He scanned the info streaming across the display, his eyes moving from one platform to another, trying to determine if one was the headquarters of the orbital forces. He couldn't explain all the added firepower, but he was still willing to bet that whoever was crewing those things were mostly novices, revolutionaries who'd hurriedly figured out how to operate the planet's defense grid, perhaps aided by a few prisoners or turncoats from the original crews.

His mind raced, wondering how he could turn inexperience

against his adversaries. Even as he considered his options, *Carcajou* shook hard, and a shower of sparks flew across the bridge. He swung his head around, his eyes finding the overloaded panel. It wasn't a vital station, and none of his people on the bridge seemed to be injured. It would take another half minute at least for damage control reports to flow in from the rest of the ship.

This isn't going to work, he thought, just as he heard his bridge officers shout out a cheer. One of the forts had been bracketed between three of his approaching vessels, and a shot from one of them took it in a critical area. There had been a moderate explosion, and a blast of escaping gas from one section of the hull…but now, perhaps half a minute later, the entire thing vanished in a thermonuclear explosion.

The celebration was short-lived, however. Denisov's ships had taken a beating just getting into range, and now all the fire from the platforms and the laser buoys was blasting away at his entire fleet. *Vipere* went first, in an explosion no less dramatic than that which had accompanied the fortress's demise. Then *Guerrier* sent out a code black transmission. The ship didn't disappear in the fury of a thermonuclear explosion, but there was no response to any efforts to communicate, nor any detectable energy output. Denisov knew that the ship was a wreck, and that her entire crew was likely dead.

He watched as another of the fortresses succumbed, reduced to a useless hulk like *Guerrier*, a shattered and holed hull remaining in its place. His ships were targeting the laser buoys as the range decreased, and they'd taken down about ten of the weapons. But the return fire was taking its toll.

Denisov knew what defeat would mean. It had taken Villeneuve nearly two years to scrape up enough ships to mount a credible assault on the rebellious planet. He wasn't likely to be terribly understanding to an admiral who'd gotten that relentlessly-assembled fleet shot to pieces with nothing to show for it all. But Denisov had always been very analytical, able to follow a battle moment by moment and project such things as loss ratios and expected damage rates forward. And that skill was telling him one thing, no matter how he tried to look at it.

His force wasn't going to make it. They would damage the planet's defensive array, probably badly. But there would be enough of it left to repel the troop transports…and his ships would be spent, destroyed or crippled. All the rebels needed to do was hang onto enough orbital strength to keep the troops from landing, and they would retain control of the planet…and of the factories they appeared to have somehow repurposed to build additional defenses.

Worse, if he didn't pull out *now*, there would be no turning back. He could get his fleet out now, at least he thought he could. But, he didn't have much time. Delaying, even for a few minutes more, would make a choice just as certainly as giving an order now.

"All ships…reverse thrust. The fleet is to withdraw."

There was a pause. Then, his tactical officer responded, uncertainty in his voice. "Mmm…yes, sir." Denisov wasn't the only one with an idea of how Gaston Villieneuve would respond to the fleet returning without completing its mission.

But Denisov had no intention of heading back to Montmirail in failure and disgrace. A frontal assault wasn't going to get the job done…but that didn't mean there weren't other options. He had to find another way to cripple the enemy defenses, and the spark of an idea was forming in his mind. Villieneuve wanted the rebellion on Barroux crushed, but Denisov knew the Union's ruler didn't particularly care about collateral damage.

Even a *lot* of collateral damage.

Chapter Thirty

"Squadron leaders, you're responsible for keeping your people in formation. We've got four targets, and we're going in one after another, like a pile driver. Bombers on the inside, interceptors outside. These bastards haven't launched yet, but it could happen any second, so be ready for anything." Stockton was in his cockpit, feeling edgy, even scared...but also disturbingly at home. He'd rejoiced at the end of the Union War as enthusiastically as any spacer in the fleet, but sometime in the two years since, he'd come to accept that a part of him deep down craved war...even needed it. It was, in a sense, his natural habitat, and as much as he craved peace, he was out of place when he got it. There was nothing in the universe he did as well as killing people with his fighter. Nothing he would *ever* do as well.

Four targets seemed like a pathetically small force for the hundreds of fighters he was leading, but he'd seen the enemy's weapons, and the damage they were doing to the Confederation's largest and toughest battleships. He could only guess what their fighters could do...or what deadly close-in defenses those ships had ready to blast his ships to atoms.

He shoved his arm to the side, angling his thrust to bring his ship around. He didn't have a place in the attacking formation, at least not a formal one. He was in command of the whole shooting match. He'd been the fleet's strike force commander since the expedition had left Megara, but this was the first combat situation. He hadn't expected to see his fighters engaged in an actual battle during the mission, at least nothing more than facing off against some leftover old tech that was still functioning…but here they were, about to go in against a group of ships that were ravaging the fleet, killing its people. If that wasn't war, Stockton didn't know what was.

His instinct was to link up with the weakest of the four columns moving in against the enemy ships…but there was no weakest. He'd handpicked almost the fleet's entire strike complement, and save for a small contingent of rookies—themselves the pick of the newest class—he had the cream of the Confederation's fighter corps with him. They didn't need his help to take on four enemy ships no bigger than small cruisers.

He found himself heading toward the end grouping, the one that included the Alliance pilots. He didn't expect any problems between the now-allied forces. His veterans had fought alongside the Palatians at the Bottleneck, and they'd seen just how good the Alliance pilots were. But, if there was any place in his powerful formation that called for his presence, it was there. The Alliance and Confederation were allies now, but their pilots had different flying styles, and the Palatians' rigid structure of honor and conduct sometimes made the fit between the two sides a bit of a rough one.

Besides, he felt he owed it to Jovi Grachus to watch over the Palatians. His thoughts often drifted to the Alliance pilot, even two years after her death. His recollections were painful, memories of his anger and hatred toward her clashing with the regret he now felt at her death. It was only after she was gone that he'd realized just how similar the two of them had been.

Suddenly, the chatter on the comm line increased, pulling his thoughts back to the present. Stockton's eyes flashed down to the small screen on his fighter's dashboard. It took him a few seconds to realize what had happened. One of the large blue ovals representing Confederation battleships was gone. For an instant, he thought it might be *Dauntless*, but then his eye caught the flagship, right where she belonged. She'd taken some damage, but all in all, she was still in good shape.

Formidable…

He concentrated his scanners to the rear, searching…but there was nothing except a heavy cloud of hard radiation where the great battleship had been. *Formidable* had lost containment, and her reactors had unleashed thermonuclear fury, consuming the massive vessel…and everyone on it.

His mind raced, trying to recall if he knew anyone on *Formidable*, but he couldn't come up with any names or faces. The battleship was—had been—one of the newest in the fleet, commissioned six months after the end of the war, and until today, unblooded in combat. Her first battle had proven to be her last.

He felt anger moving in, replacing shock. Wherever those ships were from, whoever was aboard or had sent them…there wasn't a doubt remaining, nor the slightest hesitation. To Jake Stockton, they were enemies. And, he only knew one way to deal with enemies.

"All squadron leaders, bring your birds up to full acceleration. We're going in, and we're going in hard."

* * *

Stu Weldon turned around, reaching out frantically and grabbing hold of the table as a vicious dizzy spell took him. He barely managed to stay on his feet, and he closed his eyes and stood still for a moment, taking in a few deep breaths as the sensation receded. He didn't know if the dizziness was caused by the virus or by the immense quantities of simulants and other drugs he'd taken to keep himself functioning. None of what he'd taken had affected the disease in the slightest—he'd already tried every antiviral known to Confederation medicine on a dozen patients, to no avail. But for the first time since his research had begun, he felt he was onto something. As long as he could stay conscious long enough to finish developing the treatment.

The drugs he'd been taking had ravaged his body, he knew that, and they hadn't cured a single symptom of the disease the Master had called the Plague. They just combatted—very temporarily—the weakness the virus was creating as it battled his immune system.

He opened his eyes again, taking another breath, and then he leaned forward, lowering his eyes to the high-powered microscope on the table. He could hardly see the virus specimens, even with the scope on maximum magnification. Isolating them had proven to be immensely difficult. They were tiny even by the standards of the microscopic universe, less than one-millionth the size of a typical cell. The contagion's extreme ability to penetrate most protective gear had as much to do with size as anything else. The virus's size allowed it to work its way through otherwise impermeable barriers. It also made research, and any attempts to combat it, that much harder.

The Master had given him the idea he was pursuing now. He'd already been analyzing the blood of the locals, trying to determine what it was that protected them from the deadly pathogen. At first, he'd wondered if it was something in the native food, or some other factor that affected the people living on the planet. Then, after speaking with the Master, he realized the utter simplicity of it. There was a genetic immunity factor, one that appeared to be extremely rare—even non-existent—in those from the Rim, but perhaps more common in people living closer to the empire's old core.

Even more likely, it had been rare on this planet as well, and on all others on which the bacteriological weapon had been unleashed…but the disease had killed anyone who hadn't possessed it. Everyone living on the planet now—and possibly on countless others—was descended from those few survivors.

The answer was in the blood of the locals, and in their genes, he was sure of it now. And, he believed he'd found it. He looked down at the small canister on the table, at the pinkish liquid inside. He'd need more blood from the locals to make enough to treat the entire landing party, but he had enough now for a test.

Normally, he'd have picked the sickest of his patients, or

asked for volunteers. But he didn't have time for that. He was succumbing fast, and he had to keep himself going long enough to finish the job. He would take the first dose himself.

He glanced at the small injector on the table. He had no idea how the shot would affect him, what side effects it might have...or even if it would kill him instantly. It went against all his medical training to move so quickly and recklessly, but there just wasn't time for more testing and analysis. *Any* testing and analysis.

He reached down and grabbed the injector. He took a deep breath, as much to steel his courage as anything else...and then he pressed the device against his arm, feeling the strange, almost itchy sensation as several dozen micro-injectors slid into his flesh, each of them too small to cause actual pain.

He felt nothing at first, at least not beyond the vague discomfort of the shot itself. He stood where he was for a moment, and then he reached down to pick up the analyzer.

His hand made it about halfway to the device when the pain hit him. He cried out and doubled over, reaching out for the table, trying to grab onto something. He succeeded only in pulling over the table and dumping half the glassware on top of him as he fell.

He lay there on his back, wincing from the pain. It felt like fire, somewhere deep inside his body. He struggled to overcome it, to somehow get back up. He needed to examine himself, to run the analyzer. But he could hardly move. He tried to scream, but nothing came out. He just looked up at the ceiling of the small prehab structure for a few seconds.

Then, everything went dark.

*   *   *

Dauntless shook hard. It was the first hit the flagship had suffered in the fight against the enemy vessels, and Barron twisted around, instinctively leaning down to the comm to call up damage control. Fritz wasn't *Dauntless*'s chief engineer anymore, at least not officially, but as the commander of the fleet's engineering and research operation, she was still billeted on the flagship. Barron didn't have the slightest doubt she'd be in engineering by then, orders or no.

He was about to tap the controls and connect to the engineering section, when he heard Sonya Eaton already speaking to someone. He felt annoyed for an instant, and just as quickly pushed it away, replaced it with respect for his aide. She'd taken on most of Atara Travis's duties in addition to her own, and she'd managed to handle them all perfectly, even in the middle of a battle. He smiled as he realized she was speaking with Fritz.

"All systems are still operational, Admiral…including the primary batteries." She turned toward him to report the instant she disconnected from Fritz. "There are some scattered burnouts, and some significant damage to one of the bays, but otherwise…"

"We got off light." Barron finished his aide's thought, even as his eyes moved to the display, to the power gauge for the main guns. The primaries were almost ready to fire again, and Barron was impatient. He knew full well that one solid hit from those enemy beams could knock out the whole system. And, the entire fleet was still outside the maximum range of the secondary batteries. He didn't relish running another gauntlet through the enemy's fire to get back into range. He was still staring at the small bar charts on the display when they maxed out, and an instant later the telltale flickering of lights on the control center told him the guns had fired.

And missed. He sighed softly as he watched the display update. All four of *Dauntless*'s primaries had missed. He was accustomed to far better targeting, and his disappointment manifested as frustration. He knew it wasn't the fault of the ship, or her crew. He still had most of the veterans from the old *Dauntless* at their posts, and he *knew* they were the best. No, it was the enemy's evasive maneuvers, and the AI systems that ran them. The tech was better than anything his people had, and the seemingly random shifts in acceleration and vector were confounding his gunners and their targeting computers.

Barron turned toward Eaton and looked as though he was

going to say something. But then he just turned toward his own comm unit and slapped his hand down on the controls. "Gunnery, this is Admiral Barron. These ships are killing us with their evasion programs. Standard fire control isn't going to get the job done. You're veterans, all of you...you've been to hell and back. Adjust your targeting AIs, let your experience and your intuition help." He wasn't sure any of what he said really made sense, but he knew he had to do *something*. And just telling his people to do better seemed inadequate.

He also knew that he was no longer the ship's commander, that he should have given his orders to Eaton and let her pass them on. This wasn't even *his Dauntless*. That vessel, the one into which he'd poured so much of himself, was gone, blasted to dust, a legend that would live on forever in Confederation history, but nowhere else. *This* was Atara Travis's ship, and Eaton was filling in for her. But he couldn't stop himself. They could pin so many stars on his shoulders that he couldn't stand without assistance, and he would still be a ship's captain at heart. And something of the old *Dauntless*, perhaps no more even than the spirit of the people who'd served both vessels, lived on in this new incarnation. He'd be damned if he was going to sit and watch her miss with shot after shot.

He turned toward the display, his eyes moving from one icon to another. Half a dozen of his ships had some level of significant damage, and *Regency* and *Exeter* were in bad shape, not far, he was afraid, from following *Formidable* to a grisly end.

He wasn't concerned the fleet would lose the battle, not in the end. His people simply had too much of a numerical advantage. But on any kind of even basis, an analysis of the fight ship for ship or ton for ton, there was one inescapable conclusion, and it gored at him, cut into him like a blade shoved into his gut.

His people were getting crushed.

Chapter Thirty-One

Confederation Intelligence Headquarters
Port Royal City, Planet Dannith, Ventica III
315 AC

"Do it." Holsten's voice was cold, his eyes fixed, not a spark of mercy or pity in them.

The man hesitated. He was one of Confederation Intelligence's best, an agent who'd served Holsten for years, who'd shown nothing but loyalty as he was sent into one deadly situation after another. But he was clearly uncomfortable with Holsten's orders.

"Do it," Holsten repeated firmly. He was commanding his agent to do something unethical, immoral…and in the Confederation, illegal. It was an act that could send them both to the deepest, darkest prison on the Confederation's farthest and most remote frozen penal moon. For a long, long time.

And Holsten didn't care.

The agent took a deep breath and hesitated for another few seconds, looking in Holsten's general direction, but avoiding eye contact. The spymaster just stood where he was, unmoving, silent, radiating merciless intensity. Finally, the agent looked for a few more seconds toward the haggard, exhausted looking man shackled to the metal chair, and his hands tightened on the controls in front of him.

The prisoner screamed, a mournful, pathetic shriek that would have been heard for blocks around, if the room hadn't been entirely soundproof. He strained at the shackles that held him to the chair, trying to shake free from the electrodes attached to his body. But Gary Holsten had placed those clamps himself, and they were secure. They'd come off when the captive told him what he wanted to know, and not a second before.

Holsten had exceeded his authority before. He'd spied on Confederation Senators and used the dirt he'd gathered to influence—blackmail, he'd even admit—them to do what he felt had to be done. But he'd never used any of that for personal gain. Everything he had done had been for the Confederation. For all the times he'd stepped over the line, Holsten had always considered himself a true patriot.

But this was personal. Andi's survival wasn't crucial to the Confederation. She was one of his agents, and he'd lost many people over the years. The job was a dangerous one, and she'd volunteered of her own free will. But none of that mattered, not to Holsten. Not now.

Lafarge, for all her past illicit activities and the fact that she was long somewhat of an outlaw, had served the Confederation well. Her greatest contribution, a heavily-classified secret only a select few knew of in detail, had arguably saved the Confederation from utter defeat. Tyler Barron had been showered with awards and acclimations or his role in destroying the pulsar—well deserved ones, in Holsten's book—but the brilliant officer wouldn't have had the slightest chance of getting through to the enemy superweapon if Andi Lafarge hadn't found the stealth generator and brought it back to Grimaldi.

She deserved better than to be written off as the cost of a botched operation. Whatever it took, Holsten was going to get her back…even if he had to tear Dannith down brick by brick to do it.

Lafarge was his friend, and that was reason enough to him, but he also felt he owed it to Tyler Barron. No one man or woman had done as much to see the Confederation through the war to victory, or at least whatever version of victory the Senate's acquiescence had allowed. Holsten was well aware of Barron's feelings for Andi, of the tortured, on and off again dance the two had done for several years now. And he knew, as unlikely as it appeared at first glance, they were perfect for each other. Eventually, they would set aside the immense baggage they both carried and do something about it. Something lasting.

As long as he got Andi out…

"Again," he said coldly, his eyes fixed on the haggard man in the chair. Holsten didn't take torture lightly, but he'd fought against Sector Nine long enough to understand his enemy. The Union's spy agency—and they were still Sector Nine to him, whatever they'd taken to calling themselves—didn't hesitate to inflict all manner of pain and torment on its prisoners. He knew very well that more than a few of his lost agents had died in agony, interrogated for all they had to offer their enemies. And the man sitting in the chair was a Sector Nine agent. God only knew what horrors he had inflicted on his own victims. Confederation ideals were one thing, but in Holsten's mind, there was some kind of justice in what he was doing.

Or, at least, he told himself that. Because he had no intention of stopping until the prisoner gave him the location of every Sector Nine hideout on Dannith.

The agent had paused again—Holsten understood the man's reticence, but it was pissing him off nevertheless—but then he hit the switch. The prisoner screamed again, a primal howl, as his body convulsed. A few seconds later, the agent flipped the switch back, and the prisoner collapsed in the chair. Tears streamed down his face, and he gasped for air, trying to say something, but unable to get the words out.

"Are you ready to tell me what I want to know?" Holsten stepped forward and glared at the man. "Because, if you don't, I will flip this switch, and my associate and I will walk out of this room and go out for lunch, maybe a few beers. You'll be a smoking black stain on the chair by the time we come back."

The prisoner's terror was clear, but Holsten was far from certain the torture would break the Sector Nine agent, at least in the time he had. The Union's spy agency training and conditioning programs were legendary. And no one who'd served in their ranks could doubt the consequences of cooperating with the enemy, both for them, if they returned home, and for their families.

Holsten was usually very controlled and methodical in his actions. But, he could feel that slipping away. And it wasn't just his determination to rescue Andi—it had been brewing longer than that. He'd watched Van Striker and his spacers fight their way from the brink of disaster to the verge of victory, and he knew only too well the price they had paid to get there. It hadn't shocked him when the Senate ignored a century of history and naively accepted Gaston Villieneuve's peace proposal, but it had drained him of…something. All the fighting, the death, the constant struggles…and the Senate had thrown it all away, virtually guaranteeing another generation of Confederation spacers and Marines would face the horrors of war. If he couldn't see the Union defeated, couldn't contain the Senate's folly…at least he could save Andi.

"It's decision time, Rob." It was the first time he'd used the prisoner's name. The past hours had been an exercise in dehumanizing the captive, but now Holsten was going to offer the man an escape. "You don't need to suffer like this. Help us, and I'll see that you're safe. We help our friends. Tell me where your compatriots are keeping Andi Lafarge…and I will see that you are pardoned for your crimes, allowed to emigrate to the Confederation. And, I will personally see that you have a place to live and enough money to enjoy the rest of your life in peace and luxury." Holsten turned toward the small console that controlled the electrical current. "Or, you can get fried right here, like a strip of overdone bacon." He turned and leaned forward, bringing his eyes a few centimeters from the captives. "Make your choice."

It was a gamble. If he threatened to kill the prisoner and didn't, it would drain some of the power from future threats. And, if he followed through, if he electrocuted the captive, he'd lose the best potential source of intel he had to track down Andi's whereabouts.

Not to mention, adding murder to his list of crimes.

"I don't know…"

Holsten exhaled, his fists curling up in an involuntary reaction at the prisoner's stubbornness. But then, the man's voice continued, "I don't know where she is…but I know almost every safe house and hidden base we've got on Dannith."

Holsten felt the smile forming on his face. He'd done it. He'd violated countless Confederation laws to break this man, become something very similar to those he'd always despised. But he would think about all that later. Right now, he needed to find Andi.

Before it was too late.

*   *   *

"Mr. Holsten, my name is Walter Aguillar. I am chief of staff to Senator Ferrell."

"Yes, Mr…Aguillar…I'm afraid I am very occupied at the moment. Whatever you've come to tell me will just have to wait."

Holsten took a few steps past the pompous-looking official. He was wearing light body armor, and he had an assault rifle in his hand. He'd gotten what he needed from the Sector Nine agent—at least he hoped he had—and he was on his way to find Andi. The prisoner was in rough shape, but Holsten was a man of his word, at least as much as a spy could be. He couldn't send the tortured agent to the main hospital in Port Royal City, of course, but he'd taken steps to make sure the man was receiving care. If the intel the agent had provided him proved to be accurate, Holsten would follow through on every one of his promises. He would see that the Union spy—former Union spy—lived out his life in luxury and comfort.

And, if he found out the prisoner had lied to him…well, that would have another, far less pleasant, result.

"I'm afraid it can't wait, Mr. Holsten. I have a Senatorial…"

"It will *have* to wait," Holsten snapped as he turned toward rack on the wall and grabbed a utility bag full of grenades.

"I can only imagine where you're going, armed like that in

a Confederation city in time of peace, Mr. Holsten, but I can assure you, it stops now. I have a Senatorial decree ordering you to return to Megara at once to explain your actions on Dannith. You are to come with me, right…" The bureaucrat's voice vanished to silence as Holsten pulled a pistol from his belt and pointed it right between the man's eyes.

"I said it will have to wait. Make yourself comfortable… what the hell was your name again? Or don't. I don't really care. But I have something I have to do right now, so either get out of my way, or I will splatter your brains on that wall." Holsten stared at the man with a withering gaze. "Do we understand each other?"

Aguillar was stunned, and too terrified to respond, but he did manage to nod his head slightly, something Holsten was willing to take as an answer. The spy chief turned and walked toward the door, and as the gun moved from Aguillar's face, the bureaucrat recovered some small measure of his courage, and he shouted after Holsten. "Disregarding a Senatorial order is a federal crime, Mr. Holsten, as is pointing a weapon at an authorized representative of the Senate. In addition to the crimes you have no doubt committed here. You are in a great deal of trouble, Mr. Holsten. A great deal. You will…"

Holsten just ignored it all. He stepped through the door and out into the hall, waving toward the Marines lined up against the wall. He had to go find Andi, and nothing was going to stop him, not if every Senator on Megara lay down in front of him and tried to block the way. He half-listened to the hack's threats for a few seconds…and then the shrill voice faded away as he made his way down the corridor, to the waiting transport.

*　*　*

"Andi, you're a smart woman. You know we're running out of time."

Lafarge looked up at Lille, at least through the one eye that wasn't swollen shut. "Just kill me now, you worm. Because if you don't, and I get out of here, you can count on the fact that

I'll find you one day…and I'll kill you. Count on that." But she knew it was empty bluster. There was no depth to it. She was spent, beaten. She'd already told him everything she knew…he just hadn't believed her. It was something that cut at her insides, in its own way even more than the pain of the torture.

She'd always prided herself on being tough, resolute. Now, she knew Ricard Lille had broken her, but she had nothing to give him. All she had were her crew's fake names, which she guessed they had all abandoned the instant she disappeared. She also realized just what a pro Gary Holsten was, how careful and how meticulous in protecting vital data. She'd felt bursts of anger toward her friend that he hadn't told her more, given her some kind of currency to try and stop the torment. But she understood, and even in her wretched state, she approved.

She'd spoken only the truth to Lille in her last statement, though. If, somehow, she *did* escape, there was no question she'd hunt Lille down. There was enough of the old Andi Lafarge left inside her that she knew there was no way the two of them could live, not after what had happened. He'd finish her, right here, or by God, she'd kill him—whatever it took.

Lille smiled. "You're a hard one, Andi. Such a pity you chose the wrong side. You could have accomplished wonders with us. Still, I have to thank you. Working with somebody like you is a rare challenge, and success in such an endeavor is its own reward." He paused. "Now, tell me what I want to know, and we can stop this. I won't insult your intelligence and tell you we can let you live, but I give you my word I will finish things with one quick shot to the head. No more pain, no more suffering. Just tell me what you know."

Andi looked back up at her tormenter, barely able to hold her head up. Her vision was blurry, and being reduced down to one eye that she could open cost her any depth perception. But Lille's smile was visible enough, and it told her all she needed to know. He had won, and she had lost. She knew it…and so did he.

"I told you, I don't know anything else. Gary Holsten asked me to come to Dannith and try to hire some prospectors to search for old tech…all secretly paid for by Confederation Intelligence."

Lille shook his head. "I wish I could believe you, Andi… but I'm afraid I just don't." He turned and gestured to a white-coated man standing next to the room's sole door. "Emilio, it's time."

The man moved toward her with a large injector in his hand.

"What is that?" she asked, struggling but failing to keep the fear from her voice.

"It's just something to make you…more cooperative. I'm afraid it's quite painful. I believe the most common description has been, 'I feel like my insides are on fire." Lille shook his head. "This is what your stubbornness brings you, Andi."

"Wait a minute," she said, all attempts at hiding her panic gone now. "I told you—Gary Holsten, he wanted me to find out more about Sector Nine's operations on Dannith. That's why I went to Trencher. It's why I agreed to meet you."

Lille smiled. "That's so much better, Andi…but I'm afraid still far from enough. I regret that you have forced me to use this. In addition to being rather…unpleasant…I'm afraid it will leave you a blubbering imbecile, at least at the dosage I suspect we will have to use on you. I would have as soon allowed you to die with your wits still about you, but, alas, you have made your choice." He gestured to the man, who started moving toward her. "Goodbye, Captain Lafarge."

She could see the white-coated man coming toward her, obscuring her view of the rest of the room…and her eyes locked on the injector, coming closer…

Closer…

Chapter Thirty-Two

Nothing. No fighters launching. Not even close-in defenses worth a damn. What's going on here?

Stockton was looking straight ahead as his squadrons closed on the enemy warships. He'd been waiting for some kind of response, a flight of interceptors, some level of point defense. But, beyond a few hastily repurposed and largely ineffective light batteries, there was nothing.

He felt a coldness inside, and he couldn't set aside the fear he was leading his people into some kind of trap. Memories of vicious battles passed through his thoughts, fights against massive Union fighter wings, and worse, the deadly struggles against Palatian formations during the Alliance civil war. This enemy was more advanced than any he'd fought before, and he knew a war with them would be a holocaust like nothing he had ever seen. With all that was just too hard to believe he'd discovered a weakness in their defenses so potentially devastating.

The warships were moderate in size, and they didn't look like battleships or any other kind of carrier, so the lack of fighters made at least some sense. But the closer his formations got to the enemy vessels, the more it seemed they had never even *seen* fighters before.

It didn't take more than a quick check of the fleet status readings on his screen to see how badly these four ships were hurting Admiral Barron's battleships. The fleet's primaries were firing back now, but they were having trouble targeting the wildly-gyrating vessels. One of the enemy ships had taken a pair of hits, and Stockton was relieved to see that, however advanced they were, the opposing vessels were not immune to damage. The primaries had hit hard, even if their effect had been rather less than it might have been against a Union or Alliance adversary. The problem was connecting with more shots. He'd seen *Dauntless* manage hit percentages north of fifty percent in the past, even at long range, but the fleet as a whole was shooting below ten percent...and to Stockton's utter astonishment, he noted that the flagship and its famed crew of gunners hadn't scored any hits at all.

He watched the display, trying to follow the evasive maneuvers of the enemy ships...*his* targets now. It was going to be hard to connect, especially from any significant distance. *But if these ships are really without close-in defenses...*

He toggled the comm. "All squadrons, this is Raptor. We're going to toss the book in the can on this one." He didn't suppose that would be much of a surprise to many of his pilots. He'd been a maverick his entire career, and from everything he'd heard, his reputation had exaggerated his exploits considerably. "These ships don't seem to have much in the way of close in defenses, and we haven't seen so much as a single enemy fighter. So, we're not going to pop off those torpedoes at long range. These ships are too fast, too maneuverable. If we want to hit them, we've got to get in close...and I mean *close.*"

His eyes were fixed on the screen as he spoke. His lead squadrons were less than sixty thousand kilometers from the enemy ships, right about at the edge of long range for plasma torpedoes. A normal attack closed to around forty thousand, or even thirty thousand if the squadrons were aggressive. Any more than that, and the increased losses to defensive fire would offset any gains in accuracy.

But now there was no defensive fire. That meant the fighters could get a *lot* closer…and the torpedoes could go all the way in under power, converting to plasmas at the last instant. The enemy ships would have to evade like hell to escape the 50g thrust of the torpedoes.

"I don't want a weapon launched outside of ten thousand kilometers…and anybody who holds until under five thousand, you've got a drink coming to you in the officers' club, on me."

There was usually some chatter on the comm line, but now it was a cacophony of pilots shouting. His people were ready, and from the sounds of things, it looked like he might be out a month's pay in drinks.

He tapped his throttle, edged his vector over, maintaining his position on the outside of the formation. As usual, his bird was fitted as an interceptor, which meant it was next to useless against an enemy that had no fighters. For a moment he considered ordering his interceptor squadrons to follow the bombers in and make strafing runs. But he had over two hundred of the heavy attack ships bearing down on four enemy vessels. If fifty plasma torpedoes apiece didn't do the job, the puny lasers on his lighter interceptors weren't going to make the difference.

He hit his thrusters, decelerating sharply, holding back so he had a good vantage point as the bombing groups went in. He watched as they closed. Twenty thousand kilometers, fifteen thousand…still no enemy fighters launching. The small number of light guns firing began to hone their targeting, however, and the bombers started taking hits. Two were down, then six…but the attack force ignored the losses and continued to close. The lead formations crossed the ten-thousand-kilometer mark, and not a single ship had launched yet.

Stockton felt pride in his people, and for his part in organizing such an effective and capable force. The first squadrons launched at around eight thousand kilometers, and then the whole thing turned into some kind of makeshift competition, each successive wave coming in closer than the one before. Six thousand, five thousand…even four thousand.

Squadron launch acknowledgements echoed in his headset

now, one after the other, as scores of torpedoes lurched for-ward from the ships carrying them and zipped toward the target ships, accelerating at 50g and matching every evasive maneuver the enemy vessels could manage.

Almost every maneuver. Stockton watched in stunned silence as the four ships responded to the sudden threat of his bombers' barrage. They fired up their own engines, blasting away at—*how is it even possible?*—40g. *No…more*, he thought a few seconds later, as the readings coming in matched the 50g of his torpedoes.

He'd never heard of a manned ship hitting more than 20g for any sustained period, and even that was rare. The pressure of 50g acceleration would squash crew members like bugs. He'd never seen any force dampeners powerful enough to absorb even a meaningful fraction of that kind of thrust.

They are *ahead of us…pretty damned far ahead from the looks of it.*

He felt a chill pass down his spine. If these ships had been equipped with fighters and close-in defense networks, he shud-dered to imagine what they might have done to his wings.

He watched the barrage moving forward, heading toward the now-desperately evading enemy ships. The wild moves and almost impossibly complex changes in thrust and vector were indeed shaking many of the incoming projectiles. But enough were holding their target locks.

Stockton almost gave an order for his last waves to launch at eight thousand kilometers and not try to close further. The lead squadrons' losses had quickly ramped up. Part of it was the shorter range, he guessed, but there was another cold truth. The enemy targeting systems were adapting, and their hit ratios, even with a relatively small number of guns firing, were soaring. The fighters trying to close beyond the five-thousand-kilometer mark were giving the target ships too much time to get solid locks. The losses hadn't reached the levels he'd seen in the des-perate battles of the war, but they were becoming too high to ignore.

Stockton had almost allowed himself to believe the fight would be a walkover, one where his forces suffered no or extremely light losses. But his bombing squadrons penetrating to the closest ranges were losing ten percent or more of their number.

None of that mattered, though. One glance at the status of the fleet kept him silent. The battleships engaged in the fight were taking damage…serious damage. He *had* to see those ships destroyed, and as quickly as possible.

He watched as three-quarters of the torpedoes zipped past the enemy ships, their nav AIs unable to match the rapid evasion programs of the target vessels. But even a twenty-five percent hit rate was better than a dozen torpedoes per ship. And, for all the speed and weapons power of the enemy vessels, they were not indestructible. A single hit didn't destroy one, or even cripple it, but three or four were enough to knock one out of action… and none of the four could survive more than seven. By the time the last wave of torpedoes reached their target's positions, they encountered nothing but clouds of dust and radiation.

*   *   *

"*Vanguard* reports she can land Yellow squadron, Admiral. That should account for all the fighters." Eaton snapped out her report, crisply and coolly, much like Travis had done in her years as *Dauntless*'s first officer. Barron had dropped all pretext of sticking to the admiral's role midway through the battle, and now he was shouting out orders the way he had for six years, when he'd had a captain's insignia on his collar instead of an admiral's stars.

Dauntless's Alpha bay was in bad shape, even worse than he'd thought when the first damage assessments had come in. Several of the structural supports were severed, which was a heavy repair even in spacedock, and next to impossible in deep space. It was "next to impossible" instead of "impossible" for one reason and one alone.

Anya Fritz.

Fritz had shed the bonds of her own lofty rank as readily as Barron had. He suspected she was on her hands and knees, even then, crawling around some access tube, hunting down a power outage or undiagnosed malfunction. Fritz was the closest thing to a magician Barron had ever seen in an engineer, but even the mighty Fritzie was making her way through unfamiliar territory. The old *Dauntless* had been ripped from her as it had from him, and as much as he'd loved his old ship, he had to admit no one had known the old girl better than Fritz had.

"Captain Horace on your channel, Admiral."

Barron turned and glanced over at Eaton. She did remind him of Atara, in more ways than one…including how alert she looked, when he knew for sure she'd been on duty for at least sixteen straight hours. He felt like he was about to fall over, himself, but then he realized he probably didn't look as tired as he was either. Setting an example was part of the job, and it came almost instinctively to him.

"Put him through."

"Admiral…you wanted to speak to me?" Barron had sent a communique to *Kraken* a few minutes before. The fast cruiser had suffered a hit during the battle, and the bridge crew had advised the fleet commander that the ship's captain was off the bridge…and not accessible at the moment.

Barron had smiled at the nervous bridge officer's words. She'd sounded like she was ready to bear the brunt of some tirade he might offer in response, but instead, he just left instructions for Horace to contact him as soon as he was available.

Buck Horace was a cantankerous old officer, one who'd scared the daylights out of a first-year cadet by the name of Tyler Barron. He was also hands on, in a very literal sense, and Barron knew what "unavailable" meant. Horace was down in the bowels of *Kraken*'s right next to his engineers, riding his damage control parties, digging around in fried circuitry, and, most likely, nowhere near a comm.

"Buck…yes." Barron paused for a few seconds, a smile slipping onto his face. Horace had been on the verge of retirement, having terrorized his final class of cadets…but the war had been at a nadir, and the navy needed every experienced spacer it could get. Horace took a cut in grade along with the command of

Kraken, one of the new fast cruisers fresh off out of the shipyard, and he'd been there ever since. He'd been scheduled to hang it up once and for all, when he'd asked Barron if there was a spot for him in the White Fleet…and the newly promoted admiral jumped at the chance to get so experienced an officer in his new command.

"I don't know where these people we fought are from," Barron continued, "but they came through point delta, so there's a good chance that's the route to their base."

Barron knew perfectly well that any of the system's five transit points could lead to the enemy's home, except, probably, the one his fleet had entered through. But he had to make some guesses, and that seemed like a good one.

"It's certainly *one* way to wherever they come from." Horace's voice was low, scratchy, even more so than Barron remembered. Barron wasn't a young, inexperienced kid anymore, all full of piss and vinegar, but neither was he as easily intimidated as he had once been. Years of war had hardened him, made him into a veteran warrior and a fleet commander…but Horace *still* scared him. A little.

"Those freighters will warn their people about what happened." Barron had almost sent his ships in to destroy the enemy supply ships, but he was still clinging to some hope there was still a way to restore the peace. Perhaps letting the freighters go would send a message, one that was hopefully more effective than anything he'd managed to say earlier. "Hell, the signals from the satellites in orbit already did that. It's a pretty good bet we'll have another force coming this way eventually, and an even better wager it will have more than four warships with it." Barron was guessing about everything. He had no intel, no idea at all how many of the enemy there were, or what kind of forces they commanded. For all he knew, the four ships Stockton's fighters had destroyed were the only ones these self-proclaimed "Masters" from the Hegemony possessed. But he didn't believe that, not for a second.

"Seems like a good bet, Admiral. Our best matchup with them is fighters, for sure, especially since it looks like they may not have any of their own. Of course, there's a chance they do, and those four ships just didn't carry any...that's a possibility we have to consider. We've got to be careful about jumping to conclusions, sir."

Barron felt uncomfortable with his former teacher and superior addressing him as "admiral" and "sir." He almost told Horace to call him Tyler, but it didn't seem appropriate in front of *Dauntless*'s huge control center crew. Besides, he doubted old "Ramrod" Horace would have deviated a millimeter from the book as far as addressing superior officers, regardless of age or experience...even when the junior officer had been the only one to threaten the senior with a failing grade back at the Academy.

"I agree about careless assumptions, Buck, but it sure looks like fighters are something new to them. You're right, for sure, four cruiser-sized ships simply might not have had any squadrons, even if their line ships have thousands of fighters bursting out at the seams...but I'd guess they'd damned sure have better close-in defenses if fighters were in their arsenal. Don't you think?"

"I do, Admiral. But I still think we need to be cautious. And even if they don't have fighters, we have no idea what their heavier ships might mount. If they're going to send a force to follow up on the one we just fought, we'd better get the hell out of here, and back to warn the rest of the fleet. Or, we'd better get ready for one hell of a fight."

"We can't leave, Buck. We've got people down on the surface, and I can't bring them back aboard. Not until we get this epidemic under control."

The line was silent for a few seconds. Barron knew what was going through the older man's head. The landing party numbered in the hundreds, as opposed to tens of thousands in the fleet. And billions in the Confederation. Finally, Horace said, "You may have to make a tough choice at some point, Admiral."

Barron knew his old instructor was just telling him the hard truth, but he felt a rush of resentment anyway. He hated the idea of leaving any of his people behind—to almost certain death—but he couldn't imagine issuing the order and giving up on Atara. They'd fought together, risked their lives in the same deadly battles. He'd always known he could lose her in battle, but that was something different than just pulling out—running—and leaving her behind.

"And, if we stay? Do you have any suggestions?"

"Well, Admiral, if we stay…then we'd better be damned ready to fight."

"That's why I wanted to talk to you. I want you to take *Kraken* through transit point delta…and I want you to find a good spot near the point, and wait. I want to know if any enemy forces are coming, and I damned sure want to know with as much time as possible before they get here."

"Yes, Admiral." Barron couldn't read Horace from his tone. The old officer was cold as ice. Which was why Barron wanted him looking out for the enemy. There was no one whose judgment he trusted more, no officer he was as sure would stay calm and focused, no matter what happened.

"If you pick up anything—anything at all—you are to transit back and report. Understood?"

"Yes, understood."

"Go ahead. Get through as quickly as you can, and get positioned. Dock with one of the supply ships before you transit, and get an extra load of drones. I want as much information as possible on anything coming our way."

"Yes, Admiral."

"And, Buck…be careful."

"Always, Admiral."

Chapter Thirty-Three

CFS Dauntless
Zed-11 System
Year 315 AC

"We might be able to get enough volunteers for a skeleton crew, but it would have to be one of the battleships. Nothing else is large enough for the whole landing party." Sara Eaton sat at the opposite end of *Dauntless*'s massive conference table, as befitted her place as second in command of the fleet.

Barron looked down at the commodore, someone he considered one of his few true friends. She was right, technically, at least, but any operation to get the landing party off the surface, assuming he decided to make a run toward home before more enemy forces arrived, was more complex than it seemed at first. "We'll need volunteer pilots for the shuttles, too, not to mention backup crews for the vessel carrying everyone in case those original volunteers fall ill and can't run the ship any longer. We'll try to cordon off sections of the vessel, attempt to effectively quarantine those from the surface…but we know almost nothing about this pathogen, except that many of our people were infected despite taking significant precautions." Barron turned his head and looked down the table. He had called all his top officers together to discuss options. He knew the final decision was his, but he wanted to hear what his people thought before he made his choice.

Cilian Globus had made his own opinion clear. The enemy fleet had disregarded all attempts to communicate, save for their perfunctory demand that the fleet surrender immediately. To a Palatian, that meant only one thing, and there was a single way to deal with it. He was in favor of making a stand at the planet, or perhaps even better, pushing on forward, trying to find the route to the heart of the enemy's domains. *Striking like a cobra*, as the Palatian had put it.

Barron wasn't surprised, though it still amazed him how the prospect of battle could make a man as intelligent as Globus overlook a vast array of dangers and uncertainties in the mindless pursuit of redress for slighted honor. Barron had befriended more than one Palatian, and he'd come to respect them greatly. But, they could be their own worst enemies at times.

"We have to do something, Admiral. We can't just leave them all down there." The volume of Eaton's voice declined with each word. Barron understood. They couldn't abandon the landing party, but unless the medical teams made a major breakthrough soon, there wouldn't be any survivors on the surface to worry about. If pulling the fleet out was the right call, could he really waste valuable time—and risk infecting the crews of the shuttles and the chosen quarantine ship—to retrieve a group of people who would be all be dead soon, anyway?

Part of him knew the situation on the surface was almost hopeless. He shouldn't allow it to affect his judgment...he should pull the fleet out, go back to Megara, and advise the Admiralty of the new threat the fleet had found. But, Atara was one of those he would have to abandon, and he wasn't there yet. Intellectually, he knew he couldn't let his feelings for her influence his decision...but he just wasn't ready to abandon his friend.

"Stripping down a battleship just reduces our combat power. And running back home doesn't solve the problem. We've got a new enemy, one that threatens not only the Confederation, but the entire Rim. If we let them see us run, we're only inviting invasion. But, if we fight them here and beat them, we can gain the initiative…and give them a taste of what they will face if they invade the Rim." Globus slapped his hand down on the table as he finished his statement.

Barron looked over at his friend. He doubted anyone present had the slightest question as to the Palatian's opinion on what to do. But, the Alliance forces were only a small percentage of the fleet's combat power, and any decision Barron made to fight would mostly affect his Confederation spacers.

Barron was about to respond, but Sonya Eaton beat him to it. "Commander Globus, I respect your point of view, and I agree on the unintended effects a withdrawal might have, especially on projecting weakness to a potential enemy. If we fight and lose, we may do more to encourage that invasion of which you speak. And, we must consider another factor. The Confederation knows nothing of this threat. Nor does the Alliance… or, for that matter, the Union or any of the other Rim nations. If we fight here and are completely destroyed, they are in danger of being attacked without warning." She was seated next to Barron, and as he turned toward her and listened to her words, he suddenly realized how much she looked and sounded like her older sister. He was shocked he'd never noticed it before.

His eyes moved to the end of the table, to Sara Eaton, and back again to Sonya before he responded. "Captain Eaton is correct. Whatever we decide to do, our top priority must be getting a warning back to Megara. If the fleet remains here to fight, we must send ships back…a strong enough force to be sure it will arrive. We cannot leave the Rim without knowledge of what we have found."

A series of nods worked around the table.

"At least we agree on that. As for our other course of action, I think we need to seriously consider what we might face if we remain here…and how we would fight it."

Barron had a feeling he should order the fleet to bug out immediately, even at the cost of abandoning his people on the planet. But he didn't like running any more than Globus did. And, while he still regretted the prospect of making another enemy, he did feel a growing rage toward these "Masters" and their followers. He'd done everything possible to prevent hostilities…to no avail.

It was always best to avoid making enemies…but he also knew sometimes there just wasn't a choice.

So, if these people want a fight, I'll make sure they get one…

*   *   *

"Stu, can you hear me?"

Weldon looked up, groggily. His head felt as though a bomb had gone off inside, and his vision was weak and blurry. "Captain?"

Atara Travis allowed herself a tiny smile. "Yes, Stu, it's me. You gave us quite a scare there for a while."

"What happened?" But, even as he asked, it all started to come back. The lab…the injection. "I developed a serum from the natives' blood," he said, answering his own question. "I thought it would work." For an instant, he wondered if it had, if his loss of consciousness had simply been a side effect of the cure. But it only took a few seconds for him to realize he was still deathly ill from the disease. "I guess I was wrong." He leaned to the side, putting his arms out and trying to lift himself off the cot.

"Wait a minute, Stu…you're in no shape…"

"There's no time, Atara." He had to find a way to defeat the disease. But he knew it was already too late. He didn't have the time to start over.

Travis reached out and put her hand on his arm, helping him get to his feet. "Doctor Charles checked you out, Stu. He says you had a reaction to the drug, some kind of rejection. He thinks it's because of everything the natives have been through. He believes they've progressed off on some splinter of genetic development, too far from our own norms, that they've almost become a different species. Enough variation, at least, to prevent their blood from being a match for ours."

Weldon nodded his head. Of course…that had to be it. He'd been so hopeful the serum would work. He'd been certain he had isolated the immunity factor. But his body had rejected the drug and that had prevented proper absorption. He knew in his heart he had found the cure. But, none of the landing party could take it. "I need to see Sam right away, Captain. I think he's right, and we need to find a way to get around this. We might have a cure here...if I can just find a way to get our bodies to accept it."

Travis looked down at the ground for a few seconds. "I'm sorry, Stu. Sam Charles collapsed yesterday, right after he checked you out. We managed to get him in a medpod and into cryostasis, but he's not going to be helping you with any research."

Damn...

Weldon and Charles had been good friends, ever since their days at fleet med school. And he needed his colleague now. They'd have to try a hundred different processes to find a way to strip out whatever factors were causing the rejection. He took a deep breath. *There* has *to be a quicker way...but what?*

"I'm sorry to hear about Sam..." He paused for a few seconds, thinking about his friend. Then he turned and started walking slowly, back toward the small structure that had served as his lab.

"Are you sure you're strong enough, Stu? Maybe you should rest a little longer. Dr. Charles gave you some injections to combat the rejection, but you've been through a lot."

"There's no time, Captain. If we don't make some kind of progress now, we're all done for. We..." He paused, looking at Travis.

She looked back, waiting for him to continue. But, he just kept staring at her. "Are you all right, Doc?"

"You still don't have any symptoms?"

She was taken aback by the subject change. "Ah...no, not really. I guess it takes longer in some people."

"Does it? In who?" As far as Weldon knew, every other member of the landing party had contracted the disease. Some were still in the early stages, while others, like Bryan Rogan, were barely hanging on. The big Marine had been the first to come down with noticeable symptoms, but he was still alive, his relentless constitution refusing to quite give up.

But Atara Travis seemed utterly unaffected by the disease.

Of course…

He remembered the discussion with the Master, about the survivors all being descendants of people with natural immunity to the disease. Was it possible?

He looked at Travis again, reached out, put his hand to her face, feeling for any signs of fever. Then he leaned in and put his face right in front of hers, looking into her eyes for any signs of cloudiness, another early symptom. But there was nothing.

"Atara…you may be the answer."

"Me? Are you…"

"No, listen to me. The entire landing party is sick…all except you. The people living here all have inherited natural immunity. That means that all other genetic lines are extinct here. But if there were people immune to the disease in the old imperial gene pool, they should be present in our own population as well."

She looked confused for a few seconds, but then she said, "You think I'm immune?"

Weldon nodded. "Yes, I do. It's the only explanation for why you're not sick. And a serum derived from your blood shouldn't trigger rejection in other members of the Rim population."

"My blood type is…"

"It doesn't matter, Atara. We're not doing transfusions. We're just developing a serum from your blood." He grabbed her arm, losing all concern about rank and position. "Come with me…I need a blood sample from you, right now."

Weldon felt like death warmed over, as though he might fall over any second. But there was something inside him that hadn't been there moments before, an energy.

Hope.

*   *   *

"Very well. We'll wait another day, and then we'll make a decision. In the meantime, I want you all to contact the ships under your command…and I mean individual talks with the captains. I want every vessel ready for battle…and also fully prepared to turn around and head home…either on a moment's notice. We're dealing with something new and very dangerous now. I'm going to expect the very best everyone in the fleet has to offer." Barron paused, looking down at the table and rubbing his eyes for a moment. The meeting had gone on a long time, and the fatigue was catching up to him. He pulled his head up again, surprised at just how much effort it took, and he looked down the table as those present responded with various verbal and non-verbal acknowledgements.

Then he turned toward Sonya Eaton. "Captain, I want you to prepare an evac plan for the landing parties. I want it on my desk in six hours. It's got to be complete, and it has to be one hundred percent reliable for containing any harmful pathogens. It's also got to be something we can execute in a few hours if I give the word." He knew he'd just dumped a whole lot of unreasonable on his aide, but if anyone present was up to it, he was confident it was her.

"Yes, sir. I'll see to it at once."

"Very well," Barron said, and then he leaned back in his chair, pushing against the fuzziness trying to invade his thoughts. *I need a stim when this meeting is over.* He wished he'd taken one before. "*Kraken* is on patrol in the next system, and Captain Horace will give us a warning if any enemy forces are approaching." *Assuming they come from the same direction.* "That will give us some hours' notice, perhaps even one to two days, depending on which point they come from into the adjacent system." Horace had conducted a rough scan as soon as *Kraken* had transited, and he'd sent the cruiser's cutter back to transmit the findings. They were rough and incomplete—it would take more than one ship, plus a huge number of fighters or drones, to properly survey the entire system, tentatively named Zed-12—but they gave Barron something to go on.

There was a transit point within half a light-hour of the one leading to the Zed-11 system, where the fleet still orbited the world they'd creatively dubbed "Planet Zero." *Kraken*'s scan had detected four other points, the furthest nearly a light-day distant. It would make a big difference on the fleet's warning time, depending on the point from which enemy ships emerged into Zed-12.

"Very well…I think that's good for now. You've all got enough to keep busy." A short pause, then: "Jake, I'd like you to stay for a minute." Jake Stockton had been uncharacteristically silent during the meeting. Barron could see his star pilot had still not adapted to just how highly he'd risen in the chain of command. Stockton was in charge of eight hundred fighters, a massively powerful force under any circumstances, but against an enemy that might be vulnerable to small craft attacks, it was hard to overstate the importance of the fleet's wings.

"Yes, sir. Of course."

The others rose as a ragged group and moved toward the door. Barron leaned forward to the comm unit in front of him and toggled the flight control channel. "Stara, we just finished the meeting."

"Understood, Admiral. I'll get the shuttles ready for launch."

Barron nodded and closed the comm line. His meeting had taken considerable effort to put together, not the least of which was requiring his key officers to shuttle over to *Dauntless* from their own ships. He knew they could have used the fleetcom instead, even if the variable time lag between ships would have made exchanges slow and cumbersome, but he'd always preferred face to face meetings…especially when the stakes were as high as they were now.

He waited until the others had left, and then he turned toward Stockton. "Jake…we're still guessing on whether these…Masters…have any kind of fighters or other small craft. There's no way to know for sure, but we've got to go with our best guess…which is they don't. We're outgunned on everything else, so if we've got an edge, we damned sure need to make the most of it."

"Yes, sir. I agree." There was something in Stockton's voice, a little bit of a hitch.

"What is it, Jake?"

Stockton hesitated for a few seconds. "Well, sir…those ships didn't seem to have any significant weaponry for repelling a fighter attack. But…when we got in close it…"

"Jake, tell me what you think, even if it's a wild guess. None of us knows what we're dealing with, and we need anything we can get."

"Well, Admiral, it's just that, even with their limited armament, toward the end of the fight the effectiveness of their defenses really seemed to ramp up…almost as though…" Stockton paused again. "…as though, their computer or gunners or whatever adapted almost instantly to the threat of our bombers."

Barron looked back at his chief pilot. Stockton's statement poked at something he'd been worried about…how the enemy ships were also able to quickly adapt to nav plans designed to evade incoming fire. Barron had studied the statistics from the battle, and there was no question, at least in his mind. The enemy's hit ratio declined significantly as each new nav plan was executed…but within half a minute, it would recover to the original level. Both that fact, and the situation Stockton had described, suggested the enemy's AIs were substantially more powerful than the fleet's. Just one more advantage the Hegemony seemed to possess.

"We're going to need more randomness, Jake, abrupt changes that will make it harder for their AIs to adapt. If those ships were able to ramp up their effectiveness against your fighters with so few suitable weapons, we've got to worry if they've got other ships with heavier point defense arrays…" Barron let his voice trail off. They both knew what that would mean.

Stockton nodded. "I agree, sir. I'll have to develop a series of pre-designed plans, and let the AI issue them. It's the only way with a force this size. I'd never be able to keep up with eight hundred fighters all in real time."

"That makes sense, Jake. Do it. And whatever else you think might help. Unless I'm very mistaken, we're going to be dependent on your squadrons if it comes to another fight. Their heavy guns are just too powerful and long-ranged for us to match. Your people are going to have to hit them before they get into range…and do some serious damage. Or, we're in big trouble."

"I understand, Admiral. I will do my best."

"That's all any of us can do, Jake. And your best is pretty damned good."

Chapter Thirty-Four

Desiree Marieles watched as two of her agents pried the top off a large crate. They were in the cavernous garage of one of the buildings she'd rented for those parts of her enterprise that didn't fit her cover. She had offices in Troyus City's business district for her work as a "lobbyist," but there were multiple fronts in her war to undermine the Confederation government.

The plastic container was labeled "transport regulators," which most definitely was not what she expected it—or the six others like it—to hold. Villieneuve's message to expect the shipment had come through the Confederation's own comm networks. The transmissions originated from Plegon, a sparsely-populated and unimportant world out in the Periphery, but the actual messages had come from Montmirail. Marieles had no idea how Villieneuve got the communications across the Confederation border to Plegon for retransmission, but she'd stopped trying to figure it out. She suspected it was partially the Union leader's own genius, and partially skilled exploitation of the looseness of Confederation oversight.

She'd scanned the message twice, impressed as always by the ingeniousness of the code, which read as though it were per-

270

sonal correspondence from some Periphery farmer to distant and more sophisticated relatives on Megara...at least until she introduced the encryption key.

She heard a cracking sound, and the top of the crate fell to the floor. She looked inside, and she saw a series of neat rows of small devices of some kind, each about fifteen centimeters square. *I guess that's what a "transport regulator" looks like*, she thought, worrying for a few seconds that her people had retrieved the wrong packages. But then, one of her agents reached in and pulled out the top tray, setting it aside and revealing the true cargo below. Bars of pure platinum.

Most financial transactions were electronic, of course, even most illicit ones...and Villieneuve had sent her significant sums through the normal banking networks. But her mission was a complex one, and very dangerous. She had a number of fringe conspirators too scared to accept her normal payoffs. They didn't trust mysterious bank transfers, and it would be helpful to have utterly untraceable currency-equivalents for bribes. What they perceived as untraceable, at least. She'd have bet her last credit Villieneuve had arranged for some kind of radioactive tagging, or other way to track the metal bars. The Union's leader didn't trust anyone as far as she'd ever seen, and certainly not foreign politicians he'd bought and paid for. Any conspirator who took his bribe and betrayed him could expect an unpleasant visit shortly thereafter.

She was tense, and she waved for her people to move the crates to the storage area she'd prepared for them. She'd been playing catchup for the past week. The whole Dannith situation had set her back on her primary efforts to undermine the Confederation government. The job had more moving parts than she had expected. There were plenty of willing co-conspirators on Megara, as long as she approached them correctly, with the right propositions. Radical political groups, power-hungry politicians, entrenched government officials, wealthy magnates seeking political favor, they could all be induced to take actions that amounted to plotting against the current government...as long as it was presented to them properly.

She couldn't exactly go up to the Confeds and say, "Will you help me destabilize the government, so the Union can move in?" But she was stunned how receptive different groups were to suggestions about illegal activity—and even downright treason—to further their own positions or pet agendas. She already had several of the fringe groups in full action now, and for the past week there had been semi-violent demonstrations all across Troyus City…the very best protests money could buy.

Such activities were just the start. Now, her minions were working the other side, the law and order types. They whispered of the need to crack down, to restore peace in the streets. Soon, especially after the protests spread further—she looked over at the platinum, which would greatly assist in that endeavor—she would start suggesting remedies like temporary martial law.

The magnates would be even easier to co-opt once the scope of her operation spread beyond the capital. Work stoppages on the Iron Belt worlds would trigger harsh reprisals from planetary governments that were largely controlled by the great industrial and merchant families. Such measures had always worked to quell earlier disturbances…but those organic protests hadn't had the funding her manufactured ones would. A few bodies in the streets would help, especially if she could arrange for a couple children, or other particularly sympathetic cases, to be among the apparent victims of government reprisals.

On the core worlds, where the government and academic classes were concentrated, the disruptions would move the other way, with groups of radicalized students spreading disorder. The sympathetic authorities would be unwilling to take serious action against the rioters, even as the majority of the population became more restive and resentful. By the time she was done, millions of citizens, even on Megara, would be ready to support a firm hand, one that appeared to step out of nowhere, offering peace and quelling the radicals.

Marieles had worked around the clock for months now, and she had massive numbers of people on her effective payroll, very few of them, save the several hundred operatives she had in the field, knowing exactly for whom they were working. She'd set up dozens of front groups, organizations ranging all across the political spectrum, in some cases operating against each other, a fencing match she'd orchestrated that served to increase the unrest and tension in Megaran society.

She was surprised at how much progress she'd made...and at the amount of financial support Villieneuve had managed to send her. Her mission to the Krillians had been conducted on a shoestring, and she'd been forced to substitute lies and theatrics for actual support. The differences she was seeing now were a testament to just how much progress Villieneuve had made in the past two years toward restoring the Union economy, or at least finding new ways to drain resources from it. She knew most of the Union's systems were still in distress, some deep in outright depressions, but Villieneuve's skilled propaganda had changed everything. Workers who had risen against a government they hated because they were hungry, now grimly and determinedly shared the same meager rations as before to support a regime they were convinced would make changes, bring them a brighter and more plentiful future.

She wondered how the people of the Union would react if they knew how much of their precious production was being spent on a wild gamble to destabilize the Confederation.

She was shocked, too, at how naïve the people of the Confederation were, both the politicians, immersed in their corruption, and the people in the streets, complaining about government and social problems while repeatedly sending the same scoundrels back to political office. She was surprised at how very little difference there was at the core between Confederation politicians and those of the old Union, save, perhaps, for the range of opportunities for abuse and personal aggrandizement. The common people, for all their material plenty compared to the wretched workers of the Union, were still ready to believe almost anything if it was told to them skillfully, and to ignore even the blatant excesses of the politicians they sent back to the planetary assemblies and the Senate again and again. She hadn't forgotten what Villieneuve had told her right before she'd left Montmirail. He'd said that the Confeds talked a lot about freedom, but the instant they felt threatened, or even insecure, they would willingly trade liberty for even the vaguest, most unreliable promises of security.

By the time she was done, there would be so much chaos, the people would be clamoring for a strong hand. And, she would see they got it. Several actually, all of whom would fight each other for dominance. The politicians on Megara were held back by the relative stability of the Confederation, by the fact that they had no realistic chance of getting away with the abuses the privileged had enjoyed for so long in the Union. But, once she had shattered that stability…

She would give them that opportunity…and it would be born from the chaos in the streets. And when she was done, the Confederation would be weakened, or at least, changed at its core. And, just maybe, she could push the whole thing over, and the shining beacon of liberty and freedom on the Rim would descend into a vicious orgy of civil war and self-destruction.

Chapter Thirty-Five

CFS Dauntless
Zed-11 System
Year 315 AC

Tyler Barron awoke with a start as Sonya Eaton tapped him on the shoulder.

"Sir, I'm sorry to disturb you…" Her voice was soft, tentative, but he knew immediately something was wrong. And, as his senses returned, he realized she'd more than tapped him… she'd given him a good hard shake. That meant she'd tried gentler methods, both on the comm and standing next to him, to no avail.

"What is it, Captain?" he asked, trying hard not to sound as groggy as he felt as he lifted his head from his desk and waited for his eyes to focus. He hadn't intended to sleep, just to put his head down and close his eyes for a few minutes, but now he caught the chronometer and realized that had been nearly four hours before. He felt a burst of self-recrimination, and he wondered if he'd have allowed himself to fall asleep at his desk when he was younger. He hadn't realized what the war with the Union had drained from him. But now, with the prospect of a new conflict, he wondered if he could serve as he had before, to give all, and to stand by and issue orders as he watched so many of his people die.

He wondered if his grandfather had experienced similar feelings. The elder Barron had been a legend, one whose martial brilliance had been almost singlehandedly responsible for bringing the Confederation back from the brink of defeat. But, that had been during the second war with the Union. Barron's namesake had died in the third war, his ship trapped by a Union strike force and destroyed. Tyler had never considered that his grandfather's death could have been caused to some extent by fatigue, by the fact that he hadn't been able to enter a third war with the energy and determination he'd brought to the first. At least, he'd never considered it until now.

Barron's head was heavy, his thoughts still foggy. He'd been trying to hold off taking another stim. He could feel the effects of the ones he'd been sucking down like candy over the past few days, and he suspected he was going to need more of them in the near future, but, still, four hours of sleep seemed like an irresponsible decadence.

"It's Captain Horace, sir. He sent his cutter back through the transit point with a communique for you." Eaton paused for a few seconds. "It is designated classified, your eyes only, sir."

Barron wondered why Horace would classify a report, but then he remembered what a hard-ass the old officer was. He could only think of one thing that could be in the transmission, and, if it was what he guessed, it was time to make a final decision. *I guess old "Ramrod" Horace figured I'd want to make that myself, or at least get a head start before half the fleet offered opinions.*

"I'll listen to it here." He reached out, fumbling around on his desk, still trying to get the sleep out of his head.

Eaton leaned forward, and tapped at the controls of the comm unit, taking over for his rough efforts. "On your headset, sir?"

"No, put it on speaker, Captain." There was no one else in the room but Eaton and himself…and she was doing a damned fine job of filling in for Atara Travis. He'd never have kept anything from Atara, and he wasn't going to do it from Eaton either. He needed at least one close confidante, an aide—a friend—he could trust to give him an honest opinion. "Sit, Captain. Listen in." He suspected they both knew what Horace's transmission would say.

Barron flipped the switch and activated the comm unit. "Admiral Barron, we have detected enemy forces emerging from this system's gamma transit point."

At least the gamma point is on the other side of the system. We should have a couple days before they can reach us here.

"I, unfortunately, have limited scanning information at this range. As I send this transmission, ships are still emerging…" Horace hesitated, which sent a chill down Barron's spine. He'd never known his old instructor to be unnerved by anything. "… and we are picking up several large contacts, Admiral. We can't get exact mass readings this far out, but my best guess is, the biggest ships substantially out-mass *Dauntless* and the other *Repulse*-class battleships.

The words hit Barron like a bat. This new enemy—the Hegemony, they called themselves—had superior technology… and now, it seemed, also ships larger than the Confederation's biggest. He looked up, his eyes finding Eaton's. He could see the shock in her expression, and he knew she was thinking the same thing he was.

He felt the urge to flee, to issue a fleet order and bolt for the transit point leading back to the Confederation. There were reasons to run, besides whatever role the natural desire for survival was playing in his thoughts. Megara *had* to be warned. The Confederation faced a grave new threat, and Admiral Striker and the others needed to know as soon as possible what the White Fleet had found.

It all made sense…until he thought about leaving his people on the surface. There was no coldly rational argument to make that a consideration. A few hundred people were nothing compared to the tens of thousands in the fleet…or the billions back in the Confederation. But Atara's face was there in his thoughts, resolutely staring up at the sky, almost as if she could see the fleet leaving, abandoning her and the others to the enemy's mercy.

But he was the fleet's commander and the Confederation's senior representative first, and Atara Travis's friend second. It *had* to be that way…and she would have been the first one to scold him if he ever forgot that. But that perspective hardly offered clarity. Warning the Confederation was essential, but that wouldn't take the whole fleet. He could send dispatches back to Megara…and still stand and fight. The Confederation was a peaceful nation, in its ideals if not in its actual history. But there was little cause for optimism with this new adversary. If they truly considered themselves to be superior to all other groups of humans, was there any chance for peace?

And do I dare show fear in front of them, weakness?

He remembered Globus's words at the meeting, the Alliance commander's urgings that the fleet must present a show of strength. He'd discounted the argument as Palatian bluster when he'd first heard it.

But now he remembered his mission seven years before, the deadly trip the old *Dauntless* had taken to Santis, to meet an invader…and to show strength in a situation where weakness would invite invasion and war. His people had fought a desperate battle there, and sent the only message to the Palatians that they could understand. The strength his people had shown, at such terrible cost, had prevented a war…and led years later to the Confederation-Palatian Alliance, turning an enemy into a friend.

From what he'd seen so far of the Hegemony, he doubted a show of strength, no matter how firm, would prevent a conflict…but it just might delay it. If the fleet turned tail and ran, the enemy might pursue. They might push forward to the Rim at once, and invade the Confederation immediately. If Barron could hurt the enemy here, show them that the Confederation would be no easy conquest…perhaps he could buy time. The Hegemony seemed utterly convinced of its superiority, but Barron had seen no signs of the codes of honor or martial traditions that so shaped the Alliance, and sometimes led the Palatians into foolish endeavors. If he could hit them hard enough, give them a bloody nose, maybe they would pause.

That just might give Admiral Striker enough time to get all the demobilized ships back into service…and to get word to

Vian Tulus. He was sure the Alliance's new Imperator would take his warning seriously, and send the battered remnants of the Palatian fleet to fight alongside the Confederation forces.

If we can just buy enough time…

He'd been listening to the rest of Horace's report, mostly numbers of ships, estimated masses, and notes on the formation. The officer was perhaps the hardest Barron had ever known, and also one of the most meticulous. Barron wasn't sure all the information was helpful, but he never remembered a combat situation where he'd suffered for having too much knowledge. Still, he reached out and turned off the comm. He'd heard all he needed to hear for now…and he'd made a decision.

"Captain, send a communications drone back through the transit point. *Kraken* is to return to this system at once. Instruct Captain Horace to launch all his remaining drones first, with programming to send one back every two hours, and also as the enemy fleet hits any range bands he feels are significant."

"Yes, sir." Eaton stood up abruptly, turning to move toward the door.

"Sonya?"

"Sir?"

"As soon as you send the drone, I want you to get the task force commanders on the fleetcom." He'd ordered the fleet formation condensed, and most of the ships were now within reasonable comm distance of *Dauntless*. There were still some outliers, and the communications would be difficult and cumbersome to an extent…but he had to talk to his commanders. Immediately.

"Yes, sir." He could hear defiance in her voice, building, pushing back against the fear.

He leaned back and watched her leave, and then he let out a long, deep exhale. He, too, felt his determination growing, the anger at these people and their attitudes, at the way they treated the natives of Planet Zero…and how they'd ignored his every effort to seek a peaceful solution.

"Admiral…" That quickly, Eaton's voice was on the comm. "…all commanders on fleetcom now, sir…awaiting your transmission."

"Very well," he said, his hand moving toward the controls, pausing for a few seconds above the switch, thinking about what he wanted to say. The time for discussion had passed. His words now were for those who served him, to rally them for the fight, to awaken the warriors he knew lived inside each of them.

The fleet was going to prepare for battle, and he was going to make damned sure everyone was ready, from his highest commanders, to the stewards drafted into damage control duties. They weren't going to turn around and run. He'd shown strength once before in a similar situation, perhaps on a vastly smaller scale than the battle that loomed in front of him here, but, still…the memory nagged at him. He knew what might have happened if *Dauntless* had run at Santis, if he'd shown weakness rather than strength to an Alliance ready to strike.

No, he wasn't going to run. He wasn't going to abandon his people on the surface…and he damned sure wasn't going to do anything to feed the notions of superiority the Masters of the Hegemony so clearly felt.

If they were so much more capable, they could show him. They could take on all the White Fleet had to give, the sweat and blood of its battle-hardened ships and veteran crew…and then they could see how their theories of genetic superiority held up.

He didn't know if his people could win, but he was damned sure they would put up one hell of a fight…and whatever happened, they would give the Hegemony's forces a taste of what awaited them if they invaded the Confederation.

Chapter Thirty-Six

Planet Zero
Zed-11 System
Year 315 AC

Stu Weldon turned to the side and stumbled, reaching out and grabbing at the table in a fruitless effort to stay his fall. He landed hard on the ground, dropping the canister he'd been holding.

Travis jumped up from the chair she'd been sitting in and pulled the needle from her arm, wincing slightly as she did. She raced across the room and bent down over the doctor. "Stu... are you all right?"

"Just a little dizzy..." His words were soft, slurred. She could see he was barely conscious. He looked up at her. "Stim..."

She shook her head. "You just had one an hour ago. You saw the test results." Weldon had done a quick scan on himself, checking the damage he'd done by shooting up on industrial strength stims for as long as he had. The results were grim. There was no way to be sure which would be the dosage that would kill him. It might be the next, or the third or fourth after that, but it wouldn't be much longer.

"Going to die anyway...got to keep going..."

Travis was resistant at first, her thoughts fixed on protecting the doctor, her friend, from himself. But Weldon's logic was, unfortunately, flawless. He needed the stims because of the disease that was killing him, and in the end, it really didn't matter which did the job first. At least if he kept going, there was a chance, however vanishing, that he might succeed at his seemingly impossible job.

Travis finally nodded, making herself a bit lightheaded as well. She'd given Weldon as much blood as he'd been willing to take. The doctor, despite the grim fate that awaited him—and all the others who were still clinging to life—had refused to allow her to endanger herself, at least beyond a little dizziness.

"Okay," she said, still not feeling great about it. She reached over to the table, pulling up the injector and checking to make sure it held another dose. She paused for a few seconds, unsure if Weldon was going to get up and inject himself, but the doctor just lay where he was, looking almost like he was in a stupor. She reached down, holding the injector, and stopped just short of his arm. She didn't want to do it. She was well aware it could kill Weldon, and she had no idea of the lasting health effects of such abuse of very powerful stimulants. But the facts remained...unless he could make this new serum work, and do it quickly, he was as good as dead. He'd sent his findings up to the fleet, of course, and she didn't doubt the med teams were working feverishly there, but they didn't have her blood...and she was the only one in the landing party who had not fallen ill.

She shoved the injector against his upper arm and heard the click as the tiny needles shot into his flesh, giving the dying doctor yet another 10cc of the potent drug. He sat where he was, almost still for perhaps fifteen or twenty seconds as his energy returned. Then he stood up, clearly still struggling with the soreness she knew was affecting every muscle in his body. He'd refused painkillers, wanting to stay as sharp as he could.

He propped himself up on his arms, leaning on the desk for a few seconds and taking two or three deep breaths. Then he reached out and picked up a small vial. He slid it into a machine sitting on the table, and flipped a switch. A clear liquid from a second container poured into the vial, and the machine shook the container, thoroughly mixing the two substances.

He turned and looked over at Travis. "Well, Atara...this should be it. I followed the same procedure I did before, only this time with your blood. If this doesn't work, I'm afraid it's over. I have no idea where else to go from here."

Travis felt her stomach tighten. The idea of watching everyone in the landing party die, including Weldon, was upsetting. But, there was something else there too, and she was ashamed by it. She thought about herself, about being stuck on the planet after the rest of the landing party was gone, alone with only the locals...and the Master she knew she couldn't watch around the clock. Even now, she had two very sick Marines watching him, but it wouldn't be long before he could simply walk out of the hut where she had him confined. What would he do? Order the locals to tear her to pieces? She wasn't sure how that would go... they seemed as intimated by her and the rest of the landing party as by the Master. But she wasn't anxious to find out.

But you will...if Weldon's serum doesn't work. You know you can't go back. There's no proof you're truly immune, and even if you are, you have no idea if you can carry this plague back with you even though you're not sick. It will tear Tyler apart...but he'll have to leave you here, alone...

She tried to use shame to drive the thoughts from her mind, but they remained nevertheless. The idea of being marooned in such a strange and alien place terrified her as none of the deadly battles she fought ever had. It was taking all she had to maintain her control, to hold back the panic trying to take her.

Yes, tell your dying friend that you're upset because you will be stuck here alone...after he's dead. Pull yourself together, Atara...

"Well, we'd better see if it works." She glanced down at the table for a few seconds. "Are you sure you want to test it on yourself? We could bring in one of the others if..."

"It has to be me, Atara. For the same reason as before. If it works, I'll have to find a way to make more...somehow. I've got maybe a dozen doses here, but we're going to need a lot more than that." He left unspoken that meant he would need more of her blood, a lot more. And quickly.

She just nodded. There was no use worrying about how much blood she could give, not until they knew the serum worked.

She stood and watched as Weldon took the injector and moved it toward himself. He paused for a moment and looked over at Travis. "Whatever happens, Atara, thank you for your assistance. Thanks for...everything."

Travis wanted to answer, but all she could manage was a nod, and a mostly successful effort to hold back the tears trying to well up in her eyes. Weldon had been *Dauntless*'s chief medical officer from the day she and Barron had set foot on the now-legendary vessel. He'd become a close friend since then, one of the very few she had, and now she knew she would see if he'd managed to create a miracle of sorts...or if she was going to have to watch him die on this shithole planet.

He managed to give her a frail smile...and then he injected himself with the drug.

* * *

"Commander Globus reports his ships are in position, Admiral." Sonya Eaton was at her chair in the control center. Barron was looking over, watching her lean forward, somehow keeping track of nearly half a dozen small screens feeding her information on the fleet deployment in progress. Her own job was an immense load, but now she was doing everything Atara would have handled as well, except for actually commanding *Dauntless*. Barron himself had taken on that responsibility, and he felt a little guilty for how anxious he was to wear that hat with Atara trapped down on the surface. The magnificent new battleship wasn't *his Dauntless*, and he'd sworn she never could be. But he'd come to appreciate the new vessel. She might not be the ship he'd always remember as his first command, but she was a fitting successor.

She's not your successor...she's Atara's ship. You're just standing in.

"Very well, Captain." Barron might have been amused at how quickly Globus had gotten his Alliance forces ready for the fight that was coming. The veteran commander was a very intelligent man, Barron had seen that firsthand...and a reasonable one, too, at times. But he had the weakness for battle that was so ingrained in his people. The Hegemony had attacked first, and to Globus, their conduct was an insult to the fleet. Barron had come to know his Alliance comrades very well, and if he'd learned one thing, it was: don't insult a Palatian…not unless you're looking for a fight to the death.

He glanced down at his own comm unit, thinking he should talk to Fritz before the enemy arrived. The primary duty of her new role had been to analyze any old tech the fleet found, but instead of piles of artifacts, the expedition had stumbled onto something it hadn't wanted or expected; a new enemy. Anya Fritz could do the most good now by taking personal charge of the flagship's damage control…and, hopefully, keeping the big ship going for as long as possible, just as she had on the old *Dauntless*.

He was about to reach down to the unit when the lift doors opened, and none other than Captain Anya Fritz stepped out into the control room.

Barron looked with a start. He couldn't remember Fritz ever setting foot on the old *Dauntless*'s bridge, though he was sure she must have upon occasion. She'd always considered the engineering sections to be her domain, and save for moving around from one damaged section of the ship to another, she generally stayed within those invisible borders.

"Fritzie, I was just about to comm you. I want you to take over *Dauntless*'s engineering teams during the battle. There's not much you can do fleet-wide in the middle of a fight, so let's focus your magic on this ship."

"Yes, sir, of course. I'd assumed I would do that." She was right, of course. She was in command of engineering operations fleet-wide, which meant she could assign herself to *Dauntless*. But there was something else on her mind, too. He wasn't sure what, but she seemed edgy.

"Is there something wrong, Fritzie?"

"No, sir…we just had an idea, and I…" She hesitated.

"We, Fritzie? Who's 'we?'"

"Well, sir…"

"Admiral, I've got Commodore Eaton on your line." Barron

turned his head. It always seemed a bit surprising to him when Sonya Eaton referred to her sister so impersonally. Both of the Eatons were consummate professionals, and he'd be the first one to sing either of their praises.

He glanced back at Fritz. "Put her on speaker, Captain."

"Admiral…"

"Yes, Commodore. I'm here with Captain Fritz. What is it?"

"I was talking with…Captain Fritz earlier, and…"

"And, clearly the two of you are plotting something, so one of you come out already and say it."

"We want to mine the space just this side of the transit point, Admiral," Eaton blurted out. Fritz was standing in the same spot, nodding.

Barron looked at Fritz for a second, and then he adjusted the microphone on his headset. "We haven't used mines in fifty years…" He found that he wasn't sure whether to say "Commodore" or "Captain," so he didn't finish the sentence.

Mines had been a key weapon half a century earlier, one that had been extensively used to defend transit points against assault. But the Confederation had developed methods for sending out pulses from their ships that detonated the mines before a ship reached them…and it had taken Sector Nine less than a year to steal that knowledge for Union use. Within a decade, every Rim nation possessed the countermeasures to battle mine-fields…using the same technology that had rendered missiles ineffective in space combat.

"Sir," Fritz said nervously, "this is only a guess, but just because we developed the technology to deal with mines doesn't mean these people have. We don't know much about the… Masters…" She said the word with considerable distaste in her tone. "…but it's a reasonable guess that, living so close to the center of the Cataclysm, they haven't had to deal with as many surviving neighbors as we have…or the number of desperate wars we've fought. Struggles like that are a catalyst for weapons development…one they might have lacked."

"But their technology is ahead of ours."

"Yes, Admiral, but that doesn't mean they developed all the

same things we have." It was Eaton this time, and Fritz nodded as the commodore spoke. "We only developed our anti-mine tech because of our constant wars against the Union. If we'd been at peace for the past century, we might have developed different things...but we'd probably never have even researched countermeasures for theoretical minefields."

Barron understood what his two officers were saying, but he still wasn't convinced. "But, their technology is clearly sufficient to develop the same countermeasures we did."

"Yes, sir," Fritz said, "but not before this coming battle. We're not suggesting we have a long-term edge against the Masters...but we just might have a way to get a jump here and now."

Barron was beginning to agree...and he was ready to take any advantage he could get. "But, we don't have mines. As far as I know, the Confederation hasn't produced any in more than forty years."

"I...ah...well, sir...I cobbled some together." Fritz stood where she was, but she didn't look directly at Barron.

"You what?"

"Well, Admiral...you did put me in charge of fleet engineering...and we do have a lot of extra equipment, especially on the supply ships." She paused. "I managed to put a hundred and twenty mines together...not enough for a proper field, but the way I see it—the way Commodore Eaton and I see it—any of those ships we can take out, or even damage, is worth the effort."

Barron looked back at his engineer, amazed not at her suggestion, but that somehow, despite all the miracles he'd seen her perform, he still managed to underestimate her sometimes. "Do it, Fritzie...and Commodore." He paused, holding back a smile the best he could. "Fritzie, you get those mines ready to go. If we're going to get them in place before the enemy transits into this system, we don't have much time. Sara...this was your idea, too, so you figure out the positioning. Put them wherever you think they'll do the most good."

"Yes, sir."

"Yes, sir."

The two answered, almost simultaneously.

"Then get it done." He turned and shook his head, once again grateful for the people he had around him.

*   *   *

"Why is it always you?" Stara Sinclair almost always kept her emotions in check, but not now. Stockton hadn't expected her to like his plan, but he was surprised when she blew up at him. She'd calmed down some since then, but she was still clearly upset.

"You know why it's me, Stara." Stockton understood her reaction—at least, he thought he did. He didn't suspect it was easy to be in a relationship with him, especially considering his reputation for what people had charitably described as craziness. He'd been wild as a younger pilot, even he could admit that. But he'd grown out of that—and had been promoted above it, too. It had been two years since he'd done anything more dangerous than flying around in training missions.

Then, suddenly, he realized. Stara had been steeled up to face the realities of war back then, but the new threat was just sinking in. She didn't have her defenses up, and the idea of him blasting through the transit point to stand alone before an entire attacking fleet, slipping away only at the last second, was too much for her to accept.

But, she didn't have a choice. Stockton had told Admiral Barron he would do it, and that was the last word as far as he was concerned. Even if he hadn't promised the admiral, he understood the threat menacing the fleet, the danger the entire Confederation and all of its neighbors faced. He agreed with Barron, and with the Palatians. The best thing the fleet could do was give this new enemy a bloody nose. Hopefully, it would make them rethink things, bring them to the bargaining table… and even if it didn't, it might give them pause, buy some time. His mission was the best way to accomplish that, maybe the only way.

Close-in transit point defenses were rare in war, for a vari-

ety of reasons, not the least of which was, without knowing an
attacking fleet's vector and velocity, it was impossible to place
defensive ships. A force could deploy right at the point, only
to watch a fleet come through at 0.01c and zip past and out
of range in a matter of seconds. But Stockton could scan the
approaching fleet, and the longer he stayed—the closer he cut
it—the better and more accurate his nav information would be
when he zipped back into Zed-11 and sent his report to the
fleet.

Stara fell silent as the two walked down the corridor and out
onto the landing bay. She'd argued with him, but even when
she'd been most upset, he was sure she knew he had to go. She
was as much a veteran as he was, and she knew the stakes just
as well. It hurt him to see how worried she was, how much his
mission was hurting her. It was a long unanswered question…
what's worse, going into danger, or waiting to see if a loved one returns?
He didn't pretend, even to himself, that he had any great wisdom in such matters, but he knew that mystery didn't apply here,
not really. Stara wouldn't be safe on some well-protected planet
somewhere…she'd be at her station on *Dauntless*, going into
battle with the rest of the fleet. And he was damned committed to do whatever he could to help the fleet gain an edge. Help
Dauntless—and Stara—make it through.

"I'll be back…I'm always back." He'd said such things all his
life, but now it even sounded hollow to him. He'd seen too many
people die. One day, he suspected, he would leave after spewing
that kind of bluster…and he wouldn't come back.

But that's not this time, he told himself. If he didn't get back, he
couldn't report…and if he didn't report, Barron wouldn't know
where to position his ships.

He stopped next to his fighter, scanning it quickly, his eyes
going to the modifications the engineering teams had quickly
made. She was like a bird he'd flown once before, on an even
longer mission. She carried twice the fuel of a normal Lightning, and a host of extra scanning and communications gear.

All that came at a cost, though, and in this case that was
weapons. All of them, even the targeting computer. He was

going to fly his fighter and hold his ground right in front of the enemy fleet…and he wouldn't have a laser hot enough to light a candle.

He turned toward Stara. "I'll be back…" He almost said, "I promise," but he had enough of the pilot's superstition left in him to hold back, not to tempt fortune's wrath. "I love you," he finally said softly.

She looked back at him, her face still, clearly struggling to hold back her emotions. "I love you, too," she said. "I'll take you through the launch sequence." Then she just turned and left, heading back to the control center.

Stockton watched her go, just for a few seconds. Then he turned and climbed up the ladder, hopping into his cockpit.

He regretted the fact that the fleet had found a new enemy, that the peace his comrades had enjoyed for two years had been shattered. But as he sat in the confines of the fighter, waiting for Stara's voice to come on the comm, he had a thought…one he found disturbing, but also one he knew was true.

It felt like home.

Chapter Thirty-Seven

Andi felt pressure against the skin on her arm. Devices like the injector were normally painless, but her captors had worked her over so many times that every square millimeter of her body was sore. The tiny pinpricks only inflamed the pain she'd been feeling more or less constantly for weeks now, and she cried out, hating herself for giving the bastards the satisfaction. She was ready to tell them whatever they wanted to know to get them to stop, even without the drug, and that realization had obliterated her sense of self-worth. She'd liked to believe she was unbreakable, that no enemy could shatter her will to resist, but now she only wished she had something, anything to tell them, just to end the torment…even though she doubted they'd stop even then. None of that really mattered anymore, except to feed her self-loathing. She didn't know anything, at least nothing they seemed to be after.

The pain in her arm spread, and she realized it was the drug, moving through her bloodstream. It wouldn't kill her, she was sure enough of that, but Lille's words echoed in her head, and she imagined herself a vegetable, or a meek, useless shell of what she'd been. Better to die, far better. She regretted that she hadn't fought back harder when she'd had the strength, forced her captors to kill her…but then, that would have been a form of surrender, too, at least while there had still be a chance for her to escape. Or for Gary Holsten to find her.

Even as she thought of Holsten, she heard sounds, banging at first, and then gunfire. She was dreaming—she was sure of it—imagining the rescue attempt she'd waited and hoped for. But, she didn't believe it anymore. Her captors were too good. Ricard Lille was the best Sector Nine had.

I guess I should feel honored…

There was more gunfire now, some kind of automatic weapon, and then an explosion, one that sent a cloud of dust dropping from the room's low ceiling.

For an instant, she was confused, surprised at how real her dream seemed to be…and, then she realized…

It's real. There's some kind of fight going on.

She opened her eyes, tried to focus. Everything was a blur. She'd been in bad enough shape, but now she could feel the drug taking hold. Even as she realized there was a battle in progress all around her, that perhaps Holsten's people had finally found her, she felt herself slipping from reality, her perceptions drifting away. She tried to fight it, but she found herself giving in, *wanting* to yield, to escape the pain.

She struggled through the pain to pull herself back, to hang onto what little remained of herself. She closed her eyes tightly, then opened them again and squinted, trying to see what was happening.

The sounds of fighting were louder now, closer. And she could see the agent in the room with her, staring at the stairs leading up from the cellar where she'd been held. Lille…

Her eyes caught her tormentor, ducking through a small door, barely a meter high.

An escape route. No…you don't get away. You don't survive, bastard…

But she knew there was nothing she could do, even as her hatred for Lille gave her flagging energy a boost. She was still looking when he turned around and gestured to one of the men standing in the room. "Kill her," he said.

The words echoed in her ears, in her mind. She could barely keep her thoughts functioning, to see through the pain, but she'd heard Lille's command, and she knew what it meant. She tried to get up, to lunge toward her captors…her executioners, but there was nothing. Her legs wouldn't move, nor her arms. The drug had her almost paralyzed. All she could do was shift her head to the side…enough to see the arm of one of the men rising…and the pistol it held.

She struggled to move, to force her body forward in a last lunge at her killers. She wanted to die as a fighter, resisting to the last—not an animal, led to slaughter. But her muscles didn't respond, and she sat frozen, in helpless agony as the man pointed his pistol.

And fired.

She heard the gunshot…but she didn't feel anything. She waited for her body to fall, for the pain, for the blood pouring out of her…for death to take her. But then, there was another shot, and another. Still nothing. She just sat where she was, paralyzed…and watching as her would-be killer fell forward, landing face down, his gun skittering across the floor.

There were more shots now, automatic fire, and all around the room she could see shadows, and then people, figured dressed in some kind of combat fatigues, with heavy body armor. *Soldiers of some kind…no, those are Confederation Marines…*

She felt herself slipping away, the drug sapping what remained of her strength. She tried desperately to cling to consciousness, to call out to whoever was attacking her captors. But there was nothing left, nothing but the growing darkness.

* * *

Gary Holsten stood in the hospital room, looking down at the figure in the bed. He'd always liked Andi Lafarge, and respected her, too…her independence, her drive, the raw intelligence that was so much stronger than most people knew. She was as close to him as anyone was, save perhaps Van Striker, and he was aware just how important she was to another of his most important friends, Tyler Barron.

He'd recruited her because he trusted her, both her loyalty and her ability to handle any crisis she encountered. She'd been up against danger most of her adult life, and Holsten had truly believed he could keep her safe on Dannith.

But he hadn't expected the Union's intelligence agency to have recovered so quickly…and he certainly hadn't bargained with Andi meeting an adversary like Ricard Lille almost immediately after arriving on Dannith.

Holsten knew Lille, at least he *knew of* the Sector Nine killer. Lille was Gaston Villieneuve's right hand, and based on what little intel Holsten had managed to gather on the mysterious assassin, the two men were actually friends. He still believed Andi could have handled almost any agent she was up against, but Lille was something entirely different. For all her adventures, and the fights and dangers she'd faced, Andi was new to espionage…and Ricard Lille was, by all accounts, the very best on either side.

He was still watching her, as he had been for hours now, when she finally stirred. She was hurt, badly. Broken ribs, a shattered ulna, internal bleeding, a ruptured lung, more contusions than he could easily count…the list went on and on. But all of that was treatable. It was the drug that worried him, the one they had given her. It had wreaked havoc on her system, and for a while he had worried there would be brain damage. But the doctors—and he'd rounded up every surgeon and physician on Dannith worth the name, bringing some of them to the hospital along with a Marine escort—had assured him they'd intervened in time. She would be groggy, and there would be more pain. But she would recover…completely.

He was relieved, but, looking at her, he still had trouble believing it, and whatever the long-term prognosis, he knew his friend had an extended and painful recovery ahead of her. And, he knew it was his fault.

"Gary…" Her voice was thin, labored. She looked up at him, her eyes cloudy, unfocused.

"I'm here, Andi." He tried to sound strong, to keep the regret and sadness from his words. She didn't need that now. She needed a hand she trusted, one that could lead her back. The doctors might save her life, bring her back to physical health, but Holsten had seen enough broken, tortured agents to know that Andi faced other challenges. She would need support, people she trusted and who cared about her. Most of all, he suspected, she would need Tyler Barron...but he had been one of the prime movers in sending Barron hundreds of lightyears away. It would be months before he returned, even years.

"Thanks...for...rescuing...me..." He could see her trying to move her head up, extend her arm toward him, but she gave up and let both drop back to the bed, wincing in pain.

"You have to take it easy, Andi. You're going to be all right, as good as new." He wondered if his words were empty, or if he truly believed she was strong enough to find her way back. He was scared for her...but he knew better than to bet against Andi Lafarge. "You're going to have to rest."

"Tyler?"

Holsten sighed softly. "He's with the White Fleet, Andi. You remember..."

She looked confused for a moment, but then she nodded, or at least something close to a small nod. "White Fleet...yes, I... remember."

"Andi, you're going to be in the hospital for a while, but I don't want you to worry about anything." He turned and gestured to an armed woman in combat dress and armor, standing just inside the door. "There will be a squad of Marines on duty here, and outside your room around the clock. No one will hurt you again."

She looked at Holsten, and he could see her eyes were a little brighter than they'd been. "Thank you...Gary." Then, she stared at him for a for a few seconds, a look of clarity replacing the confused expression she'd worn since she'd awakened. "Not... your...fault..."

He appreciated her words...but they cut through him like a knife, as well. She was absolving him, but if it hadn't been for him, she'd still be on Tellurus, in her big, beautiful villa. She might be bored, but she wouldn't be lying in bed, battered to death's door…and no doubt, struggling with memories he couldn't even imagine.

He would feel guilty for recruiting her for as long as he lived, and his only solace was that he had done everything necessary to save her. Whatever the eventual cost…

Even as he thought about it, he heard a commotion out in the hall. He knew what it was, or at least he had a good idea, and he didn't think Andi needed to see it.

"I'll be back to check on you later, Andi." He leaned down and kissed her on the forehead. "You get some rest…and don't worry about anything. No one can get to you here."

She managed a thin smile, all the response he needed. Then, he turned around and walked out into the hall.

The Marines in Andi's detail were standing in front of the door, tense, holding their weapons, but not pointing them at anyone. Yet. They had formed a rough line—one that included Colonel Peterson, he realized. Facing them were other uniformed personnel. *Port Royal City police.*

And behind the police, most of whom carried heavy riot gear, were Walter Aguillar and his collection of Troyus City parasites. The Senatorial aide wore an obnoxious smile, one Holsten desperately wanted to slap off his face.

"You are under arrest, Mr. Holsten, for the offenses listed in this Senate Order, and for your efforts in resisting apprehension. You will come with me now. My orders are very clear. I am to bring you to Megara to answer the charges against you."

Holsten felt his defiance rising. He was about to hurl an insult at the sleazy piece of shit when Peterson beat him to it.

"Mr. Holsten is under our protection." His tone was hard, cold…everything a fop like Aguillar probably expected—and likely feared—from a veteran warrior like Peterson.

"Do not interfere, Colonel," Aguillar managed to say, making a partially successful effort to hide the fear in his voice. "This doesn't concern you."

"The hell it doesn't, you useless piece of Troyus City garbage." Peterson arched back and, though it hadn't seemed possible, he stood up straighter than he had been. He was almost a full head taller than Aguillar. His hand was at his side, resting on the holster that held what Holsten could only imagine was a well-worn pistol.

Aguillar looked queasy, as though he might throw up any moment, but the aide impressed Holsten by only taking one step back.

"Captain, prepare your officers." It was another voice. Holsten could see the man standing behind the police, and he recognized him immediately. Stanford Beresford, the president of the Dannith Planetary Assembly…and a politician who'd spent every waking moment over the past weeks railing against the blockade and the Marines bashing down doors all over the planet.

The police looked nervous, and Holsten could see most of them looking over at the Marines. But, one by one, they drew their weapons.

"Marines, at the ready." Peterson's voice was crisp, his tone in every way that of a combat veteran. Jonathan Peterson had fought against Foudre Rouge…Holsten didn't imagine the Marine was the slightest bit intimidated by a bunch of local cops and Senatorial lapdog guards, even if they outnumbered his people by better than two to one.

"I'm warning you, Colonel. You have one last chance to stand down…or I'll have you arrested as well.

Holsten was surprised at Aguillar's burst of courage, and he winced instinctively, having some idea what the Marine's response would be.

"You listen to me, you pampered piece of garbage. You may think you're a tough guy, coming here with your bullshit orders and this crowd of enforcers, but you ain't got nothing more than a mob fit to scold a bunch of kids on a playground. My Marines have seen things that would make you wet the pants of that fancy suit you've got on."

Aguillar stood silently for a moment. Holsten suspected the Senatorial errand boy was trying to steel up his courage, to convince himself Confederation Marines would never open fire on a group of local police and a representative of the Senate. Holsten might have thought that, too, but he knew Peterson well, and he wasn't so sure anymore.

"It's up to you. What's it gonna be?" Peterson raised his hand, and the Marines brought their rifles up, not quite aiming at the police, but definitely at the ready.

Holsten was gratified that his friend would go so far to protect him. He didn't doubt the ten Marines could wipe out the two dozen or so police and Lictors, and probably in three seconds without taking any losses.

At least losses on the spot. But such an action would be treason. They'd lose their careers, and that would be just the start. They would probably spend the rest of their lives in the stockade. Jon Peterson might even mount the scaffold. Holsten was grateful, to his friend, to the Marines. But he couldn't be the reason Confederation Marines clashed with civilian law enforcement personnel. It was hard to even imagine the damage *that* would do to the Confederation, to the delicate balance that made the whole thing work when every other nation on the Rim embraced some form of total or partial autocracy.

He'd done what he had to do for Andi. But she was safe now...and as defiant as he'd always been, he wasn't ready to be the reason the Confederation military killed Confederation civilians.

"No, Jon. Stand your Marines down." He paused, taking a shallow breath. "I'll go with them."

"Gary...you can't..."

"It's okay, Jon. Don't worry...getting me back to Megara isn't the end of the story, I can promise you that." He thought of the files he had, the dirt on members of the Senate. They were vile creatures, many of them, and they didn't deserve to hold the high offices they did. *And, if they push this too far, more than a few of them will lose those positions they lied and cheated and stole to get.* "Stand down, my friend. Please."

Holsten turned toward Peterson and forced a smile. "Please, Jon."

The colonel hesitated, but finally he nodded to Holsten, and then he put out a hand, lowering it. The Marines brought their rifles down, holding them at their sides.

"These Marines are not to get so much as a note in their files." Holsten's eyes were fixed on Aguillar's. Even as a man about to become a prisoner, Holsten's force of will rushed over the aide with the power of a tidal wave.

"We only want you. As long as these Marines stand down, we have no interest in them."

"Then I will come." He turned and looked back toward Peterson. "Jon, do one thing for me. Watch out for Andi... please."

"I will, Gary." Peterson's voice was somber, as emotional as Holsten had ever heard it. He'd always considered the Marine to be a friend, but he realized now there were certain times in life when you found out just who you could count on when you most needed help. Holsten would never forget Colonel Jonathan Peterson was firmly in that group.

"All right, let's go," he said to Aguillar, making sure his voice showed as little respect as possible. "Some of the people who sent you here are in for a rude awakening when I get back to Troyus City."

Chapter Thirty-Eight

Ten Thousand Kilometers from Transit Point Alpha
Zed-12 System
Year 315 AC

Stockton sat in the cockpit, twisting his body to the side, trying to work out the kinks. He'd been in his fighter for almost sixteen hours, which was nothing compared to the great multi-system journey he'd made years before, but it was still enough to get really uncomfortable. Stockton had fought in more battles than he could easily count, but he still remembered that very long flight as the most challenging thing he'd ever done. Lightnings weren't designed for such long duration missions, and the assortment of modifications needed to provide sufficient life support and fuel, not to mention addressing food needs and the accommodation of bodily functions, were extensive.

He'd been watching the Hegemony fleet moving toward the transit point, recording every move, every burst of thrust. Maybe someone back on *Dauntless* could make something of it all in terms of estimating enemy capabilities. It was clear enough just watching that the enemy had greater thrust capability than the Confederation vessels. That would be a strong edge in any fight, and combined with their longer ranged weapons, it laid a major problem at Admiral Barron's feet.

But if they really don't have fighters…that's an edge for us…

His thoughts had looped around, various versions of this kind of logic moving in and out of his mind. The topic wasn't nearly interesting enough to *really* make the hours go by—but it was better than seeing how many consecutive seconds he could count before his mind wandered.

He reached out, poking at the controls on his panel, double checking his status. The AI had done it already, but he was happier checking himself. First, it gave him something to do…and second, he would need everything his fighter could give him when it was time to sprint back to the transit point.

He'd brought a drone with him into Zed-12, though he still wasn't sure how Anya Fritz had managed to attach the thing to his fighter. He'd sent it back a couple hours before, with most of the data the fleet would need. His purpose now was to stay in position, and monitor any changes in enemy dispositions prior to transit. At least he wouldn't have the drone hanging off his ship on the way back. His fighter had handled like shit with that thing hanging off it…and the trip back would have a lot less room for error.

His eyes moved to the screen, watching as the approaching ships came closer. They didn't seem to be decelerating much, which probably meant they were going to come through at a relatively high velocity. That made sense. It was a precaution against a transit point defense on the other side…at least it was if the defenders didn't have current information on the attackers' velocity and vector.

It was almost time to go. Actually, by mission parameters, it was past time, but Stockton knew the longer he waited, the better his final data would be. His squadrons would launch as soon as he transited back and gave the order, and they would move to the positions he transmitted. If everything went according to plan, the enemy ships would zip out of the transit point, through the minefield Eaton and Fritz had laid, and straight into seven hundred twenty-four waiting fighters. The Hegemony forces would be heavily battered before they got close to a Confederation battleship.

Stockton was taking a chance with his strike forces, gambling that the enemy truly did not have its own squadrons. Fully two-thirds of his wings were outfitted as bombers, a deadly wave of immense destructive capacity if his bet was right...and a mass of sitting ducks if those ships coming on were, indeed, loaded up with their own fighters.

He looked back at the screens, checking the enemy ships as they got closer. His fighter wasn't as fast as an unmodified Lightning, he reminded himself. *Don't cut this too close...*

He flipped a row of switches, powering up his reactor. He'd been operating on minimal power, doing as little as possible to draw attention to himself, but now it was time to get his engines online. He double checked his course back to the transit point. Everything looked good.

He did one last scan of the enemy fleet...everything seemed unchanged. He'd already crunched the numbers, and he had the orders ready to transmit to his squadrons, who were waiting in the launch bays for him to return and give the final command.

He waited another few minutes, knowing he really *was* cutting it close. He didn't know the maximum acceleration of the Hegemony ships, and all it would take was their equivalent of a Confederation fast escort racing forward to intercept his ship short of transit. Getting the latest data was important, but the risk-reward relationship was shifting.

It was time.

He pulled on the throttle, bringing his ship around to line up his engines along his course to the transit point. Then he pulled back, slowly at first, just until he confirmed his engines were back online and firing properly. He slammed the controls all the way back and felt the force of acceleration slam into him as his fighter blasted hard for the transit point.

He didn't know if the enemy would pursue him, or it they would change their plans based on his presence...but they were getting close to the point now. Even with their superior thrust capacity, they could only modify things so much. Stockton was confident he had what he needed to put a hurt on them as they emerged.

He could see the wall of ships getting closer. For an instant, he thought several small vessels were accelerating toward him, but then he shook his head. They'd just repositioned themselves in the formation.

He looked straight ahead as he neared the point, bracing himself for the transit. The move between systems was more unpleasant in the confines of a fighter, which lacked the heavy shielding of larger vessels. He took a few deep breaths as his ship approached...and then he held his breath as his fighter slipped into the strange alternate reality of the tube.

The trip between systems only took a few seconds, but it seemed longer to Stockton, sitting there, trying to deal with the incomprehensible sensations of the strange space in the tube. The feeling wasn't pain, nor sickness, but it was decidedly uncomfortable, a sense of...wrongness.

Then, with a small flash of light, he emerged into the normal space of the Zed-11 system. He shook his head, trying to banish the disorientation as he waited for his systems to reboot. He put his hand to the side of his headset, his fingers on the activation controls, waiting for the row of green lights that would tell him his ship and its comm systems were back online.

The seconds passed, seeming longer for the tension he felt, the anxiety of the impending battle. Then he saw the lights flick on, and the displays on his panel came back to life.

His finger pushed against the button on the headset's earpiece. "*Dauntless* flight control, this is Raptor. I'm transmitting the latest enemy nav information. I project entry into the system in six minutes, twenty seconds." A short pause, then: "Fleet order...all squadrons launch. Repeat, all squadrons launch."

* * *

Atara lay back in the chair, her breath soft, shallow. She'd tried to get up twice, despite Weldon's strict instructions to stay where she was...and each time she'd fallen back into her seat, almost losing the contents of her stomach as the room spun around her.

She'd insisted Weldon take—her exact words were—*as much*

blood as he could without outright killing her. The doctor had hesitated, insisting that it was dangerous to draw too much, but
she'd reminded him that the lives of hundreds of their comrades depended on his producing as much serum as possible…
and then she outright ordered him to do it. There just wasn't
hadn't been any time to waste.

Atara had been shocked at how quickly Weldon himself had
recovered. The doctor had been deathly ill, barely clinging to
consciousness with the aid of deadly stim overdoses. But he
recovered at a rapid rate after injecting himself with the serum
derived from Atara's blood. He'd convulsed in pain at first, giving her a few minutes of worry and despair, but then the pain
subsided, and she could tell in a few minutes something was
happening. His fever broke almost at once, and the black lesions
on his skin, another sign of the terrible disease, began to dry
out and fall off within just a couple hours. By evening, maybe
six hours after he injected himself, he seemed almost normal.
Indeed, his only symptoms remaining were those caused by the
stims. By morning, a series of blood tests had confirmed. The
virus was gone.

Atara didn't know whether the problem applied to blood
from everyone on Planet Zero, or the Masters and survivors
on other worlds of the coreward region, but there wasn't time
for proper analysis, and Weldon's near fatal reaction to the first
reckless experiment hardly recommended more trial and error.
As far as she knew, right now, she was the only source of the
immunity factor that could save the landing party. And there
were a lot of them still sick, every one of them dying.

Weldon was trying to refine his formula, to stretch out the
blood she could supply…and he was pumping her full of retinol
and every other drug he could think of to spur increased blood
production in her body.

"I think I can get forty doses from the blood you were able
to provide. That doesn't get us through this nightmare, but giving it to the forty most dire cases will give us a little more time."
Weldon paused. "That is, of course, assuming the worst ones
aren't too far gone, even for the serum."

"Then let's not waste time. Go. The sickest ones are in cryostasis…that's going to complicate things a little, isn't it?"

"It will slow them down. I just don't have enough ambulatory staff to handle the medpods."

She leaned forward yet again, struggling to get to her feet.

"Atara, you're too weak to stand up, and certainly to help me by playing medtech with the pods."

"Give me one of those stims you were taking."

"No…you're too weak."

"Weaker than you were?" She angled her head and stared at him, a wordless message that he shouldn't even bother to try to tell her she was.

"No, perhaps not, but…"

"No buts. You know it's the only option. We've got, what, two dozen of the landing party still on their feet? And every one of them is sick, too, except you and me. So, let's cut the shit and give me one of those injections…and then we can go save our people."

She glared across the room, watching as he finally just nodded and turned to pick up the injector. She took a deep breath as he crossed the room to give her the shot. She knew she was right. There was no choice, none save watching her people die… and, to Atara Travis that was no option at all, not when there was any hope of saving them.

And, Bryan Rogan was at the top of that list. The big Marine had somehow endured, refusing to give up his fragile hold on life, even as men and women infected far later than Rogan had died every day. Rogan was one of Atara's true friends, and the idea of her blood providing a cure too late to save him was more than she wanted to imagine.

Hang on, Bryan…we're coming…

* * *

Stockton's fighter zipped through space, heading back toward the designated assembly area of the fleet's combined squadrons. He could see clouds of small craft converging as his fighter barreled toward the rendezvous point. The wings were far more densely concentrated than he'd ever seen in a major battle…but he was betting everything on the enemy's lack of their own squadrons, and he wanted his force focused, ready to hit the Hegemony ships hard.

Stockton had hoped the enemy wouldn't have any vessels bigger than those the fleet had already met and destroyed, but his scanning mission to Zed-12 had dashed those thoughts. He'd picked up numerous large contacts, even bigger than the new *Dauntless*…and those could only be battleships. The smaller vessels his people had faced had been tough enough. He knew it would take all his squadrons had to hurt the behemoths he knew were coming.

His eyes dropped to the screen displaying the data streaming in from the transit point drones. There were enhanced energy levels, but nothing else. No transits after his, no vessels coming through.

And then, one appeared. It was large, one of the big ones he'd presumed to be a battleship. It was half again as long as *Dauntless*, and his best guess was, it out-massed the fleet's flagship by at least two million tons, probably three million.

He was surprised. He'd expected something smaller, a scout-ship or frigate equivalent. But the Hegemony seemed to show no signs of caution. He wondered if they could be that certain of their invincible superiority…and then he thought about the aspect of the question that really scared him. Were they really *that* good?

More ships began to come through, one after the other. He analyzed their velocities and vectors, and he let out a breath of relief. The enemy ships were on exactly the course he'd projected.

He tapped his throttle and decelerated, beginning to bring his ship around to form up with his wings. He didn't have a single weapon aboard, but he'd be damned if he was going to run back to *Dauntless* and land while his people were about to go in. Lasers or no lasers, Jake "Raptor" Stockton was going to lead the attack.

There were almost two dozen ships through already, including five of the big ones, and Stockton reached out and tapped at his controls, overlaying the minefield on his scanner. The lead enemy ships were just entering the area, and he waited, noting they hadn't sent out any signals yet to detonate the mines.

Is it possible it's that simple? They've never faced mines before...so they don't have the countermeasures every Rim nation does?

He wished the fleet had carried more of the ordnance, that they hadn't been limited to the small number of makeshift mines Fritz and her crew had been able to throw together. But, anything was better than nothing, and his eyes were fixed on the display as the first of the enemy ships encountered one of the deadly weapons.

The ship didn't actually strike the mine...the percentage chance of something like that was vanishingly small with the distances involved in interplanetary navigation and combat. But, the massive nuclear warhead detonated less than three-quarters of a kilometer from the Hegemony battleship. The great vessel staggered, hit by massive waves of intensely hard radiation. In some areas, the alloy of the ship's hull buckled and melted as intense energy poured over the vessel. Gashes appeared in the armor, and great geysers of air and fluids blasted out into space, freezing almost instantly into long pillars that floated out from the stricken vessel like massive spears thrown into the void.

Stockton felt a smile forming on his lips as he saw the damage. He'd enjoyed two years of peace, but he'd always known that he was a creature of war. He craved peace...but he needed an enemy. Now, he had one, and from all he'd seen about them, they were even more detestable than the Union. The predator in him was alive again, in control, awakened from two years of hibernation. His grin widened as a second mine exploded, triggered by one of the smaller enemy ships. The vessel was a bit farther away, and the damage less severe...but every bit helped.

He sat in the cockpit, all thoughts of his discomfort and soreness gone now, and he watched as nearly two dozen mines detonated over the next few minutes. Ship after ship was impacted, at least two of them suffering what appeared to be serious damage. He tried to imagine the arrogant Masters, so utterly convinced of their superiority, communicating frantically as their ships triggered one nuclear detonation after another. He could pick up the signals back and forth between the ships, but the encryption had defied all attempts at decoding, at least so far.

He watched as the approaching force passed through the last of the mined area, and moved toward his waiting squadrons. His eyes narrowed, focused on the screen as the enemy's leading ships continued forward. He was watching for any evasive maneuvers, any course changes he'd have to match, but the wall of ships just kept coming forward.

He waited as another minute passed by, then ninety seconds. The enemy was coming on, just as he'd projected. It was time.

He flipped on his comm line, setting the channel to the entire strike force. "Attention all units, this is Raptor." He might have used his name and rank, but there wasn't a pilot in the force—or in the entire Confederation—who didn't know who Raptor was. "Here they come. These people don't seem to know what fighters can do, so we're going to give them a lesson now, one they'll never forget." He reached out, putting his hand on his ship's throttle. He didn't have a gun hot enough to cook his lunch, but he was going in with his people anyway. "Squadron leaders, you all know your positions. Bombers...this is your show. With any luck, you'll get the chance to hit these ships without worrying about interceptors, so take your time and focus. I want those torpedoes planted right into the guts of these ships. You've all seen what their heavy guns do to our capital ships, so keep that in mind when you're launching. Your comrades on the mother ships need you to hit this force hard, before they can get into range and rake our battleships."

Stockton tightened his grip on the throttle. "You're all veterans...you know what to do." That wasn't technically true. He had a few rookies in the strike force, but the vast majority of his people had seen action against the Union.

He took a deep breath and glanced down at his screen again. The enemy fleet was large, powerful...and he knew just how deadly those ships were. He was confident his wings would savage the Hegemony forces…but he didn't know if it would be enough. His squadrons would have the advantage now, but once they'd completed their runs, the surviving enemy ships would close and rake the fleet with deadly beams, long before *Dauntless* and the other battleships were able to return fire. He didn't know exactly how much damage his people had to cause to even things out…at least beyond the disturbingly non-specific "a lot."

He inhaled again, holding the breath for a few seconds before exhaling hard. Then he nodded, a gesture to himself, and he tapped the comm again.

"Let's go," he said, his voice cold, grim. "All squadrons… attack."

Chapter Thirty-Nine

Stockton brought his fighter around, angling toward the massive battleship sixty thousand kilometers directly ahead of him. At least, he assumed anything bigger than the huge new *Dauntless* had to be a battleship…though for all he really knew, the enemy considered the ship a frigate, and somewhere they had vessels three or four times the size.

That wasn't something he wanted to dwell on, not while his people were coming in against the largest, most powerful ship they'd ever faced. The imperial planetkiller had been larger, but that had been inoperative, and Stockton had no doubt that the vessel in front of him was completely ready for action.

He had two bomber squadrons coming in against the vessel, approaching along distinct vectors. He'd planned out every detail of the attack, and he'd allowed for any possibility. Simultaneous squadron assaults were difficult to execute and were intended mostly to overwhelm a target's point defense capability. The Hegemony vessels seemed to lack the dedicated anti-fighter batteries that Confederation vessels—and all other warships of the Rim nations—mounted. But, he'd seen the escort ships in the previous fight repurpose their smaller guns to close-in

310

defense…and he'd watched them make it work after a fashion, adapting, steadily increasing their kill rate. He wasn't going to let his guard down, not for an instant.

The squadron leaders acknowledged their bombers were in position.

"Yellow Lightning squadron, ready for attack run."

"Gold Vipers, ready."

Stockton took one last look at the scanner. Then he said, simply, "You may begin your attacks, Lightnings, Vipers."

He brought his own ship around, adjusting his vector to match those of the Gold Vipers. It wasn't an intentional preference. The Vipers were the closest to his position…and he intended to go in with the attack on way or another. *Dauntless*'s pilots, including the legendary Blue squadron, were on the far side of the formation. His instinct had been to fly over there, to join up with his old command. But, he knew they didn't need him. He'd forged the Blues into a deadly weapon, as he had all of *Dauntless*'s wings. It hurt to think they didn't need him anymore, but he knew it was true. He could do more with less experienced squadrons, like the Vipers and the Lightnings.

He positioned himself in the middle of the attacking squadron and tapped the throttle, matching his velocity with that of the bombers. He looked down at his screen. He had nothing of his own to throw against the enemy ship…but he could watch, study, analyze. He'd seen the enemy learning in the last battle, watched them figure out almost immediately how to counter his fighters. Now, *he* would watch…and learn exactly what the Hegemony ships could do.

Then he could figure out how to counter it. How to best destroy the enemy.

The target ship was just ahead, and even as he rechecked the range, his scanners flashed to life. The enemy was firing its weapons. For an instant, Stockton thought they might be using point defense batteries, but the pulses were too heavy, the firing angles too imprecise. The enemy was doing the same thing the earlier ships had, repurposing its smaller batteries…but the battleship had a *lot* more guns than the cruisers or escorts had.

"Evasive maneuvers going in…I don't want anyone getting careless. Those guns aren't optimized for anti-fighter operations, but a hit will kill you just as dead as a point defense laser." Stockton's hand moved to the side, following his own orders. Blundering into a clumsily-targeted laser blast wasn't the example he wanted to set for his pilots.

"And don't forget…these ships are faster and more maneuverable than our own." He didn't know that for certain about the battleships, but he'd seen the thrust levels the cruisers had employed, and it seemed a reasonable assumption that the big capital ships were also faster than their Confederation counterparts. "So, we're going in…all the way in. I don't want a torpedo launched outside ten thousand kilometers. And, six thousand would be better."

His eyes moved to the screen, watching the wave of bombers as they made their final approaches. The Vipers and Lightnings were coming in from different angles, one approaching the Hegemony ship's starboard side and the other, the port.

He watched as the ships formed up into three lines, a third of the vessels accelerating slightly and a third decelerating. Each squadron was coming in on a narrow angle, heading right for the massive ship's midsection. Stockton glanced at the range display…fifteen thousand kilometers. Very close by normal standards, but not for this fight. He'd already promised every pilot in the strike force that he'd skin them alive if they launched a torpedo from fifteen thousand.

The bombers moved closer in, and as they did, they began to take losses. One of the Vipers was hit first, followed by two of the Lightnings. The effectiveness of the enemy targeting was improving with each passing moment.

How could they analyze our approach and capabilities so quickly?

"I said evasive maneuvers!" he roared into the comm as he watched the second Lightning ship hit. The first two fighters had been destroyed, but the last one took a glancing blow, and it spiraled out of the attack formation. Stockton didn't know if the pilot would regain control and manage to limp back to the mothership in his damaged fighter, or if he would have to ditch…but his gut told him the survival chances of any pilots who ejected in this battle were damned poor.

The fire from the target ship increased in frequency. At first, Stockton was concerned the ship had more batteries than he'd expected, but then he realized the rate of fire had increased. It was just another jarring example of the enemy's technological advantage…most likely superior energy generation and transmission, something that had confounded Confederation engineers for two generations.

His eyes remained fixed as the first line of bombers slipped in under ten thousand kilometers. The Lightnings were about two seconds ahead of the Vipers, but the two squadrons had come very close to executing the synchronous assaults he'd ordered. The limited fire from the target ship was indeed split between the two squadrons. Stockton was grateful for that, especially as he saw another of the Vipers hit, a bird no more than four thousand kilometers from his position—practically on top of him by the standards of space combat.

He checked his scanners, looking for a pod, any clue to suggest the pilot had escaped, but there was nothing.

The fire was heavier now, and the destruction of a ship so close by jarred him against being careless. His modified Lightning handled in a way he'd charitably describe as "like a pig," and he focused again on making himself a difficult target. He had no real reason to be where he was, save for the fact that he couldn't bring himself to watch more than seven hundred fighters under his command attack while he held back. He suspected Admiral Barron would give him a tongue-lashing over when he returned to *Dauntless*…

His lead ships were under seven thousand kilometers and moving at almost five hundred kilometers per second. Against a vessel with a proper point defense array, he knew the squadrons would have been virtually wiped out by now, but his force, despite the losses it had suffered, was largely intact.

He felt a wave of pride in his people, in the determination with which they were following his orders. All their training told them to launch their torpedoes from ranges vastly farther out…

but they understood that the realities of combat had changed with the discovery of the Hegemony. The enemy ships were too maneuverable—not a single torpedo would hit from twenty or thirty thousand kilometers.

He watched as the first line of bombers let their torpedoes fly, the small devices accelerating at 50g for a few seconds, blasting hard toward the target. Then, almost simultaneously, the doomed AIs directing each of them triggered the reactions that converted their entire mass to energy, transforming each projectile into a super-hot plasma heading right for the enemy vessel.

The ship fired its engines, a last ditch evasive maneuver to escape from the path of the deadly projectiles. The plasmas had consumed the mechanical drones that had carried them, and now they were fixed on a direct, unchangeable path. That gave the target a chance to evade...and the Hegemony ship made the best of it, blasting its own engines at nearly 50g, lunging forward as a cluster of plasmas zipped by behind it, right through the space it had occupied seconds before.

But it couldn't escape all the weapons. Stockton watched as the first plasma struck the battleship. The hit was in a secondary area—at least, he knew it would have been secondary on a Confederation ship—and it failed to penetrate deeply into the ship. But, the second and third hits, and then the fourth, smashed directly into the hull amidships.

Stockton checked the readings. As best he could tell, the first hit had barely penetrated the great ship's heavy armor...but the next two ripped right through, and a few seconds later he could see the plumes on his scanner, internal explosions blasting back out through the hull.

He had no idea how the ships were organized, where their reactors or other vital systems were located...but Raptor Stockton knew a bad hit when he saw one. The enemy's thrust dropped almost immediately, and two more plasmas—shots that would have missed had the thrust not dipped—smacked into the rear of the ship, just above the engines.

Stockton was excited as he saw the two impacts, and then again as his readings showed thrust dropping to...he watched, waited, and the numbers on his screen dipped to zero. They had knocked out the ship's engines!

"Good shooting, Lightnings, Vipers…damned good shooting. Now, get back to base and refuel and rearm. There's a lot of fighting left to do."

He brought his ship around, making a pass close by the enemy ship. It was dangerous—stupid, he suspected Stara would call it—but he wanted better scanning data. And, as he zipped by, he saw that the batteries that had fired at his people were all silent now. He didn't know how badly the ship was really hurt, but he knew enough to put a big evil smile on his face.

A predator's grin.

*   *   *

Atara looked down at Bryan Rogan. The Marine was weak, pale…but she'd never seen him looking better. Twelve hours before, the big man had barely been alive, hanging on by a thread in cryostasis. Now, he was out of the medpod, lying on a cot in one of the portable shelters Doc Weldon had turned into a makeshift hospital.

It was a strange feeling, to know that Rogan was alive because of her blood. It was nothing she'd done, of course, no act of heroism in battle that had saved so many of her comrades, but she still felt good about it…all except for the fact that she hadn't been able to give enough blood to save them all.

She was leaning forward, one hand gripping the cane Weldon had fashioned for her, and the other on the wall behind Rogan's bed. She was shaky—Weldon had argued with her for some time before he'd agreed to let her get up and walk around the camp at all—but she could feel her strength coming back. Slowly.

"You saved his life, Atara." Weldon walked through the door and into the open area of the room. He waved his arm around the space, gesturing to the dozen other cots. Each of them held a member of the landing party who, hours before, had been at death's door. "You saved all of them."

"*We* saved them." She'd take credit for supplying the blood, but it was Weldon's brilliance and tireless work that was primarily responsible for the serum. *Dauntless*'s surgeon, even sick, exhausted, and strung out on stims, had beaten every medical team in the fleet to find a cure for the ancient plague.

She sighed softly and frowned. "We saved *some* of them." The good feeling slipped away, even as she turned her head up from the sleeping Rogan and looked over at Weldon. They'd saved the sickest forty…but the others were in only slightly better shape, and they were deteriorating fast. She'd give more blood as soon as she could, but she knew it was going to be too late.

"Stu…"

Weldon looked over at her. From the expression on his face, she could tell he knew what she was thinking. "We'll do all we can, Atara. We've freed up more medpods, and with cryostatis, I can…"

"That's not good enough, Stu. You've got to take more blood now. Enough for at least another round of the serum."

"No, Atara…that's not possible. The risk to you is…"

"More than it's been in battle?"

"Atara…please."

"No, I'm serious, Stu. What about blood substitutes? You need the DNA in my blood, but I just need to have something pumping through my veins."

"It's not that simple. The substitute works for transfusions, in limited quantities, but it can't replace all of your blood. I've already taken nearly twice the amount considered safe. I don't dare take any more, not for at least a few days."

"And how many of our people will be die over those couple days? Comrades your serum can save?"

"I'll keep as many alive as I can, Atara."

"That's not an answer." She paused. "I'm willing to take some risks, Stu. We have to do more…we have to try something." She looked right at him. "Whatever that entails."

Weldon hesitated, looking uncomfortable.

"That's an order, Stu."

He remained silent for a moment. Finally, he said, "There's one thing, Atara…but it is dangerous. Very dangerous."

"Let's do it. Now."

"Atara…"

"Now, Stu." She leaned onto the cane and stepped slowly toward the doctor, something less than steady on her feet.

"I can put you in a medpod, and have the system take over as much of your bodily functions as possible. I can draw more blood—most of what's still there—and have the pod inject you with some drug treatments, something a little stronger than what I've been giving you already to spur blood production." He paused and looked at her, the uncertainty clear in his expression. "It will be very rough on your system, Atara. You could suffer permanent damage." Another pause. "You could die."

"Things have been trying to kill me for the last seven years, Stu, and I haven't run from a fight yet. I'm not about to start now. Let's get started."

Weldon stood still, looking for a time as though he might continue arguing, but then he just nodded and said, "All right, Atara…if you insist on doing this, we have to get you into a pod. I have to put you in an induced coma." A pause. "Are you sure about this?"

"I'm sure." Her voice was firm, at least it felt that way. But inside she was scared, in a way she'd never been against an external enemy. She trusted Weldon as much as she did anyone, but allowing herself to become helpless went against every instinct she had. She'd come from a place where helplessness was a virtual death sentence.

But there was no choice. She wouldn't stand by and watch her people die—she couldn't—and her blood was the only way to save them.

Chapter Forty

Denisov sat quietly, looking out at his bridge crew as *Carcajou* approached Barroux. They were edgy. It wasn't surprising, and he couldn't deny that he felt it too. The last time his fleet had approached the rebel planet, they'd taken one hell of a beating, and they'd pulled back just in time to avoid a catastrophe. Going back, heading into those deadly guns that had blasted his ships so savagely, seemed like the sheerest folly.

Only, his ships weren't going back all the way. At least not right away. He had another way to fight the rebels and their orbital defenses, one he'd worked his crews to the bone to create. One he'd pulled from the system's asteroid belt, and brought to Barroux to unleash immense destruction.

He'd picked out several dozen asteroids, small enough that his engineers had been able to create makeshift drives on each of them. It was rough, and he suspected most of those who'd worked on the project doubted that it would work. He'd even doubted it at times. But there was no way another frontal assault could succeed, not even with the damage his forces had done to the orbital defenses in the earlier fight. That left two options—

318

his plan, as crazy as it seemed, or going back to Montmirail and telling Gaston Villieneuve that Barroux was still in the hands of rebels and traitors.

Denisov could see the asteroids moving. Their velocities were low, at least by the normal standards of space travel. They were powered by really nothing more than a series of nuclear bombs situated to create the needed vectors toward Barroux's orbital fortresses. But the asteroid belt was quite close to the planet, and the speeds of the massive chunks of rock were more than adequate to turn them into devastating kinetic energy weapons.

He knew the targeting would be difficult. The warheads he'd placed to direct the asteroids as they approached Barroux were hardly precision thrusters. Still, he was confident that at least some of the projectiles would hit their targets. The vast amount of dust and smaller chunks of rock released by collisions and nuclear explosions would wreak havoc on the laser buoys, blocking much of their fire as his warships moved up behind the asteroids and finished off whatever was left.

There would be collateral damage, most likely an enormous amount. Many of the asteroids would continue past the high-level orbit of the defenses and enter the planet's atmosphere. That would represent a disaster of almost unimaginable proportions, an extinction-level event for Barroux. Denisov didn't relish the idea of killing millions, of throwing a civilized, industrialized world back into the stone age. But he knew enough about what was happening in the Union to realize he didn't have a choice. Not if *he* wanted to survive.

Denisov wasn't a politician, and he had no wish to be one. But, he was sure of one thing. Villieneuve didn't give a shit about Barroux's people, nor even its industrial production. He cared about having active rebels defying the Union's authority... and setting an example for others to do the same. A cataclysmic end to Barroux's pretensions at independence might even serve Villieneuve's needs more effectively than a conventional assault and the planet's quiet return into the fold.

"The lead wave is approaching planetary orbit, Admiral."

Denisov turned toward the officer, but he didn't respond.

He just nodded. He was doing what he had to do, but he wondered how many officers in history had caused the sort of devastation he was about to unleash on Barroux.

He felt as though he should be issuing frantic orders, but everything had already been planned, and all the pieces were in place. His fleet was right behind the asteroids, ready to hit the remaining fortresses during the moment of peak disruption.

Carcajou's weapons were prepped, as they were on every ship in the fleet. His people were nervous about hitting those defenses again, but he suspected most of them also craved revenge for the losses the fleet had suffered, for their comrades who had died. That was good. It would serve his purposes now.

He could see the enemy fortresses firing, and he smiled. *Good luck blasting those asteroids.* The guns on the orbital platforms were powerful, and they outranged anything the ships of his fleet mounted…but they didn't have a chance of affecting anything with the mass and momentum of the great chunks of rock moving toward them. The hits blasted off small chunks, but that only aided the attackers, creating clouds of dust that degraded the laser fire from the buoys. He wondered if the rebels who'd taken control of the forts realized they were helping his plan, but then that was the beauty of the whole thing…what else could they do? They couldn't just let the asteroids come toward them unopposed, toward the planet below and its helpless billions.

Denisov had never expected to commit genocide, and he was still fighting to justify what he was doing. He doubted Gaston Villieneuve would have the same reservations, but it had taken all of Denisov's discipline—and his self-delusion, too—to fend off the urge to stop the attack. Now, at least, his self-control was superfluous. There was no way to divert the asteroids, not anymore. It was far too late.

Not a single station had been hit yet, nor had a rock the size of his fist entered the atmosphere. But there was a cold inevitability to it all now. Barroux's rebels could surrender, throw down their weapons and beg for mercy…but it would all be to no avail. Their fates were sealed.

Denisov stared straight ahead, watching, waiting…and trying to hold back the humanity that threatened to consume him.

I have wrought this. I have destroyed a world.

* * *

"What the hell is going on?" Remy Caron stood in his make-shift control center, trying to make sense of the reports coming in.

"I don't know, First Protector. The orbital scans confirm the enemy ships have returned, but…"

"But what?"

"There are other contacts. The orbital stations report meteors, asteroids…a dozen of them, no more. Several dozen. All heading toward Barroux."

"That's impossible," Caron shouted.

Caron was angry, but as Hoover stood and watched Barroux's dictator pacing around the command center, shouting out pointless and repetitive commands, he realized that the man was just plain scared. He found Remy's behavior loathsome. After all the brutality he'd inflicted, the thousands—*no, probably millions*—who'd died under his short rule, the man had no courage.

Hoover had seen only Remy Caron, the merciless strongman of a communist revolution, but he'd heard stories of another man, a lowly factory worker, one who'd been reluctant to even join the uprisings against Union rule. His years with Confederation Intelligence had shown him many things, and it had stripped him of any doubts on the level of depravity to which human beings could sink. He suspected Caron had risen initially by circumstance, and then found himself in a position of power that overwhelmed him. After a lifetime of helpless obedience to his Union masters, he just plain liked the taste of power…and he craved more, longed to safeguard what he'd gained, whatever the cost. That was all conjecture, but Hoover would have bet a small fortune he was close to the mark.

Hoover had seen such things elsewhere, though Caron seemed to have become so corrupted very quickly. He hated working to support the dictator and his regime as much as Breen did, but he was in charge, and he understood that the Confederation's interests outweighed his—or his second's—personal feelings. Still, he felt anger watching Caron storm around the control center, and he was sorry he hadn't been able to side with the resistance.

He felt a touch of sadness, too. He didn't doubt Remy Caron could have been a tremendous leader for his people, that he could have brought them freedom, prosperity. But, instead, he'd become what he had fought against, and his principles were sacrificed to the lust for power, the cravings for the luxury the defeated Union leaders had left behind.

Hoover wished he could accomplish his mission by supporting the resistance, but Caron was the one in charge, and the Confederation wanted Barroux to hold out as long as possible. *If only…*

His thought was interrupted by a loud sound, coming from out in the street. It was an explosion, he realized, as the muffled sounds of gunfire erupted outside the building.

Caron spun around, gesturing toward his guards standing against the wall. "Go find out what's going on out there!"

Hoover stood still, his training taking charge. His expression was impassive, the perfect poker face as he evaluated the situation. His first thought was that Union forces had somehow gotten through, but he quickly realized that was impossible. He was at a loss for a moment, and then it came to him, a few seconds before Ami Delacorte raced into the room, a column of her armed troopers right behind her.

"It's Bernard and his rabble," she said, gesturing around the room, directing the soldiers to various positions around the room. "They're attacking the command post." She moved toward the far doorway and looked into the hallway beyond. "You three," she shouted down the corridor, "get in position and cover that door." She looked back toward Caron. "The filthy traitors…hitting us when we're trying to defend the planet. But, don't worry…we'll make this an opportunity to wipe them out, every last one of them."

Hoover was surprised, at first, but then it all started to make sense. He'd underestimated Bernard, but now his respect for the rebel grew. The resistance didn't have the strength to take on Caron and Delacorte's forces planet-wide, or even in the capital. *But a decapitation strike...*

Delacorte's reassuring words to Caron, he suspected the resistance fighters outside had a good chance.

A damned good chance.

He turned and glanced back toward Breen, and instantly, he knew she was thinking the same thing. It was a good bet she was also plotting how to help the fighters outside. Hoover still wasn't sure that was the right move for defending Barroux, but if the Union forces were hurling asteroids at the planet, he wasn't sure it mattered anymore.

Still, any wrong move, even the right move taken too soon, would mean instant death. He shook his head slightly, a signal to Breen to hold tight.

The gunfire outside was heavier now. He suspected both sides were engaged in an intense firefight. Despite his determination to remain impartial, to keep his focus on the mission, he found himself rooting for the resistance. He'd seen more than a few firefights, and while experienced, trained troops like Marines or Foudre Rouge were well-drilled in assault tactics, such things tended to bog down between less skilled fighters.

He watched Delacorte, saw the animation in her movement, the rage radiating from her body. If he'd had any doubt before that she was insane, it was gone. But, still, he stayed where he was, waiting. She might be crazy, but that didn't mean she wasn't capable, even brilliant. And he knew already that she was utterly ruthless.

The fighting continued, and he thought the sounds were coming closer. It was hard to be sure, but another glance at Delacorte more of less confirmed it. She didn't look scared... he wasn't sure he'd ever seen her scared. There were occasional advantages to insanity. But she was tense, and her tone became increasingly harsh as she shouted out commands to her soldiers.

Hoover was still trying to get a good feel for the status of things outside when the whole building shook. He stumbled, struggling to stay on his feet, as debris fell all around the room from the ceiling. He heard the sounds of part of the building coming down, and then gunfire, much louder than it had been before.

They're breaking in...Bernard and his people just might pull this off...

He felt a burst of satisfaction, but it was tempered by cold analysis. If the resistance fighters got to the control room, he knew what would happen. They'd been victimized, their allies and comrades murdered, their families brutalized by Delacorte's thugs. They would come in, guns blazing, and they wouldn't stop until everyone there was dead.

The sudden realization of how poor a chance he had of surviving the counter-revolution distracted him. He'd been on dangerous missions before, and escaped a few of those by the slimmest of margins, but now, he realized he could be minutes away from his own death. He glanced again toward Breen, wondering if she'd given any thought to how the current fight was likely to end. Even if Bernard's people didn't just shoot everyone indiscriminately, he couldn't imagine the resistance leader would be well disposed to him, or to his people. He'd turned the man down flat when he'd come looking for help, and he'd given the resistance every reason to categorize him as an ally of the current regime. He put some hope into the notion that the resistance wouldn't want to alienate the Confederation, but he also wondered if Bernard had seen through the true purpose of his mission, the cold reality that he wasn't there to help the people of Barroux at all, other than to make them the most effective barbs against a resurgent Union.

There was another explosion, and one of the walls blasted open, sending debris flying all around the room. He saw a chunk of metal hit Silvia Breen, and he raced over as the spy dropped to the floor with a thud. For an instant, he was sure she was dead, but when he got to her side, he could see that she was still breathing. He tried to see if she had any wounds, but all he could find was a gash on the head where the chunk of metal had hit her. He couldn't be sure, but he thought she'd be okay...unless, of course, they were all shot in the next few minutes.

The battle raged around the room, and within a minute, perhaps two, there were dozens of bodies littering the floor. The resistance fighters were suffering the worst, mostly because their weapons were older, less effective. But they seemed to have the numbers, and Hoover was willing to bet they also had the drive of men and women who understood how fleeting their advantage was. Delacorte had no doubt called in reserves from all over the city, and that meant time wasn't an ally to the resistance.

Hoover watched as the battle continued, and then, suddenly, he saw Henri Bernard. The resistance leader was crouched behind a pile of debris. It was partial cover, but a position that had a weak side. And Ami Delacorte was standing on that side, bringing her weapon up to bear.

Hoover had spent weeks—months—arguing with Breen, resisting her constant harangues to aid the resistance. But now, something took over inside him. Before he even knew what he was doing, he had leapt to his feet and lunged forward. He was stumbling across the room, off balance…right toward Delacorte.

She saw him, too late, and she turned to shoot. But he slammed into her first, the two of them dropping together. Bernard reacted, turning toward the spot he'd ignored until an instant before. His arm flashed up, and he fired three times in rapid succession. Hoover gritted his teeth, waited for the pain of impact. But there was none. He hit the ground and brought himself back up in a combat role, and spun his head around, trying to figure out what had happened.

Delacorte was lying on her back, her eyes wide open, transfixed, seeming to stare at the ceiling. But they were blank. A chunk of her skull was missing, and he could see the exposed gray of brain matter, covered with a wet sheen of blood.

He hesitated, just for a second, but by the time he raised his head, he could see two fighters, Delacorte's people, aiming their rifles right at him. He'd survived two close calls, but it didn't look like three was in the cards.

*I'm dead…*it was the only thought that went through his mind.

Then, he heard the shots, automatic fire…but there was no

pain. Nothing.

He watched in stunned silence as his two would-be killers fell back to the ground, their bodies riddled with half a dozen bullet holes each.

He turned, still stunned, and he saw three of Bernard's people, standing across the room, their guns still aiming at the spot Delacorte's people had occupied until seconds before.

Two of the resistance fighters just stood where they were, but the third looked at him and nodded once, right before he turned and plunged back into the battle.

Chapter Forty-One

Sara Eaton stood in front of her chair in the center of *Repulse*'s command center. She knew she should be in her seat, her harness securely buckled across her body. But she'd never had an easy time sitting still in battle, and the residual effects of the wounds she suffered in the campaign around Arcurton early in the war had made remaining seated too long downright torturous.

She'd been watching Jake Stockton's squadrons launching their bombing runs on the Hegemony ships. Stockton had tried to target the enemy battleships but, in at least half a dozen instances, enemy escorts had interposed themselves, taking the brunt of the assault in those spots.

The enemy ships were tough...and that was putting it lightly. She watched as Hegemony vessels, both escorts and battleships, soaked up enough damage that would have reduced their Confederation counterparts to clouds of super-heated gas. But Jake Stockton was a relentless warrior, and his spirit had infected his entire fighter corps. His pilots brought their bombers in one after the other, closing to unheard of ranges before they launched their weapons.

The enemy ships had considerably more thrust than anything in the White Fleet, and their navigation AIs seemed to be superior as well. Despite the courage of Stockton's pilots, many of the torpedoes missed, evaded by last-second moves more powerful and better planned than any she'd ever seen before. But the bombing runs had done their jobs nevertheless. At least half of the incoming ships were damaged, and some badly. The plasma torpedoes had claimed four ships outright, but they'd all been cruiser-sized vessels, like those present in the initial battle. None of the enemy battleships had been destroyed, though Eaton had identified two she thought looked close. Both were lagging the main body of the Hegemony fleet, and one was leaking atmosphere and fluids badly.

"Three hundred thousand kilometers to enemy's lead ships, Commodore."

Eaton waved toward the tactical station and nodded. "Acknowledged." Her mind was too occupied for more than that. She was staring at the display, at the enemy ships moving steadily toward the fleet. They would fire before her ships were in range to respond, that was a certainty. The screen was marked at the distances where the enemy escorts had opened fire, but Eaton's eyes were on the large icons, the massive battleships at the center of the Hegemony formation. She was sure those giant ships would outrange the cruisers the fleet had fought before, and that their guns would be stronger, more powerful. But she had no idea whether that would be two hundred eighty thousand kilometers, or two-fifty...or two hundred.

Whatever the distance turned out to be, it would decide the battle. The bombing runs had hurt the enemy, and the White Fleet outnumbered the approaching force. If her ships, and the others of the fleet, could close before they'd suffered crippling damage, they had a chance. If not...well, that wasn't something she wanted to think about.

We need to move forward now, at full thrust. We've got to minimize the time before we can return fire.

The strategy sessions before the fight had been contentious ones. Many of the fleet's senior officers had wanted to pull back, to give the bombing squadrons time to return to their mother ships and rearm for a second strike. Others, and she had been the leader of this group, argued that the enemy's superior thrust capacity would allow them to catch the fleet while the fighters were still half refueled in the bays. The extra time it would take the Hegemony to close against retreating ships would only lengthen the period during which they could fire but the fleet's ships could not.

Cilian Globus had been her ally in the debate, though his reasoning had differed from her analytical and mathematical arguments. Eaton would have been all for the plan to pull back slowly if she'd thought it had a chance of working, but to the Palatians, that tactic carried the taint of dishonor. The Alliance officers clamored to push forward and hit the enemy with as much force as possible, a position based on warrior code rather than on any real data.

Eaton had expected Barron to come down on her side. He *had* agreed, more or less, but he'd been distracted in a way she'd never seen before, and he'd hesitated to make a final decision and issue the orders.

Eaton knew the fleet's famous commander was worried about the people on the surface, but she was sure there was something more than that on his mind. She'd considered it for a while, and, finally she'd come up with an answer. It was the impending battle, and what it portended. Tyler Barron had set out in command of a great exploration fleet, his mission to seek out old technology and improve the Confederation's knowledge of the old empire. He'd no doubt expected dangers, but he couldn't have been ready for what the fleet had found.

A new war, one that might be very dangerous and deadly indeed…and it had started on Barron's watch. She understood her friend's hesitancy, his reluctance to order the fleet forward to finish the battle, one way or another. But she also knew there was no choice. Barron had done nothing to provoke the enemy, and if the fighting here spread to a longer and wider war, he would have no fault in any of it.

That's easy to say, but would you listen to that if you were in Tyler's place?

She wanted to help her friend, but there was nothing to do. And, as she watched the enemy's lead ships close to two hundred eighty thousand kilometers, she knew it didn't matter. The only important thing now was to do whatever gave the fleet the best chance at victory…and that meant moving forward now.

She turned toward the comm station. "Get me *Dauntless*…

"Commodore…Admiral Barron is on the fleetcom line now."

"On speaker, Lieutenant."

The officer's hands moved over his workstation, and a few seconds later, Tyler Barron's voice was blaring through *Repulse*'s control center speakers.

"All ships, all crews…this is Admiral Barron. We came here in peace, as researchers, explorers…and yet, we have found a new enemy. It was my desire to seek peaceful relations, but that has proven to be impossible. So, if war is inevitable, it is time for us to set aside wishes for peace, and to focus on what must be done now. If a war must be fought, our only concern is to win it, at all costs. So, the order is simple. All ships, maximum thrust. Advance and close on the enemy. Conduct maximum evasive maneuvers…and the instant your weapons are in range, open fire with every watt of power you can throw their way. You are all veterans, and you know what to do. Go now, into the fight… and we will win the victory, as we have so many times before."

Repulse's control center was silent. Once again, Eaton was amazed at the effect Tyler Barron could have on his subordinates—her crew, of course, but even her. She turned toward the nav station. "You heard the orders, Commander. Full thrust… take us into battle."

The bridge erupted into a grim but enthusiastic cheer. Whatever lay ahead, her people were ready.

*   *   *

"I want all batteries powered up and ready to fire the instant we enter range." Cilian Globus stood on *Fortiter*'s bridge, snapping out commands to his tactical officer. "The enemy has the edge on speed and maneuverability, but we are Palatians, and the blood of warriors flows through our veins. Targeting will be key here. Use your experience, your skill, your intuition…but hit those bastards, and hit them hard."

Fortiter shook as another one of the enemy's beams struck the ship. Globus was playing the role his people needed him to play, acting as though none of the enemy's actions worried him. But the range differential between his ships and the Hegemony vessels was a huge problem, and he knew it. His ships were all damaged already, and not a single one had yet fired a shot. The situation was even worse on his force than on the Confeds', whose primaries also outranged the weaponry of *Fortiter* and his other ships.

The technology behind the enemy beams still hadn't been fully explained, despite the best efforts of the fleet's scientists and engineering teams. Even the legendary Anya Fritz, whose reputation had reached as far as the Alliance, had come up blank so far. But there had been a terrible revelation in this battle. Those deadly energy weapons were something akin to secondary batteries, and their battleships packed an even greater punch, one that had been absent from the cruisers the fleet had faced earlier.

Globus had seen the effects of the enemy's devastating primary weapons. They weren't the mystery the beams were, at least not superficially. The Confederation had developed its own railgun systems, and even the perennially behind-the-curve Alliance had produced some models. But none of the Rim powers had managed to achieve the acceleration rates necessary to weaponize the devices over the ranges at play in space combat. At a range of one hundred thousand kilometers, a ship had less than a third of a second to react to a laser or other weapon traveling at light speed. Even the fastest railgun-launched projectiles in the Rim moved at only fifteen-thousand kilometers per second. They would take a full ten seconds to reach the target, and give a nav AI time for a quick nap before launching evasive maneuvers.

The Hegemony weapon solved that problem in a very

straightforward way, if one that reached far beyond current Confederation technology levels. Somehow, the weapons accelerated the projectiles to nearly twenty-five percent of light speed, cutting the reaction time at one hundred thousand kilometers to more like a second and a quarter. They didn't quite match light-based weaponry in accuracy, but they came close enough to make evasion far from a sure thing.

Globus had watched in horror as the Confederation battleship *Indefatigable* took the first hit from one of the weapons. The shot had been an imperfect one, more of a glancing blow than a direct hit, but as the reports flowed in, Globus realized the ship had been virtually crippled. A huge section of the vessel's aft had been torn away…or simply vaporized. The Palatian was a warrior and not a scientist, but he had some idea of the kinetic energy a projectile traveling at near-relativistic speeds imparted to its target…and he shuddered to imagine what a direct hit would do to *Fortiter*, or any of the fleet's capital ships.

There appeared to be one saving grace. The rate of fire of the weapon appeared to be very slow, and only the largest Hegemony ships seemed to mount it. That didn't help a ship unfortunate enough to take one of the deadly hits, but it did give the fleet as a whole a chance. The support systems supplying that kind of power *had* to be fragile, which meant the more the fleet could pound away at those Hegemony battleships, the likelier they were to take the railguns out of the equation.

"One minute to firing range, Commander."

Globus turned and gestured his acknowledgement. His bridge officers had all seen the effects of the enemy railguns, and they all knew that one could fire on the Alliance flagship at any moment. But they were calm, focused, keeping their fears deep inside. They were Palatian warriors, and Globus expected—and would tolerate—nothing less from them. But that didn't stop him from feeling pride. A Palatian's life was a hard one in many ways, and duty and honor stood above all other considerations. It was how he had lived his life, and how his children would, and their children. Cilian Globus was unable to imagine an Alliance that deviated from its ideals.

The way is the way…

He could see on the display that the Confederation battle-ships had already opened fire, at least the ones that still had operational primary batteries. That was about half of them, he noted as his eyes moved across the screen. Cilian had seen those batteries slicing into Red Alliance ships during the civil war, and he'd watched as the weapons utterly obliterated Palatia's vaunted orbital defenses. But they were fragile, the immense systems of energy transmission that powered them highly subject to break-down. Significant progress had been made in toughening up the systems, but some of the fragility still remained.

The Confederation fire was beginning to have an effect, but the enemy ships were so maneuverable, they reduced the hit rate far below normal. The targeting against the Hegemony vessels was falling short, a third, and perhaps less, of the hit rates he'd seen against the Union fleet at the Bottleneck.

Still, when those particle accelerator beams hit, even the advanced and high-tech Hegemony vessels took damage…and those ships had already been savaged by Jake Stockton's bomb-ing attacks. Globus knew the squadrons, including the ones from his own ships, were the only thing giving the fleet a chance. They'd done their part, and now it was up to the battleships like *Fortiter* to finish the job.

He watched the display as the distance to the lead enemy ships dropped steadily, his hands closing slowly into fists as the numbers slipped below his batteries' maximum range.

He turned toward the tactical station, staring across the bridge for a few seconds. Then, he said, simply, "All ships… open fire."

* * *

"I want everybody landed in fifteen minutes…I don't care what it takes or what the bay crews have to do." Stockton was nearly shouting, more a reflection of the adrenaline flowing through him than any real anger. "And tell Chief Evans—and the other crew chiefs in the fleet—they're not only going to turn these ships around in record time, they're going to convert the interceptors to bombing kits."

"We're doing the best we can, Jake...but the evasive maneuvers are interfering with landing operations. It's going to be more than fifteen minutes, I can tell you that much. You'd better plan on getting partial forces back out, because you're never going to get all your birds back aboard in time."

Stockton felt his face heat up, a flush of anger. The voice on his comm was Stara's, and his rage wasn't targeted at her, just at the hard lesson in reality she was giving him. But he couldn't hold it back. "You tell those idiots in the bays that my ships are coming in, and we're coming in fast. And, every damned battleship in this fleet better be ready for that."

His tone was raw, angry...and he immediately regretted unleashing it on her. But he could see the raging fight the fleet was in, and he knew the battle was a desperate one. Even with Barron's leadership, and whatever tricks or tactical wizardry the admiral might try, his gut told him they were going to lose... unless he could get another fighter strike out.

He shook his head. That need he felt...it didn't change reality. The fleet's battleships were executing wild nav programs to evade the fire from the Hegemony ships. That was good tactics, and the only way the fleet had a chance to survive the enemy's incoming fire...but it played havoc with landing fighters. His pilots had to approach motherships that were changing their velocities and vectors every few seconds, and at times, in intervals of even less than a second. The only way to land was to connect with the ship's main nav control, and to sync up with the evasion programs...but that was a damned difficult thing for a fighter pilot to do. Stockton knew he'd lose people trying to get his birds back into their bays, but there was no choice. His fighters were the only advantage the fleet had.

"All right, listen up..." He was on the command channel, speaking to his squadron commanders and above. "...we're going to have to land while our motherships are bouncing around like crazy, trying to avoid that incoming fire. That means one hell of a tricky landing. Wing commanders, line up your squadrons, one after the other. I want the most experienced ones landing first. That way, we get them back out the fastest, and…" He hesitated, just for an instant. "…that way, we're bringing in the pilots most likely to land. WE can't risk leaving our best squadrons stuck out here if somebody loses it on landing and trashes a bay." *Which will almost certainly happen.* "Let's go…get it done."

Stockton didn't particularly like his cold-blooded approach, but he knew what he had to do, and there was no sense thinking about it any further. "Ships already equipped as bombers first… we're going to be able to launch those without escorts, and I want maximum turnaround." He really wanted to send his entire strike force back in one combined attack, but that just wasn't possible. The fleet needed whatever attack power he could get out there…as quickly as possible. Besides, waiting would only mean more bays knocked out of action and fighters destroyed as their mother ships took damage in the fight.

"*Dauntless* wing," he said after he flipped the comm back to the channel for the flagship's group, "we're going in one squadron at a time. Blues first…then Scarlet Eagles, Reds, Yellows, and then Greens." He'd violated his own rule about bomber-fitted squadrons landing first. The Blues were the best he had, and he wanted them back out first. "I want everybody sharp as a razor here. *Dauntless* is jerking all over the place with evasive maneuvers, and you need to link your AIs with the main navcom and match those shifts." A short pause. "I'm going in first, and the rest of you follow."

Stockton had intended to stay where he was, but the landing was so dangerous, he decided to go first…to lead the way. Besides, he'd flown around without a weapon during the first strike…and he was determined to draw some blood with the second.

He angled his throttle, his other hand flipping switches to link his own system with *Dauntless*'s navcom. A small blue light flicked on, confirming the link. He could feel the fighter shifting on its own as his onboard AI took over, matching the moves *Dauntless*'s main system transmitted.

Stockton always hated allowing a computer to fly his ship,

and now was no different, but he knew there was no choice. Only the AI could read and execute the exact vectors and thrust strengths and angles coming in from *Dauntless*'s navcom. The problem was the delay caused by transmission and execution of the maneuver, which put the fighter and the landing platform slightly out of sync. In the end, a pilot's "feel," his intuition was what made the combat landing work…and Stockton was the best.

He glided his ship toward *Dauntless*, feeling the fighter jerk hard as the AI swung it around and blasted thrust in different directions. The fighter was coming in for a landing, and that meant it couldn't just match the big vessel's moves. It had to maintain its approach vector, line up with the opening to the landing bay.

Dauntless shook hard, as yet another enemy beam slammed into its side. Stockton was close enough now for visual contact, and he could see the gash in the ship's white metal exterior. Explosions blasted up from inside. Stockton had a career of experience in assessing the severity of hits, and he could see that last one had been bad. Not critical, perhaps, but it had almost certainly knocked out some systems.

And killed some crew. Comrades of his. Friends.

He gripped the throttle as his ship moved toward the battleship, ready to adjust the AI's course. *Dauntless* was gyrating now, spinning around and firing thrusters as she lurched back to bring her guns to bear on the enemy. The dance was a complex one, almost impossible for a human mind to follow, but it was one the ship's AI executed well…as Stockton's scanners confirmed by displaying two more enemy beams, both of them missing *Dauntless* by a few hundred meters.

He could see the bay opening coming up…on his screen and also through the cockpit. Relative to *Dauntless*'s course and velocity, he was approaching slowly. His ship seemed to crawl forward as it blasted its engines to restore alignment.

Dauntless's evasive maneuvers were heavier than any he'd seen before. He understood…the enemy's targeting was just too good, and Admiral Barron was doing everything possible to protect his ships. But it made landing fighters that much harder.

Stockton had known he'd lose pilots in the combat landing operation, but he could feel that number rising now. He'd ordered all his people to come in at minimal velocity. He didn't want some pilot losing it and smashing into a bay at high speed. That would just be a gift to the enemy. But, even at a crawl, a fighter missing the opening and hitting the hull was going to be a real problem, especially for the pilot of that ship.

Stockton's hand tightened around the controls, and he shifted his arm slightly, keeping his course aligned with the bay opening. He could feel the sweat running down his back, and for all his veteran's coolness under fire, his heart was pounding hard enough that he could feel it in his chest.

Dauntless jerked hard to port, and the opening shifted away, coming back half into his field of view a second later as the AI reacted to the battleship's evasive maneuver. He moved his arm again, slightly, a minor adjustment…and his ship zipped through the opening and came down on the landing pad. He was a little off to the side, as opposed to his usual "right on target," but it was close enough.

He reached down, pulling the release that opened his cockpit as he unhooked his harnesses. Then he jumped up, climbing out onto the fighter's stubby wing before the flight crew had even gotten the portable ladder in place.

He scrambled down as soon as they set it against his ship, and as he climbed down, his eyes darted all around until they settled on who he was looking for.

"Chief," he yelled, jumping down the last few rungs of the ladder and jogging across the deck toward the large, perennially grouchy man who ruled *Dauntless*'s flight decks like a dictator. Evans had a reputation for scaring even officers who outranked him, but Stockton was like a man possessed. He knew to what extent the battle rested on him, and on his squadrons, but he wasn't about to take shit from anyone, not even the legendary Chief Evans.

"I want these fighters coming in refit and ready to go…and Chief, I mean instantly. Do you understand me?" Evans was technically in Stara's chain of command and not Stockton's. Pilots on the flight deck were mostly expected to stand around and wait for their birds to be cleared for takeoff. But Stockton didn't have time for that shit…not now.

Evans stood still for an instant, even as several members of *Dauntless*'s flight crew gathered around, cowering a bit before the crackling rage of their terrifying boss. They'd seen Evans explode at far less, and even Stockton's high rank seemed unlikely to quiet the storm that was coming.

But Evans just nodded, and said, "Yes, sir."

And with that, the legend of Jake "Raptor" Stockton grew yet again.

* * *

"The cure was a success, sir. I've treated the last of the infected parties, and the virus should be completely eradicated in even the sickest of them within two to three days." *Dauntless* shook from another hit as Doc Weldon's words came over the comm. Almost immediately, the control center lights flickered as the flagship's quad primary battery returned the fire. The new *Dauntless* packed not only double the number of main guns her predecessor had carried, but the whole system was a damned sight more durable, too, with multiple backups for the energy transmission system.

"That's wonderful news, Stu. I can't tell you what a fantastic job you've done, or how grateful I am." Barron had been focused entirely on the battle when Weldon's comm had come in. He'd almost refused the call until the battle was over. Now his attention was almost entirely on his gifted chief surgeon and on the incredible news he'd just delivered.

"Thank you, sir." Weldon's voice was somber, hesitant.

"Cheer up Doc…you licked it. You should be proud." Barron was concerned about the battle, very concerned. But, Weldon sounded somehow…down…and it was almost automatic for him to support his people, especially when they'd accomplished the near impossible. Barron didn't know what was bothering Weldon...*perhaps the people who died before he completed the serum?*

"Yes, sir...but Atara..."

Barron felt his blood run cold. The last he'd heard, Atara hadn't even shown any signs of the disease. Had she become sick? Not responded to the serum? He could feel his stomach tightening...even more than it had been already. "What is it?"

"She has an immunity, and I used blood samples from her to develop the serum. But...we needed more, Admiral, much more." Weldon paused, and his discomfort was palpable even over the comm. "She insisted...she ordered me."

"What happened?" Barron's tone was harsher now, demanding.

"Saving everyone required so much blood...I put her into one of the medpods, but, well, it was too much for her, Admiral."

Barron felt as though he was going to vomit. *No, not Atara...* "What do you mean, 'too much?'"

"She's in a coma, Admiral. I've tried all I can think of, every treatment...but she hasn't responded to anything." A pause. When he continued, his tone was grim. "I don't know what else I can do, sir." He hesitated again, and Barron knew what the doctor's next words would be.

"She's dying, Admiral."

Chapter Forty-Two

"Here's the information I promised, Senator. I think you will find it very…interesting." Desiree Marieles extended her hand, dropping the small data crystal into Farrell's pudgy palm. She looked up at the Confederation politician and smiled. "I can think of no one better suited to see that these crimes are punished."

Actually, pretty much everything on the crystal was a fabrication. Holsten's extended absence from Megara had allowed her data people to plant all sorts of things into the mogul's financial records: evidence of bribes, personal perversions, and illegally feeding war business to the Holsten interests. She'd designed it all herself, created the perfect image of a man who was a vile criminal in his public and business affairs, and a hideous monster in private.

She had more to back it all up, a list of sympathetic past "victims" of Holsten's manipulations and abuses. They were also all phonies, of course, but Marieles had learned long before that actual truth was of marginal value at best. She had no doubt Holsten could discredit the accusations…his wealth and power gave him the resources and access to the media he would need.

But seeing the head of Confederation Intelligence convicted of crimes wasn't her goal. She needed to create chaos, and discrediting Holsten for long enough to prevent him from interfering with her plans...that was well worth the effort.

"I thank you again for your patriotism, Desiree. If more of our citizens were as devoted and conscientious as you, the Confederation would surely prosper." Ferrell moved slightly, bringing himself a bit closer. Marieles felt the urge to recoil, but her discipline kicked in.

"Men like Holsten threaten the freedoms we all hold dear, Senator. It is the duty of every citizen to fight such corruption." *What an imbecile.* Her cover was strong, but she'd planted triggers to warn her if anyone was poking around too much in her manufactured background. So far, there hadn't been the slightest indication the Senator, or any of the others she was dealing with, had made even a token effort to check her out. *The fools deserve what's coming to them...*

"I'm just gratified I was able to find a public servant who is a true patriot himself." She paused. "In my business, I'm afraid I see the underside of things far too often. It tends to make one cynical."

"I understand that, Desiree...but in this case, you can be assured justice will prevail. The ship carrying Mr. Holsten is approaching Megara as we speak. He will soon be in the Senate's custody, and he will be compelled to answer not only for his crimes on Dannith, but also for those you have brought to light."

Marieles smiled, her warmth and apparent sincerity a testament to her immense skill at tradecraft. *Yes, Senator...you will do just that.* Marieles didn't trust Ferrell—she didn't trust anybody—but the small part of her smile that was genuine was powered by the fact that she had a second data crystal, one she'd placed in a very secure location. Its contents were much like those in her Holsten file, with two important differences. The crimes and perversions listed on the second crystal were all true...and they all detailed the clandestine activities of one Senator Emerson Tolbert Ferrell.

Marieles knew very well that Gary Holsten had his own files on Ferrell…and she didn't have the slightest doubt that Ferrell would fold almost instantly when Holsten threatened to destroy him. When Ferrell inevitably came to her with excuses for dropping the case against Holsten…she would assure him that if he stopped the investigation, she would crush him as completely as Holsten would.

That would be a shocking moment for the arrogant, but fundamentally gutless, Senator. It was one she looked forward to with great anticipation. She imagined the instant when Ferrell realized he faced personal ruin no matter what he did. *That should give the pompous ass something to think about…other than staring at my ass.*

"Desiree, are you free this evening? I can arrange a quiet dinner at my villa. We can review this material together, and perhaps…"

"I'm so sorry, Senator. You know I'd love to have dinner with you, but I'm afraid I have another appointment. Work, sadly. It never seems to stop." She paused, forcing herself to smile coyly at the Senator. "This is pure work, I'm afraid…not like what we share."

"Soon then, Desiree."

"I will count the moments." She maintained the grin, surprising herself with just how much energy it took. Then, she said, "Please…review what I've just given you. Gary Holsten has run rampant for far too long. It's a disgrace."

"One we will end, my dear Desiree…thanks to your help."

"You're too kind, Senator. I'll see you soon." She nodded gently, and then she turned and walked away, hoping he didn't notice her pace quickening as she got away from him.

* * *

"I am told we have at last gained a controlling interest in the stock. A very well-executed effort, Gustav. The annual meeting is in four days…and at that time, you will announce your holdings, and elect a new board of directors, one entirely controlled by us." Marieles looked across the room at Gustav Shepard. That wasn't his real name, of course, any more than his position as a maverick investment manager representing offworld interests was genuine. But he looked the part of an upper class Megaran, despite the fact that he'd come from the streets of one of the Union's most backward and impoverished fringe worlds.

Shepard had been on Megara far longer than Marieles—through the entire war, in fact. His assignment then had been to spy on Confederation industrial interests and get as much data back to Montmirail as possible. His cover was very deep, so much so that Marieles had wondered if the agent might have become too attached to the privileged position his cover afforded him. From all she'd been able to discern from the files, he'd even exhibited somewhat of an actual talent for investing, and he'd taken on a fairly long list of real investors to supplement the initial funds that had come from Sector Nine and its various controlled entities. But Shepard had done everything she'd told him to do since she'd arrived, and he'd even passed the two traps she'd laid to catch him if he was betraying her.

"Thank you. It was a significant project…but we were finally able to track down a few last blocks of stock. We now control 50.32% of the company."

Marieles smiled, an expression far more genuine than those she'd managed for Ferrell's consumption. The company she now controlled, through Shepard and an impenetrable array of dummy entities, was the second largest media network on Megara. Its tentacles extended throughout the Confederation. It was a corrupt enterprise, as all such were, but its prejudices and biases had always been variable, driven more by the beliefs and vanities of its managerial ranks than by any rational agenda. Now, its dishonesty would be diverted to a single purpose…to spread exactly the "news" she wanted Megarans to see. Control of the network gave her direct access to over thirty percent of the capital's population, and billions more throughout the Confederation.

"I can't express sincerely enough my admiration and gratitude for all you have achieved here, Gustav. I can assure you I

will let…Father…know how well you have done." The name
Gaston Villieneuve wasn't commonly known in the Confederation, but Marieles was cautious by nature. Too many people in
the circles she frequented for the operation knew exactly who
Villieneuve was.

"I'm very appreciative. You've directed the mission with
great skill. I trust we will soon be able to move forward from
these preparatory operations…and at last launch Black Dawn."

"Soon, Gustav…hopefully." Marieles had to admit to herself, she'd enjoyed far greater success than she'd imagined possible. But she wasn't one to get carried away. Black Dawn was
still a long way from completion. Perhaps not quite as long as it
had been, but far from a guaranteed success. "Meanwhile, you
know how to proceed."

She stood still, quiet for a moment. "I have to go. I have
another meeting…a very critical one."

She now had assets in the media, industry, law enforcement,
and the Senate. But she needed the military. That had been the
toughest one. The Confederation armed forces were full of
career officers and spacers, and she'd found far less corruption
in their ranks than she'd expected.

But now, she believed she'd found just what she was looking
for, an officer…pliable enough…to play the role she'd prepared.
Admiral Torrance Whitten wore three stars on his uniform, but
he'd never commanded a force larger than a pack of convoy
escorts. He owed his rank, and the absurd cluster of unearned
decorations he wore on his chest, to his Senator-father's wealth
and power.

Marieles's eyes had widened when she'd first read his profile.
Whitten was almost perfect for her plans, a high-ranking officer from a highly-placed family, bitter because he felt he'd been
unfairly overlooked for promotions and *real* command positions.
She suspected there were reasons for that, and almost certainly,
Whitten was somewhat less than…tactically gifted. Hell, she'd
realized that just from reading the file.

Resentful, pompous, full of himself…she couldn't imagine a
better asset if she'd created one from thin air. She was confident

she could swing him, but she knew her game had to be perfect.

Let him complain, she reminded herself. *Let him tell you how unfair it has all been, how his rivals have derailed his career. Don't even bring up that subject until he does.*

She glanced down at the tablet in her hand, rereading the small summary and looking at the photo. Whitten might be a narcissistic idiot who'd managed to sideline a career that had been handed to him on a silver platter, but he was easy enough on the eyes; tall, trim, dark hair and eyes…just what she liked.

Unlike the disgusting Ferrell, she would handle this one very personally. She would bribe him, console him, gradually offer him the chance at revenge against those who had injured him…and a way to get him the rank and power he so rightfully deserved.

Seduction was very much *on* the table with this one…

Chapter Forty-Three

CFS Dauntless
Zed-11 System
Year 315 AC

Barron stared at the display, determinedly pushing his thoughts back to the battle, away from his friend down on the surface, barely clinging to life.

Dying...Doc said she's dying...

The thought of her lying silent in a medpod, her body simply giving out, seemed wrong to him. She was a warrior like he was—if she had to die, it should be in action. Where he could be at her side.

But she'd saved almost two hundred of her comrades, her sacrifice giving them all a chance to escape the deadly disease. As soon as Doc Weldon cleared the last of the landing party, Barron could bring them all back up to the fleet and get the hell out of this system...and go home to warn the entire Rim that the fleet had found a deadly new enemy.

Assuming we survive this battle...

That was far from a sure thing. The fleet was barely holding its own. He owed that mostly to Jake Stockton and his squadrons. Anya Fritz's mines and Stockton's fighter strikes had caused enough damage to equalize the fight between Barron's battleships and the technologically superior Hegemony vessels.

Even now, his people worked feverishly to deliver death and destruction to the enemy. Sweating gunners labored at their panels, supervising and adjusting the targeting of the AIs, trying to recognize patterns in the enemy moves. *Dauntless*'s teams were used to being the best, pounding their enemies relentlessly with hit after hit. But the maneuverability of the Hegemony vessels defied their skills, and reduced their hit ratio to one more befitting a group of rookie trainees instead of the deadliest veterans in space.

Or at least the deadliest on the Rim.

Barron leaned back in his chair, staring at the display. He'd been a flag officer for several years now, but he still had to remind himself at times that he was responsible for an entire fleet and not just a single vessel. That was harder now, since he'd filled in for Atara and taken direct command of the battleship.

But the fleet didn't need anything from him, not now, not really. There were no elaborate tactics, no ruses of war that would make a difference. The enemy ships were faster, more maneuverable…and the fleets were already nose to nose, blasting away at each other. The battle was in the crews' hands now. And every one of them giving his or her best…of that much, Barron was certain.

It was frustrating, but there was still nothing for him to do but watch.

Dauntless shook again, another of the enemy beams connecting. The flagship had been spared a hit from the deadly railguns, but Barron knew it could happen at any time. *Dauntless* had taken considerable damage, but her primaries had held out during the entire approach. Now, at point blank range, he'd switched over to the more numerous and quicker-firing secondaries. *Dauntless* was locked in a duel with one of the big enemy vessels, and the ships were moving toward each other, cutting the already short range to knife-fighting distance. It was a death struggle, a duel only one ship could survive, and Barron flashed back to the battle years before with Katrine Rigellus and *Invictus*. The old *Dauntless* had won that desperate fight, though only by the slimmest of margins. For all the skill and dedication of his people,

Barron had never deceived himself that the slim difference in that fight had been bravery or training. In that, the two sides were evenly matched. Nor had his tactical capability exceeded that of his brilliant rival—Katrine Rigellus had been a brilliant tactician.

No, fortune had favored him that day and condemned his noble enemy. And the luck that had saved him then had been with him on many occasions since. He wondered if he could count on such favor again...or if he'd used up his generous allotment, if he'd come so far from home only to meet defeat and death.

"Admiral, Captain Stockton reports he's launching Blue and Scarlet Eagle squadrons...both fitted out for bombing missions."

Sonya Eaton's voice pulled him from his recollections. "Very well. Give Captain Stockton my best wish..." He paused. "No, put me on the channel with the launching squadrons."

"Yes, sir." A few seconds later: "On your line, Admiral."

"Blues and Eagles...this is Admiral Barron. I know most of you are used to launching as interceptors, but right now, we need you to bomb the hell out of those enemy battleships. You're the best pilots on *Dauntless*...the best in the whole damned fleet, but you know that already. What some of you may not know, are the names of the aces that have preceded you, and who are no longer here. Your squadrons have fought for *Dauntless* in a seemingly endless series of desperate fights...and those fallen heroes are all here with you today."

He was speaking, of course, mostly at least, of pilots who had been killed in action, though his mind drifted to the Eagles' former commander, Dirk "Warrior" Timmons. Timmons had been the only pilot Barron had ever met who rivaled Stockton in daring and skill. But, Timmons had lost both legs in a terrible crash in the old *Dauntless*'s landing bay. He'd mastered his prostheses, and Barron had no doubt the pilot *could* fly, perhaps as well as ever. But regulations had cost him his active wings, and Timmons was back at the Academy know, teaching new pilots. Barron suddenly wished Warrior was where he belonged, in the cockpit of a fighter...alongside his onetime rival and now friend, Raptor.

"And you're out there today with Raptor, the best pilot who has ever lived...so go out there and show the enemy what Confederation aces can do."

Barron reached down and cut the line...and a few seconds later, he felt the familiar vibrations, as *Dauntless*'s launch catapults send her elite squadrons back into the fray.

* * *

"It's the energy transmission lines, Commodore. We've lost power to all the guns on the port broadside."

Damn! Sara Eaton slammed her fist against her thigh. She was usually a block of ice on the bridge, hiding her emotions—certainly ones like frustration and fear, at least—from her crew. But she knew just how close the battle was. The fleet needed every ship in the line, and *Repulse* was one of its heaviest ships.

"Fire up the positioning jets. Bring the starboard guns around to bear. And revise our evasion plan to account for the new aspect."

"Yes, Commodore." The nav officer had paused for an instant before responding, and Eaton knew why. The change in bearing would require a reprogramming of the evasive maneuvers, and there was no way that could be implemented without reducing effectiveness, at least for a short time. At the range *Repulse* had closed to, even one extra hit from those enemy beams—and God, forbid, one of the railguns—could make the difference between her ship surviving the fight or not.

Assuming any of us survive...

"Executing, Commodore."

Before she could respond, Eaton felt a series of slight vibrations, one after the other. Fighters launching.

"Very well, Commander," she replied, a few seconds later than normal. She thought about her squadrons. The enhanced evasive maneuvers were playing havoc with fighter operations, and she suspected the bearing change she'd just ordered—and which flight control knew nothing about —would make things worse. Still, her launch bay crews were getting at least some ships out, even if the wild gyrations in *Repulse*'s thrust meant they were scattered all over the place.

She imagined the disorganization, which was hardly limited to *Repulse*'s fighters, was gutting the effectiveness of the bombing runs. But then she glanced up at the display and saw clusters of bombers moving in, at least a dozen of them against the enemy ship closest to *Repulse*. They were from different squadrons, intermixed and coming in from all angles. And yet, somehow they were making it work.

She knew exactly how. Jake Stockton. She'd been surprised when Barron had promoted his strike force leader and put him in overall command of the entire fleet's fighters. Eaton had been a ship commander before she'd become a commodore, and she understood that any captain would be disgruntled, at least, to lose a portion of command authority over his or her vessel. For the battleships, that damned sure included the fighter wings.

But, Stockton was proving the wisdom of Barron's move, as he had been since the first enemy ships had arrived. His wings had recognized their advantage immediately, and they'd been pounding it home ever since. Eaton knew the fleet would have been obliterated already if it hadn't been for the initial bombing runs, and now, Stockton was turning the chaos into a coordinated assault, one that was keeping the fleet in the fight.

She saw that *Repulse* had completed its reorientation, and before the nav officer could report to that effect, she turned toward the tactical station and said, "Starboard batteries…open fire!"

* * *

"All right, tactical force omega…we're going in now, and we're gonna go right down that thing's throat." Jake Stockton took a deep breath and tightened his grip around his ship's controls. He was used to flying an interceptor, and he found the bloated and clumsy bombing kit to be a major drag on maneuverability. He sympathized with bomber pilots in a way he wasn't sure he had before, especially when they had to go up against more maneuverable interceptors. *At least that's not a concern here...*

"Mustang six and eight, you're drifting out of position. Tighten up and get in line. Red six, kick up your thrust a notch... you're lagging." He had a force of nineteen bombers, one that was made up of parts of five different squadrons, from three different battleships. It was, in technical military terms, a complete mess. But, it was what he had, and if he had to tell every one of them where to fly and how, then that was what he would do. Whatever it took, that big bastard of a ship up ahead was going to get a good pounding.

Stockton had scanned the entire Hegemony fleet...and he'd come to one conclusion that was really not much more than a guess. The ship in front of his small force of bombers was the enemy flagship, and it was also one of the Hegemony ships that had suffered the least damage so far.

He had almost two hundred fighters back in space now, all that the battered ships of the fleet had been able to refit and launch. He figured a few more might trickle out, but most of those still absent were trapped in damaged bays or stuck aboard crippled ships unable to rearm and refuel them. He'd done the best he could to organize the disordered attacks...and then he'd picked out the largest battleship as the premier target in the enemy's line. He was also personally leading the assault.

"Form up on me...and, whatever happens, go off my lead." He pulled back on the throttle, feeling the thrust slam him back into his seat. His fighters were close to the target already, well within plasma torpedo range. But, Stockton and his people were going to take their weapons in a damned sight closer before launching.

He could see the big ship on his scanner, the size of the icon increasing as the range dropped below twenty thousand and continued down. His velocity was over five hundred kilometers per second, and he was still accelerating.

He began mixing up his straight-line thrust with evasive maneuvers, and he tapped the comm again as he saw the enemy battleship open up with its light guns. "Remember, they may not have dedicated point defense arrays, but they've got weapons... and one hell of an AI targeting suite. Keep moving, remember your evasion patterns. Anybody who gets blown away on this run is going to be in deep trouble with me, so watch yourselves."

He angled his vector a few degrees, and then back again, bouncing around without seriously altering his course toward the target ship. He could see his pilots emulating his actions, weaving all over the display...but, one of them was hit nevertheless, and the symbol disappeared from his scanner as he was watching.

The range was under ten thousand now, and the fire was thicker, heavier. He saw a pulse go by, perhaps five hundred meters from his fighter. That was far enough to be well out of the danger zone...but close enough in terms of space battle to add to the sweat soaking the inside of his flight suit.

"Pay attention, all of you. We're in the kill zone here, and that works both ways. Stay focused...and let's get this done."

Six thousand kilometers.

He glanced quickly to the long-range scanner, a quick check on his other groups, and on the battle as a whole. The two lines were locked in a deadly slugging match, and all along the front, small forces of bombers were slipping in, trying to make a difference with their runs.

The numbers on his screen continued to drop, slipping under five thousand. It was beyond point-blank range, closer than he'd ever led an attack in...but he still held his fire. He was going to go closer...close enough to slam his torpedo right into that thing's hull, without giving the bastards a chance to even think about evading.

He angled his thrust again, his ship bouncing around so wildly, it challenged even his cast iron veteran's stomach. Still, he drove forward, increasing his velocity. He was on a course directly for the hulking ship, and at less than four thousand meters, he had about seven seconds before his bombing run became a suicide attack.

He held steady, his hand gripping the throttle so tightly, his fingers were white. He could feel the sweat on his palms, and he gripped even harder, struggling to keep his hand from sliding around. His torpedo was ready, armed…and just as the range counted down to twenty-five hundred, he squeezed the firing stud.

He'd pre-programmed the torpedo to fire up the reaction and convert to energy the instant it cleared his fighter, so now he had nothing to worry about except pulling his bird up, and clearing the enemy ship. He hit full power, blasting hard to change his vector to a clear heading. He had to drop the evasive maneuvers for a few seconds, and he could almost feel the enemy batteries targeting his suddenly predictable ship, but nothing happened. His fighter zipped right by the massive Hegemony vessel… and he watched as the torpedo slammed into its target, dead on amidships.

He let out a loud howl, grateful that his comm was off. For all his wildness, he'd come to understand, and mostly to embrace, his new command role. His people needed more out of him than a reckless role model teaching them to laugh at death. They needed a leader…and he'd promised himself that was just what they would get.

He looked at the screen and smiled as his bombers, one by one, followed his course in, holding their torpedoes to the last second, and then sending them right into the enemy vessel. At such a close range, the Hegemony ship only managed to evade a few. His attack force lost two more ships, though it looked like one of the pilots, at least, had managed to eject…and, when it was all over, they had scored no less than ten hits.

Stockton punched at the keys on his control panel, pulling up the damage assessments. The reports were a combination of scanning data and educated guesses by his ship's AI. But he didn't need any of that now. The energy readings suddenly spiked right off the scale, and the giant ship vanished in an explosion so furious, for a few seconds, it seemed like the system had acquired a second star.

* * *

"All ships, full thrust directly ahead. Now." Cilian Globus
stood in the middle of *Fortiter*'s bridge, holding onto one of
the structural supports and somehow managing to appear unaffected by the feeling of 4g that remained after the ship's dampeners absorbed as much thrust as they could.

He'd been watching the bombing runs all along the line.
Some groups of fighters had as few as three or four, and others
were decently organized makeshift squadrons. But whatever the
size or the composition, they all surged forward like the wrath
of God. Not one single fighter held back or failed to attack with
a vigor that left even the veteran Palatian commander with nothing but silent respect. No words would have sufficed to praise
the heroism and determination he was witnessing.

And that he would follow.

"We're going in. I want us close enough to these bastards to
hit them with a club." Even as he spoke, *Fortiter* shook again—
another hit. He shrugged it off. The fight had come down to
the end, and now it would be for warriors to finish it. The battle
wouldn't be won now by lasers or particle accelerators, or even
super-advanced railguns. It was the hearts of men and women
that mattered now…at least that was how Globus saw it. He
stood firm where he was, his Palatian blood boiling.

His four battleships were all damaged, two of them badly.
But every one still had at least some thrust capacity, and they
were all blasting at full now, weapons firing ceaselessly as the
distance slipped with each passing second.

Ten thousand kilometers…unheard of for capital ships. But
still he kept his force moving in. Nine thousand.

He could see *Fortiter*'s batteries' hit ratios increasing. Even
the enemy's superior thrust and AI capabilities were of limited
value at so close a range.

Globus was scared, though as a Palatian Patrician, he'd never
admit it, not even to himself. But, he was exhilarated, too, and
he could feel the tide turning. Thanks to the work of the fighter
squadrons, the victory was there for the taking. He was sure of

it, and he wouldn't let up, not until the enemy turned tail and ran back where they'd come from.

He looked at the display again. Seven thousand kilometers.

Fortiter's batteries fired again, and he could see the hits slamming into the target vessel...and great geysers erupting from the gaping wounds they created, the long streams of gases and fluids flash freezing in the frigid cold of space.

Six thousand kilometers.

He smiled and whispered to himself a phrase he'd spoken since childhood...and one that said everything that mattered.

"The way is the way..."

Chapter Forty-Four

PUV Carcajou
Approaching Barroux
Rhian System
Union Year 219 (315 AC)

Denisov sat quietly on *Carcajou*'s bridge, watching the cataclysmic destruction he'd unleashed. He'd always considered himself a professional naval officer and not some kind of sadist or mass murderer. He'd silently detested the brutal and totalitarian aspects of the Union's government, as so many long-term professionals in the navy did. But now he realized he'd crossed a line, one that would brand him forever. One that made him what he'd always despised.

He suspected the specific definition of a mass murderer varied with different factors—situation, provocation…but, mostly, the number of dead. The death toll on Barroux would be in the millions—if not the billions—and he was pretty sure that guaranteed him a spot on anyone's list.

He watched as the massive chunks of rock slipped into Barroux's orbital track. A few struck fortresses, obliterating them in an instant before continuing down toward the atmosphere. And, right behind the wave of destruction came Denisov's fleet. His ships closed on the distracted and damaged fortresses, destroying those the asteroids had spared. The dust and other interference affected their fire, but the stations' focus on trying to stop the asteroids allowed his ships to close to stunningly close range.

He leaned back in his chair, pushing away the feelings of guilt for what he had done. He'd had no choice...he told himself that again and again, and, in a sense, it was true. Retreating to Montmirail would have meant facing Gaston Villieneuve's wrath. The man's brutal rage could have consumed many of Denisov's officers, and even their families. But, for all the truth in his internal defense, he wondered if it could justify the millions who were about to die. History's greatest tyrants, its most infamous killers, all had their own justifications.

He shrugged, pushing the thoughts away. There would be time for self-recrimination later. Now, he had a job to do. He'd defeated Barroux's previously impregnable orbital defenses. It was time to secure the planet.

Barroux's people would die by the millions as the asteroids came down from the sky, blasting the surface like some enraged deity's wrath unchained. But there would be survivors, probably many millions of them. Planetary populations were extremely difficult to exterminate entirely. And, that population, whatever remained of it, had to be brought under Union control.

"Lieutenant...the transports are to advance and enter orbit."

"Yes, sir."

It was time. Barroux had escaped the Union's grasp for nearly three years...but all that was over now. Those planets that had looked on, encouraged by Barroux's rebellion, would learn a new lesson from that planet's agony. Denisov was ashamed of his central role in bringing that about, but he knew Gaston Villieneuve would approve whole-heartedly.

"All units are to prepare for landing operations. The ground assault will commence immediately after the last impacts."

*   *   *

Hoover stumbled toward the door, struggling as he carried Breen's unconscious body over his shoulders. He'd been surprised when Bernard's resistance fighters had saved his life, but then, he had just done the same for the rebel commander, so perhaps it had been payback of a sort. Whatever it was, he knew he had to get the hell out of the building. It looked like Bernard's decapitation strike had succeeded, but that didn't change the fact that Delacorte had already sent for help. Hundreds, if not thousands, of soldiers loyal to Caron were no doubt on the way.

There was also another concern, one even deadlier than Caron's people. Union forces. The information he'd gleaned in the moments before the strike had been far from conclusive... but they were profoundly disturbing. If the Union fleet was doing what he thought they were, it was going to be hard to find a safe refuge anywhere on Barroux.

He was about to duck through the doorway, or, more accurately, the gaping hole where the door had been moments before...when he saw Caron.

Several of Bernard's people had cornered the "First Protector" of Barroux, and it looked like Caron's murderous regime was about to end in a rather final way. One of the resistance fighters shoved the butt of his rifle into Caron's gut, and he doubled over and dropped to his knees, coughing up blood.

Hoover knew Caron deserved what he was about to get. He couldn't even imagine the amount of blood on the man's hands. But if Bernard's people just murdered the captive Caron, they would be going down the same road as the last regime. He turned and walked back into the room.

"Stop," he said, moving toward the fighters who were still beating Caron. "Stop that."

"Who the hell are you?" One of the soldiers turned to face him, holding a pistol in one hand, and a long, notched blade in the other. The knife was covered with a bright sheen of blood.

Hoover stopped, leaning down and putting Breen gently on the floor. He moved slowly, in a way that made it clear he wasn't reaching for a weapon. "I'm Mike Hoover...Confederation Intelligence. Congratulations on the success of your strike. But you can't just murder that man."

"Says you." The man glared at him, and Hoover could see

his fingers tightening around the knife. "This bastard had my brother killed...and his wife and children, too. He's a piece of pig shit, and it's way past time he got what's coming to him. So, get lost...while you still can."

Hoover could hear the rage in the man's words, feel his need for vengeance. But he stayed where he was. "I'm not saying he doesn't deserve to die...but you have to do it right. You can't just beat him to death right here."

"I can do whatever the hell I want, asshole...and then I can do the same to..."

"Raines...stand down. You will not threaten Agent Hoover." Hoover recognized Bernard's voice.

"Yes, sir." The fighter backed down immediately. His expression was sullen, but he obeyed Bernard without question.

Hoover turned to face the resistance leader, just as Bernard said, "I understood why you turned me down earlier, Agent Hoover, but I'm somewhat at a loss as to why you feel you must defend our good First Protector here. All of these men and women have lost friends and relatives to Caron's death squads. So, tell me, why should I order them to spare him?"

Hoover suddenly felt uncomfortable, and he wondered how he would react if those dear to him had been slain by Caron's people. *I'd probably be cutting his heart out right now...*

"I didn't say you should spare him. I said you shouldn't murder him here. Bring him somewhere, conduct some kind of trial. You spoke earlier of the Confederation as an inspiration. Well, no matter how terrible the crime, in the Confederation, the accused gets a trial before punishment is inflicted."

Hoover knew he was painting an optimistic image, one that was untrue far too often. He was well aware that many people were denied fair trials in the Confederation, that corruption and abuse were nearly as endemic as they were in the Union. It was the "nearly" that made all the difference, though.

"We're not exactly in a position to conduct a trial, Agent Hoover. Until a few hours ago, we were all in hiding, being hunted night and day. I don't even know the status of things right now. I sent teams to secure crucial installations, but our communications are out. Delacorte's people are probably jamming us."

Hoover thought about the scanner reports that came in just before the assault. "I know why your comm is out…and it has nothing to do with the late Ami Delacorte or her enforcers. The Union forces are back, and this time they're bombarding Barroux with asteroids."

"With what?" Bernard looked confused.

"They're hurling huge rocks down at your planet…it's probably the disturbance in the atmosphere that is interfering with your communications."

"What do we care if a few space boulders are coming toward the planet? Better than nuclear warheads, at least."

"No…it's not better. You don't understand the kinetic energy a ten-kilometer asteroid can release. Each one will be like thousands of nuclear detonations…and there may be several dozen projectiles of this nature. It will be Armageddon all across the planet. You have to collect your people now…and get them out of here. Out of the city. If I'm right, virtually everything manmade on Barroux will be destroyed, possibly within minutes. Getting to the wilderness is your only hope."

Hoover knew he sounded crazy, and he was stunned when Bernard just nodded his assent. Then, the resistance leader turned and shouted for his fighters to get out of the building and form up in the street…and he shocked Hoover again when he ordered his people to bring Caron with them. Alive.

Hoover reached down to pick up Breen, just as two of Bernard's people beat him to it. "Come with us, Agent Hoover," Bernard said. "My people will carry your associate. We will go to our refuges in the hills outside the city."

Hoover just nodded…and then he followed Bernard and the two men carrying Breen out into the street.

*　*　*

Hoover looked down from the high ridgeline, toward the smoldering orange glow that had once been Barroux City. The

planet's capital had escaped a direct hit from one of the asteroid impacts, but that hadn't spared it from the shockwaves and
thermal blasts. The city had become a raging inferno, and it had
been reduced utterly to ruins as, Hoover suspected, had just
about every other built up area on the planet. Forests all around
were on fire as well, the old growth trees lighting up the dust-
obscured sky…or already reduced to ashes.

The resistance hideout had proven to be a lucky spot, one
well-situated to offer shelter and protection. The high ridgelines
offered significant cover from the blast waves that had leveled
the capital. The sky was as hazy and choked by dust and smoke
as it was anywhere, but all things considered, it was just about
the best place to be.

Hoover had been out three times already, a risky move with
residual impacts still occurring and roving bands of desperate
survivors wandering out from the city. But he was responsible
for the entire Confederation contingent—his own people, and
the crew of the last smuggler's ship who'd been trapped on Barroux by the Union blockade. He'd managed to find three of his
own people, and four of the ship's crew, but that left more than
twenty missing.

Bernard had sent out a dozen patrols of his own, and save
for the two that hadn't returned, they all reported the same thing
that Hoover had seen. Nothing but blasted ruins, as far as the
eye could see.

A few of the scattered bands of survivors had joined up
with the resistance forces, and Bernard had ordered his people
to share their dwindling rations and water supplies with the refugees. Hoover was impressed with the humanity of it all, but he
wondered if, for all his blustering about Confederation ideals, he
wouldn't have kept what he had for his own people. There was
no way of knowing what food and supplies would be retriev-
able, and it wouldn't be long before the stunned groups of survivors turned feral and started killing each other for scraps of
stale bread.

Hoover turned and walked back into the makeshift camp,
toward the small shelter Bernard had made his headquarters. He

had to have a long talk with the resistance commander. Bernard had been focused on defeating Remy Caron and his people, and now on providing whatever aid he could to the desperate survivors, but there was another problem, one Hoover knew would push Bernard's fighters to the brink.

The scouting parties had reported something other than destruction and scattered refugees. Soldiers, heavily armed and armored, were moving around the formerly inhabited areas, rounding up any survivors they came into contact with. The descriptions were all the same: black body armor, perfect unison in their marches, and long, fully-automatic rifles that also launched grenades.

Bernard's people didn't recognize the soldiers by sight, but Hoover did…and he knew the resistance warriors would know them, too, as soon as he spoke their name.

Foudre Rouge.

Chapter Forty-Five

Barron walked slowly across the catwalk, looking out over the open area of *Dauntless*'s main engineering section. The immense reactors that powered the enormous vessel were situated just below, and the engines that produced its thrust lay to the aft. It was a larger space by far than that on the previous *Dauntless*, and better laid out, too. His old ship had served well, and he would never forget her...but the class had been a little haphazard in its design, and decades of service and refits to bring the old girl up to modern standards had created somewhat of a chaotic rabbit warren of passageways and access tubes.

The new ship was now like the old in one important way, however. Everywhere Barron looked, he could see the scars of battle. The pristine shininess of the new vessel was gone. Burned out equipment, gashes in the bulkhead, even a blackened area where an internal fire had gotten out of control... they all served to mark the new *Dauntless* as a veteran of battle.

Some of his people had died in that fight...and that was at the forefront of his mind. *Dauntless* had suffered thirty-one fatalities in the two battles against the Hegemony forces, and for all the pain that caused, he knew the flagship had escaped lightly.

Six battleships and fourteen escort ships had been destroyed outright in the battle, most with the loss of all hands. And the majority of the other ships had suffered losses far in excess of *Dauntless*'s.

Cilian Globus's Alliance ships had probably taken the worst of it. Globus had pushed his vessels hard, driven them almost to hull to hull contact, pouncing on the enemy battleships hard on the heels of Stockton's bombing runs. He'd lost one of his four battleships outright, and each of the other three had taken major damage, with no fewer than two hundred dead on any of them.

Barron was grateful for the heroism of his Alliance comrades, and for the courage all his people had displayed. But, he knew the victory—if he could convince himself to call such a bloody nightmare a victory—was owed almost entirely to Jake Stockton and his pilots.

Stockton had led his disordered and disorganized wings against the enemy battle line at the height of the deadly struggle, and he'd sent them in, wave after wave, closing beyond point-blank range and planting their plasma torpedoes right into the guts of the Hegemony ships. The squadrons had been nothing short of heroic...including one pilot, a Lieutenant Eve Grenner, who had taken her damaged ship and blasted it right for one of the enemy battleships, activating the plasma torpedo stuck in her bomb bay and slamming into the Hegemony vessel as a sphere of pure energy. Barron had used his semi-viceregal powers as head of the White Fleet to posthumously award her the Confederation Star, all the while thinking how meaningless such gestures really were in the wake of a fine comrade's death.

The Hegemony fleet had finally had enough, and its battered remains turned and fled...and then, Barron had done something that still gnawed at him. He'd immediately ordered his ships to pursue, to maintain contact by any means possible, and to make sure not a single enemy ship escaped, whatever the cost. He suspected the order, and the intensity with which it had been given, had increased Globus's already lofty respect for him, but there was more than honor and vengeance in his reasoning. Vengeance meant almost nothing to him, not now… not when he was facing the reality that he'd found a deadly new enemy, a grave threat to the Confederation, and to all the other Rim nations.

It was that reality, and his realization of how difficult it would be to fight the war that was likely coming, that had spurred him to mercilessly hunt down and destroy the enemy survivors. His ships had been at a disadvantage in thrust, weapon power, AI sophistication…almost everything that affected the outcome of a battle. Save for the fighters. Barron had no idea of the enemy's communications potential, no way of knowing what information had already been transmitted up the line. But he did know that he needed to maintain the mystery of the fighter squadrons in any way possible, to prevent new enemy forces from studying what had happened and developing tactics to counter the wings. It was the only choice that made sense.

It was also a choice that had cost him hundreds more of his own people, and three more of his ships. But as far as the fleet's scanners could determine, the pursuit, which stretched to the transit point and into the Zed-12 system, had been a success. Not a single Hegemony ship had escaped.

"We've got crews working around the clock, Admiral. We've got thrust up to seventy percent. I'll deny I said it if you tell anyone else, but in a pinch, I think I can get you eighty. The primaries are still out, but we should have them up and running by tomorrow. Three of the secondary turrets are still out. I think we'll have two of them online by around the time the primaries are back. The third's pretty much done, at least this side of spacedock." Fritz had come walking down the catwalk from the other direction.

"Well done, Fritzie, as always." Barron's tone was a bit distracted. He'd seen the remains of the crew from that last turret—they had been nearly obliterated. "I appreciate your diving in on *Dauntless*'s repairs, but I need you to keep the damage control crews on the other ships working at something like your normal amazing pace, too.

"I'm on it, sir. We should have every ship in the fleet at least reasonably operational within thirty-six hours."

"That's good, Fritzie…do anything you can to keep us to that schedule…or even shorten it. I'd like to get out of here before any new enemy forces show up."

"I'll see to it, sir. I'll even try to get that thirty-six down below thirty."

"Watch out, Fritzie…you know once you put something like that in my head, I'm going to hold you to it."

She just smiled.

He'd have bet his last credit on her beating thirty hours.

* * *

"Is that a power surge at the transit point?" Buck Horace was pacing across *Kraken*'s bridge. His ship was back in Zed-12, on patrol again to warn the fleet if more enemy forces arrived. It had been quiet, not so much as an errant meteor slipping through any of the system's transit points. Horace knew the withdrawal orders could come at any time. The landing parties had been retrieved, and the post-battle repairs were almost complete enough to allow the fleet to head back home, bringing the news of another enemy—and possibly another war—back to Megara. But, he was determined not to let his guard drop, not for an instant. Not until his ship was back in Zed-11.

"It appears to be normal fluctuation, sir. Strong, but within typical parameters."

Horace's response was something between muttering and a grunt. He was considered a grouchy old cuss, to put it lightly, and he'd run his spacers on *Kraken* harder than he had his cadets at the Academy. His people on *Kraken* were no doubt tired, but most of them had quickly become devoted to the captain who'd shown them just how good they could be. They could complain about him, quietly grumble when he wasn't around, but God help some loudmouth from another ship who had anything negative to say about the old man.

"I want the scanners focused on that point, Lieutenant. And I want a short spread of drones launched." He knew they all probably thought he was being paranoid—and maybe he was—but *Kraken* was about to leave the system, and the fleet was preparing for the voyage back home. In his experience, that was the time when things went to crap.

"Yes, Captain." A moment later. "Drones, ready to launch."

"Launch...lock on to them as soon as they're clear, and feed the data to my station." He walked back across the bridge, dropping hard into his chair.

"Yes, sir."

Horace reached out and punched at the controls below his small screen. Barron would send word soon, he was sure of it...the orders for Kraken to return and rejoin the fleet for the journey home. But, until then, he was going to watch that transit point like a hawk.

* * *

Barron stood outside the entrance to sickbay, struggling to make himself step through the doorway. He'd been to see Atara every day since the landing parties had been certified free of the disease and shuttled back up to the fleet. But every minute he'd spent at her side had been a torment. Atara Travis had been one of the strongest, most alive people he'd ever known, and it was difficult beyond words to watch her lying in a coma, motionless inside her frigid medpod.

He knew he should be grateful she was alive...if "alive" was even how he'd characterize her condition. Doc Weldon had all but assured him his friend would be dead by now, but she'd clung stubbornly to life, shocking *Dauntless*'s entire medical team. Weldon finally changed his prediction, though he was very clear he didn't expect her to improve much either. *It's a possibility*...that was what Weldon had told Barron when the admiral had asked about her chances of recovering. But his words were heavily shadowed by doubt.

He was about to step through the hatch when a large man came out, walking slowly and supporting himself with a cane.

"Admiral," he said, struggling to quickly straighten his posture.

"At ease, Bryan…please. The last thing I want is to see you tumbling over trying to salute or something." Rogan had always been very formal in Barron's presence, and even now, barely able to stand, he was the same old Marine he'd been years before, when a new captain showed up to take command of a ship called *Dauntless.*

"Yes, sir." Rogan's voice was stronger than it had been two days earlier, when Barron had last talked to him. The Marine still looked a bit shaky, but Doc Weldon had assured him Rogan was completely recovered from the disease. His lingering weakness had more to do with his extended stretch in cryostasis than with the pathogen that had come so close to killing him. "Are you here to see Captain Travis, Admiral?"

Barron nodded. "Yes…I'm not sure it helps anything, but I wouldn't forgive myself if I didn't get down here at least once a day."

"It helps, sir. I'm sure it does."

"Thank you, Bryan." His first thought was that Rogan was trying to humor him, to make him feel a little bit better. But Bryan Rogan was the most honest person Barron had ever known…and realizing that made him feel a little better. "I think you should go get some rest, Bryan. I need you back, as soon as possible."

"I'm ready, sir…for whatever you need."

Barron looked at the Marine, barely able to hold himself up with the cane…and then he realized Rogan was dead serious. "I know that, Bryan." Barron managed a smile. "Now, go get some rest."

He stood where he was for a few more seconds, and then he slipped into sickbay. Weldon was standing in the main room, issuing orders to a group of medtechs. He turned as soon as he realized Barron was there.

"Any changes, Doc?" Barron already knew the answer from Weldon's expression.

"Nothing, sir. But no worsening, either. Which, considering the circumstances, is its own bit of good news.

Barron wasn't sure he bought the doctor's positive spin, but he nodded, and then he walked across the room and slipped into the small alcove that held Travis in her medpod.

She looked the same as she had every time he'd come: still, lifeless. She was alive—he knew that much, at least—but each time he came and saw her in the same state, he lost a little more hope.

"Atara...I'm so sorry I let you go down there in my place..." He knew there was no logic to the statement. In all likelihood, he lacked her natural immunity...and that meant he would have died with all the others. In a sense, it had been a stroke of fortune that she had been part of the landing party, that her natural resistance to the disease was able to save hundreds of her comrades.

Just, please, not at the cost of her own life...

He moved next to the pod, reaching out and putting his hand on the cold glass. There was nothing he could do, nothing he could say. All he could do was be there, even though he knew she couldn't tell. Her brain function was still active, but she was deep in a coma.

He sat for a while, ten minutes, twenty...he lost a sense of it. Then, Weldon came in. "Admiral, it's the control center. They need to speak with you." Weldon's voice was deadly serious. "Now."

Barron leapt up and jogged out into the main room, leaning over the comm. "Barron here."

"Admiral..." It was Sonya Eaton's voice, and there was definitely something wrong. "Captain Horace just transited back from Zed-12, sir. *Kraken* picked up enemy forces entering from the system's alpha transit point. He reports..." She paused, and Barron's blood went cold. "...he reports it appears to be a larger force than the previous one." Barron heard the words, but he grappled with their true meaning. *Larger than the previous one?*

Another silence...and then, almost an answer to his thought. "Substantially larger, sir."

Chapter Forty-Six

CFS Dauntless
Zed-11 System
Year 315 AC

"The enemy forces are crossing the Zed-12 system at a high velocity. We can wrap up necessary repairs and head for the transit point leading toward home, but it's likely enemy forces will enter this system before we're able to get every ship out...and, even if we can, it will be by the slimmest of margins. Our best efforts at masking our drive trails will be insufficient to prevent the enemy from scanning the direction in which we headed." Sara Eaton stood in *Dauntless*'s conference room, looking as tense as she sounded.

Barron had called his officers back for another face to face meeting. He'd justified it because Fritz and her people needed a few more hours anyway to get the final repairs completed anyway...but there was more to it than that. They weren't all going to make it out of Zed-11, and he felt that the parting he saw coming was best done face to face.

"It will be like giving them a roadmap back to the Rim...at least if they're smart and aggressive enough to pursue immediately. They're faster than we are, and they'll be able to stay with the fleet, note each transit point we use. If we can't lose them here, we won't get another chance. We'll get back to warn the Admiralty…and the threat will be hours behind us." Sonya Eaton added her thoughts to her older sister's report, and, again, Barron was struck by how similar they were to each other. They didn't so much look the same, but their demeanor, their coolness under fire…it was like watching the same officer in two different places.

"That's something we can't do." Barron's voice was deep, raw. He leaned forward and put his hands on the table, pushing himself to his feet as he spoke. "We must get a warning home. That is of the utmost urgency, and that warning must arrive before any enemy can follow. Hopefully, significantly before." He was silent for a moment, thinking…though he knew he'd made his decision. He was grim, and he could feel it bearing down on him. "Commodore Eaton…you'll take command of a small force, all ships with full thrust capacity, or close to it, and you will return to Megara immediately to warn the Admiralty and the Senate." He looked over at Globus. "Cilian, you must go, too. This is a threat to all of us, and you need to get to Palatia and report to Imperator Tulus as quickly as possible. I know he'll listen to you."

Globus looked as though he was going to argue, but he remained silent.

"I'll take the rest of the fleet and transit into Zed-12 to intercept the Hegemony fleet there. We will conduct a running fight, relying heavily on fighter attacks, and then, after we've bought enough time for the returning force to get out of the system, we will pull back…we'll fly through another transit point, hopefully baiting the enemy to follow us, and conclude that our home systems lie in that direction."

The room was silent. Barron's plan would mean a few of their number would return home, while most of the rest of the fleet—and its spacers—would buy the time to make good that escape, very likely at the cost of their lives.

Cilian Globus shifted in his seat. "Admiral, my forces will stay. We will not run, certainly not while our comrades and allies remain to fight."

Barron sighed softly. He'd been expecting the argument…

and he was ready for it. As ready as he could be. "Cilian…no one is happy with the situation. But there's more than courage or honor at stake here. The Hegemony is a threat to the Confederation and to the Alliance. We've all seen their technology. We're outmatched at every turn. We must get a warning back. A Hegemony invasion is likely to be cataclysmic in any case…if our forces are not ready, we have no chance."

"Sir…" The Palatian looked partially convinced, but he was still arguing. "…I agree that we must send a warning, but it does not…"

"You've served alongside Vian Tulus your entire life, Cilian. You are as brothers. He must receive the warning from a source he trusts without question. He must hear this from you." There was a short silence, then Barron added, "Duty first, Cilian. Would you see Palatia attacked and destroyed, and your people enslaved, to stay here and fight? Is that honor? It is the way?" Barron almost felt guilty. Defending their homeworld was nearly a religion in the Alliance, and any mention of Palatians being enslaved harkened back to the shame of that world's past. It was a cheap shot…but Barron suspected it would work.

Globus just sat quietly. The Palatian looked extremely unhappy, and Barron realized he *had* gotten through to him. Then, he turned toward Eaton. "Commodore, your reports suggest that *Repulse* has close to one hundred percent thrust generation…and your weapons arrays are also in reasonable condition. You will choose two other battleships, and whatever escorts you feel you will need. I don't need to tell you, time is of the essence. I want your force to move out within the next three hours." Barron knew that was an unreasonable time, almost impossible. But it was all he had.

"Admiral…" Eaton was shaking her head. "There has to be another way."

Barron looked back at her, his face cold, impassive. "But there isn't…and you know it."

His expression softened, and he looked out at his officers. "I want to tell you all what an honor it has been to command a force like this one. We had hoped to discover technology and a better insight into the past...and instead we found disaster. We're going to need to fight to survive. But that misfortune was not the fault of any officer or spacer in this fleet. For those of you who will be leaving for Megara, remember, there's no shame in this. Your job is the most important one, and you will carry with you the future of all our people."

He paused and took a deep breath. "And, for those who remain here with me, we will do what we must to hold the line and allow Commodore Eaton's ships to escape. Our efforts will be dangerous, and costly, but this is *not* a suicide mission. We will use fighter attacks to slow the enemy, and to pick off their ships. Our heavier vessels will fall back, act as launch and landing platforms while remaining out of reach of the enemy's main guns...and then, we will withdraw. The enemy will likely allow us to withdraw...they'll want to track us back home. And, we will accommodate them, because they will follow us into darkness and the unknown. Anywhere but back to our home, our worlds, and our loved ones..."

Barron was silent again. Then, he said, simply. "It's time... and I know each of you will do what you must. As you have so many times before."

* * *

"Do you know what you're saying, Commodore?" Barron couldn't ever recall being angry with Sara Eaton...until now.

"Yes, sir...and I speak for us all."

Barron stared at the small group in front of him. Sara Eaton, Cilian Globus...and five other top commanders from the fleet.

"You're talking about mutiny. Do you understand what you're doing? Do you realize the consequences?"

"Admiral..." Globus took a step forward, and he stared right at Barron. "...Tyler...you have to understand. You have to *think*. You have counseled me before to set aside honor when it conflicts with duty. Well, my friend—and I say this at the risk of damaging that valued friendship—you are pursuing your own vanity when you insist on staying with the fleet. *You must* go back to the Confederation. No one else can fill your shoes there."

Barron refused to accept any of it. He hated himself enough for ordering most of his people to remain behind…he couldn't imagine leaving them to that fate while he escaped and returned to Megara.

"I want you all to listen to me, all of you, and listen well. This fleet, and every single one of you, is under my command. I've heard your arguments…and I have rejected them. Now, follow your orders, or by God, I will have every one of you hauled to the brig."

"That's what you'll have to do, sir." It was Sara Eaton again. "I'm your second in command, Admiral, and I'm telling you that you've lost sight of your duty." She paused. "And I will not go back as you ordered. You can lock me in the brig,—or you can invoke wartime penalties and throw me out the airlock—but I am *not* going back while you stay here."

"You *are* going back, Commodore…if I have to order a squad of Marines to drag you back to your ship. Is that understood?"

"No, Admiral Barron. I won't go. You'll have to order the Marines to shoot me. And even if they get me into the ship, as soon as we've transited out of the system, I will turn around and come back."

Barron felt a surge of anger. He wanted to scream, to punch the wall. He'd never faced insubordination from his officers, and the fury was close to overwhelming him. He couldn't imagine ordering his Marines to drag Sara Eaton to the brig, much less shoot her or eject her from an airlock. But she wasn't giving in… and she clearly had almost all his senior officers on his side. If he couldn't defuse the situation, he wouldn't have a flag officer left at his or her post.

He turned toward Globus. "You too? You can craft whatever explanations you want, but it changes nothing. I never thought I would see you abandon your honor, Cilian. Could anything be worth that?"

"Yes, Tyler…if what I'm doing costs me my honor, so be it. Any Palatian has one duty, supreme among all. We have fought for it for nearly seventy years. Tarkus Vennius died for it. The home world, Palatia, must be safeguarded at all costs. Without the Confederation fully mobilized and ready to fight with us, the Rim will surely fall." Globus paused, and Barron could see the pain it caused for an Alliance commander to admit that his people couldn't win a fight alone. "No one is better positioned to ensure the Confederation is prepared. It's your destiny, as the descendant of the first Admiral Barron, as your people's hero in the last war against the Union."

"He's right, sir." It was Sara Eaton again, and Barron could see Sonya standing behind her sister, nodding her agreement. "You know how things are back home...the Senate, the war weariness. You saw what happened with the Union War—the Senate was ready to do anything to avoid further conflict. I don't have your standing, sir, and I certainly don't have the adoration of the people the way you do. Admiral Striker is going to need all the help he can get to make sure this threat is taken seriously. It's not just about what the Confederation does...it's about when. Months of debate and deal-making in the Senate could cost us the time we need to get ready." She paused, staring at him plaintively. "You know what a deadly struggle we face, Admiral. We haven't discussed it, but we all know we could be looking at total defeat at the hands of the Hegemony. Billions dead, and the rest enslaved by a group of madmen who think they're some kind of gods. Is your 'honor' worth that, Tyler? Would you make the struggle—and possibly the sacrifice—of every man and woman in this fleet meaningless...because you sent me home and didn't go yourself? Didn't do your *real* duty?"

Barron felt as though he'd been run over by a heavy transport. Eaton had come at him with both barrels blazing, and, for all the instinctive resistance that rose up inside him, somewhere, deep down, he knew she was right. It was another burden of his legacy, more weight from the Barron name and from his own success in the Union War. He knew that, because he'd struggled so hard to deflect the credit and fame to the others who'd fought at his side. The Senate had already thrown away the victory his people had sweated and bled and died to win...and left the next generation to likely face a new war against the Union. How much would they resist a war against an unknown enemy, if the message came from anyone but their appointed hero?

He wanted to argue, but he couldn't come up with the words. He had to go back, his officers were right…he knew that now. And he had to leave most of the fleet behind, to hold back the enemy and prevent them from just following him back to Megara. How could he look them in the eye, order them to stay when he was going back?

How would he ever be able to look *himself* in the eye? He knew what he had to do…and he also knew he would never forgive himself for doing it. *Could* never forgive himself.

He turned toward Eaton. "Sara…if I go back, you're…" He couldn't force the words from his mouth.

"I'll stay, Tyler. I can do the job we need here, make a vital difference. I can't do that back on Megara."

Barron felt hollow. He was grateful for Eaton's cooperation, and yet it made the guilt worse, too. "Sara…"

"It's okay, Tyler. We all know what has to happen here." She paused. "I can promise you, as you yourself said, this is no suicide mission. We're going to pick that fleet apart with fighter strikes, and then we'll bolt off across space. We'll lead them on the greatest chase to nothing this side of the galaxy has ever seen."

It was a strong plan, one that had a very good chance of working…and buying the time the Confederation needed. Sara Eaton was a talented officer, one he trusted to lead his people through the fight about to come. But, the ruse was the most desperate he'd ever conceived—he'd known that when he'd planned on enacting it himself. Either the fleet would fight in Zed-12, and be completely destroyed…or it would succeed in the running battle, and then it would flee into the depths of unknown space, with little chance of ever returning home.

The Hegemony forces could catch the fleet if they wanted to, of course. They were faster, had better acceleration, and longer ranged weapons, too. But, he'd been banking on them holding back, following the fleet off into unknown space…all the while thinking they were heading toward what they perceived as an invader's home.

Barron took a deep breath. Then, he turned toward Jake Stockton, who hadn't said a word beyond adding his voice to those urging Barron to return to the Confederation. "Jake...I don't know how to say this..."

"I'll stay, sir. I can transfer over to *Repulse*."

Barron was grateful Stockton was making it easy for him, but he had more in mind that just leaving his best pilot behind. "Thank you, Jake...but we'll need more than just that. All the squadrons have to stay. Including *Dauntless*'s...and those on the other ships going back."

Stockton nodded. "I'll see to it, sir. I'm sure we can cram a few extra Lightnings wherever we have to."

"I'd like to stay, too, sir." Stara Sinclair had been silent, but now she stepped forward, her eyes darting between Stockton and Barron. "I can be a help with fighter ops."

"Yes, you can, Stara," Barron said, his voice raw. His people were asking him to leave them behind, to abandon them to destruction...or to being lost in space, maybe forever. The thought was on the verge of destroying him. "Okay...you'll transfer over to *Repulse*. At once. We don't have much time." He barely managed to force the words out.

"Thank you, sir."

I've just consigned you to being lost for all eternity...and you thank me...

"Sara...you'll have to get back to *Repulse*, now. You've got to get the fleet on the move. If you can't intercept the enemy in Zed-12, the whole effort's a lost cause." One thing Barron knew he could never do was lead the enemy back to the Confederation. If Eaton couldn't buy enough time for his ships to escape, better they all die where they were than trace a path back to Megara.

"Yes, sir. I'll have everything underway in two hours...less, if possible."

She paused, looking across the room at Barron. He wanted to speak to her, to so many of the people in the room. But, there wasn't time...and the last thing they needed was to watch him fall apart in front of them. Finally, he just said, "Good luck, Sara. Take care of our people."

But, what he really meant was, "goodbye."

Chapter Forty-Seven

**Senatorial Transport
Entering Olyus System
Year 315 AC**

"Your dinner, Mr. Holsten." The guard set the tray down on the small metal table, and then he turned to leave. Holsten didn't respond. He just snorted a bit, a private show of disrespect for the sentry, a member of the Senate's Lictor Corps. Holsten was used to hard-edged spies and battle-hardened Marines, and he had trouble just looking at the way the pampered toy soldiers of the Confederation's highest governing body strutted around like they were something special.

Holsten sat where he was, at least until the guard had left. Part of him wanted to send the tray back untouched, a silent protest at his situation. He'd done just that for the first several days, but the truth was, it wasn't going to accomplish a thing. And, damn it all, he was hungry.

He got up and walked over to the small table, removing the top of the tray and looking down at the sad pile of unappealing food. It wasn't appetizing, especially to a man who'd been born into one of the wealthiest families in the Confederation. Holsten's baby food had been prepared by a staff of gourmet chefs, and now his jailors—that was what they were, after all, however he tried to look at it—had served him this pile of institutional slop.

But it was food—of a sort—and he was hungry. He sat, grabbed the small roll on the edge of the tray, and took a bite. It was a bit stale, but it wasn't that bad…something he was far from certain would extend to the small pile of grayish meat on the plate. He finished the roll, and then ate one of the mushy boiled potatoes. After that, he shoved the tray away in disgust.

He sighed. He'd gotten himself into the spot he was in, he realized that. He'd become obsessed with finding Andi, and he'd done just that, gotten to her just in time to save her life. But his methods had been extreme, and executed without the usual care he employed to protect himself. He was a bit surprised at how quickly the howls of protest from local officials on Dannith had reached the Senate…that was something worth checking out. Nevertheless, he imagined rare opportunity to knock him down had just been too seductive to the Senators he'd manipulated in the past.

He sat quietly for a few minutes, finding himself picking again at the least objectionable items remaining on the tray. His mind was active, despite the fatigue growing heavily on him. He'd done without much sleep for weeks as he directed the search for Andi, and now it was really hitting him. But, he also knew he had to be ready—and mentally sharp—for whatever awaited him. He'd exceeded his authority, and no doubt his enemies in the Senate would characterize that as criminal. He had committed crimes, too, at least with the interrogation of the Sector Nine prisoner—but there was no way the Senate could know about that. No, they would come at him over his blockade of Dannith, and his diversion of Peterson's Marines to the planet. And, certainly, to the way he'd used them to indiscriminately bash down doors all over Dannith. He *did* have that power, but only in times of national emergency. He suspected a pack of Senators bent on revenge would have a lot of support in their notion that the capture of a single agent was hardly a clear and present danger to the Confederation. Especially when that agent had a history of being somewhat of an outlaw until recently.

And they were right, of course. He hadn't fancied he was

saving the Confederation by looking for Andi. He'd been trying to help his friend, and nothing more.

They would try to have him removed from his position at the head of Confederation Intelligence, at least…and they might very well succeed. The war was over, and without the danger of Union invasion, he suspected the public would not be in a mood to accept such aggressive and forceful conduct by the intelligence forces and the military. Some of his adversaries would be happy just to be rid of him, to send him back to his estates and to the dissolute life many of them believed he led.

Others would want more. They would seek to have him convicted of a long list of offenses, and banished to some penal moon at the edge of nowhere. He had a partial list of those Senators…and he was adding to it steadily. *They* were his real enemies, the instigators behind this entire escapade…he was sure of that.

It would be a test of wills. Those Senators knew the secrets he had. They would try to keep him isolated, cut off from his data. But he was smarter than that, and he had trusted subordinates in place, men and women who would see to the release of all of it if he simply disappeared. It would be a bloodbath, though no actual blood would be spilled. Probably not, at least.

He *was* sure of one thing, though. Whoever was behind this, they had one hell of a battle coming. Those secret records contained dirt, files and files of dirt. Corruption, perversions, and outright crimes committed by sitting Senators. If they managed to destroy him, one thing was certain. He'd take half the damned Senate with him.

Gary Holsten wouldn't go down without a fight.

One *hell* of a fight.

* * *

Andi Lafarge tried to roll over onto her side, but pain ripped through her like a fire almost immediately. She had never slept well on her back, but she didn't have much choice now. At least not until her wounds healed.

She was in pain even when she lay still, but that wasn't the worst of it. She was a wreck from what she'd been through, mentally and emotionally. Ricard Lille had broken her. No one else was aware of that, and she hadn't known anything of real importance that she could have told him anyway…but *she* knew. And, so did he.

She knew she'd recover, physically at least. Her broken bones would mend, her contusions would gradually clear up. She'd been trussed up with stiches, and her emaciated form had been nourished with the very best nutrition an IV could deliver. She'd even graduated to solid food, and surprised herself that very morning with just how sublimely wonderful a bowl of tasteless, runny oatmeal could be. But, her wounds were more than physical, and she was far from sure she would ever be the same. Now she knew her weakness. That was a gift Lille had left her, even as he'd retreated before the assault of Gary Holsten's Marines. He'd beaten her…and both of them knew it.

Holsten…she missed him, too. She knew he blamed himself for recruiting her, and then allowing her to fall into Lille's hands. But she didn't see it that way at all. She'd lost a lot of herself, but she'd managed to hang onto enough to realize that Andromeda Lafarge did what she damned well pleased. Holsten had instigated the whole thing, but she had come of her own volition, and she didn't blame her friend for what had happened.

She had wondered where he'd gone, until Colonel Peterson had come and told her what had happened. She'd had trouble believing it at first. Her image of Holsten had always been of a man in total control of his surroundings. It was hard—almost impossible—to believe that he'd left himself vulnerable…but then she realized he'd done it to find her. She'd just seen the Marines pouring into the building, shooting down the Sector Nine agents and pulling her out of there, but Peterson had filled her in on just what lengths Holsten had gone to in order to find her. If there had been any lingering resentment in her, that news had washed it away.

Not that there was anything she could do…even if she'd been able to get out of bed. Senatorial investigations and maneuvering through the filth of Megara's political swamp were about as far from her areas of expertise as possible.

She exhaled gently, the only way she could do it without making the pain unbearable. She closed her eyes for a moment, and thought about the one person she really wanted to see... but he was far away, farther than any Confederation spacer had ever been. She wished she had gone with him, that she'd found a way to join the White Fleet on its expedition. For now, all she could do was wait...and think of him, of the times they'd spent together.

She heard voices outside the room, speaking to her Marine guards. There was something familiar about one of them...

Her head snapped to the side, a reaction that sent another tremor of pain through her body.

No...you're hallucinating. It can't be...

One of the Marines finally came through the door. "Excuse me, Captain Lafarge...I'm sorry to bother you, but we have some people out here who say they know you. They insisted I check with you."

She pulled herself up as far as she could and looked over. The Marine had a skeptical look on his face, and she could see that he'd unbuttoned the holster that held his sidearm.

"People...what people?"

"What people would be here to pick up the mess you made, Andi?"

She heard the voice, clearly...and then she saw the face, familiar as though it had been yesterday she'd last seen it.

"I told you to wait outside in the hall." The Marine had an angry scowl on his face, and his hand dropped to his side, gripping the pistol.

"No...Sergeant...I do know him. It's okay. You can let him in...and anyone else who's out there with him. They're no threat to me."

"Yes, Captain Lafarge." The Marine relaxed—a little—and he turned and nodded to the man leaning into the room.

"What are you doing here? How is it even possible?" She could feel tears welling up in her eyes, and she tried to hold them back.

"I got a message from Gary Holsten...we all did."

"All?"

"Of course all...do you think we'd leave you here to face... whatever the hell you've gotten involved with...all alone?" The man grinned, and then he walked into the room, followed by about half a dozen others.

Andi looked up and smiled broadly...as Vig Merrick and the rest of her old crew poured into the room.

* * *

"Gary Holsten slips outside the lines from time to time, there's no question about that...but he's a patriot. I've known him for years, and I've never seen him do anything for personal gain." Jon Peterson was sitting in a quiet corner of the bar, his eyes moving between looking at his companion and checking to make sure no one else was close enough to overhear what he was saying.

"I agree with you, Colonel. I don't know him as well as you do, but as far as I've ever heard, he's always done right by the Corps...and that's not something we can say about a lot of the suits in the Senate, is it?" Major Bellingham commanded the First Battalion of Peterson's division. He was also the grizzled colonel's oldest friend.

"No, it damned sure is not." Peterson shoved his ever-present cigar into his mouth and puffed hard. "Holsten's a good man...and he's smart. He'll probably get himself out of this mess." Peterson paused. "But, Greg, if he doesn't..." Peterson's voice trailed off.

"There's not much we can do if the Senate convicts him of a crime...even if it's trumped up nonsense." Bellingham picked up his beer and took a deep drink. "It's a shame. I'd wager we'd have lost the war without Holsten's efforts."

"No bet, Hank. And we don't know the half of it. Confederation Intelligence did a lot, you can bet your ass on that. Then, the Senate gave away our victory. Do you know how many of our people died to bring the Union to the brink of defeat? How many spacers in the fleet? And those paper pushers watched and cowered, and then they let the enemy just skirt away. My God, the Union still holds planets they took from us in the first war. The politicians didn't even negotiate the return of the disputed systems while we had the edge."

"That's politicians for you. But, what are a bunch of Marines going to do to change any of it?"

Peterson was silent for a moment. "I don't know, Hank, but I'll tell you one thing. I promised Gary Holsten I'd watch over Andi Lafarge until she was out of the hospital...but as soon as she is, I think I'm going to take some of that leave I've accumulated. Maybe go to Megara for a little vacation." He turned his head and stared across the table. "I know you've got as much banked leave as I do...care to come along?"

Bellingham nodded. "I think so, sir. I could use some time off...and I've never been to the capital before."

Peterson took another long puff on his cigar. "I was even thinking we might give your whole first company some leave. I'm thinking not too many of them have seen Megara either."

Chapter Forty-Eight

"Admiral…*Stingray* has just returned from Zed-6. Report coming in now."

Barron just nodded. The sound of Cumberland's voice grated on him. That wasn't fair, he knew. Elliot Cumberland was a terrific officer, a veteran and utterly dedicated to his job. But, he wasn't Sonya Eaton, and every time Barron heard his low, mildly scratchy voice, he was reminded that his previous aide wasn't there. And why.

Sonya Eaton was back with the fleet…which quite possibly meant she was dead. She'd asked to stay behind, to fight at her sister's side, and Barron hadn't been able to refuse. *Dauntless* had left the Zed-11 system over a week before, and that meant, whatever fight had developed, it was most likely over. If the plan had worked, it was *just* possible some of his people were still alive, fleeing deep into the unknown and followed by the forces of the Hegemony. That was the optimistic scenario. The other possibility, and very likely the only alternative option, was that they were dead. All of them.

Barron had been in a somber mood since *Dauntless* and its small pack of companion ships had headed back toward the

Confederation…and left their comrades and friends behind. He'd spent far less time than normal in the control center, preferring to brood in his quarters and nurse his angst into full-blown self-hatred. But, he'd come up to monitor *Stingray*'s return. He hadn't let the guilt that was consuming him interfere seriously with his duty yet. He'd sacrificed his dignity, and any respect he'd ever had for himself, to get the warning back to the Confederation…he couldn't imagine doing all that and botching the mission due to his own carelessness.

"Transmission coming in now, sir."

"On speaker." He knew he should probably listen to whatever Stingray's skipper had to say on his headset first, but he didn't care. If the enemy had managed to follow *Dauntless* and her companion vessels, he figured the rest of his people deserved to know immediately. If they were being followed, he would turn his small force around, and he would throw it at whatever Hegemony vessels were tailing them. The one thing Barron wouldn't do—*couldn't do*—was lead the enemy back home. That would probably mean death for all of them, and while Barron would regret that for his crews, he found himself shockingly unconcerned at the prospect of his own demise.

"Admiral Barron, we've completed our scan of the Zed-6 system and discovered no trace of any pursuit."

Barron almost responded, but *Stingray* was still seven light minutes from *Dauntless*'s position, making any kind of back and forth communication difficult, to say the least.

"We launched three full spreads of drones, and we scanned each inbound point for any signs of transit. All searches were negative."

He turned toward Cumberland. Or, more accurately, something like two-thirds of the way toward the officer. "Congratulate Captain Rorik on his successful completion of his mission, and order him to return to our position at full thrust."

"Yes, Admiral."

Barron sighed and leaned back for a few seconds. The report had been the same for every system his people had gone through since leaving Zed-11. He could never be *sure* the enemy didn't have some kind of stealth craft following, but it didn't seem likely.

His people had made their escape. Whatever fate had befallen the rest of the fleet, at least it hadn't been in vain. Failing some unforeseen disaster, *Dauntless* would get back to Megara with the terrible news she carried. And then Barron would see if his influence with Confederation authorities as strong as his comrades had said it was, when they'd claimed the right to face death so he could get back.

He'd been planning to wait the fourteen minutes or so until Rorik acknowledged, but then he just stood up abruptly. "I'm going down to sickbay, and then to my quarters."

"Yes, sir."

Barron walked toward the bank of lifts at the end of the control center, and he stepped inside one, snapping, "Sickbay," to the AI that controlled the system. The doors slid shut, and the car dropped swiftly down the tube.

Barron has resented the new *Dauntless* at first, unable to shed his feelings about his old ship. But, the battles out at Zed-11 had helped him past that, and he'd come to truly appreciate the abilities of the new vessel. He'd even have gone as far as to say she was a worthy successor to his first command. But now, the ship was like a prison, and he felt trapped, alone.

He stepped out of the car as the doors opened, and he walked down the wide corridor, stopping at the entrance to sickbay. He waved his hand over the sensor to open the door, and then he stepped inside.

He'd come to see Atara again, to sit next to the cold metal canister that held his closest friend. He walked across the main room and toward the small, critical care cubby that held Atara's medpod. He walked in and looked down at her still form. The utter lack of movement, even of any visible signs of breathing, unsettled him every time he came in. He knew the pod's equipment was breathing for her, oxygenating her blood while her lungs were idle. But, it was still disconcerting to watch.

Atara might have been able to pull him out of the morose state he'd been in since leaving Zed-11. If anyone could, it would have been her. But that familiar shoulder wasn't there to lean on, and the deep conversations the two had so often shared where now only slowly fading memories.

There wasn't anyone for him to talk to. Sonya Eaton had stayed behind with the fleet. Jake Stockton and Stara Sinclair, as well, to direct fighter operations. Fritzie had moved over to *Repulse*, bringing her engineering expertise and her best people to the commodore's flagship. Sara Eaton herself was in command of the desperate rearguard. Barron had never felt so alone, though he was on a ship with more than one thousand devoted crew members.

He stepped back and dropped into the small chair, the one he'd sat in every day since Atara had been brought back aboard *Dauntless*. He talked to her, indulging himself in the nonsensical notion that it somehow helped her. Perhaps if she'd simply been unconscious, his companionship, and his words, might have done something for her…but the medpod was sealed tight, and he knew she couldn't hear a thing he said.

But, he kept saying the words. He couldn't stop. Stopping would be like giving up, and his desperate hope that Atara would recover was one of the few threads keeping him out of the abyss. He wanted to believe he was there in sickbay for her… but, he knew he was there for himself, too.

"Well, Atara…what should we talk about today?" He paused. "You know who I was thinking about earlier? You remember that guy on Fritzie's staff back when we first got to *Dauntless*? The engineering team all called him 'Jazz,' remember? He was short, and he looked like he was about fourteen years old…"

*   *   *

Barron opened the door to his cabin, stepping inside and pausing for a moment. The AI snapped on the overhead lamps, but he immediately growled, "Lights off." He wanted the dark… it matched his mood.

Barron knew the arguments his officers had made back in Zed-11 were logical. With his own honors from the war, and the almost universal respect for the Barron name, he was absolutely the right one to go back and convince the Senate and the Admiralty of the new danger facing the Confederation. He would probably even play a lead role in readying the navy to face whatever was coming. The safety of the Confederation was the highest priority. The only one.

But that logic was wearing thin now. He'd looked to Atara to help him through, to the hours he'd spent next to her motionless from trying to draw strength from his old friend. Perhaps, if she'd truly been there, if he'd been able to talk to her, as he had so many times before when he was troubled…but that wasn't possible. Not now, and perhaps not ever again. In his mind, he was one thing and one thing only…the admiral who left his command. Who had abandoned his fleet to death and fled with a small group of ships. The very thought of it disgusted him, and though he'd tried to hide it, the whole thing was tearing him apart.

He walked across the room, to a small chest of drawers. He leaned down and opened the bottom one. He wasn't much of a drinker, he never had been. It had been months since he'd had anything more potent than carbonated water. But, now, Barron began to appreciate the appeal of drinking. More specifically, of drunkenness.

He pulled a bottle out from under a small pile of jackets. It had been expensive, he was sure of that, and probably vanishingly rare. He couldn't remember who had given it to him, just that it had been a gift, the kind of thing people had showered on him his entire life as a sort of homage to the Barron clan. He'd always hated that, too…but now he was going to put this particular unwanted gift to good use. He wasn't even sure why he'd brought it along—perhaps to use to toast some great discovery he'd hoped the fleet would find. But, his great mission, the vaunted White Fleet, had found nothing worthy of a toast. Just death, and war. At least, he'd found another use for the bottle. Tyler Barron was going to sit in the dark in his cabin, alone, and get absolutely shit-faced drunk.

It *had* to be better than how he felt now. If it drove away the images of the Eatons, and of Atara lying in that metal pseudo-coffin, and the tens of thousands of others he'd left behind, so much the better. He knew he should stay sharp, sober, that he had duty to perform, that the Confederation needed him. But the images were still there, tormenting him. Calling him turn-coat and a coward.

He opened the bottle and took a deep drink, almost cough-ing up half of it as the harsh liquid hit his throat. He didn't like it, neither the taste nor the feel.

But, whether he liked the taste or not, he knew it would give him what he truly wanted.

What he needed.

Epilogue

Planet Calpharon
Sigma Nordlin System

"Highest, I abase myself in your presence." The man was tall, fit, his enunciation flawless and clear. He carried himself in a lordly manner, yet he dropped to one knee and lowered his head before the woman seated in front of him.

"You may rise, Calthor." The woman spoke softly, but her voice was strong. She sat on a large seat at the end of the massive room, wearing an informal pair of light pants and a tunic, both made in a fabric so fine it made normal silk seem almost like burlap. "Speak freely. Present your report."

Her demeanor relaxed, yet attentive. Her name was Akella, though she hadn't gone by that designation in many years. She had ranked at the very top of the genetic testing for more than two decades, ever since she'd come of age and submitted to the Test. Her position was a lofty one, unique, and it carried with it honors and titles…and the rule of the Hegemony. Her people, Inferiors and Masters alike, called her, simply, "Highest."

"Highest, the invaders appear to have fled from Ghasimar. The retribution fleet engaged part of their force, yet most of their ships were able to escape."

"Surely, our forces were able to track their routes?" She showed no emotion, though there was little question the contact with other survivors of the Cataclysm was a momentous development. Her calmness was born of confidence. Akella, the Highest of the Hegemony, was utterly certain that her intellect and knowledge would serve to face any crisis. Certainly, any challenge from a new strain of Inferiors who had dared to invade Hegemony space.

"Yes, Highest. They were allowed to disengage. The fleet pursues them even now, seeking the route to their home systems."

"Very well, Calthor. We will find this cluster of survivors… and they will come to understand the order of things." Her people had long assumed that the Hegemony was all that remained of the old empire. They had sent out ships more than a century before, both Rimward and Coreward, and found nothing but dead worlds.

They apparently did not go far enough Rimward…the Highest from that time failed in his duty.

"Highest…the invaders' ships…they carry smaller vessels, crewed by no more than one or two of their people. They operate in swarms, and many of them carry weapons of significant power." Another pause. "Our ships are not optimally equipped to face such attacks. I fear we suffered considerable losses in the recent battles."

"Yes, the loss reports are indeed surprising…and disturbing. I fear I will have to take personal charge of the struggle against this enemy. There can be no more errors, no further underperformance. We must develop defensive systems to account for the enemy's weaponry. It is intolerable for these inferiors to exceed our capabilities in any way."

"Yes, Highest. As you command."

"Yet, we cannot delay our response, Calthor, waiting to refit our ships. We must find this new enemy's domain swiftly…and when we track them to their home systems, we must attack at once and bend them to our will. Our destiny is clear. We are the Masters. The old empire, and everything beyond, is ours to command. We can allow no Inferiors, technologically-advanced or not, to interfere with our place in the scheme of things."

"Yes, Highest. The advance fleet will find the route to their home worlds. I am confident."

She stared back at Calthor. She had already begun to calculate the number of permutations, the varying routes back toward the Rim that her people would have to examine if they were unable to track the invaders to their home world. She did not have reliable information on the transit network past a certain point, but there were, at the least, several hundred thousand possible routes the enemy could take. An extensive probability analysis could eliminate many of them, she knew, and likely identify a more reasonable course. But the search would still be difficult, and it would take time…unless the fleet was able to maintain its tracking, and report back.

"I concur with your actions, Calthor. The fleet is to continue its pursuit."

"Thank you, Highest. Your approval is gratifying."

She sat quietly for a moment, considering a range of variables…the likely strength of the invader, how many systems they might occupy, how long it would take to find a reliable route to their home bases. Finally, she made a decision.

"These invaders are inferior…but it appears they have many advantages over our own Inferiors. It is reasonable to assume their genetic rankings might place them in a tier between us and the upper ranges of the Arbeiter-Kriegeri stock. They could be useful additions to the Hegemony, beings truly fit to serve the Masters. Once they are suitably broken and pacified, of course."

"Indeed, Highest. I agree entirely."

The Highest was silent for a short while, perhaps half a minute. Then she turned and looked toward Calthor. "All forces are to mobilize. Immediately. The Grand Fleet will assemble and prepare for its mission." There was a short silence. "They are to be ready to move as soon as the advance fleet reports the course to the enemy's home systems."

She was again silent for a few seconds, and then she looked up and spoke, her tone imperious.

"We will destroy this Rim nation and its institutions…and extend our rule to the very edge of what was once the empire."

Appendix

Strata of the Hegemony

The Hegemony is an interstellar polity located far closer to the center of what had once been the old empire than Rimward nations such as the Confederation. The Rim nations and the Hegemony were unaware of the other's existence until the White Fleet arrived at Planet Zero and established contact.

Relatively little is known of the Hegemony, save that their technology appears to be significantly more advanced than the Confederation's in most areas, though still behind that of the old empire.

The culture of the Hegemony is based almost exclusively on genetics, with an individual's status being entirely dependent on an established method of evaluating genetic "quality." Generations of selective breeding have produced a caste of 'Masters,' who occupy an elite position above all others. There are several descending tiers below the Master class, all of which are categorized as 'Inferiors.'

The Hegemony's culture likely developed as a result of its location much closer to the center of hostilities during the Cataclysm, and the resulting fact that many surviving inhabitants of the inward systems suffered from horrific mutations and damage to genetic materials, placing a premium on any bloodlines lacking such effects.

The Rimward nations find the Hegemony's society to be almost alien in nature, while its rulers consider the inhabitants of the Confederation and other nations to be just another strain of Inferiors, fit only to obey their commands without question.

Masters

The Masters are the descendants of those few humans spared genetic damage from the nuclear, chemical, and biological warfare that destroyed the old empire during the series of events known as the Cataclysm. The Masters sit at the top of the Hegemony's societal structure and, in a sense, are its only true full members or citizens.

The Masters' culture is based almost entirely on what they call 'genetic purity and quality,' and even their leadership and ranking structure is structured solely on genetic rankings. Every master is assigned a number based on his or her place in a population-wide chromosomal analysis. An individual's designation is thus subject to change once per year, to adjust for masters dying and for new adults being added into the database. The top ten thousand individuals in each year's ratings are referred to as 'High Masters,' and they rank above the others, and are paired for breeding matchups far more frequently than the larger number of lower-rated Masters.

Masters reproduce by natural means, through strict genetic pairings, based on an extensive study of ideal matches. The central goal of Master society is to steadily improve the human race by breeding the most perfect specimens available, and relegating all others to a subservient status. The Masters consider any genetic manipulation or artificial processes like cloning, to be grievously sinful, and all such practices are banned in the Hegemony on pain of death to all involved. This belief structure traces from the experiences of the Cataclysm, and the terrible damage inflicted on the populations of imperial worlds by genetically-engineered pathogens and cloned and genetically-engineered soldiers.

All humans not designated as Masters are referred to as Inferiors, and they serve the Masters in various capacities. All Masters have the power of life and death over Inferiors. It is not a crime for a Master to kill any Inferior who has injured or offended that Master in any way.

Kriegeri

The Kriegeri are the Hegemony's soldiers. They are drawn from the pick of the populations of Inferiors on Hegemony worlds, the strongest and most physically capable specimens. Kriegeri are not genetically-modified, though in most cases, Master supervisors enforce specific breeding arrangements in selected population groups intended to increase the quality of future generations of Kriegeri stock.

The Kriegeri are trained from infancy to serve as the Hegemony's soldiers and spaceship crews, and are divided in two categories, red and gray, named for the colors of their uniforms. The 'red' Kriegeri serve aboard the Hegemony's ships, under the command of a small number of Master officers. They are surgically modified to increase their resistance to radiation and zero gravity.

The 'gray' Kriegeri are the Hegemony's ground soldiers. They are selected from large and physically powerful specimens and are subject to extensive surgical enhancements to increase strength, endurance, and dexterity. They also receive significant artificial implants, including many components of their armor, which becomes a permanent partial exoskeleton of sorts. They are trained and conditioned from childhood to obey orders and to fight. The top several percent of Kriegeri surviving twenty years of service are retired to breeding colonies, to produce the next generation of Krieger-Edel, a pool of elite specimens serving as mid-level officers and filling a command role between the ruling Masters and the rank and file Kriegeri.

Arbeiter

Arbeiter are the workers and laborers of the Hegemony. They are drawn from populations on the Hegemony's many worlds, and typically either exhibit some level of genetic damage inherited from the original survivors or simply lack genetic ratings sufficient for Master status. Arbeiter are from the same general group as the Kriegeri, though the soldier class includes the very best candidates, and the Arbeiter pool consists of the remnants.

Arbeiter are assigned roles in the Hegemony based on rigid assessments of their genetic status and ability. These positions range from supervisory posts in production facilities and similar establishments to pure physical labor, often working in difficult and hazardous conditions.

Defekts

Defekts are individuals exhibiting severe genetic damage, often populations of entire worlds. They are typically found on planets that suffered the most extensive bombardments and bacteriological attacks during the Cataclysm.

Defekts have no legal standing in the Hegemony, and they are considered completely expendable. On worlds inhabited by populations of Masters, Kriegeri, and Arbeiters, Defekts are typically assigned to the lowest level, most dangerous labor, and any excess populations are exterminated.

The largest number of Defekts exist on planets on the fringes of Hegemony space, where they are often used for such purposes as mining radioactives and other, similarly dangerous, operations. Often, the Defekts themselves have no knowledge at all of the Hegemony and regard the Masters as gods or demi-gods descending from the heavens. On such planets, the Masters often demand ores and other raw materials as offerings, and severely punish any failures or shortfalls. Pliant and obedient populations are provided with rough clothing and low-quality manufactured foodstuffs, enabling them to devote nearly all labor to the gathering of whatever material the Masters demand. Resistant population groups are exterminated, as, frequently, are Defekt populations on worlds without useful resources to exploit.

Also By Jay Allan

www.jayallanbooks.com

www.ingramcontent.com/pod-product-compliance
Lightning Source LLC
Chambersburg PA
CBHW051546250626
47157CB00001B/201